What Spooked Crazy Horse?

Best wishes,

Alex Gordon

Ringwood Publishing
Glasgow

First published in Great Britain in 2016 by

Ringwood Publishing

24 Duncan Avenue, Glasgow G14 9HN

www.ringwoodpublishing.com

ISBN 978-1-901514-34-6

British Library Cataloguing-in Publication Data

A catalogue record for this book is available from the British Library

Cover design by Douglas Colquhoun

Typeset in Times New Roman 11

Printed and bound in the UK
by
Lonsdale Direct Solutions

Acknowledgements

My sister Betty, her husband Greig and the Perrers team of Steven, Simon, Nicola, Esme and the Dunsmores of Susan, Steven, Matthew and Emily. Not forgetting June, Tommy, Sean, Tracey and Catherine.

The Millport line-up: Eddie and Margaret Hughes, John and Jeanette, Kirsty, Tom and Kath, James and Helen, Arthur and Trish, Graham and Ann, Ian, Tracey and the two Johns, Neil and Eileen, Gerry and Margaret (aka Mrs Gerry), Jim, Martin and Joan, Shirley, Big Stevie, Bobby and Jean and their John, Alasdair, Colin, Yildrum, Rio, Sarah, Terry, Tony, Alex, Bob and Margaret Caldwell, Billy, Stuart, Kath, Liz, Sandra, Janice, Janette, Lesley, Robert, Wee Willie, Nick Parker, Pete and Kathy.

Visiting squad: Gerry and Wilma, Larry and Margaret, Gibby and Liz, Alex and Margaret, Jim and Carol, Robert and Jane, Donald and Liz, Anne and Matthew.

Also the good patrons and owners of the Kelburne Bar, Frasers, The Tavern, Newton, Minstrels, the George Hotel, Elwoods, Fintry Bay tearoom and the excellent Deep Sea Chippy.

And, of course, Phil Dunshea, Managing Director of Ringwood Publishing, whose skilful and expert editing is evident throughout. Sterling work from Phil, above and beyond.

The indefatigable Sandy Jamieson, too, deserves a massive round of applause for his unstinting support and backing for me and Charlie Brock. Hopefully, Brock's got legs for a few more in the series.

My apologies if I have overlooked anyone.

In Memoriam

Lorraine, Tom Nellis and Ian 'Bunny' Rae; three wonderful characters without whose welcoming presence the world is a poorer place. Wherever you have chosen as your new home, be sure you are in my thoughts, you still make me smile. Cheers, my friends.

Dedication

Gerda, my wife, best pal, soulmate and constant source of inspiration. I've said it before – and no doubt I'll say it again – Millport has the Crocodile Rock ... I've got my wee rock.

PROLOGUE

Early morning. Friday 20 February. Five years ago.

Merchant City, Glasgow.

'Hello, Mr. Brock. Please allow me to introduce myself. My name is Time. I am not going to be around forever. Enjoy me while you can.'

The words bounced around in Charlie Brock's subconscious. They had been reverberating around in there for quite some time. Too long, in fact. His on/off girlfriend Jean, brunette, lovely and dull, was convinced he was hurtling down the slope of a full blown mid-life crisis. Today was the day, though. He knew the decision had to be made; it was now or never; no turning back. *Non, je ne regrette rien*, as Edith Piaf had warbled more than once. He might even have burst into a bout of early morning crooning, but accepted he hadn't a clue to the rest of the words of the French classic.

Deftly, he swung his legs out of bed, making sure he didn't disturb the gently-snoring Jean in the process. He was wearing garish, iris-wrecking checked pyjama bottoms that wouldn't have looked out of place adorning some unwitting fashion victim with the disconcerting wish to resemble Rupert the Bear on a golf course. Brock hadn't a clue what fate had befallen the equally tasteless top. God only knows how he acquired the gaudy nightime attire in the first place; had to be a Christmas present from some short-sighted relative with a misplaced sense of humour.

He padded across the carpeted floor of the bedroom, carefully

1

nudged the door ajar, meandered through the small hallway and into the kitchen of his two-bedroomed flat. It was February and it was cold. It was Glasgow, after all. He checked his wristwatch. 5.33am. The central heating hadn't kicked in. He would have to wait another twenty-seven minutes for comforting warmth to begin flowing through the compact apartment situated on the fourth floor of a block of flats quaintly christened 'Mayflower Towers'.

Brock checked the electric kettle to make sure it contained a sufficiency of water to take care of a cup of tea before hitting the on-switch. He had lost count of the amount of electric kettles that had been tortured en route to a shrieking end following his failure to bother with this simple procedure. He pulled a white T-shirt from the clothes horse and slipped it on, involuntarily shivering as he did so. While the kettle did its job, he moved across the hallway again to the small living room and pulled open the dark brown mock velvet curtains. Street lighting illuminated the grey, old city still in its slumber. A couple of delivery vans were dropping off their wares at newsagents, bakeries and coffee houses. There were a few pedestrians scurrying about their business, seeking refuge from the early morning frost and intrusive gusts of bitingly cold wind, huddled in coats and oversized jackets, adorned in headgear circus clowns would resist. Brock heard the kettle's switch click off.

He shuffled back through to the kitchen, picked up his usual mug, threw in a tea bag, poured in the hot water, went to the fridge for a carton of milk, didn't bother checking the sell-by date, let the tea settle for a moment, removed the bag and added the milk. He detested strong tea. His Dad used to make tea like treacle. It had been a Herculean task just to get the spoon to swirl around in the cup. He didn't take sugar. He picked up the mug, sipped quietly and declared to no-one in particular, 'Ah, best drink of the day.' It

2

was something he had muttered practically every morning of his life, even if he didn't believe it.

He made his way back through to the living room and took up his usual position in front of the window. His reflection looked back at him. 'Are you making the right decision?' it seemed to say. He glanced again. Was the reflection wearing a quizzical expression? He slurped his tea, looked out from the window and down to the streets and wasn't surprised that nothing continued to happen. He smiled as a delivery van for the *Daily News* pulled up outside Javed's newsagents. The driver got out, raced round to the back of the vehicle, carelessly swung open the doors, grabbed two large parcels and threw them haphazardly in the general direction of the newsagent's doorway.

Brock sipped again. He smiled. He knew the machine room of Scotland's top-selling daily newspaper always made sure there were several surplus copies of their product to take care of the violent buffeting they would almost mandatorily receive from the 'we-don't-give-a-shit' delivery drivers. Some unscrupulous newsagent owners sold the torn and beaten-up gratis copies that should have been discarded immediately. Brock had bought a few newspapers in his time that had given him the impression a herd of elephants had been tap-dancing on them all night. He never complained; people had to make a buck.

He watched as the white *Daily News* van took off towards the High Street. The vehicle bore the legend in big, bold capital letters, **'HAVE WE GOT NEWS FOR YOU.'** Brock had always been aware of the absence of a question mark. Maybe it was a statement. Possibly they were being ironic. Certainly, they were being ambiguous. Well, today he would have news for the *Daily News*. No question mark was required for his forthcoming statement. He was quitting his job as a sports reporter. He had had enough.

After over thirty years with the newspaper, man and boy, drunk and sober, he realised it was time to take the leap, get the redundancy deal done and dusted, empty the contents of his desk into a black bin bag, ask the copy boys nicely to sling it in the back of his ten-year-old Mercedes in the rear car park, say his farewells and head for the office pub, the Double C Bar on Glasgow's often-grim, disturbingly-exposed Broomielaw. The drinks were on him. Jean, brunette, lovely and dull, was still convinced a ferocious mid-life crisis had taken control of his being.

However, Brock was well aware every lifetime came with the guarantee of a death sentence. It was time to move on before moles took up residence.

Brock looked again at the reflection in the window. He was fifty years old and realised that, while not quite ancient, he was certainly old in today's newspaper world. Where once the employer would rely on experience, even cherish and encourage it, they now preferred youth. For one very good reason; they were the cheap option. Standards in newspaper journalism hadn't slipped, according to Brock. They had thundered uninterrupted towards hell at terminal velocity. And that's where these once-mighty organs would inevitably complete their sad path towards self-destruction: burning on Beelzebub's stove.

Brock moved back through to the kitchen and thought it better to refill the kettle. He clicked the switch to boil the water. He glimpsed again at his wristwatch. 5.58am. He was never aware of it, but he spent an inordinate amount of time looking at his time piece which was rarely removed from his left wrist. It was a newspaper thing. Brock had been brought up on deadlines.

Brock saw evidence of the collapsing standards in the newspaper trade every day. He awarded a big fat zero out of ten for the front page make-up guys at one Sunday national newspaper he had picked up recently. Under the masthead was a four-inch deep colourful blurb that ran all the way across the full seven columns of the page. It was known as a teaser, a bright eye-catcher that informed the reader there was something entertaining within the pages of the newspaper's giveaway magazine. **'MARY THOMAS'** was the name in yellow on a grey/blue background. **'Part One of her superb favourite family recipes - Inside your magazine'** was the read-out underneath the name of yet another celebrity chef.

Unfortunately, it didn't sit too well with that day's splash. **'HORSE MEAT WAS NOT FIT FOR HUMANS'** it shrieked in big fat type. The sub-deck advised, **'Health alert over Scottish link to drugged animals'**. Brock could only laugh. In the good old days, someone responsible for the front page make-up would have been put in stocks and had soggy cabbages, green, red and purple, thrown at them for about a week. If they were lucky.

Yesterday's quiz in the *Daily News* offered the lucky winner an all-expenses-paid fortnight in Blackpool. Clearly, it wasn't designed to test the intelligence of the reader to the maximum. It asked, 'How many musicians are in a string quartet? A: One; B: Twenty; C: Four.' Good luck with that, smiled Brock.

He refilled his mug, went through the precise procedure as before, something with which he had become expert as he sought to overcome far too many lingering hangovers, and padded back to the living room with his puzzled expression still reflecting from the window. He looked at himself. When he was a kid his hair had been virtually white. He still possessed photographs of himself with his Mum, Dad and sister Betty on holiday in Jersey when he was about seven years old. It was a black and white snap, but it was clear he had a suntan and his hair was the colour of driven

5

snow. He looked a little odd; a bit like a watered-down pint of Guinness. A few years on, it had turned blond and another few years later it was fair. Now grey was beginning to appear at the temples, which worried him not a jot. Maybe it would go back to white, completing the full circle. That didn't bother him, either. He had tired blue eyes, a longish thin nose and, he was convinced, a winning smile.

He was two inches over six feet, of reasonably slim build although there may have been traces of a beer belly. He had earned those extra inches round the waist, he would tell anyone who could be bothered listening. They had cost him a fortune in pints of lager over the years. 'Booze and you lose' was the slogan. Not in Brock's case; it was 'Bevvy and be heavy'. He felt fit enough, just so long as he wasn't asked to toss the caber at a Highland Games any time soon.

He swigged his tea again. There was still no stirring from Jean, who had spent most of last night trying to dissuade him from the notion that walking out on a full-time job with the nation's leading newspaper and going freelance was his brightest idea. But, after years of being tied to the *Daily News*, he was beginning to feel he had taken root on the editorial floor. And he had witnessed older colleagues being treated as nothing better than part of the furniture. Not much of a reward for their diligent efforts over the years in making the newspaper the market leader. He wasn't ready to travel that route. He knew he wouldn't change his mind. He also realised Jean, his on/off girlfriend of two years, arm candy when required, would probably seek a more stable relationship with someone she believed was more reliable.

He swigged his tea, rose the mug to his reflection and quietly said, 'Cheers!'

The reflection smiled back. 'Cheers,' it said. Brock blinked, not entirely sure if the image in the window was in sync with his precise movement.

CHAPTER ONE

Early morning. Thursday 18 November.

Sant Just Desvern, Barcelona.

Crazy Horse was more than a little perplexed. It had nothing to do with the fact he had just received news that the delivery of his Ferrari 599 GTB Fiorano would be delayed. 'Just some tweaking to be done, sir,' he had been informed by the managing director of the local franchise. Crazy Horse idly wondered what sort of 'tweaking' would be required on a top-of-the-range £200,000, 205 miles-per-hour, brand-spanking-new motor vehicle. He was fairly positive 'tweaking' wasn't a technical term.

But that wasn't the problem that was creating so much consternation to Derek Laird, aka Crazy Horse, the footballer conservatively valued at around eighty million pounds by Barcelona, one of the most famous, most regal, most loved and fanatically followed football clubs in the world. He was a golden boy of global sport; one of the highest-paid football players on the planet. A Rolls-Royce Corniche and a Porche 911 Carrera already sat side by side in the garage, which, in itself, was the average size of a bungalow in the upmarket locations of his native Glasgow.

Long gone were the days when he was forced to take 'Shanks' pony' getting from A to B. If it was good enough for Liverpool's old manager, he had always reckoned, it was good enough for him. He fully understood he didn't need two cars. Or a third. The Ferrari was bought on a whim after he realised he was one of only three first team squad members without such a flash and, admittedly, eye-catching vehicle. He had to have one; cash on delivery, whenever that might be. Just so long as his Ferrari had been 'tweaked' before its arrival.

The garage was within twenty yards of his luxurious three-storeyed, six-bedroomed detached home set in four secluded acres on the outskirts of the breathtakingly beautiful and historic city. The swimming pool had just been cleared of some scattered leaves by Xavier, the diligent attendant. The chlorined water shimmered in the sunshine. Crazy Horse sat by the side of the pool, his head in his hands; puzzled and bewildered. He thought about going inside to his games room. Or his private cinema. Or his mini-spa. He stayed put, knowing the problem would follow him wherever he went.

Derek Laird was twenty-five years old and also well aware he could retire that instant, live in the lap of luxury until he was two hundred, and never get through the reservoirs of cash tucked away safely in off-shore accounts. He hadn't a clue how much of a fortune he had amassed. He left that to others who didn't have to remove their shoes and socks when it came to counting beyond ten.

Life was good for a guy who left school at sixteen without a single qualification and worked as a labourer on the scaffolds erected around many of the delapidated buildings of Glasgow's city centre. Enjoyment and excitement back then came in the shape of playing part-time for Albion Rovers. His first take-home pay from his 'proper job' was eighty-six pounds, topped up by the fifty quid for his exertions for the team with modest means from Coatbridge. He was single, reasonably good looking with blondish hair, blue eyes and a ready smile. He had a naturally-honed, athletic torso and thighs that looked as though they could withstand the impact of an Exocet missile. He was just a shade under six-foot tall. And he possessed the most prized, excessively-craved and sought-after talent in the game of football; he could score goals. Lots of them. The Barcelona fans loved him. His bravery in packed, heaving penalty boxes, with boots and elbows flying around with reckless disregard, earned Derek Laird the nickname *Caballo Loco*, Crazy Horse.

One smart freelance photographer saw the potential for a spectacular and lucrative snap. He purchased what was advertised as a 'Superior DeLuxe Red Indian Headdress with REAL red, yellow and grey feathers' from a local fancy dress shop. The best fifty euros he ever spent. Now all he had to do was persuade Barcelona's new signing to pose wearing the headdress. There had been times in the past Derek Laird would have happily balanced precariously on top of scaffolding wearing his full Albion Rovers kit to get his picture in a newspaper. However, times had changed. His initial instinct was to say, 'Thanks, but no thanks,' when the photographer approached him with the headdress idea. It really wasn't his sort of thing. His agent, though, very quickly cottoned on to the idea and immediately appreciated the possibilities. 'Think of image rights, Derek,' he pointed out. 'Sign a few thousand of these and we'll market them all over the place. Trust me, I smell money on this. Go for it, that's my advice.'

Derek Laird had been told it was a short career and he knew he had to make money while the sun shone. His personal manager and his agent hammered it into him that, in football parlance, he would be in 'bus pass territory' soon enough. That seemed an awful long way still to travel. Somewhat reluctantly, though, he agreed to the snap. The photographer took him out to the centre spot of the Nou Camp Stadium pitch. Laird wore his Barcelona strip and his sponsored Cougar boots. And, of course, the vivid, multi-coloured headwear. The sun played its part and smiled down on the entire procedure. The lensman clicked away from practically every conceivable angle for about thirty minutes and everyone was happy. The pictures appeared in every national and local newspaper a couple of days later and, at the same time, the headdresses went on sale in shops throughout the Catalan capital: Crazy Horse was in with the bricks. All that was required next was goals on a regular basis. That was all.

Laird was worshipped wherever he went along La Rambla, the colourful tree-lined mall the footballer loved so much. The restaurants, cafes. kiosks, shops, street performers, exotic birds, flower displays, the breathtaking females: just strolling along this stretch of land seemed an adventure even when it was filled with directionless tourists. He was never allowed to pay for dinner in the city's most exclusive restaurants. Owners of the Michelin three-star and Egon Ronay-listed establishments were always delighted to pick up the tab. Crazy Horse was welcomed everywhere. His wallet was never allowed out of his pocket when he was measured for the most fashionable suits in the bespoke tailors of the city. Same story with shirts, shoes, socks and shreddies. He earned a mountain of money and he wasn't even allowed to spend it. He had four huge wardrobes in each of his six bedrooms bulging with stuff that hadn't cost him a single euro.

Females, blonde, brunette and bald, adored him and were only too happy to be photographed on his arm at the many prestigious events at which his presence was desperately sought. Admittedly, he had reservations about mixing with the city's so-called high society, the 'faces' as they were known, when he had first arrived. Quickly, though, he realised he was bright enough to buy and sell a fair percentage of the glitterati, some of whom, on a daily basis, depended on their managers and agents to tell them where, when and what to eat.

Supercilious, he knew at least, wasn't an action hero.

11

He didn't buy completely into the rock'n'roll lifestyle – drugs were a complete no-no – and he was only too aware of the out-of-control egos running amok among his fellow-sportsmen. He had been told the story about the German footballer who was about to join AS Monaco from one of the massive Milan clubs. A hitch had developed in the proposed transfer deal. The player insisted on taking his twelve racehorses with him to Monte Carlo. '*Il n'y pas de quoi,*' he was told by the Monegasques, eager for his signature. 'No problem.' The principality would provide accommodation for his horses. 'What about my camel?' asked the German. '*Il n'y pas de quoi,*' came the reply. The club were determined to land the player. 'And what about my wife's tiger?' A line had to be drawn somewhere. '*Probleme,*' he was told. AS Monaco pursued a solution to the footballer's personal travelling circus. He could still sign for the club and live outside Monte Carlo. That meant no tax breaks, though, and suddenly a transfer to AS Monaco didn't seem so appealing to the player. '*Problematik,*' he told the club. It was back to his Italian villa with its private zoo. Derek Laird preferred to live in the real world. Or as near as dammit.

An appearance from Crazy Horse was guaranteed vital prime time television and, possibly, a large colour photograph on the front page of one of the periodicals. He had become part of the city's jet-set jigsaw, eventually playing his role willingly among the divas.

Just before entering his teens, he'd had a girlfriend at primary school on Glasgow's southside. He now wondered if Mabel was even the same species as some of the lovelies he had come across, in various ways, on his travels through the millionaires' playground that was Barcelona. Mabel, he now realised, had been 'homely'. They had sat beside each other at primary school, but were forced apart when they went to a secondary school which separated boys from girls. After all, they were reaching what was known as that 'awkward' age and school authorities were keen for their pupils to fully concentrate on logarithms and splitting atoms instead of the mysterious contents of each other's undergarments.

Mabel was still around when, at the age of sixteen, Laird had made his first team debut for Albion Rovers. She was nowhere to be seen when he moved to Arsenal two years later. He had thought his signing-on fee from the London club was a year's wages. He was quoted as saying he was 'over the moon' at the move. He was swiftly picking up footballspeak. The loyal old Ford Capri, a tarted-up rust bucket with go-faster stripes , was already on its way to the scrapyard as he was whisked around the car dealerships of Mayfair. He settled for a Jaguar XJ6.

Derek Laird was in England's capital city for two seasons, long enough to score fifty-two league goals before he was whisked off to Barcelona. Arsenal could not afford to reject the forty million pounds put on the table by the Spaniards. If they had, they would have found the suitors of Laird lobbing in another five million pounds. And another five million pounds, if required. As it was, Arsenal were fairly content with the thirty-nine million nine-hundred thousand pounds profit on the Scot. This time the player's signing-on fee looked like a decade's wages. Four years earlier, he had been climbing scaffolding to deliver Pot Noodles to work mates.

And yet Crazy Horse was still perplexed. And puzzled. And anxious. 'How did this ever happen?' he asked himself over and over. 'Who saw this coming?' He knew had to get away. He had to escape. He knew he had to go somewhere, anywhere he wouldn't be recognised. And considering his face was rarely off the magazine covers, both football and fashion, and the newspapers, he also knew it was not going to be an easy task. Worse still, he was on television every time Barcelona appeared – *every* game. His was a face that would be instantly recognised by at least one and a half million Catalans. And millions more beyond.

He pondered for a while. There was that lovely little Scottish island his parents had taken him to once on holiday. He wasn't even sure they had telephones or televisions on the island. Hot and cold running water? It was an island caught in time with two speeds, he recalled: slow and stop. That place would be ideal. He had made up his mind. Crazy Horse would flee to Millport.

CHAPTER TWO

Early afternoon. Friday 19 November.

Millport, Isle of Cumbrae, North Ayrshire coast.

'Hey, Hick, you do understand if you're having sex, it is a more than reasonable assumption that there should be someone else in the room?'

'Listen, you small, vile creature, make yourself useful and go and sweep some sand off the beach.'

Hughie Edwards, landlord of the imaginatively-named Hugh's Bar, stood in front of the floor-to-ceiling front window of his pub and sighed. 'Seconds out, Round Four Million and Thirty-One.' It was one of those days when he would realise, once again, that being a barman wasn't all it was cracked up to be. The island's resident GP, Dr Algernon Pendlebury, Hickory Dickory to the local fraternity, and Vodka Joe, Hughie's best customer, were going through their daily ritual.

'A duel of wits between two unarmed opponents,' Hughie mused.

The bar owner looked across at Millport's Old Pier, the ancient structure struggling for visibility through a camouflage of grey mist. He sighed as he worked his dish towel vigorously, cleaning the same pint glass for the umpteenth time. 'It's going to be a miserable one today,' he said to Vodka Joe, who was more than pleased with today's opening barb in his verbal joust with the doc. He was also peering out at the early afternoon gloom, a light drizzle already making its presence known. 'Aye, I think I saw a

15

shaft of daylight around about six minutes past eight this morning,' he replied, smiled his trademark smile and added, 'I don't think I'll have much use for my Ray-Bans today.'

Hughie Edwards, Vodka Joe and Dr Algernon Pendlebury had just one other companion in the drinking establishment on Stuart Street, situated on Millport's deserted, windswept promenade: Bungalow Bob was the island's solitary window cleaner, had a fear of heights and would only accept work on the ground floor.

'Hick,' Bungalow Bob said. 'Can I ask a question?'

'Of course, you can. Whether or not I'll answer it is another question. By the way, you do realise I'm not a particular fan of being called Hick? I'm perfectly fine with Hickory Dickory, if you must give me a nickname.' In truth, he preferred it to Algernon; what were his parents thinking? The middle name – Ulysses – would remain secret forever.

'I was just wondering, Hick, if there was ever anyone else in the room when you were having sex.'

'Don't you start, wimpy wet-rag-and-bucket man,' Hick practically snapped. 'I've got enough on my plate with the creature in the cage. Please don't follow his lead or you, too, will be able to count your friends on one finger.'

Hickory Dickory's main claim to fame was the fact that it was a long-departed relative, at that time the island's GP by the name of Eric Redford, who had originally witnessed the rock formation that would later become the 'world famous' Crocodile Rock. To be fair, his ancestor had been somewhere south of blotto when he first noticed the way the outcrop resembled a large predatory semi-aquatic reptile with its jutting jaw and long tongue. The doc had just about collapsed through the front door of Robbie's Tavern, a pub diagonally opposite the oddly-shaped geological creation on the beach. He was barely able to stand, after a day of monumental boozing with the local fishermen, when he saw the possibilities. He had to capture the moment. He stumbled at speed in the direction of home at Kames Bay, a two-storeyed grey sandstone building he shared with his doting wife Ethel. She said nothing when he asked for paint and brushes. He crashed through the back door to the garage where he kept the suddenly sought-after accessories. Ethel realised her husband of twenty-six years had no intention of indulging in some long-overdue DIY at home. The dutiful spouse stepped aside as he returned with several pots of paint and a couple of brushes.

'A crocodile, Ethel,' he gasped excitedly. 'I've seen a crocodile.' Ethel looked at her husband with the slightest trace of sorrow in her tired brown eyes. 'Of course, you have, dear,' she said. 'Deranged old bastard,' she thought.

The following day the road sweepers were first to behold the artistry of the island's GP. 'Whit the fuck's that?' yelled Arthur. 'Beggered if Ah know,' replied Gerry. 'Ah'm no cleaning it up,' said Arthur. 'Naw, me neither,' agreed Gerry. Puzzled, they picked up the empty paint pots and brushes and threw them into the back of the council's cart. 'Ye don't suppose there's been another wee shipment of that good rum on the island, dae ye, Arthur?' The question hung in the air.

A few hundred yards along Kames Bay, Dr Eric Redford wondered why his best suit was covered in paint. Ethel wondered how long it would be before her husband was certified and carted off to the giggle factory.

His distant nephew, Dr Algernon Pendlebury, was now sitting beside the fruit machine in Hugh's Bar. Fifty-five years old, tall and thin with an unruly explosion of black hair and rimless spectacles, he was sipping a large glass of his favourite white wine, *Chataueneuf du Cumbrae*, while puzzling over the Giant Crossword in the *Gazette*. 'Five letters,' he said to no-one in particular. 'First three letters are BOO and the fifth letter is S. Clue is 'Often entertaining.'

'Boobs,' answered Bungalow Bob.

'Try "Books",' offered bar owner Hughie.

Hickory Dickory wrote in the word. 'Aye, books. Too obvious, eh? Couldn't see it for looking at it.' Dr Algernon Pendlebury was bored witless and in a playful mood. He gave his small audience the impression he possessed a mind as sharp as a sausage. But it was probably just as well he wouldn't be required to perform any delicate heart surgery that afternoon. 'Maybe another bottle might help,' he thought and nodded to himself. 'Aye, that'll do the trick.' He scoffed the remains of his glass. 'Hughie, when you've got a moment, please. *Une bouteille de votre delicieux Chateauneuf du Cumbrae, s'il vous plait.*' He held up the empty bottle.

'*Mais oui, monsieur*,' said Hughie, playing his role in the daily charade. The owner looked around the quiet bar. He liked the feel of his pub: an old-fashioned establishment with no frivolous plastic plants on display. 'A wee man's pub,' his Dad would have called it. The walls were painted a dull cream and were home to a scattering of sepia-coloured prints of some of the sea vessels that had puffed proudly along the Clyde in a bygone day. The wall opposite the bar was dominated by a large mirror promoting James R. Burns and Sons. Under a huge thistle, the legend boasted that the family had been blending the finest Scotch whisky since 1890. The bar itself was about thirty feet long. It was an original and well-worn wooden surface that curved round into a small area at the

18

front of the pub. This was Vodka's Joe's domain, his 'Window on the World'. As usual, Vodka Joe had commandeered the comfiest seat in the place, a four-foot long sofa that backed against the wall in his special corner. Hughie had bought the settee in a fire sale after a local restaurant had closed down.

Vodka Joe named his exclusive area 'Sofa So Good'. He would come in first thing in the morning, swipe Hughie's newspaper, pick up a glass of neat vodka and say, 'Sofa so good.' Then he would park his slight frame on the welcoming couch. Hughie Edwards' resident customer was liked by all, even tolerated grudgingly by Dr Algernon Pendlebury, who, under the pain of death, would never have admitted to such a notion. Vodka Joe was a facial lookalike for Bogart's movie chum Peter Lorre. But, at least, he didn't annoy everyone one by constantly and irritatingly asking 'Who's got the falcon?'

Running parallel with the bar, under the giant James R. Burns and Sons mirror, were three small wooden tables. Backing against that wall were some more sofas Hughie had bought at a knockdown price from the owner of the doomed restaurant. In his fight against the recession, the desperate restaurateur had come up with a novel 'All-you-can-eat-for-a-fiver' scheme. Bungalow Bob, not unlike a small shed in dimensions, just about wiped him out in a week. To complete the furnishings in Hugh's Bar, there were ten tall stools ranged alongside the bar. There had been some spectacular Olympic-style somersaults off these seats over the years. To break the fall of any hapless drunk, Hughie had thoughtfully invested in rock-solid wooden parquet flooring.

Beside the last of the wooden tables was the fruit machine and there was a ramp leading to the rear of the pub. Before reaching the snooker room and the ladies' loo at the back, there was a small area almost sealed off from the rest of the pub. This held a collection

19

of four or five tables where the bar owner liked to herd adults with kids. Hughie still believed children had no place in pubs. Beyond this area was the Gents, on the left of a tight corridor, and a few feet further along the entrance of the snooker room and the Ladies. Sporting participants were clearly unaware that Hughie had invested in CCTV. Balls were potted to such an extent the bar owner had thought more than once of setting up his own porn channel.

Hickory Dickory was sitting at the last of the tables opposite the bar and beside the silent fruit machine.

Vodka Joe was at his favourite spot, keeping the island under his scrutiny as he sipped quietly at his drink of choice. Bungalow Bob was looking at the back page of the *Daily News* and shaking his head fairly vehemently as he disagreed, yet again, with the Scotland football manager's latest international squad. 'Guy knows bugger all about football,' he muttered. 'Complete waste of skin. Fire the dud. Fire the dud into space.'

The island's GP, patiently awaiting his replenishment of alcohol, was contentedly humming to himself, peering at the crossword. 'Hughie,' he asked again. '*Ou est mon boutieille du vin, s'il vous plait?*'

'*Pardonnez-moi, monsieur, mon erreur,*' said the landlord, his mind elsewhere. '*Désolé*, Hick.'

'Hickory Dickory, if you don't mind,' sniffed the doc. 'You know I don't like Hick.' Hughie looked at him as he found another bottle of *Chateauneuf du Cumbrae* and pondered for a moment. Was a single digit IQ compulsory in his family?

He placed the bottle of tepid white wine on the table in front of the island's GP. 'Same price as half-an-hour ago,' smiled Hughie, accepting the payment and depositing it in the cash register he liked to call the Jewish Piano. In more intimate moments, he would call it Sammy Davis Jnr. Either way, he realised it was terribly non-PC in these enlightened times. He looked at the till and muttered, 'You're as busy as the doc. The island's far too healthy.' Hughie knew only too well there would be a few more weeks like this in the run-in to the Festive period. He expected a month of relative peace and quiet, inactivity neither he nor the Jewish Piano eagerly sought, before everything went potty again; splendid pandemonium revisiting his establishment.

Hickory Dickory nibbled on the end of the Biro. 'Here's another one, lads. A six-letter word. I've got blank, blank and then NDOM. --NDOM.'

What's the clue?' asked Hughie, adding, 'That might be helpful.'

'Oh, yes, of course,' said the doc. 'Selection process.'

'Condom,' answered Bungalow Bob.

'Try "Random",' offered bar owner Hughie.

'You're quite good at this, Hughie,' said Hickory Dickory. 'Aren't you? You've not had a sneaky look at the answers, have you, naughty boy?'

Vodka Joe was sitting minding his own business, watching a couple of swans doing their best to maintain poise and grace in the choppy Firth of Clyde about fifty yards away. At the slip, a couple of little boats strained at their moorings. He let out an audible sigh.

'Still wondering why there is only one Monopolies Commission?' asked Hughie, adding, 'A euro for them, my diminutive friend.'

'Oh, my thoughts aren't worth a euro,' grinned Vodka Joe. 'Then, again, maybe they are with the state of the euro.' He scratched his unshaven jaw. 'Do you think the euro will ever come to Millport, Hughie?'

'Don't think so, Vodka. That's us just caught up with decimalisation. Took us half-a-century, but it got here in the end.'

'Aye, it's like death,' said Vodka Joe reflectively. 'It'll get here in the end.'

'Well, cheers for that, Vodka. Was I looking far too happy?'

'Ach, you know what I mean. Days like this make you wonder what it's all about, don't they?'

'Do they?' said Hughie, puzzled at the new-found philosophy of one of the island's local worthies. 'You're not thinking about taking a header off the pier, are you?'

'What would be the point, Hughie?' shrugged Vodka Joe. 'I can swim.'

'Hey, lads, how about a bit of help with this one?' Hickory Dickory, still enjoying himself, frowned again. 'Four letters starting with 'F' and ending in 'K'. The clue is: "Used in penetration." F--K. Any clues, lads?'

'Fuck,' answered Bungalow Bob.

'Try "Fork",' offered bar owner Hughie.

'Christ, Hughie, you are good,' said the doc. 'Excellent. "Fork." Aye, now that you say it.' He jotted it down.

There were occasions when the bar owner was convinced there was enough stupidity in his establishment to start a new country.

A gust of wind shot through the narrow pub as the front door creaked open. Harry Webb, known as Cobb, and Don Kirk, two jovial locals, had fought manfully against the gales thundering along the exposed Stuart Street, the rain gathering momentum as it cascaded angrily, adorning the roads and pavements with puddles. Cobb, a tubby individual of about five feet eight inches, was wearing a large black anorak. His brown corduroy trousers were stuffed into his hiking boots. The anorak, the trousers and the boots, like their owner, had seen better days. He took off his captain's hat and chucked it onto a peg on the wall beside the door. His ruddy complexion betrayed a lifelong love affair with dark rum and Coke.

Cobb's companion, Don Kirk, was also of a bulky stature and similarly attired: a dark grey Dryzabone coat down to his ankles, denims tucked into green wellies. He removed his beanie cap and lobbed it beside his pal's captain's hat. Don possessed what Billy Connolly would often refer to as a 'Halloween Cake Face.' Big, fat and cheerful, with a nose that looked like a bashed over-ripe tomato. He, too, shared his mate's fondness for alcohol, although his chosen tipple was straight bourbon. They both worked as labourers on the farms and had done so for about thirty years, but there was little they could offer their profession on a day like this. They sought succour and shelter. And where better than Hugh's Bar?

By the time they had removed their soaked coats and hung them up beside their head gear, their drinks were already waiting for them on the bar. 'How did you know, Hughie?' laughed Cobb. 'I might have fancied a small mineral water today.' Hughie smiled, 'In your nightmares, my man.' Both farm workers settled their plump, spreading backsides on stools at the bar, clinked their glasses, said 'Cheers' to everyone and sipped noisily. It wouldn't be their last drink of the day, Hughie was sure of that.

'Struggling today, folks,' said Hickory Dickory, continuing to act the role and looking puzzled while continuing to chomp on the stem of his plastic pen. 'How about some help with this one? Five-letter word. Starts with 'P', a blank, 'N', a blank and then 'S'. 'P-N-S.' What could that be, I wonder?'

'Clue, please, Hickory Dickory,' sighed Hughie.

'Oh, aye, that might give us a chance, eh?' Hick replied. 'Let's see. Says here "Mainly out of view". What does that mean?'

'Penis,' answered Bungalow Bob, adding swiftly, 'Unless he's a flasher, of course.'

'Try "Pants",' offered bar owner Hughie.

'My God, Hughie,' Hickory Dickory practically exclaimed. 'You are good. Pants. Yes, that's right. Could have been penis, I suppose. "Mainly out of view." Aye, that might have been penis.'

'I've got a date tonight,' boomed Cobb, who hadn't quite kept pace with the changes in female underwear over the last decade or so. He was quite happy to announce his forthcoming romantic interlude.

'You been on that rhino powder?' asked his mate.

'Tried that; didn't work,' said Cobb. 'Just gave me the irresistible urge to charge head down at cars.'

Hughie moved to the middle of the bar. 'So, you've found a lovely wench, at last, Cobb?' he said, still frantically rubbing at a pint pot.

'Maybe I have, Hughie,' grinned the farm worker, who liked the nickname Cobb. He was well aware it could have been much worse. It could have been Cliff, after Cliff Richard. He knew the pop singer had been born with the name Harry Webb before being forced to change it to keep up with groovy trend of the late fifties. No-one would buy a record by a bloke called Harry Webb when they could choose from Elvis, Fabian, Adam Faith, Dion, Conway Twitty, Screamin' Jay Hawkins and other exotics. Cobb was more of a Perry Como man and couldn't abide the ruckus kicked up be these rock'n'roll characters, who clearly knew nothing about music as they went about assaulting your eardrums while shaking their arses in the faces of screaming females. 'Lucky buggers,' he thought.

He sipped his dark rum and Coke and smirked naughtily, a man in his sixties being transported back to pre-pubescent times. 'Aye, maybe I've found a lass, Hughie, to share my bed. We're going down the Legion tonight. They're selling dark rum at fifty pence a shot. Could be a good night all round, if you know what I mean, eh?'

'Do we know the lady in question, Cobb?' queried the bar owner.

'Och, of course, you do, Hughie. She works in the Twilight Cafe along at Kames Bay. It's Carrie. You know Carrie?'

Hughie made sure his smile remained firmly in place. 'Dirty Carrie' was her nickname, and she was known fairly intimately by the entire male population of Millport, with the possible exception of himself, Cobb, Hickory Dickory and Vodka Joe (who only had eyes for Gina Lollobrigida). Hughie was aware she had more baggage than Heathrow Airport. Apparently, Dirty Carrie's idea of commitment was to stay overnight. It was often said black widow spiders enjoyed more enduring romances.

'Oh, good luck, Cobb,' said the bar owner, accidentally cracking the glass he was cleaning. If we never see you again, Cobb, he thought, we'll all know you've fallen into the Dark

Hole of Cumbrae. Dirty Carrie, apparently, was a fully paid-up member of the Tragic Circle. It was rumoured entire platoons had gone missing around Carrie's nether regions. The alarm was raised when the ten members of the Cumbrae Pipe Band, including two grannies, went AWOL a few years ago, but, thankfully, they surfaced at Fintry Bay after a day of indulging in homemade firewater. The drummer had never sounded better. Hughie had been given a red flag about Dirty Carrie's reputation when he first set foot on the island thirteen years ago. Since then, he had given her a wide berth. Not an easy task when her backside was the size of a small continent. Hughie had seen tugs turn quicker.

'Watch yourself with that glass, Hughie,' said Cobb. 'You can't be too careful.'

'Ditto,' muttered Hughie.

'I'm not doing too well, at all, today.' Hickory Dickory had re-entered the land of the living after five minutes in his own personal netherworld while pondering the latest clue. 'Anyone help with this one, please?' He cleared his throat. 'Five-letter word and the clue is "Rhythmical throbbing". I've got 'P' and 'U', a blank, 'S' and another blank. PU-S-. "Rhythmical throbbing." Anyone?'

'Pussy,' said Bungalow Bob.

'Try "Pulse",' offered bar owner Hughie.

'Good grief,' said Hickory Dickory. 'Fits perfectly, straight in there.'

'You sure it's not "pussy"?' asked Bungalow Bob.

Don Kirk ordered up another couple of drinks for himself and his buddy. 'Better watch what I'm drinking today,' said Cobb, with an element of 'nudge, nudge, know what I mean?' 'I'll probably stop at about fifteen,' he added.

Hughie poured the drinks and set them up on the bar. 'Great name, Don Kirk,' he said to Don Kirk. 'I've never asked, but were you, in fact, christened Donald? It's not another crazy nickname thought up on this island by locals who haven't enough to occupy their minds? I still feel sorry for old Albert Ross. He has to go through life answering to 'Hanging Around My Neck'.

'No, my Dad, God Rest His Soul, was at Dunkirk when it was evacuated in 1940. He used to tell me he stood with the water up to his shoulders for hours waiting for a vessel to get him to safety. Reckons he was one of the last off the beach. He promised to name his first born after that place in France. Remember that Winston Churchill speech? "We shall fight on the beaches"? My Dad, God Rest His Soul, would have a couple of drinks on Hogmanay and every time the clock struck midnight that was the first thing he would say. "We shall fight on the beaches". And then he would wish me and my Mum, God Rest Her Soul, a Happy New Year. Same every Hogmanay without fail. So, no surprise when I was christened Donald and it was quickly shortened to Don.'

'Good story,' nodded Hughie. 'Any others in the family?' he asked by way of conversation.

'Aye, there's my younger sister.'

'Really? I didn't know you had a sister. What's her name?'

'Dawn,' came the reply.

Hughie almost cracked another glass. 'I'll have to get off this island before my brain turns to bird seed,' he promised himself for only the umpteenth time that day.

'Getting near to completion, chaps, and that's it,' said Hickory Dickory. 'I've got a four-letter word here starts with a 'C' and ends in a 'P'. The clue is "Cultivated plants". C--P.'

'Crap,' said Bungalow Bob.

Try "Crop",' offered bar owner Hughie.

'Top of the class, Hughie,' said Hickory Dickory. 'Gold star in your jotter.' The doc gave a satisfying grin. 'Right, lads, I've only got one to go and that's me finished the crossword.' He put the emphasis on the word 'me'.

'Right, here goes,' he said. 'This should be easy, but I'm not at my best today.'

'When are you ever at your best?' thought Hughie, Bungalow Bob, Vodka Joe, Cobb Webb and Don Kirk in unison without speaking a word.

'Okay, three-letter word that ends in 'X'. Something something 'X'. And the clue is, "Very important in numbers".'

'Sex,' said Bungalow Bob.

'Why would that be very important in numbers?' asked the GP.

'Have you never had a threesome?' shot back Bungalow Bob, who had never had a threesome.

'Try "Six",' offered bar owner Hughie.

Hickory Dickory jotted down the letters 'S' and 'I'. 'You're a genius, Hughie,' he said admiringly. 'A bloody genius.' Then the frown returned to his face. 'Why is 'six' very important in numbers?' he asked.

'I'm taking a wild stab in the dark here, Hick,' said Hughie, 'but it might not be possible to get from the number five to the number seven without a number six in between. Just a thought.'

Hickory Dickory chewed on the pen and said nothing. 'Hughie's on fire today,' he thought.

Hughie moved to the other end of the bar to keep Vodka Joe company as he counted seagulls. 'Here's something to cheer you up, Vodka,' beamed Hughie, feverishly rubbing the pint glass with the dishtowel. 'Charlie Brock's coming down for a few days. Phoned last night to warn me.'

'Charlie Brock,' smiled Vodka Joe. 'Big-time celebrity down here now, isn't he? Solved the island's only shooting. Poor old Wild Bill Hickok. Sherlock Holmes, eat your heart out, here comes Charlie Brock.'

'Aye, it's never quiet when Brock's around,' replied Hughie, holding the glass up to the light, inspecting it closely. Satisfied, he placed it back with the rest of the other pint glasses on the ledge under the bar and selected another for some hearty rubbing. He began zealously cleaning the jar. He added, 'Wonder what will happen this time?'

'Strange things seem to occur when Charlie Brock's around,' nodded Vodka Joe.

CHAPTER THREE

Late evening. Friday 19 November.

Nou Camp Stadium, Barcelona.

Derek Laird summoned all the power in his sturdy frame into one vital split-second of contact and launched a shot of awesome ferocity high into the opposition's net; the rigging bulged with the explosive impact of the speeding ball before the startled, stranded goalkeeper could move a muscle.

'GGOOOOOOOOOOOOOOOOAAAAAAAAAAALLLLLL!' screamed the Spanish television commentator with his customary ear-destroying yell. The giant electric scoreboards behind both goals at the three-tiered Nou Camp Stadium simultaneously beamed, 'BARCELONA 1 REAL MADRID 0'.

Caballo Loco, aka Crazy Horse, had pounced again with his thirty-third goal of a rewarding campaign. As the ball nestled behind the opposing goalkeeper, over 93,000 fans went wild with delirium. *'Salva Caballa Loco!'* screamed the Barcelona supporters in frenzied unison. The small pocket of visiting Real Madrid fans were struck dumb, silenced by the stunning twenty-five yard volley from the Scot that would surely win the game with only seconds remaining to play. Crazy Horse's timing was as perfect as his strike. His blondish hair was picked out by the dazzling floodlights as he leapt high to punch the air in his usual salute. The Barcelona support worshipped him in their home at the Nou Camp, more of a cathedral than a mere football ground. This was a special place: their citadel, their fortress. They saluted their

Golden Boy as only Catalans can.

Derek Laird, who had long since shed his original unoriginal nickname Degsy, had been astute enough five years previously to get these fans onside even before he had kicked a ball in anger following his transfer from Arsenal. As was the normal practice, the club had opened the doors of their massive bowl of a stadium to introduce their summer signings to the fans. The Scot was one of three expensive captures the previous month, the others being a German midfielder, Gunter Overath, and a Mexican central defender, Hugo Ramirez.

The football club's manager, a rotund, amiable little man named Rafael Castillo, led the newly-acquired players onto the impeccable surface to be greeted by feverish noise from the supporters. Laird tried his best to look calm, acting like this was all so normal to him. He looked up at the vast bowl and thought, 'Shit! What have I got myself into? Can I really play at this level?' Three years earlier he had been playing for Albion Rovers in the Scottish Second Division. Two men and a dog watched them on matchday. Laird looked again at the sun-drenched, densely-populated terracings. He guessed there might be about seventy to eighty thousand people in the ground. It would take Albion Rovers a few decades to attract such numbers.

Manager Castillo, bald with a large and untrimmed moustache that dominated his face, was wildly overweight. Laird looked at him. He had been told his new team coach had once been the mesmerising midfield general of Barcelona. *El Mago*. The Magician. 'What the hell happened to you?' he thought. 'What the hell am I doing here?' he added. The Scot looked at the German, Overath. He appeared composed, completely at ease. He had cost £50 million from Bayern Munich. The Mexican, Ramirez, gave the impression of being slightly apprehensive. He had played only

31

one season with Sporting de Gijón, who were hardly giants of the Spanish game. He was the bargain of the trio; he had cost a mere £12 million. The manager was handed a microphone as he stepped into the centre circle to rapturous applause from the fans. From somewhere under his overgrown facial foliage, his unseen lips moved as he spoke to the supporters. One by one, he ushered the new players forward to take the salute of the fans.

The German, Overath, was first up. He was nonchalant, extremely confident. He was every inch a perfect specimen of a sportsman. His long blond hair just about nestled on his shoulders and he had Hollwood's idea of a perfect smile. His teeth gleamed as he waved to the cheering supporters. He said nothing before returning to take his stance beside his new team-mates. The Mexican, Ramirez, was next up. Clearly, this was all new to this player. Nervously, he took a small bow before returning hastily to the relative safety of the centre circle. He, too, remained silent. Manager Castillo shouted something into the microphone and the supporters cheered wildly again. 'What did he say?' thought Laird. 'Last and least, here's the Scottish guy?'

Derek Laird stepped forward to be embraced by an ecstatic support. They hadn't even seen him live in action and here he was being hailed as an all-conquering hero. 'Jeezus,' he thought. 'I never got this treatment when I scored my first hat-trick for Arsenal.' He waved back to the supporters. As he returned to the centre circle, he stopped to have a word with his manager. Castillo handed the Scot the microphone. Laird might have been wearing a hard hat, climbing scaffolding on some of Glasgow's disintegrating council estates and delivering lunchtime snacks to his work mates only a few years earlier, but he was blessed with a streetwise knowledge that couldn't be purchased anywhere.

With a new-found confidence, the applause of the supporters

taking him to a safer place, Laird stepped forward again. The photographers were snapping away from every conceivable angle, capturing him wearing the latest Barcelona strip. Some of the snappers were lying flat at his feet, shooting up at him. For a moment he thought, 'Wonder what that'll look like?' Then he lifted the microphone.

'*Estic molt content d'haver signat amb et Futbol Club Barcelona. Prometo jugar el meu mullor futbol per al club y per vosaltres, la mullor aficio. Prometo marcar gols per aquest gran equip de futbol. Gracies.*'

He kept it short and simple. 'I am very happy to have signed for Barcelona Football Club. I promise to play my very best for this club and you, the wonderful supporters. I promise I will score goals for this great football team. Thank you.'

The stadium was in uproar. Laird had delivered the address in Catalan, not Spanish. There was a subtle difference. It had taken him a month to learn the exact words and to master the difficult dialect. He knew he had to get the pronunciation absolutely spot on. He had hired a private language tutor. She just happened to be Catalan, a Barcelona supporter and very pretty. She wouldn't accept a euro in payment, but she was quite happy to have the Scot for company. Intimately. Every night for a month. Laird didn't recall education at Dougrie Terrace Primary School in Glasgow's southside ever being so enjoyable. He was convinced his old headmistress Miss Flynn had been a man. The moustache was the giveaway.

Laird waved once again to the frenzied support. 'They love me,' he thought. 'I am going to enjoy it here.'

But that was five years ago. Things had changed. Quite dramatically, too.

CHAPER FOUR

Early morning. Sunday 21 November.

Glasgow.

The irresistible aroma of bacon and fried eggs wafted around Charlie Brock's kitchen, his senses bombarded by the inviting bouquet of his soon-to-be-devoured Sunday morning cooked breakfast.

The journalist looked out from his fourth-storey two-bedroom flat in Glasgow's Merchant City and smiled. The hands on the clock on the kitchen wall informed him it was just nudging beyond seven o'clock on a grey, cold and uninviting morning. He stretched his arms and arched his back and yawned loudly. No hangover this morning. He had taken an attack of brains the previous evening, left his cronies in the Double C Bar on the Broomielaw at a respectable hour and made his way home.

At one point he had thought he was going to get lucky with barmaid Julie, until a reject from the World Wrestling Association turned up. Brock was convinced the interloper had muscles on his eyelashes. He realised he was a poor second in the chat-up stakes when the Giant Haystacks lookalike took notice of Julie's revealing top, a top which displayed her ample charms to some effect.

'Dae ye want to get yer gums roon this?', the behemoth asked in some mangled, tortured tongue as he proudly pointed to the bulge in the crotch of his tight jeans. Julie checked out the hump. She looked impressed, Brock observed sadly. In the same instant he accepted a shag with the Double C barmaid was out of the question. He also wondered if Mr. Muscles had stuffed a mattress down the front of his trousers. 'Another night on the substitutes' bench for Happy Harry,' thought Brock as he drained his pint of lager.

It had been a good, old Saturday night chinwag with R.I.P. and El Cid, who were his two best friends in the whole, wide world. Two guys he would trust with his laptop. R.I.P. was, in fact, Griff Stewart, the Chief News Reporter of the *Daily News*, and El Cid was Detective Inspector Harry Booth of Police Scotland CID. Lifelong mates without a secret among them. Five years earlier, when Brock had quit the *Daily News*, he knew he would lose a host of so-called friends among the journalists. R.I.P. was never going to be among the deserters.

In the past, Brock had known the feeling of a version of abandonment. His two marriages, to Irene and Wendy, hadn't quite made it to the finishing line. 'Two's not bad for a start. Maybe third time lucky,' he had told himself eleven years ago, after Wendy had ordered him to pack his toothbrush and bid his final farewell. Both break-ups had been remarkably amicable. No bad feelings; just individuals realising a mistake had been made somewhere along the line in the meeting of minds and personalities. Brock was now fifty-five years old and often wondered if there would ever be a Mrs Brock the Third. There had been a few dalliances, but nothing serious. It wasn't something that overly worried him. *Que sera, sera*; whatever will be, will be.

Brock smiled as he momentarily reminisced. Then, for the sixth time that evening, the sports journalist chinked his pint pot with that of El Cid and R.I.P.'s brandy glass – 'Gentleman's measure, thank you very much' – and said, 'Cheers, we can't go on meeting like this.' Normally it was greeted with the dual response of, 'Get some new material, mate.' He knew he never would. They knew he never would.

Brock informed his friends his afternoon had been spent in Greenock as he reported on the Morton versus Livingston First Division encounter at depressed, rundown Cappielow Park. It had ended goalless with both sets of players obviously suffering from an infliction that brought on a stubborn form of slow motion and an apparent aversion to providing anything remotely resembling entertainment. The highlight of the day came from the announcer at half-time. 'Last week's Golden Goal wasn't won, so there is a rollover this week,' he had told a couple of hundred stupefied spectators. 'The jackpot now stands at £7.' Brock thought, 'Some punter is going to get lucky tonight. That'll cover a pint of Guinness, a poke of chips and a couple of pickled onions. Maybe a blow job, too.' He was well aware they knew how to enjoy themselves in Greenock.

Brock was happy the marriages of his two pals had endured through the years. El Cid had been R.I.P.'s best man when the newspaperman signed the dotted line with Anna; R.I.P. was asked to return the compliment when the cop tied the knot with Lynda. El Cid was godfather to R.I.P.'s only child, a son called John, now twenty-four years old. And it was an identical situation when El Cid became a father for the one and only time: a daughter named Eileen, now twenty-three years old. 'Wouldn't it be ironic if John and Eileen got together?' the newspaperman often thought. 'It's bad enough having you as a mate without being a fuckin' relative, as well,' the cop always replied. Brock often wondered if becoming a dad might have kept one of his marriages intact. He didn't dwell on that, either. *Que sera, sera.*

'Enjoy the game today, pal?' El Cid had asked, drawing on his pint of heavy at the podium in the Budgie Cage of the Double

C pub. Saturday night and the place was virtually empty. 'They should rename this place Nobody's Inn,' Brock had said often enough over the past few years. In a former life, in happier times, it had been the office pub for the journalists and printers of the *Daily News* and the *Sunday News*, both based just around the corner on Walloch Street. Once upon a time, it had been a pulsating, buoyant, achingly busy boozer. Then along came a new owner for the newspaper group – 'Fatso', as he was endearingly known to most, if not all, of his freshly-acquired employees – who had turned everything on its head in one fell swoop. He ripped the heart and soul out of everything he touched. No-one grieved when Fatso disappeared in mysterious circumstances, amid speculation he owed an awful lot of money to several countries and some very shady characters, with arms dealers being mentioned in dispatches. It was often mooted that he might still be alive, having faked his own death. The private jet that had been carrying him to Bermuda, where he would visually terrorise locals on the exclusive beaches with his gross obesity and his XXXXXXXXXL garish floral shorts, had gone down in a mountain range just twenty minutes short of the holiday island. 'Maybe he just became an extra mountain,' stated Brock many times over the years. 'Who would know the difference?'

'Enjoy the game?' he asked the cop with a heavy degree of irony. 'I've had better times at a drunken, shortsighted dentist's.' El Cid could have anticipated the reply. It was fair to say Brock, having covered Scottish football for almost forty years, was becoming somewhat less than enthusiastic about his matchday trips to Greenock, Coatbridge, Kirkcaldy, Larbert and even Maryhill, where his favourite team Partick Thistle went about their business. 'Why don't you just chuck it?' asked the cop. Brock slurped noisily on his pint of lager and then answered, 'Irene and

Wendy. Good housekeepers.' El Cid laughed. He had heard the line before, of course, but it still made him smile.

'You had a good week? What's happening on the mean streets of the city?' asked the freelance sports reporter. 'Very, very quiet, I'm delighted to tell you,' answered El Cid. 'No axe murders this week. No drive-by shootings. We've got Christmas coming up fast. Tis the season to be jolly? Aye, right. Everything will begin to kick off when the doting parents go in search of cash to buy Junior the latest in whatever technology they are flogging these days. The must-have gift for an eight year old, "Let's Kill Every Motherfucker" for their game station. "That's what he wants and that's what he'll get. Only the best for Junior." Then they knock over an OAP's gaff in Newton Mearns and rob her of her life savings. So, this is the lull before the storm. I'm enjoying it while I can.'

'Aye, if it's quiet for you, El Cid, it's dead for us, too,' said R.I.P. The Chief News Reporter earned his nickname from Brock when he was regularly first on the scene at an unsuspecting family home to break the news of a horrible murder or a tragic accident, relating the details to a parent, a wife, a husband, a partner, a relative or a friend of the newly-deceased. It wasn't a role in his job he cared for. The newsman sighed, 'World news is helping us out at the moment because there's zilch happening on the home front. A wee World War Three would help. Mind you, our wonderful proprietors wouldn't know a good story if it came up and stuck the head on their balls. And don't blame the Editor. Vic Bernard is as good as they come. And Martin Gilhooley is the best News Editor I've ever worked with, so don't point the finger at him, either. No, all the decisions are coming from London. They're the ones to blame. Fatso's gone to be replaced by Fatso Two. They change the look of the newspapers every now and again and there's no rhyme or reason to what they come up with. They spend millions in bringing in new software to keep up with the changing times and, before you know where you are, the newspaper looks like a bloody comic.'

R.I.P. slowly shook his head. 'Daft giveaways and even dafter competitions dominate the front page these days. At the bottom of the page you might get lucky and notice that there is a little cross reference that informs you "Voting has been scrapped in Britain and all taxes have been abolished. Turn to pages such and such for the full story." However, if you're really, really lucky you might **"WIN A GORILLA." Or "YOU CAN BECOME PRESIDENT OF THE UNITED STATES OF AMERICA."** And then they'll ask you three simple questions. "Turtle wax was invented to polish which items? A: Cars; B: Shoes; C: Turtles." Then you've got to telephone the special hotline number before 7pm to have a chance to take over the planet's superpower and enjoy life making world-altering decisions in the White House while wondering what would happen if you pressed the big red button on the giant oak desk in the Oval Office. "Last week I was sweeping the streets of Cumbernauld for a living," said the lucky winner. "Now I've got the chance to obliterate China." And they wonder why circulation is plummeting towards the earth's core.'

'I thought you might have had the splash last week, R.I.P.' said Brock. 'Good story you had about the six year old kid who stole his daddy's Rolls-Royce and drove it from Whitecraigs to Sauchiehall Street and mowed down about thirty pedestrians before crashing it through the window of that pet shop. Terrapins all over the place.'

'Aye, I got unlucky with that one,' sighed the newspaperman. 'Nobody actually died. A couple of elderly ladies will never walk again, but that was it. Oh, and the newspaper seller on the corner will have to learn how to cope with one arm. So, no, there was no chance of that story getting on the front page. Not when I was up against **"WIN BRAD PITT AND ANGELINA JOLIE FOR LIFE".** You can't compete with that.' He smiled and added, 'I wonder how they'll enjoy life on Barra.'

Brock put up another three drinks on the podium. 'How much booze have we scoffed at this very location, gentlemen? Could you imagine how much money we would all have in the bank if we were teetotallers?' El Cid shook his head vigorously, 'Doesn't bear thinking about, does it?' R.I.P. chipped in, 'Mind you, we have had some great times have we not? Cheers!' They clinked their glasses and greedily scoffed the contents. 'God bless Mr Lager,' said Brock, looking at his wristwatch. It was just before nine o'clock. 'I think I'll make this my last, guys,' he said. 'It doesn't look as though Happy Harry will be entering the porthole of Miss Julie now Mr. Universe is on the scene. Maybe next week ...'

'Are you heading over to Millport any time soon, Charlie?' asked the cop, changing the topic of conversation. 'That was some Country and Western Festival, wasn't it? My God, I'll never forget it. You solved the shooting of Wild Bill Hickok. Amazing. Sportswriter-turned-sleuth. Remarkable. Not just a pretty face, after all.'

'Not even a pretty face,' said R.I.P. swiftly.

'Don't you dare say Spartacus isn't a handsome chap,' laughed Brock, who many insisted had more than a passing facial resemblance to a younger Kirk Douglas. He pressed the forefinger of his right hand to the dimple on his chin and said, 'I'm Spartacus.'

'I'm Spartacus,' said El Cid.

'I'm Spartacus,' said R.I.P.

The seriously well-endowed, brawny new soon-to-be beau of

barmaid Julie looked at the sports reporter, the newspaperman and the cop. He wondered why they all had the same name.

Brock got round to answering the cop's question. 'Millport? Aye, I'll be heading over to Fantasy Island some time very soon. In fact, maybe Monday. It's always a great time of year when the island gets ready for Christmas and New Year. Mainly Hogmanay for the locals. We think we can drink? Christ, try keeping up with those guys. The women, too. They know how to get on the outside of an ocean of alcohol, I can tell you. Pretty damn impressive.'

'Aye, we noticed at the Country and Western Festival,' said R.I.P. 'Aye, impressive. That's the word.'

'Fuckin' impressive,' said El Cid. 'That's the words.'

Brock had purchased a one-bedroomed attic flat on the island five years ago as a bolthole to get away from the world and its many miseries. He had christened his flat 'Schloss Adler.' His hideaway was three stories up on Quayhead Street beside the Old Millport Pier. Schloss Adler, which translated to Castle of the Eagle, was the name of the seemingly-impregnable German fortress set high in the Bavarian mountains in Alistair MacLean's war movie and novel *Where Eagles Dare*. This was Brock's favourite film and and his favourite book. His breath was often taken away when he looked out over the rolling Firth of Clyde towards Largs. 'Is there a more beautiful country than Scotland?' he would often ask himself; a rhetorical question if ever there was one, as far as he was concerned.

'I'll need to get over for a few days,' he told his drinking partners. 'I'll need to batten down the hatches. The Schloss Adler is quite exposed, as you know. It can take some hammering when the old Firth gets its dander up. I've seen the seawater clatter off my back windows. Incredible sight. The Firth wallops off the rocks below and sends showers all the way up three storeys. Did you ever see *Ryan's Daughter*? That scene when the villagers are going into the sea to get the shipment of weapons that are being washed ashore after a ship had been wrecked on the rocks? They filmed that in a storm. Some truly wonderful scenes. Old Leo McKern almost getting washed away. Fantastic stuff. It can be like that in Millport. Honest. I've seen spray flying from one end of the promenade, hitting the white walls at the seafront, and going right across the road and battering off the windows of the pubs and shops on the other side.'

Brock took another welcoming sip of ale. 'God bless Mr Beer,' he said before adding ruefully, 'Mind you, climbing up Cardiff Street these days can play havoc with the knee joints.'

'You're just getting old, Brock,' said R.I.P. 'Face it, lad, you'll need the fire brigade on standby when you light the candles on your next birthday cake. Maybe not a bad idea to have Red Adair in the vicinity.'

'Just remember, my old friend, we all age at exactly the same rate.' Brock smiled and added, 'There, that's another three seconds gone for all of us.'

Brock smacked his lips as he finished his beer and placed the empty glass on the bar. 'See you later, Julie,' he said. She smiled. Rambo of the Magic Todger scowled.

'Okay, lads, I will bid you both a fond *adieu*. I'm off to pick up a black pudding supper.' He stopped and thought about the eruption in Mountain Man's nether regions. 'Maybe, I'll stick to fish tonight,' he corrected. 'Aye, one of Luigi's specials. And then it's feet up, a couple of bottles of lager and I'll spend a pleasant evening in the company of Messrs Lineker and Co. Then I'll be off to get some kip.'

'Remember to put on the boxing gloves,' smiled the cop.

'The boxing gloves?' replied Brock. 'Oh, I wore them out months ago.'

He grinned and added, 'Always leave them laughing. That's what they say, isn't it? Easier to make someone cry than laugh. Okay, here's tonight's offering.'

'Try to keep it short, Brock,' said R.I.P. 'I'm hoping to have an early night myself.'

'Okay, said Brock. 'Here goes. Julius Caesar is desperate to find out the identity of Spartacus. He's beaten up the slaves, tortured them, fed them to the lions, crucified them. The lot. But they still won't break. He seeks out the advice of Marcellus, who is the most sadistic bastard in the world. The Emperor asks his torturer-in-chief what he should do next. Marcellus sneered and went off to devise a plan so sickening and so evil even Caesar felt a lurch in his gut when it was presented to him. Twelve slaves were to be stripped and taken down to the edge of the river's estuary. There, they would be forced to dig individual holes for themselves. They were ordered to stand upright in the pits and Roman soldiers covered them with sand, just the slaves' heads visible on the surface.'

'I thought you were going to keep this short?' asked R.I.P. 'I'm due back at the desk on Monday and I've still to go home and change.'

Brock ignored the interruption and continued. 'All the slaves were buried and set out in a long row about six yards apart. Only twelve heads could be seen. Caesar and Marcellus and the Roman legion watched from about one hundred yards away. The tide slowly started to come in. Fiendishly, Marcellus rubbed his hands.

"This will make them talk," he assured Caesar. They watched as the heads began moving from side to side in unison. The heads were rhythmically keeping in time with each other. Slowly at first and then they picked up speed. All the heads were swaying from side to side. "What is happening?" asked Caesar. "Are they pleading for clemency? Do they ask for mercy? Are they ready to tell me the identity of Spartacus at long last?" Excitedly, the Roman Emperor ordered a Centurian down to the water's edge to discover what was happening. As the Centurian crept closer he could see the heads still moving from side to side. He could hear a noise coming from the slaves. He ventured a little further forward until he could make out the sound above the beating waves. The soldier wondered what they were saying. He edged closer. Then he could hear more clearly the sound coming from the twelve heads. The slaves appeared to be singing.'

'*Oh, we do like to be beside the seaside. Oh, we do like to be beside the sea ...*'

The newspaperman and the cop groaned. Rambo, clearly puzzled, scratched his head and crotch simultaneously. Brock smiled, bade farewell to his companions, turned up the collar of his tan leather coat, pushed open the heavy door of the pub, stepped out into the bitter chill of a November evening on Glasgow's Broomielaw, leaned into the unforgiving gusts and headed for home.

He was still humming, '*Oh, we do like to be beside the seaside*' as he reached Luigi's Fish Emporium in the Merchant City.

CHAPTER FIVE

Early afternoon. Sunday 21 November.

Border Control, Perpignan, France.

BIENVENUE EN FRANCE

WELCOME TO FRANCE

BIENVENIDO A FRANCIA

WILLKOMMEN IN FRANKREICH

BENVENUTO UN FRANCIA

The large black letters on the white background of the cast iron sign at the French passport control at Perpignan looked more than merely welcoming as Derek Laird slowly edged the ten-year-old Peugeot 206 forward. He had taken the same route dozens of times over the past five years since signing for Barcelona. Not once had a border control officer bothered to inspect his passport. Not once.

'Please don't let today be the day,' he thought as he pulled down his New York Yankees baseball cap and made sure his fake moustache was still in place. He wondered just how false it looked. His good friend Ricardo assured him it appeared to be perfectly natural and maybe he should think about actually growing a real one in the future. There were two cars in front of him in his designated lane as he headed for border control. Two officers were on duty.

The first vehicle, fully occupied with what looked like a family, Dad, Mum, son and daughter, was waved through without even as much a perfunctory glance at the driver, his car, its registration or his passport. Laird had performed in front of millions in packed stadiums throughout the world for club and country and had never come even remotely close to feeling this anxious. As Ricardo would have said, he was 'sweating like a rapist'. The car in front, with a solitary driver, was motioned forward; everything being recorded on CCTV. Laird's heart skipped a beat. One of the officers asked for a passport while the other had a quick check of the vehicle.

Ricardo had assured Laird the Peugeot was not stolen – 'One careful lady owner, honest, Derek' – and the footballer realised how much trust he had placed in his little friend, who had insisted he should remain positive at this juncture. 'Yes, remember the story of the man who jumped off the top of the Empire State Building,' he urged. 'As he was passing each window, he was heard to say, "So far, so good". You must think like this.' Laird didn't need a reminder of how that particular tale concluded.

The car in front was motioned forward, everything in order. It probably took an entire three minutes for the check, but it felt like hours to Laird. He put the car into first gear and crawled forward. He was told by Ricardo to act normally, always face the officers, not to look away. Anything could spark their suspicions. '*Arretez-vous, s'il vous plait,*' ordered the guard. One of the officers had disappeared into his glass-fronted hut, the other glanced at Laird, who looked him straight in the eye and smiled. He had his passport at the ready. The immigration guard put out his right hand. '*Documentation, s'il vous plait.*' Laird could feel his heart pounding in his rib cage. A quick flip to his photograph, Laird looking stern-faced and minus any follicle adornment, and the guard handed the document back to Laird. '*Bien. Au revoir,*' he said, stifling a yawn while waving the car through.

'*I love Paris in the springtime. I love Paris in the fall. But I love Paris in the winter most of all,*' hummed Laird, looking again as he passed the sign to his left. '*Bienvenue en France,* right enough,' he grinned. 'Next stop Calais. Dover here I come and then it's back home. Hope it's all plain sailing.' He got his wish. With extraordinary ease, he escaped detection at the passport controls and wondered idly if there was a future in smuggling drugs. The Peugot 206 made it all the way to Largs before being abandoned. Ricardo had assured Laird the car was 'untraceable'. He took him at his word.

Only twenty-four hours beforehand, Derek Laird, aka Crazy Horse to his adoring Barcelona legions, had made his decision. After an agonising few days, he accepted he had little option. He had to escape the goldfish bowl; it was imperative he had some time to himself. This was no nervous breakdown or mental meltdown, although he wouldn't blame anyone who drew those conclusions. And he was certain there would be a few who would. He understood so-called friends would be selling their stories to the newspapers about the REAL Derek Laird, the man away from the spotlight. He realised, too, it would be a lot of bullshit.

This was an obstacle only he could overcome, but he needed some time away to clear his head. That was the easy decision; the next one would prove to be a lot more problematic.

Unknown even to his personal manager, Laird had maintained a separate bank account. There were another five dotted around, some offshore, but this one was for the footballer's exclusive use and there was little point in his personal manager, an extremely polite Englishman by the name of Timothy Smythe-Cooke, knowing anything about it. 'Too many Smythe-Cookes spoil the broth,' thought Laird often. Anyway, his manager had enough to be getting on with making certain the footballer would be well

47

taken care of in his dotage. And Timothy Smythe-Cooke, Mr. Fifteen Per Cent, wouldn't do too badly out of the Derek Laird's earnings, either.

Once they realised it was all legal and above board and taxes would be met, Barcelona's paymasters had agreed to lodge a percentage of their employee's wages into a specified account and another reasonable amount into other accounts where Smythe-Cooke would keep a wary eye on his investment. Laird knew other players operated the same system with their football clubs.

His agent, another Englishman by the name of William Telfer – who never got the joke about the crossbow and the apple – took care of what was known as 'extra contracts', image rights, public appearances, endorsements and so on. He was Mr. Twelve-And-A-Half Per Cent, so everyone was winning and slices of pie were being divvied up on a monthly basis. A telephone call to his 'private' bank told Laird he had around £16 million available. To move such an amount undetected would be virtually impossible, appreciated the footballer who had learned a thing or two about the world of finance since taking his last step off the scaffolds in Glasgow. However, a sum of around £1 million would escape the radar. He had arranged to pay a personal visit to his bank later in the afternoon. Laird had requested four bundles of cash in equal amounts in sterling, dollars, yen and bhat. His bank manager, who just happened to be another Barcelona fan and always eager to assist, assured his favourite footballer the money would be available any time he wanted to call for it. 'Leave all the arrangements to me,' he emphasised. And knew not to ask why Derek Laird wanted hard cash in the currency of Britain, the United States, Japan and Thailand. It was none of his business. He didn't even enquire why Laird requested that the UK currency did not go above a £50 note.

Laird knew he could get away with calling it 'fun money' for a couple of days in Las Vegas. The gambling capital of the world, plonked by gangsters in the Nevada Desert, was now the haunt of the footballer. It had once been Marbella. Then it was Aya Napia. Now it was Vegas because it did what it said on the tin. 'What happens in Vegas, stays in Vegas.' And it was true. Laird had gone twice with his Barcelona team-mates. They were relatively well behaved compared with footballers from other countries, mainly England. In Vegas, they shed all inhibitions, went for it and, most importantly, got away with it. They were small fish in a big pond when the Hollywood legends were in town. They thrived on their anonymity before running home to their families, often leaving a trail of mayhem behind them. No-one would ever know. Good old Vegas.

Bugsy Segal's old hunting ground didn't even enter into Laird's mind when he thought about pulling his disappearing act. He knew an individual could vanish over there forever if you crossed the wrong people. Laird had every intention of returning to Barcelona before too long. He just had to sort out something extremely important before doing so. Well, it was extremely important to him.

'Reeeeeeecaaaardo here.' It was the usual answer from Ricardo Osario on his private mobile. 'Crazzzeeeee Horse! What a fuckin' goal! How's the old torpedo dangling, my good man?'

Derek Laird had met Ricardo Osario within a few days of signing for Barcelona. He liked him immediately. He was brash and colourful; a real character. 'You want anything, and I mean ANYTHING, I'm your man, you dig?' said Ricardo by way of introduction. 'Just ask for Reeeeecaaaardo.' He was about five foot six inches, but his weight was probably more in proportion to someone about two feet taller, reckoned Laird. He was plump, to be polite. You couldn't miss this guy. He wore a short-sleeved bright yellow shirt adorned with prints of hula-hula girls. Disturbingly, the buttons were undone just about down to his navel. Laird guessed he had about six or seven chunky gold chains around his neck, all differing in length. Lime green, extremely loose shorts flapped around his knees and white socks covered most of his shins. He wore red sandals. Dark sunglasses were shoved back on his shaven head, green eyes sparkled in a swarthy, happy roly-poly face. He had a broad smile as he spoke. 'Derek Laird. Scotland. Great country. My grandparents came from Glasgow.' Vigorously, he shook Laird's hand. Laird didn't believe him for a minute.

Not much later, he discovered that Ricardo Osario was any nationality he chose to be on any given day. On the first day of meeting, he was Chilean. A couple of days later he was Paraguayan. Laird spent a few hours in his company one afternoon when his new-found friend started off as a Mexican, moved to become an Argentine and finally settled on Peruvian. 'Keep 'em guessing,' said Ricardo, with a wink. But Laird trusted him and would prove that on this particular morning.

'Ricardo, we must meet,' he said, making the call from a public telephone box. 'I've got to see you as soon as possible. It's very important.'

'I hear you and I'm with you, man. Where and when?' Ricardo Osario knew when someone was in distress and his usual flash act came to an abrupt halt.

'I'll see you at the Salamanca. Okay?'

'I'll be there,' replied Ricardo. It was one of their favourite eating places at the harbour. 'Give me half-an-hour.'

Ricardo was as good as his word, even five minutes early. 'What's the problem, man? Ricardo is here to the rescue.'

Laird realised he had no time to waste. He and the rest of the Barcelona players had the day off after his winning goal against Real Madrid. He knew he had to make the next few hours count. Ricardo settled into a booth inside the restaurant, famous locally for its large portions of paella. 'Must be important if we're hiding in here,' he said.

'It's important, Ricardo,' answered Laird. '*Very* important. I need your help.'

'I told you on the first day I would be here for you,' said Ricardo. 'Anything. Here I am.'

'I need a car ...'

'You need a car like a reindeer needs a hat rack.'

'No, listen, Ricardo. This is serious. Okay? I need a car. Not a new one, nothing flash, something that will blend in with the traffic.'

'No Ferrari? No Porsche? No Bentley?' Ricardo couldn't help himself.

'Absolutely not; nothing like that. Just an ordinary car. Something that won't attract attention. And, Ricardo, it must be clean.'

His friend momentarily looked disappointed. 'Have I ever let you down, man? Ever?'

'Sorry, Ricardo, my head's all over the place at the moment. I know you won't disappoint. But I need that car. Today. As soon as possible.'

'May I ask a question?'

'I'd prefer if you didn't,' said Laird. 'I don't want to lie to you.

What I will say is that I must disappear for a while. How long I don't know. I will be back, but I have to sort something out and I need to do it on my own. It's not anything I can dump on anyone else. I've got myself into something and I've got to get myself out of it.'

Ricardo's question was out before he knew it. 'Is it a girl? Pregnant? I can fix that for you, too. I know good people ...'

'No, trust me, it's not a girl,' replied Laird. 'I promise I will tell you when the time is right. You have my word.'

'That is good enough for me, Derek.'

Laird realised that was one of the first times in the past five years his friend had given him his Christian name. He smiled. 'Sorry to be mysterious, but you are the only one I trust at the moment. No-one at the club knows. None of the players. Not even the manager. None of the directors. My personal manager doesn't know and neither does my agent or any of the other guys. Only you.'

'I am privileged, Derek,' said Ricardo, looking across the table, waving away a waiter at the same time. 'Give us twenty minutes, Manuel. Okay?' The waiter shrugged and moved to another booth.

'I need a car today,' repeated Laird. 'And I have to ask for another favour.'

'Consider it done.' Ricardo shifting closer across the table, moving a giant salt cellar out of the way. 'I'll throw in UK registration plates, as well. Free and for nothing. You might need them. Yes?'

The footballer nodded and then dipped into his back pocket and produced his wallet.

Ricardo backed away. 'No, no money, please ...'

If Laird had entertained even the merest thought that his friend would be disloyal it vanished in an instant.

'I must square you up for the car. Remember, Ricardo, just an ordinary car. But you can help me with this, too. I know you have good friends out there. You have earned their trust. Mine, too.'

Laird took out four different debit cards and spread them on the table. He picked up a pen and four pieces of paper. He wrote the four-digit numbers on the separate scraps of paper. Carefully, he produced four paper clips and attached the relevant pieces of paper with the numbers to each card. He looked at his friend who stared back quizzically.

'These numbers will activate the individual cards. Please don't get them mixed up.'

'You want me to take four of your cards and do what?' queried Ricardo.

'I want you to give a card and its number to each of the friends you trust the most. I know you have a lot of friends who travel a lot. I have never asked what they get up to. None of my business. But they do move around quite a bit, don't they?'

'Yes, of course. That is my secret. Of course, I have airline crew, yes, pilots included, ferry skippers and many more I do work with. As you say, Derek, they move around a bit. A little something here, a little something there.' Ricardo looked at Laird, flashed a wide-mouthed smile and winked. 'That is my business. Maybe best you don't know.'

'Agreed,' replied Laird. 'I'm trusting you to pass on these cards to four of your, er, associates and tell them to use them at ATMs wherever they find themselves tomorrow. Tell them to help themselves to 1,000 euros each. That will make it worth their time, I think. Please do not choose anyone going to France or Britain. I'll trust you to pick the right people, those who won't get too greedy. I don't want my manager noticing and sending out the SAS after me. Once they've used the cards, please tell them to get rid of them, cut them up, whatever, but just make sure they disappear. I'll sort out everything when I get back.'

'Free money! That will NOT be a problem, Derek,' grinned Ricardo. 'I'll give my, what did you call them, "associates", these cards and you have my word they will be activated tomorrow. And you also have my word they will not go above 1,000 euros.' He winked again. 'My associates are trustworthy people.'

Ricardo shot a hand across the table and took that of Laird. 'Shake on the deal, Derek. It's as good as done. Your car will be with you within a couple of hours. That soon enough?'

'That'll be fine,' said Laird. 'Something with a full tank of petrol that won't fall apart when it runs over an empty cigarette packet.'

'You offend me, sir,' said Ricardo mockingly. 'There's a car I've been looking at as a runaround that might be perfect. No point in having a flash car in the middle of Barcelona, is there? Everything's got a dent in it, the drivers are lunatics, *non compos mentis*. Panel beaters must earn as much as you.'

'Or you,' replied Laird.

'Is there anything else?'

'I think that's it,' answered the footballer.

'So, you don't think a disposable telephone would come in handy, my friend?' smiled Ricardo. 'Maybe two? Use yours and everyone will know where you are on this planet in minutes.

You're not very good at this, are you?'

Laird looked across the table at his companion. He wondered what he really did for a living. 'Hadn't thought of that. Can you sort that out?'

'You insult me, my friend.' grinned Ricardo. 'Manuel!' he shouted at the hovering waiter. 'Two hungry men over here.'

CHAPTER SIX

Late morning. Monday 22 November.

Glasgow.

Charlie Brock slung a couple of denim shirts into a holdall. They were kept company by a laptop, a pair of faded blue Levi's jeans, a couple of cotton crew necks, a scattering of T-shirts, a few pairs of socks and an assortment of boxer shorts. He fitted in a bundle of tea bags and a pint carton of milk.

He was wearing a dark blue marino wool polo neck sweater, a pair of light fawn chinos, black socks and slip-on brown deck shoes. He had a quick look around the apartment to make sure he hadn't left anything switched on that shouldn't be switched on. A quick shufty round the kitchen. Everything in order. He picked up the holdall, walked down his small hallway, grabbed his knee-length tan leather jacket off the peg and said to no-one, 'Ready or not, Millport here I come.'

Central Railway Station was a brisk fifteen minutes' walk away from his flat in Glasgow's Merchant City. He bought a return ticket for the 11am train to Largs. Brock decided he would have a couple of pints and lunch in McKinlay's Bar just across from the Largs Railway Station. He had always fancied Willy. She was one good-looking dame. And she never failed to deliver with her steak and ale pie. He was told they were home-made and he had no reason to ever doubt the word of Willy, a blonde, full-breasted barmaid he had known for years; way back to when they were both kids holidaying on Millport with their parents, the same fortnight every year for about ten years. She was known as Wilhelmina back then, of course. They practically grew up together as holiday mates. He remembered a stolen kiss one afternoon in the bus shelter at West Bay. They had giggled excitedly. He had been nine at the time, Willy two years younger.

'She's wearing exceptionally well,' thought Brock immediately as he stepped through the door of McKinlay's to see Willy behind the bar. 'Fifty-three going on twenty. The Joanna Lumley gene.' She looked up from pulling a pint of heavy and flashed a dazzling smile, her violet eyes coming alive, clearly happy to see her old friend. She pointed to a quiet part of the pub at the back and Brock followed her directions. He was delighted to note that Willy still resolutely refused to wear anything as cumbersome as a bra. And she still possessed a figure that allowed her to continue wearing skimpy tops that sometimes exposed a large and pert nipple every now and again as she stooped behind the bar. He appreciated that. So did all the male customers in McKinlay's, each of whom appeared to have two inches of tallywhacker hanging out of each ear.

After the usual greetings, the sports journalist was forced to take a sharp intake of breath.

'Charlie, how come you've never tried to slip me a crippler?' asked Willy, suddenly, quietly and without warning, as she poured him his first pint of the day. The train journey had been relatively dull. As were that day's newspapers. As were his fellow-passengers. As were the weather prospects. But Willy had brought some excitement into his tired, old life within minutes of walking into the bar. 'You know I would have liked that, don't you?' she added with a radiant smile.

'I got that impression,' said Brock, trying desperately to

recover his composure. He was a man of the world, after all. A sports reporter, for fuck's sake. Following a moment's hesitation, he managed to summon up, 'One snag, Willy, you're married. And I just happen to like your other half, Wee Tommy. So, a missed opportunity, I'm afraid. I'll have to live with it.'

'I would still give you one, Charlie,' said Willy, leaning closer, her top opening wide, her right boob practically in full view. Her off-the-shoulder little white cotton number had come loose; *very* loose. Charlie couldn't help gazing at the splendid pendulum of flesh that swung to and fro as Willy bent over to wash some pint glasses in the basin at the bar immediately in front of him. He felt like saying something profound and witty along the lines of, 'Well, that's made my day' or something equally inane. What would Michael Caine say in such a circumstance? He couldn't find the words as he gawped at his friend's right breast, the nipple now in sight. 'Surely, she knows what she's doing?' he pondered. 'She must know I'm looking. Should I be looking?' Willy kept sploshing around in front of him, the breast heaving from side to side. 'Like what you see, Charlie?' she said without looking up. Then she smiled teasingly.

Brock, acting nonchalant as best he could, swallowed a mouthful of lager, smiled and nodded. He couldn't conjure up a single word.

'I've got another like that one right over here,' said Willy, abruptly straightening up in front of Brock. Thankfully, Brock and Willy were in a secluded corner of the thirty-foot horseshoe-shaped bar that had a gantry down the centre obscuring the view of the locals who were standing at the opposite end, watching the lunchtime sports update and missing Willy's impromptu boob show behind the optics.

'What are you trying to do, give me a heart attack?' muttered Brock, any pretence at cool totally gone. How would Steve McQueen have handled this situation?

Willy tossed her long, blonde hair back and chuckled again. 'This is for your eyes only, Charlie boy. My cheating husband hasn't seen me naked for years. Doesn't seem interested.' She didn't look too perturbed about the misdemeanours of her errant spouse.

'Can't understand that, Willy,' said a still-startled Brock with genuine feeling. 'You're all woman. Christ, are you *all* woman.'

'If I had known you were in town I might have worn the old suspenders and the black sheer stockings,' smiled Willy, her eyes positively dancing with mischief. 'Would you have liked that, Charlie boy?' Brock's head was elsewhere. 'Had that really happened?' he thought. It had been one of the most wondrous sights Brock had witnessed in recent times. Years, maybe. Willy continued to smile invitingly and added, 'I thought you looked as though you needed cheering up. Did I succeed?'

'What do you think, Willy?' he replied. Brock was close to passing out.

Willy winked. 'That little bastard husband of mine has been shagging the florist. I wouldn't mind, but she looks like the back end of a train wreck. It's been going on for about three years. I've just found out. He doesn't know that I know. I've been a good girl for far too long, Charlie boy.' Willy giggled heartily. Brock wondered what was coming next.

'Oh, I've seen you looking, you old perv, when I bend over behind the bar. I've given you a wee flash every now and again, given you a wee glimpse of my strawberries because I like you.

59

Always have. Now what are you going to do about it?'

Apart from a mild splutter, Brock was silent. His love life looked like taking an upward turn, in more ways than one. His luck was changing. He pondered for a moment, 'Should I put on the Lottery tonight?'

'I take it you're going to Millport?' Willy enquired matter-of-factly. 'How long are you going to be on the island, Charlie boy?'

'About nine inches,' he replied, smiling, thinking Sean Connery as Bond would have been proud of such a retort.

'That I've got to see,' said Willy. 'I take it you're not expecting company. Or am I being presumptuous? How about I come over tonight? I'll tell my nicompoop of a husband I'm going to see Caroline. You remember my friend Caroline from Millport, don't you?'

'Don't think I've had the pleasure,' answered Brock.

'Of course, you haven't,' said the barmaid. 'No-one's had the pleasure. I've just invented her. My straying spouse won't mind. He'll see it as an ideal opportunity to shove his miniscule dick up Pammy the Weed. A whole night with Pammy the Weed. Lucky him. And I'll be with you, Charlie boy. And do you know something?'

'I'm terrified to ask,' said Brock, his mouth drying rapidly.

'I'm going to fuck you senseless,' smiled Willy.

'Oh, good,' gulped Brock.

He forgot to order his steak and ale pie.

CHAPTER SEVEN

Early afternoon. Monday 22 November.

Double C Bar, Broomielaw, Glasgow.

'Why don't we surprise Brock?' asked Griff Stewart, Chief News Reporter of the *Daily News*.

'That's not a bad idea,' replied Harry Booth, Detective Inspector of Police Scotland CID.

'Aye, he won't get too many surprises at his age and stage,' said the newspaperman.

'Careful, R.I.P.' said the cop. 'We're all around the same age. There's a bit of mileage in all of us yet. The tank's not completely empty. Plenty of marrow in the old bone. Still a bit of mischief in the groins. Don't you be saying my future's behind me. You and I are still a couple of good-looking hombres. People think we're brothers, so you've got to be one handsome bastard. Mind you, I think your hair is thinning a bit quicker than mine.'

'At least, mine is the same colour as the original,' said the reporter. 'You're getting a bit grey there, mate. Maybe you should try one of those products they advertise on the telly. You know the one I'm talking about? The guy looks in the mirror and his hair is practically the colour of pure snow. He spreads some gel on his napper, rinses it and – hey, presto! – ten seconds later he's back to being jet black.'

'I'll try that as soon as you promise to get a hair-weave thing. Remember that old manager? The German bloke? Can't remember his name. It'll come back to me. He used to advertise some sort of miracle grow ...'

'I thought that was for your garden?'

'... that guaranteed you a full head of hair in about a week? I don't know why he bothered, mind you. He had a kisser like a well-spanked arse.'

'Aye, they used to call him Potato Face, didn't they? The head the size of a belly, only not as attractive. You're right. He would have been better off growing the hair down his face. We could have called him Herr Face.'

The newspaperman and the cop, having both completed early shifts in their honest toil for their respective employers for another day, laughed out loud and clinked their glasses at the podium of the Budgie Cage of the Double C Bar, their favourite drinking den, on Glasgow's Broomielaw. Apart from their Birth Certificates dictating something else altogether, they could have been a couple of mischievous schoolkids. Dedicated in their chosen professions, doolally during time off for good behaviour.

'Ach, we're old codgers, El Cid,' continued the reporter. 'If we're lucky, we might get a nod off a rocking horse.'

'Speak for yourself,' said the cop. 'I'm sure I was getting the eye from that female in here on Saturday night. The one who was playing the puggy.'

'That was a bleedin' bloke,' said R.I.P. 'What were you drinking? What are they putting in the heavy in this pub? Mineral water for you from now on, my old mate.' He smiled and said, 'Anyway, it's just as well we're happily married, isn't it? Seriously, though, it would be good to fix up Brock with a nice bird, wouldn't it? He's not getting much action down there below the belly button at the moment. Hasn't had a carpet burn on his knees for at least a couple of months. Poor soul hasn't experienced the sensation of a squeaking mattress for ages.'

'Aye, and that's him over to Millport on his own to "batten down the hatches", as he says, before the ills of winter are inflicted upon his sacred isle,' said the newsman.

'Could probably do with the company,' agreed the cop.

'Aye, not much to do over there apart from swim in booze and consume fish suppers. He doesn't even ride a bike, does he? Do you know I read somewhere recently that there are fifteen hundred bicycles for hire on that island? It's got a population of something like fourteen hundred. It's got more bicycles than people. That says a lot about that island. Get your priorities right. Do you know the islanders have got a new name for Millport? Barbados With Bikes, they're calling it.' He sighed and added, 'I blame it on the inbreeding. You know what they say over there, don't you? It's like incest or country dancing; you should give it a try at least once because you never know you might like it.'

'And all the good women are taken, as well,' observed El Cid. 'Try having an affair on that island. Ten miles in circumference and everyone knows each other's business.'

'Aye, sexual suicide,' frowned the newspaperman.

'I take it you've got some time off due, R.I.P?' asked the cop. 'I think I've still got to squeeze in five days before the turn of the year. They've changed the bloody rules again. If you don't take your allocated quota inside twelve months, that's your tough luck. We can't carry them over into a new year any more.'

'Use them or lose them, eh? Same with us. I checked my diary this morning. I've got five days, too, by coincidence. I'll have a word with Anna and see if I can get a free pass for a couple of days. Might take over the sticks. Fancy a round of golf?'

'In November? In Millport? Are you going for Optimist of the Year?' Pause for thought. 'Okay, we can play it by ear.'

'Better if you use clubs.'

The cop ignored the lame jest, displaying the disdain it so richly deserved. He added, 'Lynda will probably be happy to get rid of me for a few days. Same every year. Christmas is on the horizon and she starts to panic. "What will I get Eileen?" Or "Do you think Aunt Lucy would like another cardigan from Laura Ashley?" Or "How about a nice pair of slippers for Uncle Bert? Did you see the ones he was wearing last year? His toes were practically popping through them." On and on and on. I catch a word every now and again and nod. She's not talking to me, she's talking *at* me. Know what I mean?'

'Listen, my old thief-taker, that's not exclusive to the Booth household. And my sister's brood seem to be extending by the minute. My niece now has five kids. FIVE KIDS. Christ, I remember her when she was in a pram. And it won't be long before they grow up and have five kids. And then ...'

'You'll be dead, my old friend,' interrupted the cop.

'Aye, I suppose I've got that to look forward to,' sighed the newspaperman. 'My idea of hell would be playing the role of Santa Claus in a packed department store at Christmas. All those horrible, grotty, wee kids pulling at your beard, farting loudly on your knee, peeing everywhere, being sick down your costume that's already been worn by about a hundred diseased deadbeats. I hope to God I go to heaven.'

'You won't know anyone up there. All your friends and

relatives will be down in "The Big Fire", as my mother used to call it, on a spit beside Adolf, Ghenghis, Saddam, Osama, Gadaffi, Idi, the guy who invented Big Brother and that newspaper owner Charlie despised so much. What was his name again?'

'Fatso,' said R.I.P.

'No, his real name.'

'That WAS his real name,' laughed the newspaperman. 'You know like Pele? Or Columbo? Or Liberace? Or Sting? Or Moses? He was born, his parents saw this mound of blubber with eyes and called him Fatso.'

'Izatso?'

'No, Fatso.'

They both laughed like a couple of kids. 'Right,' said El Cid. 'Are we on? Fancy a couple of days on Brock's island? Over at the Schloss Adler?'

'Aye, why not?' replied R.I.P. 'A wee break will do us both the world of good. A couple of drinks in Hughie's, a few fish suppers from the Hippy Chippy and, maybe, a wee round of golf, a shot on the bikes. Sounds idyllic. I'm well up for that.'

'Will we let Charlie know we're coming over?' asked the cop.

'No, let's surprise him,' replied the newspaperman. 'I think he'll enjoy the company. Save him getting bored.'

'Aye, let's surprise him. As you say, he probably doesn't get too many surprises these days.'

CHAPTER EIGHT

Late afternoon. Monday 22 November.

Millport, Isle of Cumbrae.

'Here comes Charlie,' said Hughie Edwards, genial mine host of Hugh's Bar in Millport. 'He's looking happy enough. Wonder what's put a smile on his face?'

Automatically, the bar owner began pouring a pint of lager. Charlie Brock, with the fierce wind and rain buffeting him, crossed over at an angle from the harbour slip to Stuart Street and waved cheerily at the front window of the pub. He couldn't see in through the glass, but he knew the punters in the bar could see out. He had dumped his holdall in the flat, didn't bother to unpack, hit the switch for hot water, clicked on a couple of wall-mounted radiators, had a quick check in the fridge – a couple of bottles of lager had managed to escape attention on his last visit – and noted there were still five bottles of reasonable plonk in the wine rack. He smiled. He couldn't get the vision of Willy out of his mind.

He would make sure he never repeated that phrase out loud.

Brock pushed open the main door of the pub and shook off some of the persistent rain that had greeted his arrival. 'You've got a grin as wide as the Clyde,' observed Hughie. 'You look as though you'll need plastic surgery to get rid of that smile. Partick Thistle signed Ronaldo?' The bar owner set down the pint of lager at the very spot on the bar he knew his journalist pal favoured. Vodka Joe had his 'Window on the World' and Brock had his place at the corner of the bar. He shook his mate's hand; a good, firm handshake.

'Great to see you, Charlie. To what do we owe the honour this time? Down to solve another murder? Show the beat cop how it's done? Foil a bank raid by the Mob? Prevent some angry grannie from knocking over the post office? Find out who stole Wee Jeannie's bike?' They laughed. Then Hughie asked, 'You know Fiona's left, don't you? Wee Fiona Anderson? The beat cop who found the body of Wild Bill? Aye, she's back on the mainland, the cop shop at Greenock. Aye, I'll miss her sharp mind, straight talking, complete fairness, her witty repartee, her two-handed drinking and, of course, her enormous bazookas.'

Hughie paused and smiled at the recollection before continuing. 'We've got a bloke now. Nice guy. Terry Watson over from Maryhill. He seems as happy as a pig in the proverbial. I informed him he might find the weekends here a wee bit quieter than he was used to. He told me that was what he was looking forward to. No-one with a meat cleaver attempting to make sure his head parted company with his shoulders. And, more importantly, he's happy to look the other way, too, when we're having a wee lock-in.'

'Still breaking the law, then?' smiled Brock. 'I might have to put you at the top of my 'to do' list.'

'Please, boss, If you're taking me down to the cells remember not to mark my face,' said Hughie, mockingly. 'I'll squeal. Just keep the rubberhose away from my face.'

Brock, still thinking of Willy, guffawed loudly. 'I'll note your comments, but can't promise anything.'

He took a sip of lager and smacked his lips. Hughie said, 'The first of the day is always the best.'

Brock grinned again. 'Actually, I must confess, Hughie, I

stopped over at McKinlay's and had a couple in there before I got on the ferry.' Idly, he asked, 'You know Willy, don't you? The barmaid at McKinlay's?'

'Aye, I know Willy,' nodded Hughie. 'Everybody knows Willy. Everybody would like to know Willy a lot better. If she ever wants a full-time job in this pub I would be more than happy to accommodate her.'

Brock returned his smile. 'I bet you would, you dirty old bastard. Wait until I tell Maggie.'

'Honestly, Charlie, she would bring in the punters by the score,' said Hughie with an earnest expression, imagining the Jewish Piano at full pelt on a daily basis. 'She's a looker, that's for sure, but she's great at her job, too. Can't take that away from her.' He squinted at his mate and said, 'You know her well, don't you? I'm told you were kids down here during the Glasgow Fair for years.'

'Aye, I think you could say I know her well,' replied Brock, grinning from ear to ear. He didn't add that he was about to get to know her a little bit better than he did when he had left his flat earlier that day.

'See you've brought the Glasgow weather with you.' Vodka Joe, seated in his reserved spot, raised his glass to welcome Brock.

'November in Scotland, Vodka Joe,' said the sports reporter. 'What can you expect? We must be used to it by now. If you want a rainbow, you've got to suffer the rain, my friend. You can put away the sun tan oil for at least another month.'

Brock looked through the window at the leaden skies and the swollen clouds and realised the weather had deteriorated in the past half-hour. 'What's happened to Largs?' he asked. 'It was there a minute ago.'

'Aye, that can happen,' said Vodka Joe, who was a bit of an expert on these things considering he spent most of his waking hours sitting in the corner of Hugh's Bar gazing across the Firth. 'It's not going to get any better, either. Nature's water tap is on for the day. I'll just have to stay indoors.' In his twenty years on the island hardly anyone had witnessed Vodka Joe venture past the Newton Beach, half-a-mile from Hugh's drinking emporium. He got to his feet, shuffled to the bar and pointed to the upturned vodka bottle on the gantry. He never had to ask for his favourite tipple. Hughie, through thirteen years of habit, immediately placed a glass under the well-used optic. 'Aye, that's the stuff I want,' said Vodka Joe. 'Don't want to surprise my mouth.' There was only one time Vodka Joe flummoxed Hughie and the entire island by switching from vodka to whisky. Millport was in uproar. It was the biggest news to hit the island since the new owner, a young, long-haired guy from London, slapped five pence on the price of a haggis supper at the Deep Blue Plaice, aka the Hippy Chippy. Vodka Joe never did explain why he switched drinks for an entire week. It was another of the great Millport mysteries.

Hughie, a lithe, fit-looking specimen of five foot ten inches, floppy fair hair and Buddy Holly glasses, poured Vodka Joe his drink, looked at Brock's pint, noted the contents were disappearing at a rapid rate, picked up an empty tumbler and began pulling another beer for his mate. 'On the house, lads,' said Hughie, turning to pour himself a brandy and port. 'Cheers,' he said and Brock chinked his glass.

'What would you say if I told you Willy might be in this very establishment tonight?' asked the journalist.

Hughie took the glass away from his lips mid-sip. He looked at Brock somewhat quizzically. His eyes narrowed. 'What would I say if Willy might be in this very establishment tonight?' he repeated. 'She would be welcomed with open arms.' He paused and asked, 'Coming over to see you? I would say you were a lucky bastard is what I would say. A big, lucky bastard.' He added quickly, 'Is she staying the night up at Schloss Adler?'

Brock scratched his chin. 'Could be,' he said.

'Big, lucky, jammy bastard,' said the bar owner. Very quickly, he asked, 'What age is Willy now? Hard to tell. Obviously, got to be around our age group.'

'She's just turned fifty-three,' said Brock. 'I'm two years older and you're another year adrift. You're ancient, mate.'

'And why should a living man ever complain?' pondered Hughie, momentarily adopting a philosophical approach to the conversation that swiftly returned to Willy. 'Doesn't even look forty-three. Make that thirty-three, in fact. Good-looking female for her age. Look at Twiggy. Good grief, she's over sixty. Have you seen her on those TV adverts? Fantastic! And what about Helen Mirren? Wow, what a figure! Joan Collins, too. What age is she? Eighty? Ninety? One hundred and ten? I wouldn't kick her out of bed, I can tell you.'

'Just wait until I tell Maggie,' broke in Brock, but his pal was on a roll and took no notice.

'I saw an interview with Joan Collins in a magazine a couple of weeks ago. She was celebrating some anniversary with her husband who's over thirty years younger than her. I had to laugh when I read the bit about even her friends expressing their concerns about the age gap. Do you know what she said, Charlie? "If he dies, he dies ..." As long as I've got a face there will be somewhere for that woman to sit. Same with Willy. No offence. She's not one of those eighteen/sixty-five jobs you get. You know what I mean? The bird looks eighteen years old from the back, but when she turns round she's sixty-five.' He went quiet and, in hushed tones, asked, 'Is Willy not still married? To Wee Tommy? I heard a tale about him a while ago.'

'That he's shagging Pammy the florist? Or Pammy the Weed, as Willy has rechristened her.'

'Aye, that's it. I heard it, but I didn't believe it. Why the hell would you mess about with another woman when you're married to Willy? She's still Miss World material. She's on some youth drug Maggie doesn't know about.'

Brock was distracted for a moment as a vision came to mind. Willy. He said nothing.

'Daft wee bugger, Tommy,' continued Hughie. 'What was it Paul Newman said when he was asked about why he had stayed faithful to Joanne Woodward? "Why eat hamburger when you've got steak at home?" Something like that? You know, Willy looks a wee bit like Joanne Woodward in her prime.'

Brock imagined Joanne Woodward topless and said nothing.

'So, Willy might be having a wee sleepover, is she?' grinned Hughie, adding, 'And my old friend might be having a wee leg over? Lucky big bastard.'

Hughie shook his head and positively chortled. 'I was over at Largs just the other day to pick up a few things for the pub. Too expensive to buy stuff down here. At least, Dick Turpin had the good manners to wear a mask when he robbed you. Do you know it's about ten quid dearer for a three-litre box of very ordinary red or white wine than it is over in Largs? You complain and you're told, "It's island prices." They must be importing the stuff straight from Monte Carlo on Prince Albert's personal yacht.'

71

Hughie sipped his brandy and port and let out a sigh. He continued, 'I popped into McKinlay's and Willy was behind the bar. Fair brightened up my day, I can tell you. There was almost a round of applause every time she bent over. Never wears a bra, that girl, may the Good Lord be praised. Big Eric was over at the same time, too. We were having a pint at the bar when Eric suddenly spluttered and splashed some of his beer down his shirt. "Christ," he told me, "I've just seen Willy's left tit." And with that, he was off to the loo leaving a vapor trail behind him. Was in there for about half-an-hour. It was the only cludgie that was in use and there was a queue of about six desperate blokes waiting to have a dump. Big Eric ignored the frantic battering on the door. Eventually, he came out, said, "That's better." Then he picked up his pint and continued to drink. Come to think of it, he had the same sort of grin you've got on your smug kisser just now. Did you get a swatch at Willy's marimbas?'

'You're on a fishing expedition, my friend,' smirked Brock, with a great deal of self-satisfaction. 'Put your rod away.'

'I know where I would like to put my rod,' sighed Hughie, adding, 'No offence. You lucky big bastard.'

Bungalow Bob pushed open the door of the pub. 'Shit!' he bellowed. 'Look at this bloody weather. How am I supposed to make a living? How can you wash windows in a fuckin' storm? My missus wants a new duvet for Christmas. How am I going to get the money for that?' The island's window cleaner took off his bright yellow nylon puffer jacket and began to shake it wildly. Rainwater flew everywhere.

'Just what we need, Bungalow,' said Hughie. 'Now it's as wet in here as it is out there. Thanks.'

'Sorry, Hughie, I wasn't thinking.' Not for the first time Brock wondered about the window cleaner's nickname. Maybe it had nothing to do with his fear of heights. Maybe it had everything to do with having nothing up top.

'Thanks,' echoed Vodka Joe from the corner. 'I don't normally take water in my vodka.'

'Sorry, Vodka Joe, didn't see you there.'

'I'm ALWAYS here,' protested Vodka Joe. 'Where else would I be?'

'Try the rest, come back to the best.' The bar owner's self-satisfied smirk evaporated when Vodka Joe added, 'Hughie's vodka is ten pence cheaper than anywhere else on the island. That's why I'm always here. Mind you, I've heard of those other brands.' He took a swig and asked, 'What exactly am I drinking, Hughie?'

'The best there is, Vodka Joe,' replied Hughie, 'and that's all you need to know.' He looked sideways at the upturned vodka bottle on the gantry. 'RASPUTNIK,' he noted to himself, shrugging his shoulders at the same time. He walked back to the bar beside Brock and picked up his brandy and port. 'No, I've never heard of it, either,' said the bar owner. 'It's seventy-five per cent cheaper than the other stuff.'

'Just so long as wee Vodka Joe doesn't go blind, you'll be okay,' said Brock.

'Wee Vodka Joe's likely to go blind for another reason altogether,' answered Hughie. 'Just ask him about Gina Lollobrigida.'

Hughie's smile suddenly turned upside down. 'Aw, hell,' he said, 'here comes Boring Brian. The expert in sabotaging enjoyment. He's about to flog us all to death with lethargy. Prepare for the vortex of doom. You would have thought he had a crossword to do

73

on a day like this. Do the world a favour and stay at home. Wash his hair, something like that. If you listen carefully, Charlie, you'll hear snapping noises followed by squeals coming from the cellar.'

'Snapping noises followed by squeals?'

'Aye, that's the mice throwing themselves into the traps when they detect his footsteps coming in this direction.'

Brock shook his head. Vodka Joe also caught sight of the looming Brian. 'Here comes the guy who is constantly upstaged by his own moustache,' he announced.

'Do you know, Charlie,' Hughie continued, 'he was telling me a story the other day about a female who told him she never wanted to be in his company again? Her exact words were, "I never want to see you again as long as I live."'

'Come on, Hughie, we've all been told that at some time in our life.'

'Aye, but she hadn't even been introduced to him at that point. And there was the other female who informed him if they were the last man and woman on earth they would be the last man and woman on earth.'

Once more uninvited rain swept in through the door as Boring Brian made his entrance. He wondered why the pub had gone so silent. Eventually, Hughie said, 'Hi, BB, how are you today?'

'A wee bit moist,' came the reply. 'Aye, just a tad damp.'

Brock looked at him. 'You're not one for exaggeration, are you?' he said. 'You're soaked to the skin.'

'Oh, it'll dry in. Eventually,' said Boring Brian, his sodden black hair stuck to his skull. He took off his anorak and hung it on a peg at the door. 'I've just seen a cloud that is the spitting image of Elvis Presley,' he said. 'And I almost stepped in a puddle in George Street.' He ruminated for a moment. 'A usual, Hughie, if you don't mind.'

'I could do wi' a top-up,' came the voice from the corner. 'Guess what I'm drinking?' Boring Brian looked over his shoulder. 'Oh, Vodka Joe, didn't see you there. Yours is always a vodka.'

'Cheers, mate, don't mind if I do,' said Vodka Joe cheerily. Boring Brian looked puzzled. 'Hughie, did I just ask him if he wanted a drink?' Hughie laughed, 'I think you might have.'

'Oh, well, I better get him a vodka, then, I suppose. Small, mind you.' He practically sobbed. Brock wondered if Boring Brian had ever fancied employment as an undertaker. He had all the attributes to make a genuine success in that profession. The guy in the wooden box would probably look more cheerful in comparison. Probably had more to smile about, as well, when Brock thought about it. Suddenly, the sports reporter snapped his fingers and pointed to the island's merchant of gloom. 'Walter Matthau!' He exclaimed. 'That's who you remind me of. Walter Matthau.'

'Not George Clooney, then?' chipped in Hughie.

Boring Brian turned to look at his reflection on the large wall-mounted mirror opposite the bar. It had been presented to the pub in another century from a whisky distillers that had long since gone to the big cask in the sky. Boring Brian peered at himself. He said, 'Can't see it myself, Brock. Was he not a bit on the lugubrious side? You know, a wee bit dull? Mournful, even? He was in *Grumpy Old Men*, wasn't he?'

Boring Brian looked again at his reflection. 'No, don't see it myself.' He paused. 'More of a Les Dawson man. I think. Now he was funny.'

'Not Norman Wisdom, then?' asked Brock. Boring Brian looked thoughtful for a moment. 'No, didn't find him funny. All that tripping himself up, spilling his drink, toppling over tables, his trousers falling down to his ankles and being dragged across a lawn by a runaway mower. Who would laugh at that?'

'The whole of Albania,' answered Brock.

'Albania?' queried Boring Brian, repeating, 'Albania? That must be a dull wee place.'

'Maybe it is, but they still loved Norman Wisdom. They've got a life-sized statue of him in their town square.'

'Must be about four feet high, then?' threw in Hughie. 'Honestly, Brock, was he big in Albania?'

'Aye, it's the truth. They loved him over there. Seriously. They had a day of mourning when he died. He was buried in a matchbox, apparently.'

Boring Brian, a mite befuddled by the information that had just come his way, waddled back to the bar to pick up his pint of beer. Hughie winked at Brock and mimicked, 'Ah, nectar from the gods,' at the same time the chronically-tiresome imbiber spoke those very words. 'He'll go onto gin and tonic as soon as he's finished that,' whispered the bar owner. 'You sure?' asked Brock. 'As sure as Muhammad Ali isn't about to be welcomed into the Ku Klux Klan any time soon.'

Brock looked around the bar, a dramatically-changed scene from when he was last on the island, the Country and Western Festival. He had arrived on the morning of the last day of August and returned on the afternoon of Monday, September the third. In between, he had assisted Police Scotland CID in capturing the killer of Wild Bill Hickok. He was quite chuffed with himself. That was more than two months ago and the island, that had groaned under the weight of twelve thousand cowboys and cowgirls – and one Red Indian – was now reminiscent of Aberdeen on Flag Day. Actually, he thought that comparison might be a bit unkind, considering he had never been in Aberdeen on Flag Day.

'Another pint, please, Hughie,' said Brock as he drained his drink. He just couldn't get images of Willy out of his mind. Again, he reminded himself not to say that out loud. 'One for yourself and a wee scatter for the troops.'

'Last of the big spenders,' laughed the bar owner.

'Aye, I can afford to go crazy over the next few days,' grinned Brock. 'I've just had a payment in from my old mates at the *News* for five match reports and a couple of wee stories they used last month. Something in from the *Mail*. And the *Post*, too. Not bad; keep me going.'

'Oh, thanks, Brock,' said Boring Brian. 'I'll have a gin and tonic, please, Hughie.'

Brock and Hughie smirked in unison. Boring Brian wondered what he had said that was so funny. 'Maybe I should take my act on the road,' he thought, briefly, to himself. A wee voice inside his head said, 'Don't be so fuckin' daft.'

'Cheers,' chorused Vodka Joe and Bungalow Bob as they hoisted their drinks to their lips. 'Enjoy,' said Brock. He pondered for a moment. 'Whatever happened to that guy who used to drink in here and organised the boat trips?' he asked. 'That bloke you called Mr. Jinx? I didn't see him at the Country and Western Festival.'

'Did I forget to tell you?' said Hughie. 'Sorry. He's dead. Aye,

Mr. Jinx's dead.'

'What are you talking about?' replied Brock. 'He was only in his late thirties, early forties.'

'Aye, sad that,' said Hughie. 'Hit by a speeding burger van in Largs in June. Killed outright. Not the luckiest individual I've ever met, that's for sure. He always insisted fast food would kill him.'

Brock looked to see if his mate was indulging in some stand-up comedy. Hughie remained stoney-faced.

'I knocked on Tam Neill's door to see if he was coming out to play,' Brock broke the momentary silence. Neill was his neighbour, living on the first floor at the Schloss Adler. He was edging towards ninety years old and, in his heyday, could outdrink any man, woman or animal on the island. Brock had met him five years ago, only hours after getting the keys to his bolthole. 'So, you're my new neeboor,' asked the irascible OAP. 'Welcome to Alcatraz.' He shook his hand warmly and asked, without warning, 'Celtic or Rangers?' That question again. It had followed Brock around all of his life. 'Partick Thistle,' he answered. 'Oh, a Celtic or Rangers fan without the bus fare, then?' smiled Old Tam. An instant friendship was struck there and then. Old Tam favoured McIntosh's on Cardiff Street for his afternoon tipple: a large Glenmorangie in copious numbers. He would rumble into the pub, slap a pound coin on the bar and tell owner Alasdair, 'Throw me out when that's finished.' Never failed to get a laugh.

Old Tam had lived alone since the death of his wife Annie in 1995. 'Went to sleep and never woke up,' he informed Brock early on. 'Loved that bloody wummin.' And then he would swallow hard as another large whisky said hello to its new surroundings. Brock laughed, 'You know, Hughie, I was walking along the front with Old Tam one day, heading down to the Mitre for his morning bowl of soup, when we met that tall female who's always immaculate ...'

'Diana,' said Hughie, as though there was only one female on the island who took care of her appearance.

'Aye,' said Brock, 'Diana, that's her name. Old Tam introduced me to her and told me she used to be a dancer in the White Heather Club. Remember that Scottish dancing programme on television years ago? A hooch here, a wheech there, tartan everywhere? Apparently, Diana used to be one of the lead dancers. It was easy to see why because she was still a fit-looking woman, although I would have guessed her age at around the mid-sixties. It was a nice day and she was wearing shorts. Old Tam was eyeing her up. She said, "How do you like my legs, Tam?" He didn't even pause. "I'd like them behind your neck!" She giggled and walked on. "I've just made her day," he said with that wee glint in his eye. Anyway, I knocked on his door, but there was no reply. I take it he's okay?'

'Aye, he's fine,' said Hughie, 'nothing to worry about. Old Tam will see us all off, you can be sure of that. He's down in Bournemouth for a few weeks over the Christmas period to spend some time with his daughter and his grandkids. Threatening to come back early in January to terrorise the island again.'

Brock nodded in the direction of the gantry and said, 'I see you're already getting ready for the festivities, then.'

A blackboard was hanging by a piece of string next to the Rasputnik vodka bottle. Hughie had scrawled on it in chalk:

HOGMANAY TIMETABLE

7.30pm: FOOD

8.00pm: DRINK

12.05am: BRAWL

Changing the subject, the bar owner asked, 'Anyway, sportswriter/sleuth, what's new on the football front? Who are St. Mirren going to buy? If the Jags have got Ronaldo, I suppose we'll have to make do with Messi.' He grinned and took another swig of his brandy and port.

'Very quiet, Hughie, to tell you the truth,' answered Brock. 'Wouldn't mind a nice, big exclusive, flog it to the highest bidder. Then the fish suppers are on me for the rest of the week. Sadly, if it's happening out there, I sure as hell don't have a clue. Sometimes stories just drop on your lap. It's happened to me a couple of times. That's the way it is in this game.'

Brock drained the remnants of his glass and sighed, 'You never know what's around the corner.'

CHAPTER NINE

Early evening. Monday 22 November.

Millport, Isle of Cumbrae.

'So, when can we expect the lovely Willy to grace us with her presence, Charlie?' enquired a cheerful Hughie Edwards as he poured Brock another pint of lager. The sports journalist, leaning against the bar, checked his wristwatch. It was just a shade after six o'clock on a miserable evening weatherwise. The rain continued to lash down as the colourful fairy lights on the cables that stretched from Quayhead along the promenade to Kames Bay rattled in the whistling wind.

'She finishes her shift in about an hour,' he replied. 'By the time she gets home, gets changed, throws a couple of things into an overnight bag, catches the ferry ... let's see ... oh, probably sometime next week.'

Both laughed. 'Aye, if she's anything like Maggie, it'll take her about a month to make up her mind about what knickers to take,' grinned the bar owner. 'Maybe you'll get lucky and Willy won't burden herself with anything as cumbersome as underwear.' He looked contemplatively at his friend for a moment before adding, 'Thankfully, my missus doesn't have too many decisions to make when she's helping out in here. Her main job is to make sure the ice cubes stay cold. And she's not very good at that. I don't even ask her to make a cup of tea for fear of her burning the water.'

He added quickly, 'Please don't tell her I said that. When Maggie's in a bad mood, everyone knows about it.'

'How bad?'

'Rip-the-heads-off-fluffy-kittens bad.'

'Now that *is* bad. Why don't you put a smile on her face and take her out?'

'Aye, I've thought about it often enough,' nodded Hughie. 'A bullet between the eyes should do the trick. Anyway, enough of my Ball and Chain, when can we expect Willy to light up my little parlour? Brighten up the island, too, for that matter. You're not joking, are you? She is coming over?'

'She said so,' nodded Brock. 'No reason to doubt her word.'

'How did you pull her?' quizzed Hughie. 'Has this been going on for years and no-one's noticed? You haven't even told your old chum?'

'Didn't see it coming,' answered Brock honestly. 'Always liked her, but I've always had time for Wee Tommy, as well. I thought she was off limits, my friend.'

'And Wee Tommy's screwed up?' exclaimed Hughie without thinking.

'Well, he's screwed up Pammy the Weed, that's for sure,' returned Brock.

'I've always fancied Willy,' confessed Hughie, pouring himself another brandy and port, a reflective, faraway look in his eyes.

'Wait until I tell Maggie.'

'Ach, Maggie's got nothing to worry about,' said Hughie, shaking his head. 'I'm like the dog that chases after the bus. Wouldn't know what to do with it once I caught it.' He clinked his glass against Brock's pint pot. 'Good luck to you, big man. Lang may your rum leek or something daft like that.'

Vodka Joe, sitting in the corner, picked up his glass, looked at the inviting contents, sighed and said with a fair degree of satisfaction, 'Ah, my little friend, come and embrace your destiny,' and sipped quietly at his drink. Boring Brian stood in silence at the bar. He seemed especially interested in a particular piece of anaglypta wallpaper just above the optics. He wore black rimmed spectacles and sported what he believed to be a Clark Gable-type moustache. Even it looked tired and uninterested being forced to spend the rest of its life under his extensive snoot. He was a trifle miffed one day when someone offered to buy him one of those plastic faces with the spectacles, nose and moustache attached from a joke shop. 'But I see you've got it covered,' observed Vodka Joe.

Bungalow Bob peered at the newspaper he had already read at least twice. Sky Sports News was on the television situated on a shaky-looking shelf on the wall at the corner of the bar. The sound was turned down. Hughie looked at the screen. 'Biggest con out, that,' he said to Brock. 'Twenty-four hour sports news, my arse. They're still rerunning the stuff that was on at ten this morning. Over seven hours later and the wee info bar is still telling us Chelsea are about to sign some bloody Brazilian. The guy'll be about fifty by the time he gets round to signing.'

Hickory Dickory, the island's GP, practically burst through the front door of the pub. 'Torrential,' he gasped. 'Bloody torrential.' He was soaked. His umbrella had been blown inside out. 'Look at me,' he said. 'I've just walked fifteen minutes from the surgery and I'm wet through. Look at my coat. Look at my trousers. I couldn't get wetter if I stood under Niagra Falls.' The rain outside still skudded off the pavement and beat a wild tattoo on Hughie's front window. The doctor was about to shake his battered brolly before Hughie shouted, 'Don't even think about it, Hick.'

'Oh, aye, sorry, Hughie,' said the doc. 'And don't call me Hick.' He placed his drenched brolly against the wall beside the radiator at the side of the door. He carefully placed his sodden coat on a peg. 'I need an injection of *Chateauneuf du Cumbrae*. A bottle, please, Hughie. As quick as you like, it's urgent. I'm feeling a wee bit traumatised. *Oui, une bouteille, s'il vous plait.*'

The bar owner went to the fridge where he always kept at least four bottles for the GP's daily consumption. 'What's brought this on, Hickory Dickory? No-one's died, have they? Can't afford to lose another customer.'

The GP replied, 'Worse, Hughie.'

'What can be worse than losing another customer? Pray tell.'

The bar owner placed the bottle in front of the doc, who poured a large one and drank greedily, gulping down a full mouthful. 'I better put another in there, gentlemen. Excuse me.'

'You look as though you've seen a ghost,' added Hughie, eager to discover what had brought such a fevered reaction to the GP.

Hickory Dickory picked up his glass and took another large guzzle. 'You know old Angus Simpson, don't you?' he said finally. 'The wee fellow who works over at the grocer's at Kames Bay?'

Hughie nodded. 'Haven't seen him for ages. Thought he was dead.'

'No, he's alive okay, I can tell you that,' said the doc. 'I think I'll have to have him committed, though.'

'Committed?' asked Brock. 'Christ, if you rounded up all the loonies on this island and carted them off to the laughing academy there'd be about ten people left in Millport. And they'd all be under five.'

'Old Angus would have to be at the head of a long queue, then. He would have to be first to go,' said the doc, earnestly.

'And what has Old Angus been up to that's so serious?' asked Hughie.

Hickory Dickory swallowed another huge mouthful. He placed the half-empty glass on the bar. 'He's just turned up at the surgery with a cushion stuffed up his jeresey.' With staged dramatic timing, the doc sploshed in a refill.

Hughie looked at Brock. Brock looked at Hughie. 'And what's so terrible about that?' the bar owner enquired.

'He thinks he's pregnant,' came the answer, swiftly followed by another gulp of wine. 'Eight months gone.'

'Och, don't be so fuckin' stupid,' said Bungalow Bob. 'He's seventy, if he's a day.'

Maybe old man Simpson wouldn't be bereft of company while being invited to eat with rubber cutlery for the rest of his life. With practised ease, Hughie ignored the island's window cleaner and said, 'Aye, I could see how that might traumatise you, doc.

Hickory Dickory raised the replenished glass to his lips and smiled. He knew the island didn't realise he had a sense of humour. 'Cheers, everyone, I need this,' he said, adding with the faintest of grins, 'I do enjoy these moments of whimsical candour as once more I embark along this tortured path of life.' Reassuringly, he drained the glass.

The bar owner turned back to the sportswriter. 'I was talking to Ted over at the Georgics Hotel this morning,' he said. 'Nice guy. English. How does a bloke from Nottingham ever discover

Millport? No Scottish connection whatsoever. Sees an advert in a trade paper, comes over to the island, falls in love with it and buys himself a hotel. Just like that.'

'Aye,' said Brock, 'I've used the bar in there a couple of times. He is a neighbour, so to speak. Aye, nice guy. Always smiling. He tells me he's a Nottingham Forest fan who can now die a happy man after watching his side win the European Cup twice. Aye, quite a happy chappie.'

'Not this morning,' corrected Hughie. 'He told me a party of twelve from Devon had just cancelled their rooms for the entire Festive period. He got a phone call from one of them late last night telling him they wouldn't be coming. Naturally, he asked them why. He was told he could keep their deposit, but they had no intention of coming to an island that had so many psychopaths.'

'Psychopaths?' queried Brock. 'In Millport?' He added, 'There's no doubt there are a few who aren't rowing with all the oars in the water ...'

'A tattie short in their mince,' interjected Hughie.

'... but psychopaths? Certainly the elevator isn't going all the way to the top floor ...'

'Daft as oatcakes, most of them,' interrupted Hughie.

'... but psychopaths? Don't think so.' Brock lifted his pint to his lips and thought for a moment, which wasn't easy as an image of a topless Willy continued to dance around in his mind. He snapped his fingers and laughed. He put his pint back on the bar. He continued to giggle.

'What's so funny?' asked Hughie. 'That cancellation is going to cost Ted hundreds.'

'Psychopaths?' asked Hughie. 'I think you'll find someone from Devon hasn't picked up the Scottish dialect too well. I'll bet you they've been told about CYCLE PATHS' – he emphasised the words – 'not bloody psychopaths. Better get onto Ted and see if he can phone them and get the booking back on.'

'Psychopaths,' repeated Hughie. 'Cycle paths. Christ, you can see that something can get lost in the translation, can't you? I'll phone Ted right now.' The bar owner went to the telephone on the bar at Vodka Joe's corner to hastily relay the good news. After a minute on the blower, he returned to his spot beside the sportswriter. 'Ted says thanks, he owes you several,' smiled the bar owner. 'Brilliant! Psychopaths and cycle paths.' He shook his head, grinned broadly and picked up his brandy and port. 'Cheers, Brock, best laugh I had since I heard Ally MacLeod telling everyone that Scotland would win the World Cup in Argentina in 1978.'

Hughie sipped and then adopted a somewhat serious expression for a moment. Returning to the subject that continued to play on his friend's mind, the bar owner asked, 'I take it even Willy won't be wearing her skimpy stuff on a night like this?' Hughie could always hope. And they hadn't quite got around to slapping a tax on fantasising. Not yet, anyway.

'You never know with women, do you?' said Brock. 'I can walk through the streets of Glasgow on perishing winter mornings, frost on the ground, wind howling, wearing my big brown leather coat, Timberland boots, gloves, scarf and my beanie hat and there are all these wee lasses with their exposed midriffs and wearing daft wee slip-on shoes with no soles. Are we definitely from the same planet? Is there a factory somewhere churning out these lovely little androids who are impervious to weather conditions?'

'I think we should be told,' said Hughie, adding, 'If Willy turns up with one of the outfits she wears in McKinlay's this place will be mobbed in minutes. I'll need to build an extra loo just for Big Eric's exclusive use.'

They both laughed. Neither noticed the info bar rolling round the bottom of Sky Sports on the television. It read:

BREAKING NEWS ... DEREK LAIRD MISSING AT BARCELONA ... BREAKING NEWS ... DEREK LAIRD MISSING AT BARCELONA ...

CHAPTER TEN

Early morning. Tuesday 23 November.

Barcelona.

'*CABALLO LOCO QUE FALTA!*' shrieked the banner front page headline in *Diario Sports*, one of the leading newspapers in Barcelona.

'*CRAZY HORSE IS MISSING!*' Golden Boy Derek Laird hadn't turned up for training the previous day. No phone call. No explanation. No sign of the team's star attraction. The player's non-appearance had been immediately leaked to the press by some 'helpful' insider. The newspaper carried a large three-column, twelve-inch deep colour photograph of the Scottish footballer celebrating his spectacular winning goal against Real Madrid only four evenings before. There was a smaller head image of the team's manager, Rafael Castillo, across one column, three inches deep. The Sports Editor had purposely chosen an image of the manager looking very unhappy with a worrying frown dominating his features. It was no easy task detecting such a photograph; under his giant moustache, Rafael Castillo smiled a lot. Not in this photograph, though.

'I have no idea where my player is,' admitted manager Castillo at a hastily-arranged Press Conference in the Media Room at the Nou Camp Stadium. He was realising that if a week was a long time in politics, then a day was a lifetime in his chosen sport. He added, 'I am sure there will be a very good explanation because he is an excellent professional. He has never given us any trouble in his five years at this club. Yes, I am certain there will be a very good reason.'

'When did you first realise he was missing?' queried a reporter; an easy one to start with to get the manager talking.

'Like all the other players, he was allowed the weekend off after Friday's game,' answered Castillo. 'That, of course, is normal. We only expect some players to visit *mujer hermosa* after a game.'

The sports reporters knew *mujer hermosa*, beautiful woman, was the name of the treatment table at the Nou Camp Stadium. Some footballers were known to embrace the treatment table more often than they did their wives or girlfriends. Or, in one case, boyfriend. Crazy Horse was rarely injured and, thus, hardly ever had the requirements of *mujer hermosa*.

'So, he is not injured?' queried a reporter, firing in the expected question. Castillo, perched on a large desk with some fifty reporters sitting in casual seats in front of him, fiddled with his overgrown moustache. He had been through it all before with a particularly inquisitive Press.

'No, he is fine, as far as I am aware,' replied the manager. 'When he left the ground on Friday night he was okay. He is a very fit athlete, as you all know. How many games has he missed for us in five years?' A shrug of the shoulders, the arms extended, his hands aloft. 'Not even ten.'

The reporters nodded. One asked, 'Have you checked the hospitals?'

'Yes, of course,' answered Castillo, somewhat wearily. 'That was one of our first phone calls. We have checked with the police, too. We have given them the make of our player's cars and his registration numbers and they are looking at CCTV to try to check his movements. No luck so far. Airports, too. Nothing. Ports. Nothing. Border controls. Nothing. Mobile phone calls. Nothing unusual, but authorities are checking recent calls.' He paused. 'Can we talk about football, please, gentlemen?'

One asked what was obviously a prepared question. 'Is he still in your squad for the game against Valencia?'

'Yes, of course,' said Castillo, now chewing on the cheroot he thought made him look a little like Clint Eastwood in *A Fistful Of Dollars*. An overweight, bald Clint Eastwood, adorned with an abundance of facial furniture and chopped off at the knees. No-one had ever witnessed the cheroot lit. 'I cannot leave him out until I know for sure what is happening. To me, that is the right thing to do.'

'Any problems for the player?' asked another newspaperman.

'I have already said he is fit ...'

'No,' pressed the reporter, 'off the field. Are there any problems off the field?'

Castillo shrugged. 'I am not aware of any such problems.'

In an instant, he realised this story might head in a direction that would be less than helpful to Barcelona and its supporters' favourite player. A cartoon had recently appeared in a national newspaper of a Spanish player down on his knees with a straw sniffing along the whitewash of the eighteen-yard line. No words were necessary. The player had a penchant for cocaine and the cartoon left no room for misinterpretation. The player's caricature, his identity clear to all, was gleefully snorting away on the pitch in a stadium with sixty thousand onlookers. Clearly, as the caricature suggested, he was above the law. A day after the cartoon appeared, the player was suspended by his club and detectives took a very public interest in his activities away from football. At the age of twenty-seven, the footballer's career was effectively over.

Castillo fixed the inquisitor in his gaze. 'No, there are definitely no problems with my player. Don't waste your time looking for snakes under every rock because there are none. We all know my player does not give us any trouble.' He thought he would lighten the mood and laughed, 'Yes, he is Scottish, but even I drink more whisky than him.'

There was a small ripple of laughter. The press pack nodded in agreement. They drank more whisky than the Scot.

Castillo smiled and continued, 'And he does not have a wife to nag him, either.' He added a little disconcertingly, 'Lucky man.'

'Is there a chance you will suspend the player if he does not show up?' probed another reporter, getting the press conference back on track.

Again, the manager shrugged his shoulders. 'How can I do that?' he asked. 'There may be a good explanation for his ...' Castillo didn't want to use the word 'disappearance'. A slight hesitation before adding, '... his non-appearance.' A scowl was hidden under the facial hair disguising his lips. He added, 'No, I have no intention of suspending my player. Not until I know what is happening. He is in my pool of players for the weekend. I can only repeat he is a good boy who has never given this football club any trouble whatsoever. No trouble. No problems.'

'And no show,' smirked another reporter.

Castillo didn't like this particular newsman from *El Mundo Deportivo*. He always wanted the front page. He thrived on scandal; he liked to dish the dirt. He wasn't interested in players with hernias. Players with hookers was more his thing. The Barcelona manager didn't believe the journalist knew the first thing about football. In fact, in all his twenty-five years in the profession, he hadn't met too many sports journalists who had a clue about the game, in his opinion. In private moments, over coffee at an airport waiting for a flight to and from European games, he would mix informally with the press pack. Dictaphones would be switched off and he took the opportunity to have a word in the ear of one or two he thought were particularly useless at their chosen career path. 'How could you know anything about football when you never played?' he would often ask them. 'You don't need to be a horse to tip a Grand National winner,' was the predictable reply.

The manager looked again at the inquisitive reporter. 'Yes, of course, you are quite right. That is why I am talking to you, yes? He could be here in an hour with a perfectly acceptable and logical explanation. Who knows?' Another expansive movement of the shoulders; another chomp on the cheroot.

'So, you are not too worried?' persisted the *El Mundo Deportivo* reporter.

'Well, yes, of course, I am concerned,' replied the manager. 'I have to hope nothing serious has happened to my player. That, of course, would concern me; concern everyone at this club. Our supporters, also. We must hope my player is okay. I'm sure he is, but for one reason or another Derek did not show up for training on Monday and there is no sign of him today.'

'I take you have made every effort to contact the player?' repeated a newspaperman.

Castillo narrowed his eyes. He was used to stupid questions. 'Yes, of course, we have tried to contact him,' he sighed. 'There is no answer from his phones. We have obtained keys to his home and there is no sign of him. Everything looks perfectly normal. We have also visited his favourite hotel. They haven't seen him for a fortnight. We've tried his friends and associates.'

'And he hasn't tried to contact you or the club?' Another silly question.

'If he had done that, I would now be in a position to provide you all with answers,' sighed Castillo.

'So, he is off the radar?' asked another.

'If that's the way you want to put it, yes,' said Castillo, a little huffily. 'But I repeat once more there could be a valid reason for him not being here.'

'Is he still in the country?' asked the *El Mundo Deportivo* reporter, sensing a front page splash.

'Why wouldn't he be in the country?' said the team coach warily. 'As I have said, as a precaution, the police authorities have checked on this. They are satisfied he is in Spain. I can't see any reason that he would want to leave the country. None whatsoever.'

The press wanted to use the 'kidnap' word. That was a no-go area at this stage in questioning. It would be different, though, in another twenty-four hours or so.

While Rafael Castillo fielded a barrage of questions from the persistent reporters, Derek Laird, feted and adored by thousands, was already on his way to Scotland. The ten-year-old Peugeot 206 was up to the task.

CHAPTER ELEVEN

Early morning. Tuesday 23 November.

Largs Slip, North Ayrshire Coast.

'Apart from that, Mrs Lincoln, how did you enjoy the play?' laughed Griff Stewart, aka R.I.P., Chief News Reporter of the *Daily News*.

'Oh, come on, they can't be THAT bad,' smiled Harry Booth, aka El Cid, Detective Inspector with Police Scotland CID.

'I'm telling you, mate, they are not even THAT good!' said R.I.P. with a straight face. El Cid realised his newspaper pal had just clambered aboard his favourite subject: his perception of the appalling state of journalism worldwide.

'Honestly, El Cid, trust me,' urged R.I.P. 'If one of today's young journalists was transported back to Ford's Theatre in Washington on that fateful evening back in April 1865, that would have been his first question to the widow of the newly-assassinated President. The biggest news story in the history of the country could have taken place under his nose, but he would do his job and stick to his task. He was there as a theatre critic and nothing and no-one was going to prevent him from getting that crit of '*Our American Cousin*'. A dead President of the United States? Who cares? He had a crit to do.'

'You do like your slight exaggeration, my boy,' grinned the cop as he prepared to guide his Audi onto the ramp of the Largs-Millport ferry. The 8.45am crossing was reasonably quiet, the sedate seaside town already preparing for its late morning nap.

Five cars, a delivery van and an ambulance were in the queue in front of him. About twenty pedestrians, many laden with Morrisons shopping bags, were about to embark on the same journey. A sturdy breeze swept along the promenade; a grey, non-event day in the offing. Silently, El Cid allowed his vehicle to roll down the slip, up the ramp and onto the ferry, the Caledonian-MacBrayne employee signalling for him to take the middle of three car lanes.

'Actually, R.I.P.,' he said, 'I've got a good story for you. Remember that severed head that was found on the beach on Orkney a couple of years ago? A Turkish female, if I remember correctly. Worked in the local bakery, I think. I was sent up with a few of the team and one of the island's cops told me he was questioning some of the locals. He was on the beach when he held up the head and asked this old bloke if he recognised the face. The chap looked long and hard. Then he said, "Och, aye, I think so," and then added, "but she wasn't that tall."'

'Fuck off,' said R.I.P.

'True. Honest,' replied El Cid. 'You newspaper guys don't have the copyright on a lot of the nonsense that goes on out there. I've come across a few crackers. You think all your young reporters are a bit slow on the uptake? We've got a few cops who aren't far behind. There was one young lad who was ordered to clear a crime scene. A murder had taken place on a hilltop. After forensics had poked around, he was told to remove piles of logs and rocks strewn around the scene. He got four or five of his mates to start carrying the logs and stuff down the hill to get them out of the way. They were struggling with the stuff and, halfway down, another officer stopped them. He said to the leader of the pack, "Why don't you just roll them down the hill and save you carrying them?" The young cop looked impressed by the advice. He turned to the others. "Right, you lot," he commanded in his sternest tone of authority. "Back to the top of the hill. We're going to roll them down." True. Honest.'

'Fuck off,' said R.I.P.

The crossing took ten see-sawing minutes, the Firth of Clyde rocking backwards and forwards, dutifully obeying the demands of a furious overhead wind. The cop drove the car down the ramp onto the island, being greeted by the sign, **Failte gu EILEAN CHUMBRUAICH, Welcome to the ISLAND OF CUMBRAE**. He turned left, heading south towards the town of Millport, four miles away from the Cumbrae slip.

'This is the life,' sighed the cop. 'I love this wee place.' He pressed a button on the car door and the window wound down. 'Get that good fresh air into your lungs.' He sniffed dramatically. 'Do you think any of those cows realise it's Tuesday?' He smiled and added, 'You know, if Lynda had her way we would spend months down here.'

'Really?' said the newspaperman. 'Could you live here? No more mean streets? No more hatchet-wielding maniacs to confront on a nightly basis? No more bullets to dodge?'

'Glasgow's not that bad,' laughed El Cid. 'Been at least a month since I was attacked by a lunatic with a blow torch. Don't think I've ever dodged a bullet in my life. A couple of the wife's rolling pins, but never a bullet.' He tugged at his cheek and continued, 'No, I doubt if I could live here. Nice place, but I don't think my liver could stand it. These punters know how to shovel away the booze.'

'I suppose there are just so many rounds of golf you can fit into a day,' nodded R.I.P. 'How many times do you want to cycle round the island? How many times can you be bothered walking along the beach? No, as they say down here, I'm a mainlander. The island life is not for me. Having said that, I aim to rip the arse out of it while I'm here. I'm sure Brock will be happy to see us. A nice wee surprise.'

'And he doesn't get too many surprises at his time of life,' nodded the cop in agreement.

CHAPTER TWELVE

Early morning. Tuesday 23 November.

Millport, Isle of Cumbrae.

'Christ, Willy, I almost came there.' Charlie Brock laughed uncontrollably.

'Me, too,' said Willy, also indulging in a fit of the giggles.

Brock rolled off Willy onto his back. He sighed. 'When did you become such a brazen hussy?' he asked, smiling in satisfaction while stroking her long, tousled blonde hair.

'When did you come into the pub yesterday?' replied Willy.

'About midday,' answered Brock.

'About midday,' replied Willy.

They both chortled like kids. The two entwined in each other's arms; both naked; the bed sheets at their feet. Brock began nibbling at Willy's neck. She positively purred.

'You've made me feel like a woman again, Charlie,' she said. There was a small silence before she added in hushed tones. 'Thank you.'

'Willy,' whispered Brock, 'I think I should be thanking you. Last night was beautiful.' There was a slight pause. 'We've wasted a lot of time, haven't we?'

'Well, Charlie boy, we've now got the opportunity to make up for it.'

There was another silence for a moment or two; a joyous hush. Something quite remarkable and extraordinary had happened between two old friends. They had been gentle lovers, which surprised Brock. Willy had promised to 'fuck him senseless' and she looked as though she was about to explode with desire when she entered Hugh's Bar shortly before nine o'clock the previous evening. Without hesitating, still dripping wet and carrying an overnight bag, she made straight for Brock, standing at the bar. In her haste, Willy bumped into Boring Brian. It was the best time he had had in years.

She kissed Brock full on the lips; a long, luscious caress. Hughie Edwards looked on from the other side of the bar. Was that a tinge of the green-eyed monster called jealousy? In all likelihood, it would have been the same emotion experienced by every other red-blooded male customer with a pulse. Willy's kiss had been as defiant as it had been seductive. She would certainly have realised most of the regulars in the bar would be well acquainted with her husband Tommy. Frankly, she couldn't care less. He had Pammy the Weed and she had Charlie Brock, a guy later that night she would tell over and over again throughout their love-making that she had fancied like mad since they had been kids.

She had bowed to the demands of the severe weather, the rain still tumbling out of the dark grey skies and the wind whipping up a storm as it relentlessly bowled along the unprotected promenade. She removed a French beret, shook her head and smiled luminously. She took off her charcoal duffel coat which Brock accepted and placed with the other drenched coats and jackets that had formed a discarded sodden pile on the pegs beside the door. Brock could see the skimpy top and the short skirt had been replaced by a thick woollen red polo neck and a pair of figure-hugging dark blue jeans. The high heels had also been discarded for a pair of brown calf-length boots. She smiled and whispered, 'Don't worry, Charlie boy, I won't be wearing this stuff all night.' The sports reporter stepped back in admiration. 'Willy,' he said, 'you would look fabulous in the eye of a hurricane.' He meant it, too.

'You want to sit away from the bar?' said Brock, thoughtfully. 'Somewhere more private?'

Big Eric heard the question. He had been about to offer Willy his lap.

He was disappointed when he heard her say, 'Here's fine. It's just good to be on this side of the bar for a change.' She fumbled in her back pocket before producing a purse. 'What are you having, Charlie boy, as if I didn't know?'

'Beautiful and she pays her round,' nodded Brock. 'Looks like I'm on a winner.'

Willy pulled the journalist towards her and whispered again. 'Play your cards right and the winner will be on you.' That devastating smile again; gleaming white even teeth. Brock wondered if she had ever had a filling in her life. He guessed not. He said out loud before he could prevent himself, 'How do you make perfection more perfect?'

Willy moved her crimson lips closer to Brock's left ear. 'You are not just trying to get into my knickers, are you?' she said, quickly adding, 'That's if I've got any on, Charlie boy.'

From just along the bar, Big Eric watched and wished he possessed the ability to read lips. His eyesight was good, though, and if Willy clenched Brock's backside one more time, Big Eric knew he would have to make an emergency stop at the toilet.

Even without the skimpy top, Willy was still managing to attract an audience in Hugh's Bar. Tip-Toe Thompson had finished his shift as chef at The Pier restaurant next door and joined Big Eric, Bungalow Bob, Hickory Dickory and Boring Brian at the bar. Vodka Joe was cosily enveloped in satisfying sleep in his 'exclusive' area, world-watching and seagull-counting duties exhausted for the day.

Hughie poured Willy her ordered dry Martini and lemonade, smiled at his attractive customer and placed the glass in front of her while supplying a beer mat. He was giving her the VIP treatment. He looked at his pal Brock. 'What about you, Charlie?' he asked cheekily, with only a hint of the smile that had just been bestowed upon Willy. 'Are you saving yourself for the big night?'

Before he could say anything else, Willy intervened, 'Oh, I don't think Charlie will be allowed Brewer's Droop tonight,' she breathed in smoky tones. 'I'll make sure of that.'

Big Eric overhead the words and beat a hasty route towards the Gents.

'Jumpin Jehosophat!' The door groaned open, a fierce gust of unwelcoming wind shot through the pub and in stepped Captain America. Hughie couldn't help raising an eyebrow in surprise. Captain America, real name Tommy Cunningham, born in the local Lady Margaret Hospital some fifty years ago, had earned the moniker after spending six months in Vancouver. Why he was swiftly transformed from Tommy Cunningham into Captain America became fairly evident as soon as he opened his mouth. 'Gee, what a motherfucker of a night,' he exclaimed. 'That's as bad as an any ornery twister.'

The small, tubby owner of Millport Transport rarely stepped foot in Hugh's Bar of an evening. Hughie didn't take it personally; Captain America's flat was six yards away from Robbie's Tavern at Kames Bay and it was all of about a twenty-minute saunter to his howf. Now why would he venture out on a 'motherfucker of a night' to visit Hugh's Bar? He reckoned the presence of a very attractive lady may have played its part in persuading him to face the elements.

'You been chucked out of Robbie's?' asked Hughie, with a hint of mischief. Captain America summoned up a grin. 'Gee, ya know, sometimes a fella jus' needs a plain, good, ole change of scenery, Hubert.' He took off his drenched buckskin coat with the fringes adorning the sleeves and added it to the gathering heap on the hook. He was still wearing his soaked stetson as he stepped towards the bar. He stopped in mock astonishment. 'Ma goodness, what have we got here?' he said. Hughie thought Captain America's acting ability was on a par with that of Kermit the Frog. 'Well, Ah do declare, it's Miss Willy, ain't it? Miss Willy from across the way? Well, are you a sight for ma ol' sore eyes? Ma goodness, you are a mighty purty gal. Yessirreee.'

He stepped forward and took Willy's right hand, courteously bowed forward and planted a kiss on it.

'You wouldn't kiss that if you knew where it had been about a minute ago,' he was informed by the hand's owner. Willy then grabbed Brock by the backside.

A look of horror shot through Captain America's chubby features. He took a quick step backwards, hastily wiped his lips with a handerkerchief and said, 'Hubert, a Jack Daniels, my boy. Large. Quickly, please.' Captain America picked up his drink and made a swift retreat to sit opposite the snoozing Vodka Joe.

At that moment, Big Eric, who had been away for about a mere five minutes, something of a personal best, returned from the loo. 'That's better,' he said and moved to his spot at the bar and picked up his drink. 'Much better.'

'Fancy a job, Willy?' asked Hughie, imagining the barmaid behind his bar with her lungs hanging out and his punters trying to work out if she was wearing panties or not. The mental picture of Big Eric being stretchered home every night with exhaustion formed in his mind. 'Fancy it?' he repeated.

'Oh, you never know, Hughie, do you?' she answered. 'Strange things happen in this life.' Below the bar she moved her right hand to check out if Brock was hard. She wasn't disappointed. 'I don't think I'll be in Largs forever.' She looked at Brock. 'Maybe I'll move to Glasgow. You never know, do you?' Brock smiled and lifted the pint to his lips. 'I'll drink to that,' he found himself saying.

'Ah say, Ah think it's calming down out there,' said Captain America, only five minutes after his arrival.

'Calming down to a tempest,' said Tip-Toe Thompson, bang on the money.

'No, boy, Ah think Ah can detect it's getting just a mite better. Ah think Ah'll jus' mosey along.' He took his still-soaking buckskin coat and slipped it over his shoulders. 'Ah'll bid ya'll a wunnerful farewell,' he said, straightening his stetson. He didn't look back at Willy as he pulled his coat tight and went out to brave the storm back to Robbie's Tavern. 'Fuckin' wasted journey,' he said to himself.

'I think I've blown my chance there,' observed Willy.

'That's what you get for being honest,' laughed Brock, thoroughly enjoying the company of one of the most gorgeous females he had the good fortune to clap eyes upon. He had a fair idea of what would follow later in the evening. So, too, did his companion.

They left the bar a couple of hours later, heading towards the Hippy Chippy. 'We've got fifteen minutes before he closes,' said Brock, looking once again at his wristwatch. 9.45pm. Captain America would never have a career in meteorology, Brock decided during the couple of minutes' brisk stride from Hughie's. The weather was actually deteriorating and the isolated Island of Cumbrae, with little to protect it from the angry elements, was getting a battering that night. They made it to the Hippy Chippy just in time. 'We okay for a couple of fish suppers?' asked Brock. 'Yeh, mate, another fifteen minutes and you would have been in a right bovver,' smiled the London-born owner with the pony tail.

'Do you know why they're called pony tails?' Brock whispered to Willy.

'No idea,' she returned in hushed tones.

'Pick it up and you'll see a horse's arse underneath it,' smirked Brock.

Later, in the Schloss Adler, as they tucked into their takeaway, Brock told Willy about a marvellous incident a couple of Glasgow Fair Holidays ago when a drunken visitor arrived at the Hippy Chippy just as the shutter was going down.

'Hey, mister, can Ah get a fiss supper?' he slurred.

'Sorry, we're closed,' he was told.

'Aye, right,' came the reply. He decided to try again. 'How aboot a black puddin' supper, chief?'

'Sorry, we're closed,' he was told again.

'Aye, right,' he said. 'Well, how aboot a cauld pie supper, then?'

'Sorry, we're closed,' he was informed for the third time.

The drunk knew it was time to rethink his strategy. He came back with, 'Awright, wull ye just throw out a couple of fuckin' pickled onions?'

Brock and Willy dined regally at the table at the front window as the rain poured down in torrents, the wind whipping it around in mesmerising patterns. The puddles at the harbour front appeared to have a life of their own as they constantly changed shape. 'They look as though they've got a heartbeat,' said Willy, looking down from the top floor flat. She sipped a cold glass of Pinot Grigo. 'You didn't have to go to all this trouble, Charlie,' she said, adding, 'Sweeping me off my feet by wining and dining me. To hell with mystery adding to seduction. I want to make love to you. I have wanted to make love to you ever since I knew what making love meant.'

Brock realised she had inserted the words 'make love' instead of 'fuck'. He preferred the reference change. After draining a second bottle of white plonk, they went to bed. And they 'made love'. Four times.

'Just as well I've got a new pacemaker,' said Brock in a still moment as they cuddled in tightly, the wind and rain battering noisily at the bedroom window. The Firth of Clyde made its violent presence known, too, splattering its raging sprays against the rocks and sending showers climbing the walls.

'Heaven,' he murmured.

'Amen to that,' she replied. And they made love again.

Afterwards, with both bodies still linked, Willy nestled her chin on her left hand, her elbow on the pillow. She looked at Brock and asked gently, 'Do you remember one afternoon when we were just kids and you were playing football at West Bay?'

'I played football at West Bay EVERY day,' said Brock.

'No, there was one day when I was on my own,' said Willy, her violet eyes clearly visible in the shadows. 'I was standing behind your goal. We had met the previous year in the Nixe. I was sitting beside you. We were just kids. Then, all of a year later, you invited me to see you play. You told me you were going to play in goal for Scotland some day. Remember?'

'Aye, as a matter of fact, I do,' said Brock. 'You wanted to talk to me and I had to play football. I was frightened you might get hit with the ball. We were up against the locals and there was always a bit of niggle in those games.'

'I thought you were ignoring me. I thought you didn't like me. I stood there for about an hour, but you hardly said a word to me. I remember I went over to the old fishing pond. Remember, where we used to look for tadpoles?'

'Aye,' said Brock, a little intrigued. 'I do remember seeing you sitting there on your own. I wondered what was upsetting you. You looked as though you were crying.'

'I WAS crying, Charlie. I was ten or eleven years old and my heart was broken. I didn't think it would ever mend. I just sat by the edge of the pond and sobbed my little heart out. The boy I loved didn't love me.'

'Christ, sorry,' said Brock, apologising for an innocent action from decades gone by. 'I didn't realise, Willy ...'

'Couldn't you see how I felt? It was the last day of the holidays. I knew we were both going home. I lived in Paisley and you lived in Glasgow. We were a world apart. I wanted to talk to you that day. I wanted to let you know how I felt. I didn't want to go another year without seeing you. I didn't have your address, phone number, anything. I could have written to you and told you how I felt. The following year I looked for you. I went up to the caravan park where you stayed. I went to West Bay every morning and afternoon. There was no sign of you. Someone told me you were in Rothesay. Your parents wanted a change. You might as well have been on the moon. I lost you all because of a game of football. Stupid game, football.'

'Sorry,' said Brock again.

'And then I met that little shit Tommy and we got married when I was eighteen. Millport was the only place I had been outside Paisley. Then Tommy and I went to live in Largs. And the next time I saw you I was working in the Station Bar and you walked in with this stunning female. My heart skipped a beat. I knew it was you immediately. Those blue eyes, the dimple on your chin, the fair hair a lot longer than I remembered. And you were so tall and handsome. My breath was taken away. I almost cried. The last time I had seen you was in that bloody goal in Millport. Ten years on you simply walked into a pub and, once more, I was that wee girl sitting beside the fishing pond at West Bay sobbing her heart out.'

'Sorry.'

'I checked out your wedding ring finger and saw the gold band. I looked at the female. She wore a wedding ring, too. You were married. I was married. Your wife sat at a stool at the bar and then you turned to look at me. I didn't know what to do. I could see you focusing on me and then smiling. "Willy?" you asked.'

'Aye, I remember that,' admitted Brock. 'I introduced you to Irene, didn't I? I asked you if you were married. You showed me your wedding ring.'

'And that was that. Later, I was told you had got divorced and had remarried. A barmaid, I was told. You got the wrong barmaid, Charlie boy.'

'Wendy was okay,' he said, somewhat defensively of his ex. 'It just didn't work out. You could say I've got two successful marriages behind me.'

'And then we seemed to bump into each other quite a lot. Remember the David Bowie gig at the Barrowland? You were standing at the bar in one of the pubs at Glasgow Cross? I came in with some of my Largs cronies and stood right beside you? Christ, Charlie boy, you took my breath away again. I really liked you. I enjoyed it when you came into McKinlay's on your way to Millport. Not too happy with the array of females who were with you ...'

'There weren't that many,' said Brock. Slight pause. 'Did you never wonder why I stopped drinking in the Station Bar and moved to McKinlays, Willy?'

'The lager was two pence cheaper?'

'Aye, that's it in one,' grinned Brock. 'Nothing to do with the view.'

'I liked you and I knew you liked me, but what could I do? I was married to that little shit and I knew you liked the wee creep. So, it looked as though never the twain shall meet, eh? Another lost love story in the maze of romances gone astray.'

'Very philosophical,' said Brock, inadvertently caressing his companion's right boob and fondling her erect nipple.

'If you fiddle around long enough with that, Charlie boy, you'll eventually get Radio One. The reception's better on the other one.'

Both laughed.

'Were you surprised by me yesterday?' asked Willy, a serious tone in her question.

'No, I wouldn't say I was surprised,' replied Brock. 'Surprised? No. More shocked, stunned and amazed, I would think. And flattered, of course.'

'And here we are today in your bed in Millport. Frightening, isn't it? With West Bay just around the corner. You got any paraffin? Let's go and torch those bloody goals.'

Suddenly, his mobile shrilled. 'Bugger! I better get that,' he said, looking at his wristwatch; 9.52am. 'It might be important.' He stretched across Willy and picked up the infuriating, intrusive instrument. 'Who the hell can this be?'

R.I.P.'s name flashed up on the screen. Confused, Brock answered, wondering why his old mate was phoning. He knew R.I.P. was aware he was in Millport for a few days.

'Surprise!' cried the news reporter and repeated, 'Surprise! Guess who's in Millport and right downstairs from the Schloss Adler? Me and El Cid. Surprise!'

The cop came on, 'We haven't caught you with some voluptuous blonde, have we, Brock? We okay to come up?'

'Oh, shit,' said Brock, trying to think quickly. 'Listen, lads, just a wee bit early for me. Why don't you go over to Mrs Pastry's for a roll and sausage and I'll clean up here and see you asap? Catch you over at Hughie's. Okay?'

'I think we've surprised him,' said R.I.P.

'Caught him with his pants down, methinks,' added El CID.

110

CHAPTER THIRTEEN

Late morning. Tuesday 23 November.

Millport, Isle of Cumbrae.

'Who in their right mind would give up all that?' asked Hughie Edwards, reading the front page of the *Daily News* that informed him of the mysterious disappearance of Derek Laird from Barcelona.

'It'll be the drugs, Hughie,' surmised Vodka Joe in an instant, adopting one of his more thoughtful expressions. 'It's always the bloody drugs. Do strange things to your head. Stick to alcohol, I say. You're safe with booze. No problems with the spirits.' Vodka Joe shuffled past the bar owner, adding, 'By the way, Hughie, how did I get home last night?'

It was precisley two minutes past eleven in the morning and Hughie Edwards had just swung open the doors of Hugh's Bar. And, as on most occasions, Vodka Joe was his first customer. His glass of vodka was already waiting for him on the bar, but he was disappointed to note the bar owner was still reading the *Daily News*. Normally, he could nick the newspaper before settling into his comfortable corner at the front window of the tavern.

Vodka Joe parked his backside on the couch and repeated, 'Telling you, Hughie, it's all that cocaine stuff that does it. Me? I'm happy with vodka, but these big-time football stars, well, they want something else, don't they? Shoving all that stuff up their beaks, blowing their bloody heads off. And heroin? Don't get me started on heroin ...'

'Perish the thought,' mumbled Hughie, holding onto his newspaper while pouring change into the Jewish Piano.

'They forget where they come from,' continued Vodka Joe. 'Grow up with their arses hanging out their trousers and, once they've had all their money, it's something else that's hanging out their trousers. Do you see the birds these guys pull? Some of these blokes look like Quasimodo on a bad hair day, but they can still end up getting off with some fabulous blonde with tits the size of bouncy castles. Stoned out of their heads, don't know if it's New York or New Year and they get off with some beauty queen. Stupid bastards.' Vodka Joe added, slightly more vehemently, 'Stupid, RICH bastards!'

'It says here that Derek Laird is earning £200,000 – per week – at Barcelona,' Hughie, settling on a barside stool, informed his little pal.

'Naw, don't believe it,' said Vodka Joe. 'That's just paper talk. Two bloody hundred thousand quid for working ninety minutes a week? No chance. That's about a million quid a minute.'

'There's a photocopy of his contract in the paper,' said Hughie.

'Let's see that,' said Vodka Joe, displaying more speed than had ever been previously witnessed by any inhabitant of the island. Nimbly, he swept round to the corner of the bar. 'Let's see.' He practically ripped the newspaper out of Hughie's hands. He looked at the photo of the contract. 'Fuck me, that can't be right. Two hundred thousand quid? I've never made that in my life and that arsehole can earn it for farting about on a piece of grass for an hour-and-a-half? Fuck's sake.'

'Can I get my paper back now?' pleaded Hughie, desperate to find out more about the Scottish international player who had gone

AWOL from one of the biggest football clubs in the world. 'How does a guy like that go into hiding? Where can he go? Everyone knows who he is.'

'Howard Hughes wasn't seen for decades,' observed Vodka Joe, settling back into his personal sofa. 'And he was one of the biggest film producers in Hollywood history, wasn't he? Even punters in mud huts in the middle of the rainforest in Venezuala knew all about Howard Hughes.'

There were rare occasions when his little friend actually surprised him with his mental agility. Just the other day he had said, 'Real knowledge is to know the extent of one's ignorance.'

'Didn't realise you were a devotee of Confucius,' Hughie had said.

'Confucius? What are you talking about? That was Charlie Chan, I'm sure.'

Vodka Joe focused as a seagull desperately flapped its wings as it flew into a gust of wind. 'What about Agatha Christie?' he asked.

'Oh, aye, I had forgotten her,' said Hughie. 'She disappeared, too, didn't she? Came off the radar for about a fortnight, didn't she? Way back in the mid-twenties? The cops thought she had committed suicide, if I remember correctly. Something to do with her husband wanting a divorce. She just disappeared. I remember it now.'

'They even made a film, didn't they?' said Vodka Joe, more than content with his recollection.

'Did they?' asked Hughie, once more impressed at the range of knowledge of his hard-drinking chum.

'Aye,' said Vodka Joe. 'I've seen it. Dustin Hoffman's in it ...'

'Eh? Did he play Agatha Christie?' Hughie couldn't quite picture it.

'Naw, you're thinking of *Tootsie*.'

'Was that Dustin Hoffman?' asked the bar owner. 'I'm sure it was Robin Williams.'

'Naw, it wasn't,' said Vodka Joe, certain of his facts. 'He never made a movie. He was a singer with Oasis.'

'Christ sake, Vodka Joe, are YOU on cocaine?' said an exasperated Hughie. 'It wasn't Robbie Williams it was Robin Williams and he was a singer with Spandau Ballet.'

'Tootsie sang with Spandau Ballet?' queried Vodka Joe. 'Anyway, I think you'll find Robbie Williams was in *Mrs Doubtfire*. Or was that Charles Bronson?'

'Aw, give us peace,' said Hughie. 'Listen, if you are on this coke stuff, who's your dealer on the island? Anyone we know?'

'No, I'm happy enough with alcohol, thank you very much for asking,' said Vodka Joe. 'And I'm happy to inform you my vodka diet is working a treat – I've lost eight days already this month. Vodka and oxygen, Hughie, two of the most important things on the planet. Speaking of which, just stick another in there, as the actress said to the bishop.' He drained his glass and pushed it across the table. 'The rest of this island thinks you're a miserable bastard,' he said and added, 'But, Hughie, I don't think you're miserable.' He smiled and added, 'Is it my fault I have a liver hell-bent on suicide? Any time you're ready.'

'Done like a kipper again,' thought the bar owner as he walked over to the table to retrieve the glass. The flap allowing entrance to the optics was at the other end of the bar. Hughie sighed and took the well-worn path. He poured a glass of the most obscure

Polish vodka on the market and moved back to the top of the bar, towards the area commandeered by the island's local worthy. His newspaper had vanished. Vodka Joe now had the prized object in his possession and Hughie knew he would require dynamite to prise it from his grasp.

'There's your drink,' he said.

'Just bring it over, Hughie,' said Vodka Joe. 'Can't you see I'm busy reading the paper?'

The bar owner groaned again. He came back round to the side of the bar, placed the drink on the table in front of Vodka Joe and said, 'There you are, sir, sorry for the delay.'

'Sarcasm is the lowest form of wit, Hughie,' said the resident occupant of the couch. 'You should know that by now. My last servant died from it.'

'I'll just nip out and get another newspaper, shall I?' said Hughie. 'Any particular preference?'

Vodka Joe didn't even look up. 'Aye, I like the *Record*. That'll do. Thanks.'

Hughie walked the fifty or so yards to Crawford's the newsagents and bought a *Sun*. He was gone all of five minutes.

'Look at this, Hughie,' said Vodka Joe, still scouring the *Daily News*. 'It says here that Laird has been shagging "a gorgeous movie star, a beautiful pop singer and a busty TV presenter on a children's show". It says it right here. All at the same time.'

'He's shagging them all at the same time?' replied the bar owner. 'Must have plenty of energy. Lucky beggar.'

'No,' corrected Vodka Joe, 'not all at the same time. Not all in the same bed at the same time.' He paused momentarily before

115

pondering to himself, 'I wonder how much heroin you would need for that?'

'So, he's not been shagging them all at the same time, then?' queried Hughie.

'Naw, don't be daft. And it doesn't say "shagging", but that's what it means, doesn't it? It says, "Derek Laird has been seen escorting the gorgeous Erica Martinelli, star of the forthcoming blockbuster *Creeping Hell*."' Vodka Joe continued to read. 'Aye, it says here he was seen with this Erica bird in some swanky restaurant on a Sunday and was then photographed with Melinda Z at a cocktail party twenty-four hours later.'

'Melinda Z? What's that?' asked Hughie.

'It says here that she's a "pouting rock star". It also says her latest CD is to be called, *Let Me Squeeze Your Lemon Till The Juice Runs Down Your Leg.*'

'I'll make sure to order a copy,' said Hughie, without any great enthusiasm.

'And here's the other bird he's been shagging,' said Vodka Joe. 'She's Anna Glow ...'

'Glow?'

'That's what it says here,' said Vodka Joe. 'Anna Glow. Apparently, she's busty and has been warned by the Spanish TV authorities about her low-cut tops while working on the children's network.' Vodka Joe laughed out loud. 'It says here she has already exposed her breasts three times in the past month and now all the dads are tuning into the kids' shows. Just as well Big Eric's not Spanish. Be dead in a week with friction burns. Didn't have weans' programmes like that when I was a toddler.' He paused for a moment's thought and added, 'Mind you, I can still make a radio out of an old Corn Flakes packet.'

'It's going to be one of those days,' mused Hughie, heading behind the bar to pour himself a large brandy and port. Automatically, he moved towards the vodka optic, picked up a fresh glass and poured another for his sole customer.

Vodka Joe was still reading the *News*. 'Fuck's sake,' he practically shouted. 'This bastard has also been having it off with a "mystery brunette". He's been seen at a quiet little bistro with "another lovely". It says here a local man said, "It looked as though they were very much in love. They gazed into each other's eyes all night and hardly touched their food." So, there you have it. This wee Scottish bastard who used to mix cement or something for a living is now pumping the arses off a gorgeous film star, a rock goddess, a bird that keeps getting her tits out on kids' telly and a "mystery brunette". Is there any justice in the world?'

'No, definitely not.' Boring Brian had just joined the debate, a wave of apathy pervading the bar. 'A pint of heavy, please, Hughie, if it's not too much trouble,' he requested before adding, 'I saw a dog peeing up against the lamppost outside.' He blew his nose and added, 'Could rain again today.'

Hughie returned behind the bar and began pulling a pint. 'Good morning, BB,' he said, trying to sound cheerful on a bleak November morning, grey clouds gathering overhead, Largs, once again, about to disappear from view.

'Good morning?' asked Boring Brian. 'What's good about it? I got up about seven o'clock this morning for a cup of tea. Did you hear that bleedin' wind and rain last night? The dead couldn't sleep through that bloody racket. I went into the kitchen, switched on the kettle and, remember, I'm in my bare feet, I feel this sticky stuff under my toes. I looked down. The dog's only gone and shat all over the place, hasn't he?' He paused and added, 'Brian Jnr's never done that before. Mind you, I didn't take him out for his usual last round-up last night. Too effin' wet.'

'Aye, Brian Jnr should have held it in until the rain went off,' said Hughie.

'That's what I thought, as well, Hughie. Thoughtless little hairy-faced shitbag. No Bonio treats for Brian Jnr tonight.'

'How's Mrs BB keeping?' asked Hughie.

'Oh, Brenda? Aye, fine. Thanks for asking. Says she's staying in bed today.'

'She's not well?' asked the bar owner with a smidgeon of concern.'

'Naw, can't be bothered getting up,' replied his mirthless customer.

Hughie passed over the foaming pint. 'I must get off this island before my brain turns to bird seed,' he thought for the first time that day. He knew it wouldn't be the last occasion such a notion would come to mind.

He looked around the bar surface for his *Sun*. Nowhere to be seen. Vodka Joe, having devoured the *Daily News*, was sitting snugly in his corner with *The Sun*. Hughie moved to the top of the bar, but before he could say anything, Vodka Joe got in first. 'I thought I told you to get a *Record*?' he practically chided the bar owner.

'The glamour of this profession is beginning to dim,' thought the bar owner as he moved to the Martell optic to pour himself another much-needed shot of brandy and port.

'Who the hell needs three cars?' Vodka Joe practically shouted.

'This wanker already has a Rolls-Royce and a Porsche and has just ordered a Ferrari. He's got one of these "exclusive Ferraris being delivered within the next fortnight", it says here. Hell, would you believe there is a waiting list for this car? Years! Honest Ernie in Largs can make and sell a car in the same day.' Vodka Joe took a sip of his drink and added, 'Mind you, the cars normally fall apart the same day.' He chuckled at his wit. 'I loved that story about him not being able to fix the brakes on someone's car, so he just made the horn louder.' His eyes lit up as a thought came to mind. 'Hughie, you don't think he's dead, do you?'

'Honest Ernie?'

'Naw,' replied an irritated Vodka Joe. 'Who gives a fuck about Honest Ernie? No, this Derek Laird guy.'

'Dead?' asked the bar owner. 'He's as fit as a fiddle.' He wondered where that expression originated. 'Were fiddles particularly fit?' he mused.

'Naw,' said Vodka Joe, 'not of natural causes. Maybe bumped off by the Mob? They've got the Mafia in Spain, haven't they?'

'They've got the Mafia in MILLPORT,' answered Hughie. 'Have you seen the price of a double nugget in the Nixe these days?'

'It's possible, though,' isn't it?' Vodka Joe was warming to the thought that the Scottish international footballer might be sleeping with the fishes. He had seen *The Godfather* at least fifty times and that's what the Mob did to guys who crossed them, he knew. Luca Brasi was one of Don Corleone's enforcers who used to knock over the opposition for fun. 'Poor Luigi, he now sleeps with the fishes,' that's what he said, wasn't it? Vodka Joe liked that expression. There had been more than a few visitors to Vodka

Joe's wee island over the years he wouldn't have minded giving 'concrete overcoats', another *Cosa Nostra* expression he admired. Then he would tip the offender into the Firth off the Old Pier to 'sleep with the fishes'. Old grannies were a particular nuisance with their zimmer frames.

He smiled at the thought. Hughie wondered if Vodka Joe was having problems with wind again.

'Listen, Hughie, what if this rich bastard had agreed a wee payment to miss a penalty-kick or something?' queried Vodka Joe. 'Say the Mafia put a few million on the outcome of a game? Know what I mean? Happens all the time, doesn't it?'

'Does it?' asked Hughie.

'You're so innocent, Hughie,' Vodka Joe shook his head slowly, a resigned look on his wee face. 'Did you watch the Finlayson Cup match at West Bay in July? Do you think Largs were good enough to take five goals off Millport Amateurs? Get real, Hughie. The game was rigged. I bet you there was big money riding on it. What about Fingers Freddie's performance in goal that day? Fuckin' crap. Dodgy, I'd say. Okay, I accept he's now in his sixties, but he should have done so much better with that third goal. And, okay, he's just had his hip replaced, but he was at it, I'm sure. The game's bent. I'll bet you the game's bent.'

'Did I tell you I once got a trial with St. Mirren?' asked Boring Brian.

'So, if they can bet on a Finlayson Cup-tie, what's to stop them putting big money on a Champions' League game?' said Vodka Joe. 'What if they nobbled this Crazy Horse guy? What if he took the money and then didn't keep his part of the deal? What if they ordered him to fire the ball over the bar and he got it all wrong and blootered it into the net? Did you see his goal against Real Madrid? The ball could have gone anywhere, couldn't it? Maybe he tried to put it into the crowd and, instead, it flew into the net.'

'I think you're onto something there,' said Hughie, sarcastically.

'You really think so?' said Vodka Joe. 'That would explain everything, wouldn't it? Aye, that's it. He's sleeping with the fishes. Money won't do him any good where he's going.' He smiled at the thought.

Moments later, Griff Stewart and Harry Booth entered the bar; the newspaperman and the cop were known to Hughie Edwards after the Wild Bill Hickok 'incident' during the Country and Western Carnival.

'Did I tell you I once got a trial with St. Mirren?' asked Boring Brian.

CHAPTER FOURTEEN

Late morning. Tuesday 23 November.

Millport, Isle of Cumbrae.

Brock practically skipped down the five sets of the spiral staircase on his way to the front door of the tenement close. He still had a spring in his step when he crossed from Quayhead Street, waved happily at the dozing coach driver in the vehicle parked at the harbourside and prepared to walk into Hugh's Bar. 'Be careful what you say, my boy,' he told himself.

Brock composed himself, sucked in a lungful of cold North Ayrshire air and pushed open the door to the pub.

'Tell us about this blonde bird,' ordered R.I.P. The door didn't even have time to close behind Brock.

'Aye, the big blonde with the splendid knockers,' said El Cid.

Brock refused to be put out of his stride. 'What blonde bird?' he asked.

'The one who almost ripped your arse off last night,' said Boring Brian.

'Jeezus, it's true,' thought Brock, 'you can't keep anything quiet down here for long.' He paused and said, 'Nothing much to tell, R.I.P. Just an old friend.'

'I wish I had an old friend like that,' chipped in Boring Brian. 'One that wanted to wrench my backside from ...'

'Did you tell my friends you once had a trial with St. Mirren,

Brian?' countered Brock.

Boring Brian was suddenly animated. He turned to the cop and the newsman. 'Did I ...'

'No offence, mate, but we're not interested,' interrupted El Cid with a finality that rendered any protest futile. 'Tell us later. We've got some juicy stuff to uncover here.' He looked at Brock. 'Fess up, Charlie, what went on in the Schloss Adler last night? Your secret's safe with me. I'm a cop.'

Hughie passed a freshly-poured pint of lager in front of his pal. He threw him a lifeline. 'Did you hear that Derek Laird has vanished from Barcelona? It's in the paper. Here.' He pushed the *Daily News* in front of Brock. The sportswriter didn't get the chance to pick it up. El Cid was well versed in dealing with stalling tactics. 'Laird will still be missing in half an hour,' he said. 'This is important. Come on, then, Charlie. The blonde? Who is she?'

'I told you, El Cid, she's an old friend,' replied Brock, realising he was in for a bumpy ride. And R.I.P. had yet to throw in his tuppence worth.

'Her name's Willy. She was down visiting a friend, a *girl* friend, and she popped in here to have a quick drink.' Brock was determined in his quest to protect Willy's reputation, but he was on the ropes. And he knew it. 'She saw me and came over to say hello and ...'

'Tried to remove your rear end from the rest of your body.' Boring Brian was still a bit miffed about being denied the opportunity to regale the occupants of the bar with the tale of his trial for St. Mirren.

'I don't recall that,' said Brock.

'I'll never forget it,' said Boring Brian. 'Big Eric spent most of the night in the loo.'

'You don't get out much, do you?' fired back Brock, beginning to bristle.

'A lot of people say that,' replied Boring Brian. 'I get out enough. I could be rearranging my sock drawer at the moment, but I'm here, ain't I?' He smiled and added, 'And I was here when that blonde bit attempted to split you cheeks.'

'How is your arse for love bites this morning, then, Brock?' R.I.P. had joined the attack.

'Right, let's get it from the top,' said El Cid in his best grilling-a-suspect timbre.

Brock took a sip of his beer, smacked his lips and looked at the back page of the newspaper kindly provided by Hughie. 'Christ,' he said, 'this doesn't sound like Derek. I know this lad. Met him lots of times when he was with Albion Rovers. Good lad. I've done a few interviews with him. Talked to him a few months ago, as a matter of fact.'

'You can tell us about that later, Charlie,' said El Cid, the terrier with a bone. Brock silently vowed to pay his next parking ticket if his cop pal ever became a traffic warden.

'What have you got to hide?' asked R.I.P. 'You're free and single. You can come and go as you please. No big deal if you're bonking a blonde bird with large booby-doos.'

El Cid's eyes narrowed. 'Well, if you've got nothing to hide and you're keeping mum that can only mean one thing. *She's* got something to hide and you're shielding her. Right or wrong, Brock?'

The bar door creaked open and in stepped Willy, windswept

and gorgeous, blonde hair blowing wildly in the gust that was accompanying her into the pub. Her entrance was greeted with silence.

'Am I interrupting something, boys?' she said, all wide-eyed and innocent. She turned to Brock and smiled. 'Oh, fancy bumping into you again, Charlie. Isn't life full of coincidences?'

'Would that be the Guinness Book of Coincidences, young lady?' chuckled El Cid.

'Dry Martini and lemonade?' asked Hughie, already making his way to the optics.

'That would be lovely,' replied Willy, hanging her charcoal duffel coat on the peg at the door. She could feel everyone's eyes burning into her. 'A bit wild out there.'

'Aye, could chuck it down later,' said Boring Brian. 'I wonder if someone in authority would allow us to cancel today.'

She ran her fingers through her hair and turned to walk to the corner of the bar beside Brock. R.I.P. reckoned she sashayed more than walked. Willy was wearing a tight pink V-neck long-sleeved top with a white T-shirt underneath. It was obvious to all she wasn't wearing a bra. 'Christ,' thought El Cid. 'She could have hung up her coat on The Pointer Sisters.'

She was wearing a fresh pair of blue jeans and the same brown ankle-length boots as last night. 'Thank you, Hughie,' she said as she picked up her Dry Martini and lemonade. 'I'm ready for this.'

'I'll bet you are,' thought R.I.P. He looked at Brock and said, 'You look ready for yours, too, my old mate.'

'Lucky big bastard,' thought Hughie, not for the first time in recent hours.

'So, you know our good chum, Charlie, do you, young lady?' El Cid was back on attack after being momentarily derailed. 'Willy? I don't think he's ever mentioned you to us. Has he, Griff?'

'No. Never,' said the newspaperman, sitting in the opposite corner from a silent Vodka Joe, both fascinated by Willy's rear end.

Brock stepped forward from the bar. 'Where are my manners?' he said. 'Harry Booth, this is Willy Pearson ...'

'Willy Tyler,' she corrected. Brock realised immediately she had reverted to her maiden name.

'Sorry, my mistake,' said Brock. He turned to where his old newspaper colleague was sitting on a stool. 'And this is Griff Stewart. Watch what you say in front of these two, Willy,' he grinned. 'Harry is a Detective Inspector with the C.I.D. and is also known as El Cid.' He turned once more to his other pal and said, 'Griff is Chief News reporter with the *Daily News* and we know him as R.I.P. I'll explain later. Okay, gentle people, that's the pleasantries out of the way. Everyone knows each other, nothing to get excited about, all friends together and no need to mention the war.'

'That was in *Fawlty Towers*,' said Boring Brian. 'I almost laughed. By the way, did I tell you about the size of the snail I saw on Crichton Street this morning? Absolute monster.'

'And, Willy, how do you know Charlie?' El Cid, finding it increasingly easy to ignore the guy with the joke face at the bar, was in interrogation mode.

'Oh, that's a long story, Harry,' said Willy, taking another swig of her Dry Martini and lemonade and making a conscious effort not to fondle Brock's backside, achingly close to her right hand as they stood at the bar.

126

El Cid looked at the clock above the door. 'It's just twenty minutes past noon,' he observed. 'We've got all day. And all night. We're staying for a couple of nights. Maybe three, eh, R.I.P?'

'That's the plan,' said the *Daily News'* finest, certain he had detected a faint groan from Brock.

'You'll put us up, Charlie, won't you?' smirked the cop.

'No problem with that, is there?' added the newspaperman.

Brock wondered if they had rehearsed this double-act as soon as he said he would see them in the pub instead of inviting them upstairs to the flat. 'Couple of old nosy pests,' he thought, smiling at his pals.

'Might be a wee snag, guys,' he replied. 'I was going to do some DIY, a bit of painting to freshen the place up while I'm here. Winter coming on and all that.'

'Oh, we won't mind, will we, R.I.P?' said the cop, still grinning.

'No, we'll be happy to give you a hand,' the newspaperman laughed heartily and added, 'Actually, I like the smell of paint. I've been overcome with emulsion several times.'

'Nobody likes the smell of paint,' said Boring Brian, still waiting for an opening to tell the gathered company about his trial with St. Mirren. He would probably miss out the bit that he failed the trial. He always omitted that part.

'Ted's doing a cheap bed and breakfast deal over at the Georgics, fellas,' said Hughie, helpfully. 'About a tenner a night. You won't get better than that on the island.'

'Oh, I'm sure Charlie could do better than that, Hughie,' said El Cid.

'Aye, especially if we are going to help with the painting and decorating,' added R.I.P. 'Right, Brock?'

'Look, lads, I would like to ...'

Brock was cut off in mid-sentence by El Cid.

'And where did you sleep last night, young lady?' he asked Willy. She took another swig of her Dry Martini and lemonade, buying a bit of time. She went to the back pocket of her jeans. 'Would you set up a round for the bar, please, Hughie?' she said. 'Just what everyone's drinking, thank you. One for yourself.' She wondered if she had managed to deflect the question.

'Well, we're waiting, young lady,' repeated the cop. 'Where did YOU sleep last night?'

'You said you were going to stay with your pal, remember?' Brock broke in. 'That old school chum who stays down here. Gilmour Street? Was that it?'

'Clyde Street,' corrected Willy, thinking she might throw in something that rang of authenticity. 'Yes, Caroline. Stays over at Clyde Street.'

'Caroline on Clyde Street?' reflected the cop, enjoying himself while aware of Brock's piercing glare. Suddenly he looked at the bar owner. 'Ever heard of her, Hughie? Caroline? She come in here? You must know everybody who comes in here.' Pause. 'Everybody who DOESN'T come in here, too, I would imagine.'

'Caroline,' said the bar owner, composing himself. 'Let me think ...'

'I've never heard of her,' said Boring Brian, stroking his moustache.

'Aye, Caroline,' said Hughie. 'Know her quite well. Comes in at the weekend. Not a heavy drinker.'

El Cid rummaged around in his jacket pocket and produced a pen and notepad. He looked quite pleased with himself; he loved backing suspects into a corner. 'Right,' he said. 'I'm going to write down a couple of questions on one piece of paper and the same on another piece of paper. Okay? It'll only take me a minute, bear with me, will you?' He scribbled down three questions. 'You might want to get yourself a pen, Hughie.'

He took a piece of paper, moved to the centre of the pub and placed it on the bar surface. 'Hughie, can you come over here, please?' he asked. 'It's just a wee experiment. Won't take a minute.'

He looked at Willy. 'Can you come over to the table beside my news-gathering friend, please, young lady?'

The cop put a piece of paper in front of Hughie, walked to R.I.P.'s corner of the bar and placed another blank piece of paper in front of a slightly bemused Willy.

'This is just a wee game I like to play from time to time. Indulge me, please.' He practically chortled.

Hughie looked at the words jotted down on the paper. On separate lines, they read,

HAIR COLOUR?

SKINNY OR FAT?

TALL OR SHORT?

The bar owner looked at Willy. She looked at the bar owner. 'No conferring, please, contestants,' beamed the cop. 'Simple questions and simple answers, please. Shouldn't be too difficult. On you go, there's your starter for ten.'

Hughie hoped he was on the same wavelength as Willy. He paused. She paused. 'Come on, good people, the clock's ticking. Answers, please,' said the cop.

The bar owner scribbled his answers, as did Willy. El Cid scooped them up and moved to a neutral part of the bar beside the fruit machine. He placed the two pieces of notepaper in front of him on a table. He compared the answers. 'Oh, this IS interesting,' he said, theatrically. 'VERY interesting.' He paused. 'Willy, young lady, you say you know this Caroline from Clyde Street, eh? Went to school with her? Hughie. She comes in here every weekend? This Caroline from Clyde Street?'

He picked up a scrap of paper and looked at Willy. 'Your friend Caroline from Clyde Street has black hair, she's thin and is about 5ft 8in. Is that correct?'

Willy wondered if El Cid had been a member of the Gestapo at any stage of his career. She sipped her drink and said confidently, 'Yes, that's my friend Caroline.'

The cop eyed Hughie. 'Let's see now,' he grinned. 'Your Caroline would appear to be blonde, slightly overweight – I like that, Hughie, nice touch, never call a female fat – and she's small.' He walked down the narrow public bar, much the same way he would have expected Hercule Poirot to do as he preened himself following a particularly testing whodunnit. He fixed his fingers into the lapel of his jacket and exclaimed, 'I put it to you, young lady and bar owner, that one of you is a LIAR!'

'Oh, fuck off, El Cid,' said Brock. 'She slept at my place.'

'Ah, the truth, at last,' said the cop, still playing the Hercule Poroit role. 'Now I must ask another question. She slept AT your place? Or she slept WITH you at your place?'

'We did it four times,' said Willy, ending the brief pretension and adding with a blistering smile, 'Does that answer your question, officer?'

'Lucky, jammy, big bastard,' thought Hughie.

'Four times?' considered Boring Brian. 'I haven't done it four times in my life.'

'Ah, so Happy Harry has come out of hibernation, has he?' said the cop. 'Thank God for that, we all thought you were going over to the dark side, Brock.' He raised his glass to his sports reporting pal and said, 'Welcome back, my friend.'

'Cheers,' threw in R.I.P. 'You can never keep a good man flaccid.'

'Okay, lads, now that we have got the charades out of the way, can I have a look at the paper and find out what's happening with Derek Laird?' said Brock. 'That seems a whole lot more interesting than my love life.'

Willy returned to the corner of the bar, surreptitiously stroked Brock's backside, gently pulled his head to the side and whispered in his right ear, 'I don't know about that.' Both grinned. Boring Brian nodded to himself and thought, 'I knew I was right.' He told the assembled company, 'Look, she's at it again, trying to rip his arse off. I told you, didn't I?'

'Oh, get a life,' said Vodka Joe, stirring in the corner.

Boring Brian looked startled. 'I've got a life. What could be more exciting than getting a trial with St. Mirren?' he mumbled to himself.

CHAPTER FIFTEEN

Mid-afternoon. Tuesday 23 November.

Largs, North Ayrshire Coast.

The wind hurtled robust and unobstructed along the promenade, sweeping with it abandoned pieces of paper, discarded fish and chip cartons, empty crisp packets and other assorted debris on its wayward path.

The hovering grey clouds threatened a downpour. It was cold and it was miserable. The inhabitants of Largs, wrapped in bulky clothes to repel the ferocious gusts with umbrellas at the ready, went busily and briskly about their business. They knew precisely what to expect. No TV weather forecaster was required; a deluge was on its way. This was the North Ayrshire coast. And this was November. Derek Laird, snuggled into his parka coat, pulled up the hood and whispered, 'Thank you, God.'

One of the most famous faces in football disappeared into its winter clothing. He stood at the Largs slip, waiting for the 2.45pm ferry crossing to the Isle of Cumbrae and, he hoped, welcome anonymity. With storms on the horizon, Caledonian-MacBrayne had warned of possible cancellations to the ten-minute service. The ferry owners were always quick to pull the plug if they believed any danger threatened the safety of staff or passengers. Derek Laird stood at the slip, stamping his feet to inject some warmth into his toes. To all and sundry, he looked like any other commuter. Nothing special. Certainly, he did not resemble one of the best-paid footballers on the planet. Not the multi-million pound superstar who had vanished into thin air. Just a bloke shivering along with the rest of the passengers, some fifteen in total, waiting to get across to Millport.

'This will be memorable,' smiled a small, dumpy woman, clutching five Morrisons shopping bags. 'Ah'm aboot to risk life and limb so Ah could get five pence aff ma man's pork chops.'

Derek Laird realised she was directing her conversation towards him. He was slightly startled. 'Ah said, Ah hope ma man appreciates whit Ah dae fur him,' she grinned, her headscarf struggling to stay on her head as the wind tried desperately to remove the garment and whisk it along the front.

'Aye, I'm sure he does,' he answered, gliding into the vernacular with ease. 'Aye, what man wouldn't, eh?'

She looked at him, only his eyes visible above his zipped-up collar and underneath his flapping fur-trimmed hood. 'Well, ye look cosy enough, son,' she grinned. 'Ah might get ma man wun o' those big coats. Ur they expensive, if ye dinnae mind me asking?'

Laird didn't want to tell his inquisitor that he had got it from Julio's in the exclusive Rambla area in Barcelona. There's no way she would have believed it had been priced at four thousand euros, but he had got it for zilch. 'Oh, this?' he said warily. 'Got this out of one of those Army Stores in Glasgow. Cost about a tenner.'

His companion for the moment looked at the sandy-coloured coat with all its zips, buttons and multude of deep pockets. She didn't want to tell him he had been done. 'Aye, very nice,' she said. 'Ah wish yer health to wear it. Looks cosy.'

The ferry lurched towards the slip and settled with a grinding sound, metal visiting concrete. The landing gear eased down and a Cal-Mac worker came forward, preparing to motion the cars onto the mainland once he was convinced the ramp was properly in position. Four vehicles emerged. Laird could see a quick confab between two blokes in Cal-Mac uniforms. 'Please don't call off the crossing,' he practically winced. One nodded and the other moved to the side and ushered the waiting six cars ahead towards the vessel. 'Ten minutes and my problems are over,' thought Laird.

Just as well Derek Laird could play football. He would never have cracked it as a clairvoyant.

About twenty yards from his left elbow, a white Ford Focus swept into the car park marked 'RESIDENTS ONLY'. The driver emerged and opened the back door. Two kids spilled out and were joined by their mum from the passenger's side. There was a quick look in the boot, a couple of shopping bags were fished out and the four headed in the general direction of Morrisons. The driver's attention was caught by the sight of the guy standing at the slip talking to an old lady, obviously preparing for the ferry across to Cumbrae. One flash of the face under the hood and he recognised him in an instant.

'Well, well,' he thought. 'If it isn't Derek Laird.'

CHAPTER SIXTEEN

Mid-afternoon. Tuesday 23 November.

Millport, Isle of Cumbrae

The inquisition over for the time being, Charlie Brock had the opportunity to relax at the bar and catch up with the news of Derek Laird's sensational vanishing act at Barcelona. Willy moved close to him and inserted a hand in one of the back pockets of his Levi's. She turned and winked seductively at Boring Brian, whose knees almost buckled.

'This just doesn't sound right,' observed Brock, smoothing out the newspaper in front of him on the bar surface.

'Oh, you're not going to do your sportswriter-turned-sleuth act again, are you?' grinned Vodka Joe. 'Surely clearing up one mystery is enough for one lifetime?'

Brock picked up the newspaper. 'Look at this,' he said. 'Derek Laird has just ordered a brand new Ferrari ...'

'Too much money,' interrupted Vodka Joe, from his corner at the window of Hugh's Bar. 'Who the hell needs three cars?'

'Forget that,' said Brock. 'Does it make any sense to order a £200,000 car and then go missing when it's just about to be wheeled up to your front door?'

'Suppose not,' said Hughie, 'hadn't really thought of that. Aye, sounds a bit daft, doesn't it?'

'Too much money,' repeated Vodka Joe, this time a little more vehemently. Brock hoped there wasn't a soap box in the vicinity.

Harry Booth, Detective Inspector of the CID, added, 'Probably stoned when he ordered it and forgot all about it. What's cash like that to a guy like him?'

'About a week's wages,' answered Vodka Joe. He looked across at Griff Stewart, Chief News Reporter of the *Daily News*, who had invaded his space in the corner of the pub. 'That's if you can believe all you read in the papers,' smirked the local worthy.

'I know I don't,' said Boring Brian. 'Newspapers are just sensation-seeking rags.' He had never really forgiven them for not mentioning his trial with St.Mirren.

'Please, guys, let me think,' pleaded Brock, a faint trace of impatience in his tone. 'I know this lad. This just doesn't sound like him one little bit. As I said, I spoke to him only a few months ago. He was talking about coming over to Scotland to spend New Year with his family. A couple of days with them and then straight back to Spain.'

'Would the club let their player go on the booze in the middle of the football season?' quizzed R.I.P.

'When I was at St. Mirren ...'

Boring Brian was cut off abruptly. 'If the fixture list allows it, I wouldn't see a problem,' replied Brock. 'Just so long as the individual doesn't go on a complete bender. And Derek Laird isn't a big boozer, anyway. The club would be well aware of that.' He paused to take a sip of his lager while receiving a peck on the cheek from the attentive Willy. She squeezed his right buttock for good measure. He beamed, suddenly content with life, and continued, 'Look, I know Barcelona really work their players hard at the start of the season. They go up to a place up in the mountains called the Collserola Hills and put their players through extreme altitude training. Derek Laird told me Spanish footballers are the most dedicated and professional he has ever worked with. Okay, the odd one might dabble with drugs, but it's not as widespread as has been reported.'

'See, I told you,' said Boring Brian, 'newspapers can get a lot of things wrong. When I was at St. Mirren ...'

'Spanish footballers don't booze a lot,' interjected Brock. 'That's just not their culture. Show them a pint of lager and they'll probably throw up. They like a nip, I do know that. Whisky is quite big in some Spanish regions, you know? They love our stuff, but they distill a lot of their own gear, too. Derek told me there was something called Doble V that was about one hundred bucks a shot. But they don't overdo it. Three whiskies a night is probably a Spanish player's idea of a wild night out on the lash. The point, though, is that the footballers will be as physically fit as is possible when the winter months come around. A couple of days' break wouldn't do any harm. All the hard work is done in the summer and they ease up in the winter. You know, it is possible to overtrain a player. I've seen it in British clubs where the old sergeant majors put their players through knackering routines throughout the season. These players are basically all tuckered out in the last fifteen or twenty minutes of games. There's nothing left in the tank.'

'Two hundred thousand pounds-a-week and they can't last an hour-and-a-half,' sniped Vodka Joe. 'Shower of pansies.'

'I never got anything like that at St. Mirren,' said Boring Brian.

No-one took any notice.

'We're getting a bit sidetracked here, folks,' said Brock. 'He's ordered a flash car, probably paid cash up front or cash on delivery and he's not around when it's delivered. Why? Barcelona were always good enough to allow the player time to visit his family in Scotland certain in the knowledge he would return at the promised time and in good nick. Same with his international appearances. He has travelled all over the place with Scotland and has always been back when expected. That shows good discipline. Of course, he's the only Spanish-based Scot in the squad, so he has to make these journeys on his own. Yet there's never been a hint of him straying. Not once. So, why disappear now? Why would an excellent professional score the winning goal one night against Real Madrid, go home and then never be seen again? It doesn't add up. Doesn't sound like the Derek Laird I ever met.'

'Maybe he's dead,' said Vodka Joe, repeating his thoughts of earlier in the day.

'Where's the body?' asked El Cid. 'The Spanish cops aren't *that* bad. Don't you think they'll have thought along those lines, as well?'

'What if he's been fitted with a concrete overcoat?' asked Vodka Joe. 'And dumped in the river? They've got rivers in Barcelona, haven't they?'

'As a matter of fact, the city is flanked by two rivers,' said R.I.P. 'I've been there once. Lovely place. There's the Llobregat and the Besos. Beautiful.'

'There you go, then,' said Vodka Joe, adding with victorious finality, 'A fuckin' choice of *two* rivers. He sleeps with the fishes. Mystery solved. He's upset the Mob and they've got rid of him. That's what I think.'

'Purely as a matter of interest, Vodka Joe,' said Brock, 'do you watch the *Godfather* movies?'

'They're up there with my favourites, Brock,' answered Vodka Joe. 'Luca Brasi is a particular hero of mine, if you must know. What a man.'

Brock looked at Willy with no little concern. 'I hope Derek Laird is okay,' he whispered. 'He's a genuinely nice lad.'

'I'm sure he'll be fine,' she replied, soothingly and somehow reassuringly. 'Don't worry.' She kissed him on the cheek.

Four miles away, a wind-blown Derek Laird stepped onto the Isle of Cumbrae for the first time in more than two decades.

CHAPTER SEVENTEEN

Mid-afternoon. Tuesday 23 November.

Daily Tribune Sports Desk, Glasgow.

Rodger James was known in the newspaper trade as Smiler. Charlie Brock and anyone who had the misfortune to venture within fifty yards of this rancid individual immediately realised it was a moniker that wasn't exactly wholly appropriate.

Brock, during an evening of over-indulging at the Double C, once memorably put it this way: 'Rodger James known as Smiler? That's a bit like discovering Vlad the Impaler had a pet name, Kookie Funster, an adorable alter-ego who took care of waifs and strays and was particularly fond of abadoned puppies.' Everyone in the Budgie Cage that evening nodded in unison.

No-one was certain Smiler actually cast a shadow.

Rodger James didn't possess anything remotely akin to an accommodating nature. He was a rottweiler with a laptop, a sports reporter who thought nothing of destroying reputations, annihilating individuals, devastating fellow human beings and, on a particularly good day, fragmenting hitherto happy marriages and relationships, driving partners to the brink of suicide. Everyone was a target. No-one was immune. Smiler took no prisoners on his quest for mass destruction of personalities.

He collected the wood, erected the gallows and provided the noose. He would even pull the lever at no extra cost.

It was obvious to all that Charlie Brock didn't care much for his Press Box colleague. Charm and Smiler had been separated at birth. The only excuse Brock could ever hazard for the brutal, ruthless, thoughtless way the *Tribune's* Chief Sports Reporter went about his business was his unfortunate physical appearance.

'God must have been in a particularly bad mood the day He put that guy on earth,' Brock would muse. 'He must have exhausted His stock of faces when Rodger James came along the conveyor belt, so he just gave him an extra arse.'

Smiler was not handsome. He was a stick-thin individual who found it outwith his scope of fashion sense to seek out clothes to fit his scrawny frame. He scaled around the six foot mark, round-shouldered, hawk-faced with mean hazel eyes. His attempt to cover his bald pate with strands of wispy grey hair fooled no-one. His hair would often be either four feet in front of him or four feet behind, depending on which way the wind was blowing. Much like Nosferatu, he skulked rather than walked. 'How could a guy with a kisser like that go to shave every morning – forced to look in the mirror, witnessing that gargoyle image peering back – and start the morning with a smile?' Mind you, Brock often wondered if there was a reflection in the mirror.

It mattered not a jot to the *Tribune* sports reporter that he was treated like a social leper by all. He wore people's collective disdain as a badge of honour. He was sixty-two years old and had been given reassurances by his equally-despised Editor, an odious character by the name of Bob Steele, that he had 'a job for life' at the *Tribune*. Brock wasn't particularly fond of Steele, either; another bloke inaptly named, and who could never understand why he was known to so many as 'Lobster'. And then someone told him the marine crustacean didn't possess a backbone.

Smiler liked Steele's style. He particularly admired his Editor's imaginative use of the German World War Two Luger he kept locked away in the top left hand drawer of his desk. The large square windows of Steele's office on the second floor of the *Tribune* office in the heart of Glasgow's city centre looked directly onto the car park. That was unfortunate for reporters and other employees when the Editor was wont to display his displeasure at any individual who had incurred his wrath. The mortal sin for any reporter was missing a story that would crop up in rival publications. Such a professional malfunction would normally mean the Luger being removed from the drawer, the windows being opened wide and Steele, a grinning, bullying predator, sitting on his swivel chair awaiting the arrival of the unfortunate who had messed up.

When the hapless hack, guilty as charged without the hint of a trial, locked his car's doors and loomed into view, he knew to fear the worst. The Editor would fix the culprit in his sights, point the Luger in his direction and shout 'Bang!'. The guilty party was then expected to collapse to the ground and remain in a prone position until Steele blew a whistle to inform him or her it was okay to get back to their feet. The perceived transgressor never complained, being mainly thankful for the fact the revolver wasn't loaded with real bullets. On a daily basis, employees of the *Tribune* would drive into the newspaper's car park to witness it littered with the bodies of those who had fallen foul of their Editor. It was quite clear why Smiler was in awe of his master.

One former Scotland international footballer, a personal friend of Brock, had been turned over in typical fashion by the *Tribune's* reprobate reporter, a man who didn't do decent journalists any favours in his endless pursuit of heaping misery on unsuspecting sportsmen. This particular footballer, a bloke called Jimmy Thomas, had been on holiday in Benidorm with his family and couldn't believe his ears when he received a telephone call from one of his team-mates to inform him he was all over the front and back pages of the *Tribune* back home after an 'exclusive interview' with Smiler.

The footballer, it was revealed, hated the sight of the club's manager, believed the chairman lacked ambition, didn't trust the board of directors, rated a fair percentage of his colleagues in the dressing room as 'merely moderate', 'distinctly average' or 'downright crap' and would, in the near future, be contemplating asking for a transfer.

The footballer was aghast. He telephoned his only friend in the Press, Charlie Brock, who had been on the staff at the *Daily News* at the time

'Fuck's sake, Charlie, what am I going to do?' he asked frantically, his voice trembling. Unfortunately, Brock had heard it all before.

'Did you talk to Smiler?'

'I couldn't get away from him. He was lying in the lounger right beside me at the pool.'

'You were in the same hotel?'

'Aye, no luck. I could hardly believe it when I saw him in the foyer a couple of days ago. And what could I do when he pulled up the lounger beside me? I could hardly tell him to get lost, could I?'

'I warned you about him, Jimmy.'

'Aye, fine, I know that, but I thought we were talking completely off the record. I'm on holiday, for God's sake.'

'Smiler doesn't take holidays. I bet you he had his tape recorder with him.'

'Aye, he was footering about with something under a towel when I was talking to him, but I never took much notice. Christ, did he tape everything I said?'

'I would think that was a certainty.'

'Bloody hell, Charlie. You know what it's like. I had a couple of Piña Coladas for breakfast and wasn't really concentrating on what I was saying. He was being all so matey, too. I should have smelled a rat.'

'If it looks like a rodent, smells like a rodent, there's every chance it is a rodent, Jimmy.'

'What happens next? Can I say I was misquoted? What do you think, Brock? God's sake, throw me a lifeline here.'

'Wish I could, mate. Undoubtedly, Smiler will have it all on the record, so it won't just be your word against his. It will be taped. Not one hundred per cent admissible, of course, but a heavy factor on his side.'

'I'm fucked?'

'Well and truly.'

Jimmy Thomas's holiday was ruined. He counted down the ten days before he returned home to explain himself. His manager, Big Jack Simpson, hadn't quite come back to earth, despite the reasonable lapse of time. He remained in Vesuvio mode, as Brock had accurately predicted, and refused to listen to explanations. The footballer was fined six weeks' wages and dropped from the first team for the opening couple of months of the new season. Into the bargain, he was ordered to train with the Under-16 squad. Smiler would have been more than satisfied with his handiwork.

'I'll kill that lanky bastard if I ever get a chance,' Thomas had told Brock.

'You'll have to go to the end of a long queue, Jimmy, before you get anywhere near him. Try to forget it. And, for goodness sake, don't talk to him again. If you're stuck in a lift with him for a month, please say nothing.'

'The only thing I'll ever say to him again is, "Goodbye, bastard" as I boot him off a cliff at midnight without a witness in sight.'

'Hold that warm thought, Jimmy.'

CHAPTER EIGHTEEN

Mid-afternoon. Tuesday 23 November.

Millport Slip, Isle of Cumbrae.

'Aw, thanks, son,' grinned Wee Effie MacKenzie, inadvertently dropping her hand onto the thigh of her fellow-passenger. 'You're a treasure, did you know that? A wee treasure.'

Derek Laird had elected to sit beside the chatty islander with the erupting eyebrows after assisting her onto the coach with her five bulging Morrisons shopping bags. He smiled back. 'A treasure?' he thought. 'A hidden treasure, that's for sure.'

'Aye, a treasure,' repeated Wee Effie, still snuggling into her window seat, preparing for the fifteen-minute journey that would wheel them from the Cumbrae slip to the island's capital of Millport. 'See a' the men ower here, son, they widnae gie a second thought to gien' ye a haun wi' yer shoppin'. Never wance in a' the time Ah've been here. Never the wance.' She shook her scarf-covered head. 'Oxygen thieves the lot o' them.' Warming to the theme, she added, 'They're either plain crazy or just mad.'

Derek Laird, confident he was in a safe place, had pulled back his hood. He turned to look at the lady. 'Crazy or mad? What's the difference?' he asked. He had to know.

'Aw c'mon, everyone knows,' said Wee Effie, a trace of pity betrayed in her voice at her travelling companion's ignorance. 'Crazy people have bulging eyeballs.'

'And mad folk?'

'Easy. They slaver oot the sides o' their mooth.'

'Now I know,' reflected Derek Laird, wondering how he could have gone through his entire life up to that point having eluded that morsel of knowledge.

'Mind ye, they could be drunk, tae, and they're nae use to man nor beast when they've had a few,' added Wee Effie. 'Ye widnae trust yer bags tae them when they're in thon state. Aye, they go bloody bonkers when they hit Largs, so they dae. They're no' that clever in Millport, either, but there must be something in the air in Largs. They don't fool anywan. Tell their wives they're away tae dae some shoppin' and they head straight for Smithies and get paralytic, stumble back ontae the ferry, get helped onto the coach and get let aff close to their hooses.' Wee Effie clutched her brief travelling acquaintance's thigh again. She sighed and added, 'And then they go back tae their local pubs. Ye know, they never get barred. Naebody gets barred oan this island. They'll oxter people oot the pubs, get them upstairs and leave them at their doors. Aw part o' the service. Whit a place.' She eyed up the good-looking lad who had been helpful in giving her a hand with her shopping bags. 'Ah didnae catch yer name, son.'

'I didn't throw it,' replied Laird.

'Eh? Whit?' Wee Effie looked puzzled for a moment. 'Oh, aye, very good. Ye didnae throw it. Aye, very good. Must remember that. Whit's it, anywey?'

'Murdo,' answered Laird, deciding, in an instant, to bodyswerve the question. He had no intention of giving up a morsel of information to anyone.

Wee Effie nodded thoughtfully as though carefully dissecting the information. 'Murdo,' she repeated and grinned once more.

'Aye, that's one of my favourite telly shows. Have ye heard o' it? *Murdo She Wrote*?' She giggled, happy with her impromptu attempt at banter. 'Well, Murdo, I must ask you a very important question. Okay?'

Derek Laird, wondering what was coming next, nodded. 'Go ahead.'

'Whit brings a nice big boy like you to Millport?' she asked suspiciously, possibly having watched way far too much *Murder She Wrote* and *Miss Marple* on daytime television. Her brown eyes were twinkling, barely visible under the thick dark eyebrows that were stitched in the middle and had never remotely come into contact with tweezers. Before Laird could reply, she added as a *coup de grace*, 'And November at that.'

'I don't suppose you would believe me if I told you I just need a change of scenery, would you?' He asked. 'Tell you the truth, Effie, I've been working hard for the last couple of years, without a real break, and I just want to get away from things, put my feet up and do nothing for a spell.'

Wee Effie nodded solemnly. After a moment she said, 'I know whit ye mean, son. Ma man's helluva good at daen' nothin'. Ye know, when things get on top of me – and Ah tell ye they dae every noo and then – Ah just get masel' aff to Arran. Ah can spend a day or so ower there and come back as good as new. Aye, Ah know whit yer sayin'. Even The Man Upstairs took a day's rest, did He no'? And if it good enough for Him, then it's good enough for us, eh?'

'My thoughts exactly, Effie,' answered Laird, glancing to his right as the coach passed the Lion Rock. He remembered clambering around the odd-shaped structure as a boy. He was amazed it was still standing.

'Where's a' yer stuff?' asked Wee Effie, pointing to Laird's holdall. 'Yer travelling awfy light, ur ye no'? Ah take it yer goin' tae be wi' us fur a wee while?'

'Oh, yeah. I've got other stuff over at a pal's place in Largs. This is just some gear for the next couple of days before I get organised. No problem there. Maybe my mate will bring it over.'

'And will he be as handsome as you, Murdo?' smiled Wee Effie, her hand clutching another piece of her passenger's thigh. 'Ah'm no' wan fur any of that promiscuity stuff, ye unnerstaun', but there's nuthin' wrang wi' havin' a wee look. There's no' many doon in Millport that's easy oan the eye, Ah can tell ye that. Including ma man. He's no intae that promiscuity, either.' She paused before adding, 'Well, Ah don't think he is. He has a wee peek at Page Three every day, but that's aboot it, Ah think. Mind ye, Ah've caught him eyein' up Big Aggie when she's been cleaning the stairs. An arse, oops, sorry, son, a bottom the size of the moon. An' a full moon, tae. And she still wears short skirts. Legs that look as though they wid be better aff propping up a piano. Ah don't think it's right that a wummin in her seventies should wear short skirts, dae ye?'

She didn't wait for a reply. 'Bloody Jezebel. If Ah thought for a minute that there was any hanky panky wi' her and ma Alfie he wid be walking funny for the rest of his life. Actually, when Ah think aboot it, he dis walk a wee bit funny the noo, anywey. Naw, Ah widnae staun for any o' that sort of promiscuity stuff. And Ah bet she widnae go a' the wey ower to Largs to get cheap pork chops for ma Alfie.' Another pause. 'Anyway, Murdo, is your pal as good looking as you? This wee island needs some handsome blokes.'

Laird didn't get the chance to reply. Wee Effie's eyes glazed over for a moment. 'Ma Alfie was a good-looking man, so he wis. Full head of wonderful, thick hazel hair and a lovely row of white teeth.' She smiled at the reminisce before adding, 'Noo as bald as a billiard ball and a goldfish's got merr teeth.'

Laird smiled broadly and decided to play along. 'To answer your question, Effie, my pal's a lot better looking than me.'

'He must be like that Cary Grant, then. Or Gary Cooper.' Laird was sure he detected Wee Effie swoon for a moment. As the coach crawled along the promenade, passing the Victorian and Edwardian buildings to one side and the Firth of Clyde on the other, she still had some time to continue the grilling.

'Oh, he's good lookin', tae?' she pondered. She moved closer. 'Yer no' wan a' *them,* ur ye?' She motioned with a limp wrist.

'No, no, never quite got round to that, Effie.'

'Thank the Big Man for that,' grinned Wee Effie. 'Wid be a terrible waste if ye were wan o' *them.*' She did the limp wrist routine again. Laird reckoned she had also watched a lot of Larry Grayson on the telly in the past.

She pinched another piece of thigh as the questions continued. 'And where will ye be stayin' Murdo? The Georgics has got a couple of rooms open, but they're no' daen' dinners or onythin' like that. Bar's open, though.'

'You know, Effie, I've arranged all this at such short notice I haven't had time to book anywhere. I thought I might try the caravan site.'

'Oh, ye'll no' huv ony luck there, son,' Wee Effie was shaking her head. 'Naw, sorry, but they close from October through to February these days. Everythin's shut. The office, the shop, the lot. Did ye no' ken that?'

Derek Laird, it was obvious, hadn't realised that Millport had gone into reverse since he was last on the island twenty-odd years ago. 'No, Effie, as a matter of fact, I didn't know that.'

'Ah wid let ye stay wi' me, Murdo, but ma man widnae care fur that,' she offered, adding, 'Merr's the pity.' That far-away look again as she repeated, 'As Ah telt ye, he's no' into that promiscuity stuff.' Another pause. 'Well, at least, Ah don't think he is.'

The coach rumbled towards its destination beside the Old Pier.

'Don't worry, Effie, I'll find something.' Laird sounded more confident than was his entitlement.

'Tell ye whit, son,' said Effie. 'Get yersel alang to Robbie's. Dae ye ken it? Just opposite the Crocodile Rock?'

Laird knew from memory where the island's landmark was situated and had also noticed the pub on the coach's journey along the promenade. 'Yes, I know it,' he said.

'Ask fur Hamish. He's got keys for flats and hooses a' ower the island. He keeps stacks of them fur people wi' holiday places and the like. He'll give you a good price. Aw above board, ye unnerstaun'. The folk that own the flats get their cut. Just tell him Wee Effie sent ye. He'll get ye fixed up in a jiffy, nae problem.' She smiled warmly, tugged at the strands of the headscarf under her chin and made sure it would cope with the rigours of the biting wind that awaited them as soon as they clambered from the coach. Derek Laird took the five Morrisons shopping bags from the luggage rack, stepped down onto the pavement and offered Wee Effie his hand to assist her down the two steps. 'A proper treasure,' she said. 'Ye've spoilt me, Murdo, ye really huv. Noo Ah'll get masel' up the road and get ma man's dinner oan the go.' She stepped forward and, unexpectedly, pulled Derek Laird towards her and planted a particularly wet kiss on his cheek. 'That's fur yer trouble,' she murmured. 'Pity it's no' merr.'

A genuine smile played on Laird's lips, the first for some considerable time. 'Have you got far to go?' he asked.

'Naw thanks, son, Ah'm just up the road here.' She motioned with her head towards Cardiff Street. 'First close. Ah'll tell that lazy bugger o' a man that a handsome stranger almost swept me aff ma feet. He'll probably choke on his pork chops. Serve him right. Takes me fur granted, ye know. Just cause Ah'm seventy-three.'

'I can hardly believe it,' said Laird honestly. He thought she had to be at least eighty, but kept that to himself. He said his farewells again before turning and pulling the hood of the parka back over his head, his face sinking from view. He crossed the road, heading back along Stuart Street towards Robbie's Tavern.

'See ye, son,' shouted his fleeting travelling partner. 'Remember and tell Hamish Wee Effie sent ye. He'll look efter ye.'

Laird turned and waved. He zipped the jacket right up to his nose, only his eyes visible under the fur hood, and walked into a stiff breeze.

'Brock, just how well do you know this lad Derek Laird?' asked Hughie Edwards, the bar owner looking out of his pub's large front window, taking no heed of the huddled figure walking into the wind, only a few feet from his peering glance.

'Well enough,' answered Brock, sipping at his pint, more than just a little distracted by the attentions from Willy, welcome though they were. She was in one her playful moods, her hands appearing from most angles to caress parts of his body. Boring Brian had never had it so good. Big Eric had never visited the loo so often.

Brock continued, 'Honestly, Hughie, he's a good lad. This

disappearing act just doesn't sound like him. I hope to God he's okay. I'm sure he is. He's a pretty sane guy. All that running up and down scaffolding has helped keep his feet on the ground.' He laughed at his observation. 'Oh, you know what I mean.'

'Hope you write better than you talk,' said Vodka Joe with his usual cheeky grin.

Brock smiled. 'Can't help wondering, though. Where does a guy as well known as Derek Laird go to hide? Christ, he's even instantly recognisable to wee lassies who wouldn't know a ball from a banana. How does a bloke like that vanish into thin air?'

CHAPTER NINETEEN

Late afternoon. Tuesday 23 November.

Glasgow.

Rodger James smiled through his rapidly decaying molars. The *Tribune's* Chief Sports Reporter known to all – and feared by most – as Smiler, was hatching a plan that would actually save the marriage of a well-known Scottish international footballer, a maverick figure known, in private, to have a wandering eye and a rampant libido.

The player was on the verge of completing a £12 million move from one of Edinburgh's Big Two to one of London's top sides. There was just a medical to be passed within the next few days and the player knew he would skip through that. **'JUST CAPITAL!'** roared most of the newspaper headlines, rather unimaginatively. And now he was about to find himself on the receiving end of a good deed. He swiftly realised the good deed of the newspaperman would come at a price, of course.

Smiler and favours were strangers.

The newspaperman checked the number in the bulging contact book he had heaved around with him for decades. No doubt many of the names in that book had long since gone to meet their Maker, but Smiler's list of numbers for individuals in sport, entertainment and politics was known to be frighteningly detailed. He grinned and dialed the number. It rang twice.

'Hello?'

'Good afternoon, son,' droned Smiler. 'Do you know who this is, son?'

The sports reporter had a high-pitched whine that sent dogs running for cover. It was unmistakeable.

'Aye, hello, Rodger,' answered the friendly, unsuspecting voice. 'How are things?'

'Aye, fine, son,' whispered the sports reporter. There was no preamble. 'Are you alone? Can you speak, son? Mrs Crawley's not there, is she?'

'Mrs Crawley? My mum? Oh, my wife? No, she's in town with the kids. Wee Andy's got a birthday coming up. He's six next week. More expense, eh, Rodger?'

'Son, I've got something to tell you.' The tone had become somewhat sinister.

'Okay, Rodger, fire away,' said Adam Crawley, who was looking forward with anticipation and eagerness to his new career in England. A lucrative dream about to come true.

'You sure no-one's listening, son?'

'I'm on my own, Rodger,' replied Crawley, detecting menace in the voice of the caller. Slightly exasperated, he asked, 'Look, Rodger, what can I do for you?'

'No, son, it's what *I* can do for *you*.' Again, the hint of a threat.

'Go on then, Rodger, what can *you* do for *me*?' Crawley was intrigued.

'You sure you're on your own?' repeated Smiler, the cat toying with the mouse.

'Fuck's sake, Rodger, what is it?' Crawley's patience snapped

155

in an instant.

'Oh, son, you know I don't like swearing. Oh, no, I can't condone that sort of thing, son. Let's put a halt to that right now. No blaspheming, you understand?' It bordered on an order. 'Now, are you listening?'

'Okay, Rodger, sorry. I'm having a stressful day, getting ready to move to a new club, you know the sort of thing.'

Smiler didn't have a clue about that 'sort of thing', but he did know that Adam Crawley's life was going to get a lot more traumatic in the next minute or two.

'Jennifer, son.'

Lots of silence.

'Jennifer, son,' repeated Smiler.

Another moment's silence. 'Jennifer who, Rodger? Who are we talking about?' Adam Crawley's throat had suddenly become quite parched.

'Jennifer Herriot, son. You know her quite well, don't you?' The mouse was doomed and cornered; the claws were out.

'Jennifer Herriot?' Crawley realised he was in trouble. Big trouble.

'Aye, that wee blonde lassie you met at a school's awards day. You presented her with a medal for something, didn't you? Swimming, was it? Fifteen back then, I believe. When was that, son, three years ago? Eighteen now, is she not? Nice looking girl.'

'Oh, aye, THAT Jennifer Herriot,' answered Crawley, trying to play for time, wondering what this bastard on the other end of the line was up to.

'Aye, that's the one, son. Nice big blue eyes, too. You know her VERY well, in fact, don't you?'

'Sorry, haven't a clue what your talking about, Rodger.'

'Oh, come on, son. Sure you do.' Smiler smirked satisfyingly. He envisaged himself as a great matador preparing to plunge his sword into a dying bull, to the sound of rapturous applause. Then there was a change of tone and emphasis. 'You've been giving her a seeing-to for quite a while, haven't you?'

'You've got this all wrong, Rodger,' said the footballer, his mind in turmoil, staring bug-eyed at the telephone receiver in his hand.

'No, son, I've got this all right. And you know it.'

Crawley was more than a little disturbed, but continued to attempt to play a game of bluff with a man who was a master of the art. Never bluff a bluffer. 'Must be somebody else, Rodger. Maybe another player? Someone pretending to be me? That kind of thing happens, you know. All the time.'

'Oh, I know, son, I know. But I've got photographs and the lad in them looks uncannily like you.'

Initial rage had merged with confusion and now resignation. Crawley's head imploded. Game over. 'You sure?' he said meekly.

'Oh, aye, son. I'm as sure as night follows day. It's you alright. Good snaps, I have to say. No problem with identification. Nothing like those CCTV images that could be an alien from another planet. Oh, no, son, these are the work of a professional. All very much in focus; sharp focus, too.'

Crawley said nothing. Suddenly, he felt a little queasy.

'Would you like me to describe one of them? Happy to do so,

son.' Smiler was enjoying himself.

Crawley snapped. 'Have you got your fuckin' lad in your hand, you old bastard? Are you jerking off to this, you old cunt?' The footballer had parted company with the plot.

'Now, now, son,' chided Smiler, sounding much like a schoolteacher reprimanding an errant pupil. 'Language, please. There's no need for profanities now, is there?'

'Fuck you.' Crawley, defeated and distressed, had had enough of playing games.

'Tut, tut. Language, son. What would Mrs Crawley say if she heard you talk like that? My goodness, she would be shocked, wouldn't she?' Smiler was working something loose from his right ear with the base of a pen. He allowed the merest of pauses before continuing. 'Oh, I wonder what she would say if she saw one of the photographs I have in my possession? I'm talking front page here, son. Aye, the quality is that good. Big exclusive. Every paper in the country, probably in Europe, will be falling over themselves to follow this one up. Maybe a good idea to tell Mrs Crawley before the rest of the world gets to know.'

Better idea to hand Mrs Crawley a rocket launcher and let her point it towards my groin, thought the footballer.

'Well, son, what do you think? Nice looking girl, Jennifer Herriot.' Smiler didn't curse, but he could leer with the best of them. 'Superb little body, son, you picked well with her. Lovely breasts, too, son. Well done.'

Adam Crawley felt his shoulders slump in the general direction of his ankles. Suddenly, anger welled within him. 'Where did you get those fuckin' snaps, you old bastard?'

'What have I told you about the language, son? Cursing and

swearing is for louts with no command of the English vocabulary. Keep it for the dressing room. The pictures? Well, you could tell your teenage mistress to close her bedroom curtains before she goes down on you. All that scaffolding at the offices across the street from her flat. Did you never notice it? It's been there for weeks. Perfect place to look across and into someone's bedroom. A photographer could perch there all day and snap away quite happily.'

It was Crawley's turn to smile. 'Listen, you old bastard, I just happen to know that is illegal. You can't print those fuckin' pictures because they were taken in the privacy of someone's home, so you can shove them up your skinny arse.'

'Yes, son, you're quite right, I don't have much padding in that department. Thanks for reminding me. But before you start to use some more of the obscenities that seem to form so easily on your lips, may I please enquire what you would like me to do with the OTHER pictures?'

Crawley back on the ropes again. 'What other pictures, you old sleezebag?' He was intrigued once more.

'Just a minute, son, let me sift through this wee pile. Oh, here's a nice one of you walking down Princes Street. Hand in hand. A couple of young love birds, gazing into each other's eyes. Taken earlier this year, I believe. There's a poster on a gate advertising some boy band called The Breeze. They were due to play in September, just a couple of months ago. Oh, wait a minute, son, here's another one of you kissing. More than a friendly peck between friends, I would say. Then there's this one with your hand practically up her skirt while you're sitting on a bench in Princes Street Gardens. Hunting for squirrels by any chance? Or looking for a beaver, maybe? Either way, it's an interesting snap. I've got a whole bunch of them. All taken in public and, as you seem to know the law, all perfectly above board and legal to publish. You really should have been a bit more careful, son. Mrs Crawley would be very interested to hear your explanations, I'm sure. We'll publish one of the photographs on the front page and let the reader make up his own mind. I'll write something along the lines of, "Here's golden boy Adam Crawley getting away from the pressures of preparing to move to a big London club by catching up with a glamorous blonde in Edinburgh. Mrs Crawley was in England's capital with the couple's two children, Andy and Shirley, while searching for accommodation. She says she is looking for a four-bedroomed home in Essex and life couldn't be better." That sort of thing.'

'Now, listen you old bastard, I'll have you killed. I know people ...'

'No doubt you do,' interrupted Smiler, not even a trace of nerves in his voice. Dismissing the death threat, he continued, 'You'll try to talk your way out of this, but what do you do when the OTHER pictures start to appear? The ones with you and Jennifer going at it like a couple of crazed weasels? Oh, those pictures will see the light of day, take my word for it. Here's how it works, son. My photographer can do a deal with, say, a magazine in Australia. They're not that fussy and, of course, your fame now you've cost millions will have spread to our Antipodean chums. They'll use the pictures. They still believe in "publish and be damned". Great attitude, son. And then, of course, newspapers in Britain have to respond to the pictures flying around the globe. They'll be on the net, all over the place. Our newspapers will plaster the word **"CENSORED"** over the rude parts, of course, but everyone will know what it's all about.'

The player said nothing.

'Still there, son?'

'Still here, you old bastard.'

'And have you even thought what a scandal like this would do to your commercial prospects, son? Not good, oh, not good, at all. The car deal? That'll never get into first gear. Don't think the manufacturers will want any connection with someone who is a two-timing love rat, do you? The hair product? That'll get pulled, too. That video game for kids? Don't think so. Anything else on the horizon, you can kiss goodbye.'

'I was always told you were an old shit. Now I know. You don't ever want to bump into me in a dark alleyway, you old scumbag.'

'An understandable reaction, son. Highly commendable, too. Protecting yourself and your own. Just like a wounded animal. Yes, I like that. Waste of time, of course. You've got a vile tongue and I've got the artistic pictures. Who do you think is holding the winning hand? It may interest you to know that your new club's owner is an extremely devout Roman Catholic. On first name terms with the Pope, I'm told.' Smiler paused for effect. 'What was that sound, son? Whooosh! Aye, that's your career going down the pan. Goodbye to all your dreams. You're done, son. Unless ...'

Crawley had collapsed into the chair beside the telephone. 'I'm listening,' he said, defeated.

'These photographs can go into my special file. Just like that. Oh, son, in case you are thinking of doing something silly and sending some of the heavies around to bash my head in, you can forget it. The photographer will have a set, too. And there'll be another pile with an anonymous friend. If a hair on my head is nudged sideways, those pictures will be released to everyone. Are you listening, son? You have my word on it.'

'What the fuck do you want?'

'I wouldn't mind you refraining from using bad language, son, for a start,' said Smiler. 'Now here's the deal. I will expect one genuine exclusive story from you every month. At least one. Got that? I want those dressing room secrets. I want to know the players who like little girls. Or, even better, little boys. There are skeletons all over the place in dressing rooms, are there not? Which player is fornicating with whom? I want to know about the drunks and the druggies. Who are the troublemakers. The manager? Has he got a bit on the side? Most of them do, you know. A big transfer story would be good, too.'

Smiler paused to let the demands sink in. He continued, 'In short, son, I want to know EVERYTHING that is going on in that dressing room. I'll keep my end of the bargain just so long as you keep yours. Understand, son? Let me down even once and photographs will be flying around the globe at the speed of light. Do you really want to let your adoring public know you possess a pecker that resembles a worm in a huff? Wouldn't need too much pixilating to obscure that shrunken acorn, would it, son? And I'm sure Jennifer's parents might be more than just a tad upset at their teenage daughter parading around in the nude with a leather whip in her hand and black, shiny boots up to her backside. What's that in her other hand? Is that a dildo? What was she going to do with that, son? Shove it up your back passage? Something like that? Kinky, son, very kinky.'

There was no response.

'Do we have a deal?'

'Do I have a choice?'

'No.'

'We have a deal.'

'Congratulations.'

'Congratulations? Why the fuck am I being congratulated?'

'You've just signed up for Team Smiler and we'll be a winning combination. Guaranteed.'

'How do you sleep at night, you old bastard?'

'Oh, just as well as you do, son, when you crawl back under the sheets of the marital bed after a night of swinging naked from a chandelier with your blonde nymphomaniac. Oh, yes, son, I sleep very well, indeed, thanks for asking.'

Crawley was certain he could hear cackling in the background.

'I'll give you a couple of days to digest what I've just said. It may take some time for it all to filter through. But, son, be assured of this - I have the photographs and I will use them if you don't come good. You know that, don't you?'

'Aye,' said Crawley, exhausted yet somehow strangely relieved. If he played ball, his marriage would be saved. Now he understood why Rodger James got so many exclusives for his newspaper. How many others out there were being blackmailed?

'Before you go, Rodger, can I say something?' asked the footballer in a flat tone.

'If you must, son.'

'I won't forget this.' The line went dead.

'Another good day at the office,' grinned Rodger James with deep satisfaction.

'Now let's find Crazy Horse.'

CHAPTER TWENTY

Early evening. Tuesday 23 November.

Millport, Isle of Cumbrae.

Charlie Brock and Willy made their excuses and left Hugh's Bar just before six o'clock. 'Time to go for a bite, lads,' said Brock.

'Try to restrict it to food,' said Vodka Joe, cackling gently in the corner.

Harry Booth and Griff Stewart clinked their glasses at the bar. 'Good lad, Charlie,' said the cop. 'Do you think he'll let us stay with him tonight?'

'Do you think he'll let us film him with that bird, Willy?' the newsman practically leered.

Bar owner Hughie Edwards poured a large tipple and left it on the bar. 'On the house, Vodka,' he said. The incumbent in the corner looked cosy as the wind gathered momentum outside, some of the boats in the harbour clattering violently against the walls. He was casually observing a reckless race between a newspaper's motoring pull-out and a plastic cup as they zig-zagged along the pavement. His money was on the cup. 'Have you lost the use of your legs, Hughie?' he said. The question was ignored.

'Well, lads, what's it to be tonight?' asked Hughie. 'Wild night at the Moulin Rouge? Poker at the Plaza Casino? Pole dancing at Seventh Heaven? Or a poke of chips out of the Hippy Chippy? Spoiled for choice on this island, eh?'

'Well, I do believe I will be getting on the outside of a few more brandies,' said R.I.P. 'Play it by ear after that. Anything good on Sky Sports?' he asked, stretching across the bar for the newspaper. He looked at the schedule and was clearly unimpressed. He looked again at the front page. 'What's your take on this, El Cid? This guy Crazy Horse missing? Strange, eh?'

The cop took a sip of his beer and scratched his jaw. 'No-one's mentioned kidnapping yet. I wouldn't rule that out completely. There are a lot of skint and desperate people out there. How difficult would it be to snatch a guy like Derek Laird? Presumably, everyone knows where he lives. Presumably, also, it's a quiet part of the city. Probably wouldn't be too difficult at all to snatch him. These guys aren't like pop stars who go around with armies of bodyguards to protect them. Footballers haven't reached that stage yet.'

'Kidnapping,' said the reporter. 'That's an Italian crime. Don't they have the copyright on that?'

'Kidnapping's an ANYBODY crime,' said the cop. 'Anyone who is skint and desperate, as I've just said. He could be abducted right outside the front door of his house, shoved in the boot of a car and whisked off to the mountains. Plenty of quiet places up there. I had a pain-in-the-arse sergeant who was grabbed by some locals on holiday in Ibiza one year. He was a bit pissed and making a nuisance of himself in a restaurant. He was asked politely to shut up, but he was too far gone to take notice. A couple of locals waited until he had finished his meal and was getting ready to leave when they escorted him to their truck, stuck him inside, drove for about an hour up into the hills and then booted him out in the middle of the night in the centre of precisely nowhere. Completely lost in the pitch black. Shat himself. If they can do that to some drunk just for a bit of fun, what would they do for cash?'

'Point taken, mate,' said the newspaperman. 'What about a ransom, then? There's been no mention of that yet.'

'If the kidnappers, supposing there *were* kidnappers, knew what they were doing, they might let things settle down for awhile. Normally, though, there is a ransom demand only hours after a kidnapping. Maybe they're waiting to see if the club call in the police. I would expect they have already done that. If Brock's right and Laird is a trustworthy bloke who doesn't dabble in drink or drugs, then the club will have ruled out that he is lying in a stupor behind a door somewhere. Okay, he appears to have a healthy appetite for the opposite sex ...'

'A film star, a pop singer and a children's TV presenter with the big Brad Pitts,' interrupted Vodka Joe. 'And don't forget the mystery brunette, either.'

'Right, he likes to get his leg over. All these females have been contacted, apart from the brunette. That's interesting. Who is the mystery lady? Why did he keep her a secret? He was quite happy to have his photograph taken with the others and talk openly about their so-called friendships ...'

'That's a new name for it,' interjected Vodka Joe, who, although besotted with Gina Lollibrigida, might have been persuaded to accept the offer of a night of passion with any of the footballer's 'friends'.

The cop continued, 'If you are asking for my professional opinion, I would start a search right now for that lady, the brunette. Footballers tend to stick together on nights-out, strength in numbers, that sort of thing. I bet one of Crazy Horse's team-mates knows the identity of this female. She didn't just drop in from Mars, so someone must know her. Someone is bound to have taken a photograph of both of them together. The Papparazzi got their arses kicked after Princess Di, but they're still at it. Still photographing the Royals when their guard is down.'

'A good, exclusive snap and they can retire for life. They're not big on people's privacy. And they know the rules and how to bend them. If you are out in public, then you are fair game. If you're running around naked with a handful of busty birds on a private beach, that's a different matter. That's seen as off limits. It's out in the open, but it is on private land. In the good old days no-one would have published that. But that French magazine went right ahead and used topless pictures of the high-profile princess by a poolside at a private villa and got away with it. Some editors will take their chances of not going to jail. But it says in the newspaper here that Crazy Horse and this female were spotted eating in a quiet little bistro in the hills. A pound to a penny the owner would have tipped off one of the local snappers. Bet you. Doesn't do his establishment any harm if a top footballer is spotted having dinner there. A free advertisement.'

'Happens all the time in Scotland,' observed R.I.P. 'There's one guy with a nightclub who is never off the telephone to us. It's a perfect set-up for a newspaper. You don't have to employ a photographer to follow a celeb around all day. This bloke will get in touch to give you a rundown of who's in his club that night and you just send the lensman along. Everybody's happy.' He paused, smiled and continued, 'Apart from that famous English international who was playing away. Thought he had escaped from it all in Manchester and would be safe in Glasgow. Mistake to make. The photograph of him and this bird with her tits spilling out onto the carpet was syndicated that night and appeared in every red top newspaper the following morning. My advice to these blokes is simple: the moon might be a safe place to have a fling. Even then, I'm not too sure. Photographers get everywhere. Mobile phones are dangerous things, too. Everybody's got a camera these days.'

'Right,' said El Cid, 'all we have to do now is wait for tomorrow's newspapers and there's bound to be a picture of Miss X. She might fancy a bit of publicity herself.'

'She might even be with him right now,' chucked in Hughie reasonably.

'That's another possibility,' said the cop. 'Maybe they've done a runner together.'

'Maybe they'll turn up in Gretna and get married,' said Vodka Joe.

'Highly unlikely,' said Hughie, caught in serious mode. 'Footballers like to do these things in style these days, don't they? Sell the exclusive snaps to *Hello* or another glossy magazine for millions. Can't see them getting spliced at the Gretna Anvil somehow.'

'So what are we left with?' asked El Cid. 'A famous footballer who has gone missing. Has he disappeared willingly? If so, why? What is he running away from? Where has he gone? Has he been taken away under force? What sort of line of enquiry are the Spanish cops following? Is he, in fact, still in the country? If he's not, what about passport control? This guy's face has been everywhere in recent years. He's hardly anonymous. How would a guy like that get out of Spain without being noticed? And where's the mystery female? Is she with him? Who is she?'

'Too many questions,' said R.I.P.

'And not enough answers,' replied El Cid.

'No fuckin' answers,' threw in Vodka Joe, less than helpfully.

CHAPTER TWENTY-ONE

Early evening. Tuesday 23 November.

Barcelona

It was a crisp autumnal evening in the Catalan capital as Rafael Castillo knelt in silent prayer inside the tiny, serenely quiet chapel deep within the bowels of the Nou Camp Stadium. Barcelona Football Club officials had sanctioned such a place of worship when the stadium was rebuilt in March 1954.

The football manager bowed his head in front of the statue of the Virgin Mary. Rafael Castillo was known to be an emotional individual, a team manager who cared deeply about people. A character with the ability to mix philosophy with football and who often cited Colombian writer Gabriel Garcia Márquez as an inspiration. 'He who awaits much can expect little.' Words that carried meaning for Castillo on his journey through life. He firmly gripped his rosary beads, passed through the family for generations, and prayed for the well-being of his player, Derek Laird.

Across the city, Miguel Araquistian rarely came into contact with rosary beads. In his official capacity of Comissari of La Guardia Urbana, he pondered as he sat at his untidy desk, scraps of paper, pens, notebooks, newspapers, tissues, polystyrene cups messily scattered across the surface, at Comisaria de Barcelona, a five-storeyed building on Carrer Nov de la Rambla. He was far from seeking Divine Intervention or help from above.

'*Cabron! Bastardo!*' he uttered menacingly through clenched teeth set in a firm jaw. Muggers, thieves and pickpockets were all in a day's work. Maybe a knifing or two when too much tequila or whisky had been involved. Perhaps a shooting if there was some dodgy dust in town. But the possibility, however remote, of a kidnapping? This was unusual, even in this bustling city awash with opportunists; especially, he thought, Romanians mingling with unsuspecting tourists.

'The visitors give their expensive cameras to total strangers and then go to pose with their loved ones on the streets of La Rambla, and they are surprised when the gleeful benefactor disappears into the crowds, along with their equipment?' He had told the story many times. He never understood the mentality of those who visited his beautiful city. 'Their generosity knows no bounds. They want to give away their possessions to total strangers.'

This was different, though. *Caballo Loco* was missing. The Scotsman who scored so many goals was nowhere to be seen. One minute he was scoring a dramatic late winner against Real Madrid and the next – hey presto! – gone into the wind; gone like a puff of smoke on a winter's evening. Where? Why? What had happened? Was he safe? Had he been kidnapped? And, God forbid, was he dead? 'Those fuckin' Romanians would stop at nothing,' mused Araquistian.

The policeman was arched forward in his leather seat as he looked out of the window of his office on the second floor of the city's police headquarters. It had just gone beyond six o'clock in the evening and the city he loved was still vibrant with market traders, cafe bars and sightseers. There were also thieves wandering with their quick eyes and their equally swift hands, sizing up situations in a heartbeat. American tourists were their favourites. Cameras, DVDs and video recorders were shed alarmingly and almost willingly. And then the cop would walk down two flights of stairs and past the desk at the foyer where scores of angry visitors, robbed of their goods, vented their spleen at the unfortunate incumbent on desk duty that day. That was a normal day in a busy precinct.

Caballo Loco vanishing was not in the script. Making matters worse, Señor Araquistian was a Barcelona fan.

Araquistian, six foot, bulky and overweight, or, as he liked to insist, 'nutritionally challenged', hauled himself out of his chair and paced closer to the window. He swept a hand across his dark curly hair and removed his aviator spectacles, required for poor eyesight and not merely an affectation. The crumpled jacket of his light grey suit had been chucked carelessly over the back of his chair; his tan slip-ons hadn't seen polish for some considerable time. He kept 'worry beads' in the right-hand pocket of his trousers. Without thinking, he would often play with the beads. It wasn't his most endearing trait and one that often surprised anyone witnessing it for the first time.

He padded across the marbled floor and picked up a copy of his favourite newspaper, *La Vanguardia*. A photograph of Derek Laird stared solemnly back at him. The footballer looked unusually grim and dour, a vast contrast with the photograph which had been on the back page only a few days before. That had shown Laird as he celebrated his winner against Real Madrid, the hated enemy in the eyes of Araquistian and all Catalans.

The cop perused the story for the third time that day. Nothing new to report, he thought. No leads. No information. No inside tip-offs. Nothing. The press, it appeared, had hit a brickwall. He knew the feeling; he had come to a halt at the identical obstacle. He had several trusted grasses out there only too happy to propel their grandmothers towards incarceration for the right price. Araquistian had also been known to slip a few euros into the palm of one of his eastern European 'friends' for information. He had made the usual calls to his more reliable informants. *Cero.* Zero.

He had volunteered to question two of Crazy Horse's female companions. The movie star and the pop singer. To his surprise, he found them to be intelligent and not the airheads he had anticipated. Both knew the situation with the footballer. There were to be no commitments, no promises, no ties. They were with him on his rules. Araquistian's female colleague, Maria Dominguez, of questionable sexual preferences, had interviewed the other 'bimbo', as she so eloquently put it, the children's TV presenter who seemed to have such difficulty in keeping her bosom in place and out of view when the live cameras were rolling. She merely confirmed what the other two female associates of the footballer had said. There were no strings, no problems. Anyway, it helped her TV career to be seen as often as possible in the newspapers. 'And he's good in bed, too,' she informed a clearly unimpressed Dominguez. She added with a practised smile, 'That's always a bonus.'

One extremely important part of the jigsaw was missing. Where was the mystery brunette? *Who* was the mystery brunette?

Araquistian returned and parked his ample backside on the edge of his desk. He looked again at the newspaper. There was an out-of-focus photograph of Laird and the unknown companion sitting at a dining table in a small bistro. The cop acknowledged it was probably taken by an amateur with a mobile phone. What could be seen of part of the girl's face was in profile and the snap only proved she possessed plenty of hair. It cascaded down onto her shoulders, obscuring most of her features. There was a face in there somewhere, but it was completely unidentifiable. Unfortunately, Laird and his companion had left the bistro only a handful of minutes before a paparazzi, tipped off by the opportunistic restaurateur, arrived on the scene. A professional photo could have closed that part of the case by now, an identity established.

The cop could ask his friends in the newspapers to print a full-sized photograph of the dodgy image and ask, **'HAVE YOU SEEN THIS GIRL?'**, making a plea to the public. He also knew his office would be hit by an avalanche of phone calls, emails and every social network device on the market as 'helpful' people took a guess. The girl in question had already been asked to come forward to help the police with their enquiries. So far, though, no show.

Araquistian once more swept his hand through his mane of unruly hair. 'Who are you?' he said, looking at the photograph. 'Why not come forward?' He wore a puzzled expression. He realised, of course, there could be a mountain of reasons the mystery woman hadn't stepped forward. For a start, she could be married. Maybe engaged. In another relationship. Maybe she just didn't need the hassle and wanted to remain anonymous. Araquistian shrugged, walked back to the window and began playing with the 'worry beads' in his right pocket. It wasn't a pretty sight.

A few miles away, Rafael Castillo sighed heavily, placed a cheroot in his mouth and made his way from the chapel to the Press Conference suite on first floor of the Nou Camp Stadium. He walked along the winding corridors, the walls adorned with massive murals of the club's greatest players, Kubala, Cruyff, Maradona, Ronaldinho, Figo, Stoichkov, Messi. He felt as though their eyes were drilling into him, looking down forlornly on a dead man walking. There were floor-to-ceiling prints of the European champions. One with PARIS 2006 in huge letters, another with ROME 2009 and a third with WEMBLEY 2011. The players were celebrating joyous occasions.

'*Buenos dias, el entrenador,*' said one of the club's public relations staff as she ushered Castillo into *Espacio Multimedia*, the Press Room. 'What's good about it?' he wondered as he made his way to the long wooden table that had only one seat behind it. Before he got a chance to get his rear end anywhere near it, camera bulbs immediately started flashing. 'Luckily for you lot,' he said to the crouching photographers, 'I do not suffer from epilepsy. I would be in the emergency room at *L'Esperanca*. I would have a season ticket for *L'Esperanca*.' It didn't lighten the mood of the media; they had heard the line on an almost daily basis for the past three years.

Castillo sat down and pulled his chair forward. He placed his elbows on the surface. Scattered in front of him were an assortment of mobile telephones, tape recording devices and microphones from scores of the city's newspapers, radio and TV stations. He guessed there were about two hundred inquisitors in attendance. He had been in this movie before; well, not exactly *this* movie. Yes, he had had players disappear on him before. It wasn't professional, but he knew some players could be easily led, especially when wild sex was on offer. They were athletes, fit young specimens of manhood, and he would often overlook a small indiscretion. The player would be hammered in training for the next few days and his salary would be lighter that month. Castillo was always astonished at the professionals who were only too aware of the club punishments that lay ahead, but still took the bait.

This, though, was different; very different. Derek Laird enjoyed the pleasures of the flesh, little doubt about it, but he never missed training. Not once in his five years at Barcelona and his coach for three of those years believed him to be 'a manager's dream'. Lord knows, Castillo had said it often enough. Now the 'manager's dream' had vanished without trace.

174

The press demanded an early evening update. Castillo cleared his throat. He had a prepared statement drawn up by the PR department which was passed around the reporters. Basically, it told them there was no update. That, knew the men and women from the media, would not be acceptable to their editors. They all required a grain of information to take the story forward and Castillo was right in the line of their fire. 'Take aim,' smiled the coach. 'Okay,' he said, 'who's first?'

A young reporter identified himself as Javier Sanchez from the newspaper *La Vanguardia.* 'Señor Castillo,' he said respectfully and possibly a little nervously, 'can you tell me, please, what the police are doing at the moment?'

Castillo didn't recognise the youth and wondered if this was his first Barcelona Press Conference. He could have snapped back in frustration. He didn't. 'For that information you will have to ask the police authorities. They will give you that information, I'm sure.'

The youth wasn't about to be fobbed off. Unexpectedly, he shot back. 'I take it you are in constant contact with the police authorities. Is that not the case?'

Castillo was taken slightly aback. 'A baby-faced assassin,' he thought. He looked at the inquisitor and replied, 'Yes, of course, that is the case. In fact, I believe they have a press conference of their own arranged for some time tonight. You may want to check with them.'

'When did you last hear from the police authorities?' The youth was on a roll as his more experienced colleagues let him do all the running.

'Me personally?' queried Castillo, unable to prevent an

eyebrow arching quizzically skywards. 'I am the coach of a football team. That is my concern. I still believe there will be a very good explanation to all of this from my player. Until then, the police will remain in direct contact with the club officials.' He drew breath and added, 'Believe me, I would love to be able to give you the information you and your colleagues seek. However, as you can see from the club statement, we are not in a position to do so at the moment. When there is something to say, you will all hear about it, you have my word on that. And, as you know, gentlemen, I am a man who keeps his promises. This is a very unfortunate situation, but the club and the police are working together in an attempt to come up with answers. And, as I have said all along, I believe there will be a reasonable explanation for all of this.'

'You've got nothing to tell us?' asked the youth in the front row.

Castillo could feel a growing exasperation. 'I have told you all I know. We are not hiding anything. The football club and the police authorities want this incident taken care of as swiftly as possible. Until then, we will all have to remain patient. And that includes your readers, listeners and viewers.'

'You said "incident", Señor Castillo. Has there been an incident?' Javier Sanchez was smarter than he looked.

Another sigh from Castillo. 'A poor choice of word, maybe. I know of no incident. You are the newspaperman, use your own word.'

'Oh, yes, I will, señor Castillo,' the journalist said and smiled as he scribbled in a notepad perched on his knee. *Coach Castillo hasn't got a clue*, he wrote.

CHAPTER TWENTY-TWO

11.14am. Wednesday 24 November.

Millport, Isle of Cumbrae.

Hickory Dickory, the island's rather eccentric GP, was doing what he did best. He was seated in his favourite spot beside the fruit machine at Hugh's Bar, sharing a bottle of the finest *Chateauneuf du Cumbrae* with himself. This was the doc at his most satisfied, getting on the outside of some lukewarm white wine of some indistinguishable vintage, safe in the knowledge the landlord had several more bottles with the fake labels in stock.

Seated at the table in the corner by the large front window was Vodka Joe, peering through the pages of Hughie's recently-purchased *Daily News*, mumbling all the while. Every now and again an expletive would bounce around the bar, interspersed with a 'look at the hooters on that babe'. Another unremarkable day on a quiet little island sitting doing nothing, minding its own business, was in the offing, thought the doc. Wrongly.

Hughie, with his usual dexterity, was wiping a pint glass with a well-used dish towel. The forensics people at CSI would have encountered insurmountable obstacles in attempting to lift a clean fingerprint off any of his pots. He pushed his Buddy Holly spectacles further up the bridge of his nose and squinted into some late-morning brightness, the drizzle abating for the moment. The images would soon be dimmed, Largs and Arran would fade into the background as a dull greyness enveloped the North Ayrshire coastline. 'Hurry up with that paper, will you, Vodka?' he asked his resident customer.

'Ach, give us a minute,' came the reply. It went quiet again. Hickory Dickory poured himself another large measure of plonk, picked up his morning *Gazette* and continued reading. Bar owner Hughie sighed and smiled as he had sighed and smiled on many occasions in the past. Millport moved at its own pace and no-one could bother to summon up the motivation to alter a process that had taken centuries to cultivate. The reverie was broken by the island's doctor.

'This is beyond a joke!' he exclaimed. 'This is an absolute outrage. I'm not having this.'

Hughie was intrigued; it was most unusual for the GP to be this animated at precisely 11.27 in the morning. Especially as he had only poured two glasses of *Chateauneuf du Cumbrae* after squeezing through the pub door that day, beating Vodka Joe by a nose.

'What's shattered your peace on this tranquil day in Sleepy Hollow, Hick?' asked Hughie.

'*This*!' The doctor held up the front page of the austere broadsheet, a newspaper stubbornly refusing to switch to tabloid as so many others had done over the years. His displeasure was only too evident. '*This*,' he said again, pointing to a headline on the front page and presenting it to Hughie, who readjusted his specs, wrinkled his nose and gazed across the bar.

'*New row over Ministers' expenses?*' Hughie hadn't realised the island's resident GP held such vehement views on the subject.

The doc turned the paper around. 'No, no, not that,' he said. '*This*!' He stabbed his forefinger at another headline and again turned the front page towards Hughie.

'The price of eggs to soar?'

'What?' spluttered the confused GP, turning the paper around. 'Eggs going up? Again? Liberty!' He bristled for a moment, scoffed a large portion of his wine and repeated, 'No. *This*!' He pointed once again at the article that was creating such offence.

'Scotland's finest quality newspaper?'

'What?' The doc was indignant. '*This*!' Once again he indicated the news that was so upsetting him and turned the paper towards Hughie, who was beginning to wonder how many times he would be required to shave before he ever discovered what was irking his crushed grape-devouring customer.

'Car prices continue to rise?'

An irritated doc turned the paper around again. '*This*!' he said. 'The story about the footballer going missing in Spain. Does any self-respecting editor, a professional who should have his finger on the nation's pulse, really think that is a story beholding of the front page? Does he genuinely believe they will sell papers with nonsense like this on their front page? It's little wonder circulations are falling in that industry. The front page is sacred, it's for important news ...'

'Like MPs' expenses claims, the price of eggs and cars being more expensive?' asked the bar owner, slightly incredulously.

'Important issues, Hughie; vital pieces of information,' exclaimed the doc.

'I've got a question for you, Hick,' Vodka Joe stirred from his little neuk at the front window. 'Have you ever thought about becoming a gynaecologist? Or would you not know what you were getting yourself into?'

'Oh, pipe down, little man,' said Hickory, rarely one to indulge in the frivolities that he had ascertained some time ago dominated the thought processes of his fellow late-morning imbiber. 'Go and count the waves in the Firth. Must you try to bring abject misery to everyone who is unfortunate enough to be sucked into your orbit?'

Vodka Joe pondered for a moment. 'I'll have to get back to you on that, Hick,' he said.

'Take your time. I'm having a serious conversation here.' The doc looked again at the offending article. 'This is preposterous,' he practically bellowed. 'Sport should not be on the front page, it should be tucked away at the back.' He added, 'For the ill-educated. The fortunate ones among them who can actually read.'

'You don't think that is an interesting story, then?' asked Hughie. 'A famous Scottish sportsmen, and God knows we don't have a superabundance of them these days, has vanished and no-one knows why. Is he alive? Is he dead? Has he been kidnapped? You don't think that is more of a news story than a sports story?'

'So he kicks a leather sphere around for a living. Big deal. It says here he is a goalscorer. So what? He can propel a round object twixt the uprights on some far-off land and we're all supposed to get excited when he goes AWOL?' The doc was adamant in his stance.

'He could be sleeping with the fishes. Luca Brasi could have done him in.' Vodka Joe was determined to continue with *The Godfather* theme. His observations fell on deaf ears. Immediately, he understood what it must be like to be Boring Brian.

'I abhor all sport,' said the doc, the disdain obvious in his tone. 'Wretched pastime. Tried to make me play cricket at school. I wasn't having any of that. Sport is for thugs.' He put the paper down and held up his hands and looked at his long, bony fingers. 'These hands are for violins,' he said, with an air of triumph. 'Not for violence.'

'So, by your reckoning, Hick, only cretins, nincompoops, bullies and the scum of the earth are involved in sport?' asked Hughie, still furiously cleaning a pint glass.

'Maybe not quite as harsh as that, dear boy, but you're close,' said the doc, adding, 'And stop calling me Hick. The nickname the islanders took so long to conjure up and bestow upon me is Hickory Dickory. I accept you are never going to give my proper title of Dr Algernon Pendlebury, so, that being the rather obvious case, I'll settle for the elongated version, thank you very much.'

'So the Greeks were wasting their time some three thousand years ago when they decided to gift the universe the Olympic Games?' asked Hughie, failing to disguise his smirk.

'Don't get me started on the Olympic Games, dear lad. Did you see how much it cost London to stage that useless event? Billions! People starving all over the world, folk sleeping on the streets, families getting turfed out of their houses, thousands losing their jobs, factories closing down, a recession like we have never known in our lifetime, and they squander millions on firework displays.'

The doc was working up to a full head of steam. He took another gulp of plonk. 'And for what purpose? To see people flopping about in swimming pools? Meandering around tracks? Falling into sandpits? Blasting hell out of clay pigeons? Propelling pointy things at a big circle? Throwing bits of metal? Lifting heavy things? Punching the stuffing out of a brain-dead opponent? Throwing each other around a ring? Cycling? Bloody cycling? Grannies can get round this island quicker than some of those so-called Olympians. And they don't take performance-enhancing drugs. Waste of the tax-payer's money, if you ask me.'

'What about dwarf throwing?'

'Oh, be quiet, Vodka,' snapped the doc, before adding in the same exasperated breath, 'Although I realise such an occurrence is as rare as my chances of observing old farmer Josh's pony eating with a knife and fork.' He turned his attention back to the bar owner. 'Hughie, dear lad, could you bring me another of your finest bottles of *Chateauneuf du Cumbrae*, please? This could be a long day and I think I deserve a treat.'

'You would be guaranteed a gold medal in wine guzzling.' Another offering from the corner of the bar.

'A fresh glass, too, Hughie, if you could be so kind.'

'So your belief is we should scrap all future Olympic Games?' queried the bar owner. 'We should forget all about discovering who is the best in the world at their given sport? We should leave athletes, sportsmen and sportswomen throughout the universe, without any sort of precious goal? No need to pound themselves into peak condition for the ultimate challenge on the field of sporting endeavour?'

'Couldn't have put it better myself. Waste of time. Save the money.'

'You didn't answer my question about becoming a gynaecologist. That's a job where you could always keep your hand in.' Once more Vodka Joe had his say.

'Continue reading your *News*, ruffian,' snorted the doc. 'When we require your input we will put the request in writing.'

Hughie was happily distracted when the swinging door groaned and in stepped Charlie Brock and his female companion, the graceful, charming Willy.

'Sanctuary,' cried the sportswriter, arms outstretched. 'We need sanctuary.'

'And a pint of lager for you and a Dry Martini and lemonade, if I'm not mistaken, for the young lady. You are a young lady, are you not?' smiled the barman, stopping short at batting his eyelashes.

'I was the last time I looked this morning, Hughie,' whispered Willy. 'Thank you for asking.'

Hughie placed the glasses in front of Brock and his companion. 'Where's Laurel and Hardy?' he asked.

'We left R.I.P. and El Cid snoring their fat heads off, both entwined on the sofa,' smiled Brock.

Not for the first time, the bar owner's eyebrows shot upwards.

'No, not like that,' laughed Brock. 'Just two drunks sleeping it off ...'

'Having it off,' came the voice from the corner of the bar.

'Good morning, Vodka Joe,' said Brock, craning his neck and glancing to his left. 'Sorry, didn't see you there. How are you doing?'

'I'll have one of my usual, thanks,' said Vodka Joe, who, as far everyone was aware, wasn't in the slightest defective in his hearing.

Brock smiled. 'One for our wee pal at the window, Hughie. One for yourself, too. What about Hick?'

'Oh, he's happy enough,' said the bar owner. 'That's him onto his second bottle. Let's hope no-one falls ill on the island today. They'll not get much assistance from Doctor Dolittle.'

Willy, who had decided to award herself a couple of extra days off due to her 'bad chest', as she had told her boss the previous evening, made herself comfortable on a bar stool before picking up her glass.

'Who would ever believe that?' laughed Brock. 'You with a bad chest?' Even with his two friends in the close vicinity of next door in the flat the previous evening, Willy and he had managed to make a connection. 'Three times. I'm slowing down,' Brock had said in the early hours of the morning. 'You're taking me for granted,' Willy replied, flashing one of those dazzling smiles that would have had Big Eric racing for the Gents. Brock's good humour continued upon his first visit of the day to Hughie's bar.

'What's on the agenda today, laddie and lassie?' queried Hughie. 'Anything planned?'

Brock feigned deep thought. 'So much to do, so little time. Don't take this wrong way, Hughie, but I'm not going to spend all day in your fine establishment. I'll wait for Tom and Jerry to make an appearance, buy them a couple of heart-starters and maybe go for a wee walk with Willy. If it stays dry, of course.'

'Barbeque not a possibility, then?' asked Hughie, who, in his mind, had been bestowed the precious gift of humour from above. The question hung in the air, unanswered.

'Head off to Fintry, I think, and pick up a late breakfast at McKenzie's. They still do those smashing all-day breakfasts over there, Hughie?'

'Best on the island,' answered the bar owner, 'just don't tell Tip-Toe next door. He reckons his are the best, but McKenzie's just shades it. Their fried bread makes all the difference. Probably takes a few years off your life, but well worth it.'

Brock lifted his beer, chinked Willy's glass and said, 'Here's to another eventful day on the Isle of Cumbrae.'

Vodka Joe, nestling in his 'Sofa So Good' corner and reading today's update on the puzzling disappearance of the Scottish player nicknamed Crazy Horse, paid no heed to the hooded figure that hurried past the window on his way along Stuart Street.

CHAPTER TWENTY-THREE

11.32am. Wednesday 24 November.

Millport, Isle of Cumbrae.

The waves wickedly licked the rocks around the deserted boatyard at West Bay. A small fishing trawler, neglected and sadly allowed to fall into disrepair but still defying the elements, bobbed wildly in the Firth of Clyde. 'Ideal place to go missing,' thought Derek Laird when he pushed the key into the lock of the front door of the wooden chalet, one of twenty scattered around opposite the boatyard. He had gone over twenty hours undetected on the island.

The previous afternoon, Hamish McNulty, proprietor of Robbie's Tavern, had reassured him the other nineteen holiday flats were unoccupied. 'It's November, young fella. Who'd be mad enough to want to holiday over there? Present company excepted, of course.' It was a fair point well made. Laird had pushed open the door to Number Twenty and stepped inside the cabin. It was fresh and tidy with a decent-sized living room and a kitchen just off, an adequate shower room and a double bedroom at the rear. TV and radio; no satellite and no telephone. Just the way he wanted it.

He wondered if he had been recognised by the bar owner in Robbie's. If Hamish had twigged, he certainly concealed it well. He had been more concerned with the horse racing on Channel 4. 'I backed a cert at 20 to 1,' said Hamish. 'It was still running at 10 past 3.' Laird wondered how often the bar owner had cracked that joke.

Laird had settled on one of the comfortable stools at the bar in

Robbie's. Surprisingly, he felt quite at ease in his new surroundings. Two men, both in their seventies, guessed Laird, were playing chess in an alcove in the corner. Another, wearing paint-spattered blue overalls, was at the other end of the bar, reading the *Racing Post*. No-one paid a blind bit of notice to the stranger in their midst. And that suited Derek Laird. The fake moustache had been discarded somewhere en route to Calais. His only form of disguise was to attempt to grow a beard, but he discovered he would never be one of those cool dudes with designer stubble. He realised he resembled a cross between Steptoe Snr and Shaggy from *Scooby Doo*. Not that it appeared to matter to the good patrons of Robbie's Tavern. He could have been wearing his Barcelona strip and he was convinced no-one would have given a hoot. Why anyone would want to impersonate an owl was another question altogether.

'What will it be, young fella?' Hamish deserted his post at the top of the bar beside the television set to offer assistance. 'Cash customers only, just so long as the ink is dry,' he laughed. Hamish, slight, sharp featured, grey-haired and with a ready smile, looked at Laird for a disconcerting moment. He took off his specs, pinched his nose and put them on again. 'Blind as a bat,' said the bar owner. 'Can't see a thing without them. Okay, what's your poison, young fella?'

'A pint of lager, please,' requested Laird.

'Coming right up, young man.' Hamish picked up a pint glass, shoved it under the tap and began pouring. 'This bugger's lively today,' he informed Laird. Without warning, he shot out the question, 'You're a new face. What brings you to Millport?'

'Murdo,' lied Laird, offering his hand across the bar. 'Just thought I would get away from the rat race for a wee while. Take a breather.'

Hamish passed over the beer and shook the hand of the stranger. 'Hamish McNulty,' he said. 'Landlord and duff punter, at your service.'

Before Laird got a chance to raise the tumbler to his lips, Hamish queried, 'Have I seen you before, young fella? Your face looks vaguely familiar.'

'If you know this face you must have one helluva memory,' smiled Laird. 'I've not been over in this part of the world for about twenty years. And, believe it or not, I wasn't drinking age back then. Parents had a wee caravan up at Kirkton Park. We used to come over here quite a lot.'

'And you thought you would come back and see what the Twenty-First Century has done to our wee island?'

'Aye, thought I might have a wee wander around. I see they still hire bikes at Marples. Jeez, that guy must have made a fortune out of me. Cycled round this island about a thousand times. I learned to ride a bike down here, you know.'

'*Everybody* learned to ride a bike down here. We've got to be famous for something.' Hamish thought for a moment. 'And boozing. Aye, bikes and boozing, that's us.'

Laird passed over a tenner and took a sip of his inviting pint. 'Have one on me, Hamish.'

'Can you stand a gin and tonic?'

'Sure, fill your boots.'

'I'd prefer to fill my glass,' cackled the barman. 'Cheers, young man.'

The bar owner downed the gin and tonic in three gulps and Laird reckoned it might not have been his first of the day. Hamish moved back to the top of the bar and gazed at the television set. 'I've got Serendipty in this one,' he said without turning round. 'Not a bad price, 3/1. Fell the last time I backed it.'

Laird thought it wise to let the bar owner catch up with the horse racing before asking for a place to stay. He didn't realise he would have needed a tow truck to entice Hamish away from the TV set when horse racing was on. It was all over in the space of a few minutes. 'Another fiver down the drain,' said Hamish, crunching a piece of paper and throwing it into the bin behind the bar. Laird noticed there were a few such pieces of discarded and crumpled pieces of paper in there to keep it company. 'At least it didn't fall this time. Now that's progress.'

'Freshen your glass, young fella?' McNulty sidled back down the bar and pointed to Laird's empty pint glass. 'This one's on the house. I'll keep you company.'

'Wee Effie tells me you're the guy to see about accommodation, Hamish. Is that right?'

'Aye, I'm the man with the keys. What are you looking for? A flat? Plenty of them going at this time of year. One right next door, as a matter of fact.'

'Sounds okay, Hamish, but I was looking for something maybe a wee bit quieter. Maybe catch up on my reading.'

Hamish looked at the holdall somewhat quizzically. 'How many books have you got in there, young fella?'

'About two hundred,' answered Laird, with a grin.

Hamish looked over the bar to see if there was an extension on the holdall. 'Pretty thin books, eh?'

'Actually, it's called a Kindle, Hamish. You can download

hundreds of books. They're known as ebooks.'

Hamish stared at Laird. 'Kindle? Ebooks? Don't want to be rude, young man, but what are you talking about?'

Laird eased off the bar stool, went to the holdall, rummaged around and produced his Kindle. 'There you are, Hamish,' he said. 'There are around two hundred books in there.'

Hamish looked as though he had just been informed the earth was flat. 'You're joking, aren't you? How does that work, then?'

Laird realised he may have to take a short cut in getting to his destination. 'So you click here and there and that's you ordered a book. Simple, eh?'

'Oh, aye, simple,' said Hamish, downing his gin and tonic and taking the habitual route to the top of the bar to stare once again at the TV set. 'I've got Ghostly Hush in this one. Couldn't run if it had a rocket up its arse. Good price, though, 11/1. Worth a flutter.'

Laird was just about to ask if Hamish ever picked a winner, but he stopped himself. He was reasonably sure of the answer.

A few minutes later and another crunched-up piece of paper was destined for the bin. 'At least it wasn't last,' sighed Hamish. 'Aye, right, son,' he said. 'You're looking for a bit of peace and quiet? I've got the very place for you.'

He described the wooden chalets on West Bay Road, just a couple of hundred yards from the Westland Hotel and opposite the boatyard.

'Don't worry about the hotel,' said Hamish. 'That'll be empty, too. And Old Eddie mucks about in the boatyard, but you'll hardly know he's there. I'll get the keys to Chalet Number Twenty. That's right at the back, up off the road.' He rummaged in a drawer under the till. 'I'll get you a pamphlet. Aye, here it is. And you're in luck, it was cleaned yesterday, so everything should be spic'n'span. Let's see how much they charge in November.' Hamish scanned the single plastic-embosed A4 sheet. 'It's fifty pounds-per-night, young fella. Bit steep, eh? Three hundred for the week, seven full days. It's not cheap on this island. You pay for the silence.'

Laird could have bought all twenty chalets and have money left over from his monthly income. He realised it wouldn't have been too bright to write a cheque. It had to be cash, but he also knew he had to barter. 'Three hundred pounds for a week? Wow, I hadn't budgeted for that ...'

'I can get you a cheaper place,' said Hamish, quickly, trying to be helpful.

'Let me think, Hamish,' said Laird. 'I've got a few quid tucked away in my account for a rainy day ...'

'And you can always be guaranteed a rainy day down here, young fella.'

'And it does sound good. Can I see the photograph?' Hamish passed over the A4 sheet with the information. 'That looks perfect. I'll need to see what I've got in the bank. I think I might just about cover a week.'

'Like I said, young fella, I can get you cheaper. Nice place just five minutes up the back behind the Garrison.'

'Hold it for me, will you, Hamish? I'll nick along and try the hole in the wall. I passed a Bank of Scotland on my way here. I take it everything is functional? You know, with it being so quiet?'

'It's the only bank on the island, so it better be functional, young fella, or else your old grandpa here might as well shut up shop right now.'

191

'Give me ten minutes,' said Laird, putting his Kindle back in his bag. 'Okay to leave this here? It's just shirts, jeans and the like.'

'And two hundred books,' smiled Hamish. New technology never ceased to amaze him. 'Two hundred books in a wee dod of plastic? What will they think of next?'

Laird passed no-one going or returning from the cash dispenser. He didn't touch the machine. Instead, he withdrew £500 from an inside pocket and stuffed it in his wallet. He thought it was a reasonable idea to allow the bar owner at Robbie's to believe he didn't carry large amounts of money on his person. It was a little bit of subterfuge, but he decided it was necessary.

He had come too far to trip up now.

CHAPTER TWENTY-FOUR

11.55am. Wednesday 24 November.

Millport, Isle of Cumbrae.

'Come on, Casper, let's go and frighten someone.' Willy was still boisterous. Charlie Brock had put on the white parka coat he thought made him look like the indomitable Major Smith, as played by his favourite actor, Richard Burton, in the film version of Alistair MacLean's *Where Eagles Dare*. Willy believed he resembled the cartoon character, *Casper The Friendly Ghost*.

'The friendly ghost? Well, in that case, no boos is good boos.' Brock couldn't resist; Willy groaned.

'Okay, which way?' asked Willy as they stepped through the door of the close, ready to face the rigours of a brisk early November afternoon in Millport. 'Left or right? You choose.'

'That's fine and dandy, leave all the big decisions to the man,' said Brock, pulling up the hood of the parka. Willy did likewise with her duffel coat, linking her arm between Brock's. 'There'll be no football for you today, my boy,' she laughed and gave him a peck on the cheek. He smiled back, the years rolling away. 'Let's head for Fintry Bay,' he said. 'That'll work up an appetite. Ready?' 'As ready as I'll ever be, cap'n,' responded Willy. 'Let's get rid of some cobwebs.'

To the outside world, they were just another normal, happy couple. Brock could hardly reconcile himself with the fact that this time last week he wouldn't have known if his companion was in Lagos or Largs. He wasn't complaining, though. He had no idea why it had happened, where it was going and where it would end. For the time being, though, he would enjoy it while he could. Willy thought along identical lines. Two consenting adults who had made a connection. 'Good for us,' they thought in soundless tandem.

'Willy, please don't take this the wrong way, but is all this not a little bit bizarre?' You and me, I mean? The suddeness of it all?' asked Brock.

'Bizarre?' queried Willy. 'You're the one dressed like *Casper The Friendly Ghost.*'

'I'm not going to get too much sense out of you today, am I?' The couple trudged up Cardiff Street before turning left onto West Bay Road.

'I wouldn't bet on there being a massive change in the situation tomorrow either, Casper.' She gripped his arm even tighter, snuggling into the comfort of his bulky coat as the wind picked up, whistling directly into their faces.

Derek Laird threw his mobile phone on the settee. It had been switched off for four days. He fished out one of the two disposable phones, acquired by his pal Ricardo. Automatically, he had gone to use the instrument several times. He knew it was untraceable, but had thought better of it. He didn't expect anyone to understand his actions, certainly not anyone at Barcelona Football Club or among their legion of fans. Time and again, he had picked up the phone only to change his mind. He needed time to think and he couldn't do that in the blaze of publicity that would inevitably come his way. There were certain things he did not care to be made public.

Laird moved around the chalet in a bit of a fog. Eventually, he unzipped his holdall and began decanting the contents. Neatly, he placed a pair of designer jeans on a hanger in the MFI wardrobe. Laird meticulously folded two crew neck sweaters and two polo shirts and grabbed an array of socks and boxers. He put them on the empty shelves. He lobbed a pair of black deck shoes into the bottom drawer of the wardrobe.

The previous evening, he had stopped at the local mini-market on his way back from Robbie's Tavern after picking up the keys to Chalet Number Twenty. Two grey-haired ladies he reckoned were in their seventies were working the tills. The guy from the pub with the paint-spattered blue overalls was also in the shop. He was buying what looked like lunch, a cold meat roll and four bottles of Beck's. Brock looked around the store. It had been a long time since he had had to purchase provisions for himself. There was always someone around who would take care of that role.

He hesitated for a moment before picking up a plastic basket. Bread and milk. He knew these were essentials. He popped them into the basket. What next? The hamburgers looked okay. In they went. Potatoes. A must. He picked up a pack of butter as he shuffled among the shelves and the narrow passageways. He wasn't a great drinker of alcohol, but, for no apparent reason, picked up two bottles of dry white Prosecco and six bottles of Stella Artois. He gazed around, spotted some frozen chicken legs and placed them in the basket. He stepped towards the first check-out before stopping abruptly. Tea bags! The thought came from nowhere. He located them on a shelf at the back, returned to the old lady who was smiling knowingly in his direction. She had detected the lost soul as soon as he came through the door.

'Another zombie,' she thought, a trifle unkindly. Such a sighting was rare in Millport, so it helped brighten her day when a clueless individual picked up a basket and tried to look nonchalant. She could spot them a mile off.

Laird piled the provisions into two blue plastic bags, paid and smiled. 'On your own, son?' asked the shop assistant.

'Oh, aye. That obvious, eh? Not very good at this sort of thing. I'll get the hang of it.'

'Just whistle if you need me,' said the check-out 'girl'. 'You know how to whistle, don't you?' Laird smiled back. 'Aye, I've got that bit under control.'

He turned right on his way back along the promenade with a fair idea of where the chalets were located. He walked past Hugh's Bar at a brisk pace, stopping at the newsagent only fifty yards or so beyond the pub. He picked up a couple of national newspapers and made a point of not looking at the headlines as he paid for them. The woman at the cash register could have been about ninety years old. Laird was getting a clue as to why Millport was often referred to as 'God's Waiting Room'.

'Thank you very much,' he said rather too loudly when his change arrived.

The shop assistant didn't even look at him as she pointed out, 'I may be incontinent, young man, but my hearing is still good. Thank you.'

Laird smiled wanly as he made for the door and a quick exit. Then it was onto Cardiff Street, across to West Bay, past the children's swing park, the football pitch and the helipad – that hadn't been there twenty years ago, he noted – and on towards the boatyard and the cabins directly opposite. He checked his pocket for his key and made sure it was Number Twenty. It was. He opened the door, looked around the place and was satisfied. This was the very location in which he would make the decision that would affect his entire future.

Some twenty-one hours later, Laird had brewed a cup of tea and walked through from the kitchen to stand at the large windows at the front of the chalet. He took a sip. 'This is the ideal spot to sort out my life. No-one's got a clue who I am. I'm anonymous. I'm the Invisible Man.' He gulped another mouthful and gazed across to Largs. Moments later, he was spluttering, coughing and choking, tea spurting through his nostrils.

'Jeezus! It can't be,' he practically screamed. 'It's that sports reporter bloke. Charlie Brock. What the fuck's he doing here?'

Laird peered out the window. Was that Charlie Brock? Hard to tell with that enormous hood, but it certainly looked like him. The footballer continued to stare. The object of Laird's keen attention turned to plant a kiss on the cheek of his companion, his face in full view. Laird blurted, 'Fuck's sake, it IS him.'

Completely oblivious of any commotion his actions may be creating in a nearby log cabin, Charlie Brock kissed Willy and whispered, 'Let's have a nice, quiet day without a single complication.'

CHAPTER TWENTY-FIVE

12.05pm. Wednesday 24 November.

Glasgow.

Not a pretty sight at the best of times, Rodger James was never more repulsive than when he was actually smiling. The bared teeth resembled a row of condemned buildings. His sour features just weren't structured to cope with mirth. On this occasion the Uriah Heep of the newspaper world was hideously radiant.

'You know where Derek Laird is? You better not be joking, son.'

Denis Forrest was on the other end of the telephone. 'There are people out there I will not joke with, you fuckin' creep. You're most of them.'

'Oh dear, that vile tongue of yours will get you into as much trouble as your dick one day, Denis. But tell me more about Derek Laird before you fly off the handle again. Remember at all times, I've got the pictures.'

Denis Forrest had wrestled with his conscience. It hadn't been an easy decision to make this telephone call. But his marriage depended on it. He had been a team-mate of Derek Laird in the Scottish Under-16 squad; two wide-eyed kids with ambitions, both trying to break into the big-time. Torn cruciate ligaments in his right knee ended his career before it had got off the ground. He was now training schoolboys in the Largs and Fairlie districts for a living; not quite what he had in mind when he and Laird were everyone's tip for stardom. Not once did he begrudge his friend his extraordinary rise through the footballing ranks. If anything, he held up the player as an example to schoolboys to emphasise what could be achieved in the game if they applied themselves and worked hard.

Now he was about to turn Judas and he didn't feel comfortable.

It was just a stupid two-month affair with a primary school PE teacher. It meant nothing. Just a fling. He had never cheated on Melanie before and, of course, he adored Denis Jnr and Elizabeth. He would do anything for his family. But it had been laid on a plate. For two months. And he took more than just a bite of the forbidden fruit. He gorged himself silly, all the time believing he had covered his tracks. Until ...

'Hello, son, do you know who this?' Denis Forrest didn't have a clue as he looked quizzically at the receiver. 'Sorry, mate, you're going to have to be a bit more specific. Line's not too good.'

'It's Rodger James, son. Does the name mean anything? Do you read newspapers, son?'

'Oh, right, the guy from the *Trib*? THAT Rodger James? Aye, I know the name. Surprised to hear from you. How on earth did you get my number?'

'Oh, we never give out that sort of information, son. Let's just say I've got my sources. I asked a contact and he was only too happy to help.'

'All very cloak and dagger, Mr James.'

'Oh, there's an awful lot you can hide under a cloak, son,' said Smiler. 'And there's a lot of damage you can do with a dagger. Know what I mean?'

'Sorry, Mr James, haven't a clue. What can I do for you,

anyway?'

'No, son, it's what *I* can do for *you*.' Smiler was reading from a well-worn script. 'That's a nice wife you have there. Melanie, I believe. Lovely children, too, I'm told. One big happy family. That's very gratifying. Especially in this day and age when there is far too much happening outside marriages. Know what I mean now, son?'

Denis Forrest looked as though he had been hit by a jackhammer. 'Look, Mr James, thanks for the sermon, but what's this all about? Why are you phoning me?'

'Yes, you're right, son, I haven't made myself at all clear, have I? My profuse apologies. Now if I was to mention the name Carol Lafferty would that get your attention? Would that switch on the light, son?'

Carol Lafferty, Head Physical Education teacher at Biggington Primary School in Largs. Denis Forrest said nothing.

'Did I hear a penny drop there, son? Was that what I heard?' Smiler thrived on people's misery.

'Okay, I used to know a Carol Lafferty, so what? You trying to blackmail me or something? You know what I earn? You're wasting your time, pal.'

'Blackmail? Sordid, son, very sordid. No, anything but. I have something you want and I'm going to keep it safe for you. Now do you understand? I'm a benefactor, son, not a blackmailer. My goodness, perish the thought.'

'And what have *you* got, Mr James, that *I* might want?' Forrest felt sick; he had a fair idea of the response.

'Pictures, son,' whistled Smiler. 'Plenty of them. All pin-sharp and in glorious technicolour, too. I'm looking at one just now. You're not wearing a lot of clothes; well, in fact, you're completely starkers. Outdoors. Must have been a rare good summer, eh? You're standing to attention and, by the looks of it, you're more than just a little excited. Your friend also seems to be chasing an all-over tan. She's shed her clothes, too. Now here's one with her on her knees. You're very close. Is that a microphone she's talking into? Wonder what she's looking for down there. Seems to be enjoying herself. Here's another ...'

'Okay, no need to go on.'

'Oh, you get the picture?' Smiler laughed; thankfully no-one witnessed the spectacle.

'What the fuck do you want? If it's not money, what is it?'

'Well, let's act like adults, okay, son? I realise you are out of mainstream football – what a pity – but I know you can be useful to me. You could be a good ear.'

'What the fuck does that mean? Good ear?'

'We're going to have to do something about your language. I hope you don't talk like that when you've got all those weans around about you. Tsk tsk. An ear in journalism is someone who listens in to all the gossip, like an ear to the wall. Get it?'

'I don't think there's an awful lot you'll want me to tell you about the snippets I pick up unless you want to know the name of the best cartoons on the TV or the increased price of a Tornado ice cream.'

'Oh, you do yourself an injustice, son. I know you are around when the teams go down to Inverclyde to train. I've been there; great complex. Yes, that's where all the big teams go to prepare, isn't it? Facilities second to none and we don't have too many of

201

them in this country.'

'I'm nothing more than a ballboy. I erect the goals, put out the markers and all the other menial tasks no-one else can be bothered to do.'

'Correct, son. And people will talk when you're around. You're not visible, are you? And when people talk I want you to listen. I'll give you a number and I want you to phone me immediately you hear anything. I want to know what's going on. You'll get stories, I'm sure of it.'

'And if I don't?'

'Well, you will force me into making certain Melanie gets to see these photographs I have on my desk. One day when you're at work, I'll have them dropped off. Just like that. Then you might have some explaining to do when you get home, son. Make the calls and everyone will be happy and the lovely Melanie will never need to know about your shenanigans with Miss Lafferty. Okay, son? If I don't hear anything within the next couple of months I'll understand you don't want to play ball. And that's when I'll get someone to hand deliver these snaps to Melanie. Okay, son? Have I cleared up everything now, no room for doubt?'

'No room for doubt,' repeated Forrest. And no room for manoeuvre, either, he thought.

Just over a month later he made the call.

'Isle of Cumbrae? Millport? You're sure?'

'This is my first and last call to you, you bastard. I reckon you can now destroy those pictures. Now leave me alone. Just fuck off.'

Another of Smiler's little foibles was a severe lack of trust in his fellow man. He ordered, 'No-one else must know. Okay, son? This is between you and me. As for the photographs, well, we'll wait and see. It would be a shame to destroy ALL of them. Maybe I'll hold onto a couple just in case. You understand? Can't be too careful.' He smirked. 'Imagine me telling you about being careful. How ironic is that?'

At that precise moment, Denis Forrest wasn't very fond of himself. Derek Laird, he knew, had gone into hiding for reasons best known to the player. He respected that. And now this loathsome newspaper character had the information on his whereabouts, data provided by Forrest. What could he do? If Melanie ever got sight of those photographs he realised the locks on the doors would be changed by the time he got home. 'Sorry, Derek,' he said softly to himself and hung up.

He made one more call. Les Green was a freelance sports reporter who operated in Madrid. The journalist, who had previously worked at the *Mirror* in London, had met Forrest while he was at Inverclyde covering Atletico Madrid's preparations for a Europa League encounter against Celtic in Glasgow. Green remembered Forrest from the Scottish Youth set-up and they spent a rather pleasant liquid lunch in The Norseman on the Largs promenade. Green offered Forrest his card and said, 'Stick that in your wallet; you never know when it will come in useful. I pay good money for a tip-off.' Forrest felt lower than a snake's belly, but he reckoned he might as well make something out of his revelations. Surely, this creature, Smiler, would never be able to put two and two together. He took the risk and dialled the number in Madrid. He might as well receive his thirty pieces of silver. 'Forgive me, Derek,' he whispered with a fair degree of remorse.

Back in the offices of the *Tribune*, Smiler still had the telephone stuck to his ear. He was lost in thought. Why would Derek Laird try to hide in Millport? He had seen a report recently that claimed Lord Lucan had fled to the Isle of Eigg after the murder of his nanny back in the Seventies. And Smiler was aware that Eigg made Millport look like a teeming Metropolis. So, he reckoned, if someone such as Lord Lucan, with the world and its auntie searching for him, could blend in undetected with the locals on Eigg, it would be quite possible for Derek Laird to mix with the natives in Millport.

And he didn't believe it would take too much sleuthing to track down the missing footballer.

CHAPTER TWENTY-SIX

12.26pm.Wednesday 24 November.

Millport, Isle of Cumbrae.

'Charlie? Charlie Brock?'

Brock, mystified, looked at his mobile phone. He didn't recognise the number on his screen, but, in an instant, he had identified the caller.

'Derek Laird? Is that you, Derek?' He couldn't disguise the incredulity or control the excitement in his tone.

'Aye, it's me, Charlie.' Simple as that. A footballing superstar who had vanished from one of the biggest clubs in the world was on the line. It seemed completely normal, two old friends having a chat, shooting the breeze, a bit of catch-up, whiling away a moment or so.

'Derek, how did you get my number?' An off-guard experienced hack posed the question and immediately realised it wasn't the one he should have asked. 'Where are you?' would have been more appropriate in the circumstances.

'You phoned me a few months back. Remember? I kept your number on file. Hope you don't mind.'

'No, no. Great to hear from you.' Brock's head was clearing. 'Derek, where on earth are you? The whole world is looking for you.'

'Tell me about it. I just thought I would keep my head down

for a while.'

Brock laughed. 'Christ, Derek, you like your understatements, don't you? God Almighty, man, where are you? Are you okay?'

'I'm fine, don't worry about that. I wondered if I could ask a favour?'

'Fire away, Derek. I'm more likely to help than hinder. What can I do for you?'

'Look, I know this is a big story and you could earn a few bob ...'

'You do like your understatements ...'

'... but can I ask you to sit on it? I promise I'll talk to you first. You'll get the exclusive. I'll tell you everything.' There was a small pause. 'But only when I'm ready, Charlie. I don't want to talk just now.'

'No pressure here, Derek. Just tell me where you are and I'll fly out today. Tell me it's somewhere hot. The Copacabana should be nice this time of year.'

It was Laird's turn to laugh. 'No need for that, Charlie. I thought you might fancy a couple of beers.'

'When?'

'Right now.'

'Right now?' Brock furrowed his brow. 'This minute? Derek, where the hell are you?'

'Just around the corner.'

'What corner? What are you talking about?' Brock briefly wondered if someone was playing a joke on him. The Picture Editor at the *News,* Mike McNeill, was a fair mimic and Brock had been on the receiving end of his so-called wit more than a few times. Yet it did sound like Derek Laird ...

'You walked past the old boatyard about three hours ago ...'

Now Brock was convinced.

'... with a rather attractive lady.'

'The old boatyard? Here, in Millport?' The puzzled expression was back on the face of the sports reporter. He repeated, 'Derek, where the fuck are you?'

'Do you know the timber chalets just across the road from the boatyard?'

'Know them well. Almost bought one before I acquired the Schloss Adler ...'

'The Schloss what?' It was the footballer's turn to be baffled.

'Long story. Aye, right, the timber chalets. What about them?'

'Knock twice on Number Twenty and ask for Crazy Horse. You might get a wee surprise.'

'Derek, I'm as surprised as I ever want to be right at this minute.'

'See you in about fifteen minutes, then?'

'You hear that noise? That's me knocking on the door.'

CHAPTER TWENTY-SEVEN

12.32pm. Wednesday 24 November.

Barcelona.

Miguel Araquistian, the comissari of La Guardia Urbana, was standing at the full size window on the second floor of the police headquarters at Carrer Nova de la Rambla. Vigorously, he was playing with the 'worry beads' in his right trouser pocket. He was attracting some strange glances from passers-by in La Rambla.

He was lost in thought. The shrill of the telephone on his cluttered desk broke the spell. Without a trace of urgency, he meandered lazily across the office, located the telephone under today's debris and lifted the receiver. 'Araquistian,' he answered sharply.

The voice on the other end of the line was a shade more excited. 'Crazy Horse!' came the loud exclamation. 'I know where he is!'

The cop sighed heavily. 'Not again.'

Over the past twenty-four hours he had reason to believe his department had nailed the missing Barcelona footballer on several occasions. The first lead came from Laird's bank. The manager had been anything but helpful at the start, but when Araquistian's men threatened to come back with a warrant, he opened up and, subsequently, it hadn't been the easiest of tasks to get him to close down. He kept going on about some charity funds 'maybe being misappropriated'. The cops hadn't a clue what he was chattering on about. He was relieved when he was informed they were not one bit interested in misplaced charity cash for the widows and orphans. They demanded information on Derek Laird and the bank manager could be as indiscreet as he wished, the information would not lead back to him. 'He took out exactly one million, one hundred and fifty-seven thousand, three hundred and thirty-four euros yesterday,' he said.

'And you didn't ask him why he needed such a large amount?' asked Maria Dominguez, Araquistian's right-hand operative with the questionable sexual tastes.

'That's not my business,' replied the bank manager. 'It's his money. Plus he is a very good customer.' He whispered conspiratorially, 'He gets paid very well, you know.'

Dominguez remained stoney-faced, a feat which never required a lot of effort on her part. 'Anything else?'

The bank manager was happy to be of assistance; anything to keep the police away from probing more closely into the charity money that had gone astray and somehow found its way into his account.

'Yes, this may be of interest,' he offered. 'Mr Laird asked for the money to be paid in four separate currencies. He wanted sterling, dollars, yen and bhat in equal amounts.'

'And you didn't think that was unusual?' queried the cop.

'It may be unusual for you or for me, but Mr Laird is a footballer. He lives in a different world. He is not the only footballer who has an account here. We never ask questions.'

The information was relayed to Araquistian. He swept his hand through his thick black mane. With a fair degree of exasperation, he uttered, 'Well, they never said it was going to be easy.' However, he knew it had just become even more complex. Why would Derek Laird want currency for the UK, the United States,

Japan and Thailand?

A couple of hours later the cop caught a break. A young swimming pool attendant had just been apprehended. His name was Xavier Iribar. He had tried to fence foreign currency: large amounts of dollars, yen and bhat. The 'fence', unfortunately for Xavier, was an undercover cop working to snare a gang of eastern Europeans known to be working just outside La Rambla circuit, not far from Laird's villa. It didn't take long for Xavier to break down as he sat in a small, grey interview room confronted by two plain-clothes policemen. He was a good-looking eighteen year old, with long black curly hair, lively almond eyes, a small stub nose, white even teeth and a glowing smile. One of the cops described in fairly graphic detail what happened to attractive young males in the darker recesses of some of the prison cells in the city. The spacious mouth might come in handy, he was told. The cops had a full confession in a matter of minutes.

'I was sweeping the pool,' said Xavier, 'when I saw Señor Laird driving his Porsche into the garage area. He waved over; he always waved. I liked him. I saw he was carrying a large briefcase and that was most unusual. I never saw him with one of those before. About half an hour later, I saw him leaving, being picked up by someone in a car at the gates. I didn't see who was driving – I don't even know if it was male or female – and I didn't see the make of car. I'm not very good with cars. It might have been red. I didn't notice the registration plate. Why would I? I noticed, though, he did not have his briefcase. I admit I was tempted. Señor Laird had a habit of leaving a small sidedoor unlocked. I gave him five minutes or so in case he came back unexpectedly. There was no sign. I tried the handle, the door was unlocked. I knew he normally used only one of the bedrooms on the first floor. I tried the first wardrobe. Nothing. Second. Nothing. Third. *Premio maximo!* Jackpot! I looked inside the bag, so much money. I wondered if it was real. I didn't recognise it, but it looked and felt real. I thought I would find out. I was given a name.'

His head sagged forward accompanied by a deep heavy sigh. 'And here I am.' He looked pleadingly at one of the cops. 'Please don't send me to jail.'

'Okay,' said Araquistian. 'A wild goose chase. Very clever, Crazy Horse, just a pity about the opportunist thief. So now you have a lot of sterling and you are going to the UK. England? Or home to Scotland?' Another thought, 'Or are you going to change sterling elsewhere for another currency and keep us guessing?'

The cop did not need complications. He got them, anyway. Earlier, one of the first phone calls of the day had him frantically juggling with the contents of his trouser pocket. 'Crazy Horse is where?' He practically shouted down the receiver. 'Amsterdam? How do you know? His card's been used? How much? One thousand euros?'

Fifteen minutes later. 'What? Where? Rome? Don't tell me his card has been used. Yes? How much? One thousand euros? Fuck!'

'Did you say Heraklion? Where's that? Crete? And his bank card's been used? How much? One thousand euros? Fuck!' Araquistian was beginning to wonder how many Crazy Horses there were out there.

'Berlin? Let me guess, his card has been used, yes? Let me guess again, please, one thousand euros? Yes, thank you.' The 'worry beads' were in danger of being worn out.

Ricardo Osario had kept his word. And his many friends among aircraft and shipping vessel crews had done him proud. Crazy Horse asked for confusion. And Ricardo had delivered, just as Derek Laird knew he would.

So Araquistian was not overly-excited when he got this most recent call. Once again, he was informed, 'Crazy Horse! I know where he is!'

But the cop became a bit more animated when he recognised the voice of the caller. Now the cop was interested. This was no hoax call. This was from his nephew, Javier Sanchez, a sports reporter with his favourite newspaper, *La Vanguardia*. And Little Javier, who was now about six foot tall and twenty-two years old, was making a name for himself in the media. With a modicum of assistance from his proud Uncle Miguel, of course.

'Calm down, Javier,' urged Araquistian, 'I'll still be here in five minutes. What is this you say? Crazy Horse? You know where he is? Tell me, please.'

'Yes, uncle, I know. He is in *Escocia*.' Javier Sanchez's hands were shaking as he held the telephone to his lips.

'*Escocia?* Scotland?' queried the cop, his sharp mind picking up the thread. 'That makes sense. All that UK sterling.' He paused momentarily. 'How the hell did he get there? How on earth did he get out of Spain? Border Control? Useless bastards, every one of them.'

'No matter,' said his nephew. 'He is back in *Escocia* now.'

'A moment, please, Javier,' said Araquistian. 'How did you get this information? Who else knows?'

'No-one, uncle,' replied the rookie reporter who, armed with questions provided by his helpful relative, had grilled Barcelona Head Coach Rafael Castillo only hours beforehand. 'An informant in Madrid phoned to tell me. He's a freelance journalist called Les Green. Ever heard of him?'

'Rings a bell. Please continue.'

'He's been on the payroll at *La Vanguardia* for years and gives us little snippets every now and again. He phoned five minutes ago and I just happened to be passing the phone. He was looking for my boss. I told him he was out to lunch and I didn't know when he would be back. He asked me to identify myself. I did, but I got the impression he wasn't too impressed. Obviously, he had never heard of me. He asked me a couple of other questions. I tried to convince him. Then I told him you were my uncle and what you did. I hope you don't mind. That did the trick. He asked for extra money and I told him I would take care of it. Then he told me Crazy Horse had returned to *Escocia*. He even told me where he was. Just a minute, please. I asked him to spell it out for me. It is an island called Isle of Cumbrae. I'll spell it for you, three words, I-S-L-E O-F C-U-M-B-R-A-E.'

Araquistian asked his nephew to repeat it as he scribbled on a notepad. 'Okay, got it. Where on earth is this Isle of Cumbrae?'

Javier Sanchez was slightly more advanced in new technology than his uncle. 'I've googled it. It is somewhere in the Firth of Clyde off the coast of North Ayrshire. Millport is its only town. It is very small, just 3.9 kilometres long and 2 kilometres wide. It only has a population of 1,434. It's not far from Glasgow. And Crazy Horse is there. That very place. Isn't that amazing, uncle?'

Araquistian nodded and grinned. 'It's amazing he can hide on that tiny island. How many did you say? Just over 1,400? He must be a magician, able to disappear.'

'I'm going to this island,' asserted the newspaper reporter. 'It's my story and I'm going. I'll find a way. I'll check and see if I can get flights. Such a small island, maybe not. But I AM going. This is the story that could launch my career. How I would love to shove it up the arses of some of the so-called top reporters. I'd absolutely love that.' He added firmly, 'I'm going.'

'Not without me you're not, nephew,' exclaimed the cop. Technically, he realised, no crime had been committed. So far. But he was convinced his bureau chief, Comisario Principal Sergio Pirri, could be persuaded that there had been the possibility of a kidnapping. Unlikely, he thought, but not impossible. And, besides, Señor Pirri and Señor Araquistian were good friends and golf buddies. He knew there had to be a golf course on this Scottish island, no matter how diminutive. He could scout it out. There was always the possibility of a break for him and his friend in Scotland some time in the near future. 'Do they have a summer in Scotland?' he asked his nephew.

'I think so,' said the newspaper reporter, slightly bewildered. 'Not sure.'

'Doesn't matter, nephew. Look out your passport. We're heading for Scotland. Now!'

CHAPTER TWENTY-EIGHT

12.33pm. Wednesday 24 November.

Millport, Isle of Cumbrae.

R.I.P. ordered a brandy – 'Gentleman's Measure, my good man' – and moments later hoisted the glass to his lips and looked across from the front window of Hugh's Bar. He sipped and sighed. 'What's Brock up to now?' Gazing over towards the Old Pier, he noticed Charlie Brock talking earnestly on his mobile phone. 'Thought he was going to slow down when he quit the *News*. He's never worked harder.'

El Cid, quaffing an ale, his right hand stuffed into a packet of cheese and onion crisps, agreed. 'He's never stopped, has he? Maybe we should get him his old job back. What do you think?'

'I think he might tell us both to propel our heads where the sun don't shine. He's doing okay at this freelance caper. A nice, big, juicy exclusive would go down very well, I would think. Some cash in the bank for Christmas. He's not likely to get it in Millport, though, is he?'

'He's had all the excitement he's ever going to get on this island.' Vodka Joe stirred from his light slumber in his favourite corner. 'The Wild Bill Hickok experience will keep him going until they're placing the pennies on his eyes. That's the biggest hullabaloo there's been in Millport since old Jimmy Brogan was done for drink driving. Silly sod, no-one to blame but himself. Wee Fiona warned him she was under pressure from her bosses in Glasgow. Would you believe no-one had ever failed a breathalyser on this island? Come to think of it, no-one had ever been breathalysed. Not a solitary soul. Wee Fiona knew the bevvying was going on every night, but just so long as there were no accidents, she was happy enough to turn a blind eye. Christ, she was half-cut herself most of the time she was driving her Panda.'

'Wee Fiona? Oh, aye. I remember that name. She's the island's cop?' El Cid interjected.

'WAS the island's cop,' corrected Vodka Joe. 'Aye, Fiona Anderson. Now works with the Noddy bridgade in Greenock. Smashing wee lass. She was getting a lot of grief from the high heid yins across the water and she was told someone would have to be sacrificed.'

'And Jimmy Brogan was the unfortunate bloke to make history?'

'Aye, he did that. Fiona went round every pub and hotel and implored everyone to leave their cars if they were drinking. She warned everyone to screw the bobbin. She knew all the booze bags. Christ, some of them used their cars for travelling one hundred yards or so. Hardly worth their while fiddling about with the car keys. Take them longer to locate the bloody ignition. Could have walked home. Anyway, poor old Jimmy got done.'

'I take it he wasn't in a fatal smash or anything like that?' El Cid's curiosity had been tugged.

'No, nothing like that. Nobody dead. Or even hurt. Not a scratch. But he was involved in a smash and Wee Fiona just couldn't look the other way on this occasion.'

'Lot of damage done, then, I take it?'

'No, not really. Bumper bent, rear headlights smashed ...'

'And that was enough for this guy Jimmy to be done for drink driving?'

'Well, it was Fiona's Panda, after all.'

The cop laughed. 'I suppose the guy was asking for it. That was a bit unfortunate, was it not?'

'Aye, even worse, though. Jimmy was the island's only taxi driver. He was off the road for eighteen months and his missus had to do all the driving. She wasn't best pleased, I can tell you that. Crabbit for a full year-and-a-half. Everybody gave her a wide berth. Never the life and soul of the party at the best of times. No wonder Jimmy took a wee Salvador.'

The Detective Inspector gulped down a mouthful of beer. 'Hey, newshound, what's happening with Charlie?' he asked. 'Is he heading over here? Even, more importantly, is he heading over here with the enchanting Willy? And where on earth did he find her, by the way?'

Hughie, returning after changing a barrel of Guinness in the bowels of his establishment, caught El Cid's question. 'Lucky bastard,' he smiled.

'That's Willy just coming out of the door.' The newspaperman hadn't realised he was now giving a running commentary on the movement of his sports-reporting pal and his female friend. 'Brock's put the mobile in his coat pocket. Now they're having a wee kiss. Arm-in-arm now. Where are they going? Not in this direction, anyhow. Heading round Clyde Street? No pubs there. Not like Brock to pass up some valuable drinking time. Wait a minute, they're heading up Cardiff Street. Wonder where they're off to? McIntosh's?'

'You fancy a bit of sleuthing?' El Cid could see the possibilities for some fun. 'Let's tail them, see what they're getting up to. Might catch them in the act. What do you say?' He scoffed the remainder of his beer and turned to the bar owner. 'As much as I thoroughly enjoy the delicacies and delights of your well-stocked bar, Hughie, I would like to remain upright by the time midnight is upon us. Some fresh air will be well received.'

'You don't think Brock will think we're snooping, do you?' R.I.P. was wary. 'Don't want to fall out with him. We need a roof over our heads for the next couple of nights, remember.'

'Ach, it's just a jolly wheeze. What can be so important that it will upset our old mate?'

'Point taken. Come on then, Sherlock, the game's afoot.'

CHAPTER TWENTY-NINE

12.35pm. Wednesday 23 November.

Glasgow.

With a triumphant flourish, Rodger James replaced the telephone on its cradle, leapt to his feet, grabbed his grubby gaberdine coat from the back of his chair and, in his usual annoying fingernails-scraping-down-a-blackboard nasal drone, screeched to a copy boy, 'Arrange a chariot, son. A front page beckons.'

The *Tribune's* chief sportswriter was on the move. Grinning through his personal broken-down Tombstone Territory, he could already visualise the story in the newspaper. The banner headline was already written and would shriek in giant capitals, **'I TRACK DOWN CRAZY HORSE!'** The sub-deck, in lower case, would be along the lines of, **'How I found football's missing Golden Boy'**. There would be no hint of where the information had come from. It was his source and it would remain that way. In any case, Smiler was never going to become famous for sharing the plaudits; the glory was always his and his alone. He cackled. 'Okay, Crazy Horse, here I come, my friend. You can't hide from Smiler.'

Charlie Brock often insisted it didn't matter how much you lowered the bar of expectation, Smiler would still find away of slithering under it. All of which meant little to the *Trib*'s sports reporter. Insults were oxygen to him. 'Next stop Millport,' he said to no-one in particular as he slipped into the coat. He stopped to stuff a notebook into his pocket and ignored the half-eaten sausage roll on his desktop. 'That'll still be there when I get back,' he observed. The office cleaning staff had long since refused to go within a few feet of Smiler's workplace. 'We don't want rabies,' they had informed the newspaper bosses and, after one look at the discarded mess that adorned his desk, the Health and Safety people, always fearful of unknown strains of bacteria, agreed to the cleaners' plea.

Smiler, impatient as ever, couldn't be bothered waiting for the elevator to make its way to the editorial on the second floor. He took the stairs, two at a time, as he headed for the taxi he knew would be waiting for him. When Smiler snapped his fingers it was a good idea to enquire, 'Which hoop? And how high?' He looked at his wristwatch. It was nudging 12.38pm. He smiled, realising the hourly service from Glasgow Central Station to Largs would be taking off in some twenty minutes to cover the twenty-four miles to Largs. He would be within touching distance of the Isle of Cumbrae in just over an hour.

'Then it's onto the ferry and let the fun in Millport really begin,' he snorted disgustingly, after throwing open the taxi door and settling his scrawny frame on the back seat. 'Central Station,' he grunted. 'And make it quick, no detours.' The cab driver, Larry Wilson, had been with the taxi company for three years and he knew never to question Smiler. 'Millport, eh?' he thought. 'Interesting. Very interesting.' He pointed the vehicle in the direction of Gordon Street.

As usual, Smiler had little difficulty in refraining from the pleasantries of idle chit-chat or the preposterous notion of offering a tip to the driver. He handed him a taxi chit and said with undisguised menace, 'I'll be checking that. No waiting time, right?'

As usual, Larry Wilson replied, 'No, of course not, Mr James.

No waiting time.'

They reached their destination in a matter of minutes. As Smiler prepared to step out of the cab, not bothering to observe the niceties of a 'thank you' or a 'goodbye' to the driver, he fished out his mobile phone from his top pocket. He telephoned sports desk secretary Marge Dawson. 'Arrange a hotel room in Millport tonight,' he barked just before he slammed the door behind him. Ever distrustful of leaks to the opposition, he added, 'Put it in the name of James Stewart. Okay? Let me know asap. Somewhere nice. Have they got any good hotels in Millport?' He didn't wait for a reply as he clicked off, crossing Gordon Street and heading for Central Station.

Cab driver Larry Wilson drove back towards his company's depot in Govan. Speedy Kabs had had the contract with the *Tribune* for four years and the drivers were ordered to drop everything to pick up their reporters. The newspaper workers were top priority. The drivers were told to be particularly efficient and courteous when it came to a bloke called Rodger James. He was an acquaintance of the boss of Speedy Kabs and thought nothing about making a complaint, no matter how trivial. Having lit the touchpaper James would sit back and wait for some unfortunate to be summoned, handed a P45 and dumped onto the dole. Little things like that helped Smiler make it through the day.

Before checking in again at control, Wilson pulled his taxi over on the Broomielaw to make a telephone call. He checked a card and tapped out the number.

'Hello, Mr Crawley, remember me? Larry Wilson? The taxi driver? You gave me your number last night and told me to give you a call if I thought anything was important?' He grinned. 'I think this is important.'

221

The previous evening, Adam Crawley, Scottish football's latest impending big-money export to England, had had a few drinks at a sports function in Glasgow before ordering a taxi to take him home to Morningside in Edinburgh. As so many people do, with the exception of Smiler, he chatted freely, opening up to the taxi driver, a complete stranger. Taxi drivers, bar staff and hairdressers. Was it really part of their job description to listen to the world's problems? As luck would have it, the name of Rodger James disturbed the peace as the cab radio crackled to life with the voice of a dispatcher. The *Tribune's* chief sports reporter was looking for a taxi. Urgently, as ever. Crawley growled, 'Skinny, horrible bastard.'

Larry Wilson nodded. 'Not many people appear to like that bloke, Mr Crawley. Not the most charismatic guy I've come across, anyway. You know him?'

'Aye, I know him,' replied the footballer. 'Wish I didn't.' Even though he had a few Brandy Alexanders too many, a sudden thought occurred. He said to the taxi driver, 'You must know him, eh?'

'Pick him up just about every second night. Still waiting for my first tip.'

Crawley ignored the additional comment. 'So, you know where he lives?'

'Aye, over Pollokshields way. Big stone villa.' The taxi driver grinned. 'You thinking of paying a visit? Firebomb his house? Give him a kicking or something like that? I could sell tickets. Fifty/fifty spilt. We'll make a fortune.'

Crawley took a breath before responding. 'Between you, me and your meter, I would love to kick the crap out of that stick insect, use him as a fuckin' football. Not on his front doorstep, though. I'd never get away with that.' He paused. 'Is he married, do you know?'

'Never seen a Mrs James,' answered the cabbie. 'Who the fuck would marry that streak of misery?'

Crawley went silent again for a moment. 'Listen, what's your name?'

'Larry,' replied the taxi driver. 'Larry Wilson.'

Crawley took out his wallet, worked his way through a bulge of credit and debit cards and handed a personal card to the driver. 'There's my mobile number, Larry. Don't give it out to anyone. I get any daft calls, I'll change the number overnight. Okay? Can I trust you?'

'Get me a signed Scotland top and we'll say no more.' The driver saw an opening and went for it.

'Consider it done,' said Crawley. 'I'll take care of it. But I need a favour from you. Let me know when that bastard is away from home. When he's on the road and where's he's going. Could be interesting to have some gen on this creep. I'm in Edinburgh for the next few days. I've got to tie up some loose ends. But I'll not be far away. Anything within the next day or so and I'll make sure you get the signed strip and a few quid. Tell anyone and I'll say this conversation never took place. No bragging to your mates or anything. Understand?'

'Aye, I understand okay, Mr Crawley,' answered Wilson. 'I don't like the bastard, either.'

Some eighteen-odd hours later, Larry Wilson checked the card and punched in the number. 'I think this is important, Mr Crawley.'

223

The footballer gave the taxi driver his full attention. 'Call me Adam. Okay, what's so important?'

Larry Wilson imparted his news.

Silence for a moment and then a chuckle, 'Millport? You're kidding? Why is that undernourished rake going to Millport? A bit late to top up his suntan.'

'That's what I heard him say, Adam,' added the taxi driver now cosily on first-name terms with a famous footballer. 'And just before I drove away, I heard him ordering some lackey to get him a hotel room, so, presumably, he's planning on staying one night, at least.'

Crawley was interested. 'What the fuck is he going to get up to in Millport?'

'Don't know, but I've seen him like this before,' said the cabbie. 'He's on a story, I'll bet you anything you like. He's sniffing. Defo. He was smiling that horrible smile of his through those rotten teeth. He's onto something, I'm telling you.'

Adam Crawley couldn't prevent himself from conjuring up a mental picture of Smiler grinning. He shuddered and then looked at his wristwatch. He wondered how fast he could get to Largs. He had done the journey several times when the Scottish international squad trained at the Inverclyde sports centre before a big game. He was well acquainted with the fastest route to the seaside resort. And then over to Millport.

Larry Wilson added, 'He said something about "let the fun begin". Something like that.'

'Let the fun begin, indeed,' said Adam Crawley.

CHAPTER THIRTY

12.42pm. Wednesday 24 November.

Millport, Isle of Cumbrae.

Willy linked arms with Charlie Brock once more, the early afternoon chill making its unwelcome presence obvious as it whisked around the Old Pier. 'Is it always this exciting in your life?' she queried.

'Sometimes I find it pretty much nigh impossible to catch my breath,' smiled the sports reporter. 'Only a couple of weeks ago I saw two goals at Broadwood when Clyde drew with Peterhead.'

'Seriously, though, Charlie, this guy Crazy Horse is here in Millport?' she asked. 'The bloke they've all been talking about? The bloke who's been in the newspapers and on the telly? He's here? In Millport? Is this a joke?'

'No joke, Willy,' replied Brock. 'I'm sitting on the sports story of the century. Right here. In Millport. Amazing. Fuckin' amazing.'

'So, what happens next, Scoop?'

The couple began moving in the direction of Cardiff Street, the wind whipping about and snapping at their faces. 'Let's get over to the chalets at the boatyard and have a chat with the man himself. Let's hear what he's got to say.' Brock stopped momentarily and shook his head. 'First Wild Bill Hickok and now Crazy Horse. You couldn't make it up.'

'Do you know this guy well? I heard you say in Hughie's that you knew him from his Albion Rovers days. Did you say you talked to him only a few months ago? Any clues there?'

'No, not a thing I can think of. Straightforward interview. Barcelona were due to play Manchester United in a Champions League game and I was just looking for a wee preview. He scored two goals for Arsenal at Old Trafford and I was asking him if it was it a happy hunting ground, stuff like that. We were on the phone for the best part of half an hour. He was chatty enough; absolutely no problem. If there was something worrying him he certainly hid it well.'

'Would he have told you if there was a problem?' Willy was intrigued.

'Doubt it. I would say we were friendly enough, but not at that level. I always got the impression he was quite happy in his own company. I did him a couple of wee turns when he was at Rovers. Unknown at the time, so I gave him a wee bit of publicity. Put his name in the papers, wrote a couple of pieces for some magazines. **"YOUNG SCOT FOR THE FUTURE."** That sort of thing. Got him some snaps of himself playing, too. You would have thought I had handed him a lottery win. The littlest things. We kept in touch, a phone call every now and again, a wee plug here and there. To be fair to the lad, he still kept in touch when he went to London. He phoned me to give me the story of the transfer to Arsenal. Nice exclusive for the *News*, scooped Fleet Street with that one. Colleagues across the border not too happy. Boo hoo. But, of course, the phone calls gradually became fewer and fewer; the lad had a new career. All understandable stuff. And he gave me a wee hint of the Barcelona transfer, too. Smiler was on the case and ...'

'Smiler?'

'Oh, you don't want to know, Willy. His name's Rodger James. Works for the *Trib*. I'll never introduce you to him, don't worry.

After a meeting with this guy it's mandatory to go home and burn your clothes. He once fell into quicksand and it spat him back out. You know when you roll back a rock and you see all those disgusting little bugs scurrying around and you say "Yuk"? Well, those insects look at Smiler and THEY say "Yuk". Pestokil wanted to use his image on the side of their vans. Horrible, vile guy. He's got a face like a constipated turtle.'

'What does a constipated turtle look like?'

'Smiler. All the warmth of a breeze block. Flowers wilt and die when he's within a twenty-yard radius. Puppies commit ...'

'Okay, I get the drift, Charlie. Hit a raw nerve, perchance?'

'Aye, you're right, let's stop talking about that repulsive skinny turd. He'll get his one day. Hopefully soon. I wouldn't mind being around to witness that.'

'Tell me more about Crazy Horse. I'm interested, honestly.'

'I've always found him to be a good lad. No airs or graces. There are a lot of pretentious twats in football, but, thankfully, he's not one of them. Still one of the boys. Not a big drinker, but he does like the ladies.'

'Just like George Best?'

'Well, maybe not on Bestie's scale, but he does okay, that's for sure. Maybe I'll keep you away from him.'

'Maybe you'll *have* to.'

'Hmmm, so you're only hanging around with me to meet some mega-rich handsome footballer? Then I get the elbow. I can see it all now. You want to be a WAG?'

'What on earth is a WAG?'

'Surely you know. All the birds who hang around famous footballers. They're wives and girlfriends; WAGS for short.'

The couple continued climbing the steep hill, Brock not even tempted to stop for a snifter at McIntosh's. When there was business to be taken care of, he was a professional. Anyway, if this story panned out as Brock expected and hoped, he might have enough cash to *buy* McIntosh's.

Willy broke into his brief reverie. 'And your friend Crazy Horse has plenty of these WAGS, then?'

'Well, he doesn't have a wife. Unless he's done something on the quiet.'

'Maybe that's why he's gone missing? Got drunk, got married, wakened up and thought, "My God, what have I done?" And then done a runner? Happens all the time, doesn't it? The old joke, "I've never gone to bed with a dog, but I've wakened up with a few." You know it?'

'Unfortunately, Willy, I've *lived* it.' He added swiftly, 'Not recently, of course. But I just don't see Derek Laird quite in that mould, to be honest. Just taking off like that? Too level-headed. No, as far as I'm aware, he's happy just playing the field. He's good looking, twenty-five, made a few million and probably has another six or seven years left in the tank if he takes care of himself. Going missing just doesn't fit his DNA. There's got to be a very good reason and, hopefully, we're about to find out. At least we can rule out kidnapping now, so that's a relief.' Brock stopped in his tracks as they turned the corner from Cardiff Street onto West Bay Road. 'This is just unbelievable. Truly incredible.'

He failed to notice the two figures furtively following some one hundred yards behind.

'He's up to something, R.I.P. I'm sure of it. I can feel it in my beer,' said El Cid.

'I didn't realise you worked on intuition, mate,' said the newspaperman.

'I don't. But I have the feeling that some day I will.'

CHAPTER THIRTY-ONE

12.57pm. Wednesday 24 November.

Millport, Isle of Cumbrae.

The door creaked open a couple of inches and, furtively, Derek Laird squinted through the crack. He was greeted with, 'Is Crazy Horse coming out to play, mister?' Charlie Brock and his friend, introduced moments later as Willy, were standing on the top step leading up to the front door of the little wooden chalet. So this was the place chosen as a hideaway for one of the world's best-known footballers in his attempt to vanish off the face of the planet? Without preamble, both were ushered in. Laird poked his head out for a moment and had a quick look around. Satisfied, he closed the door and clicked the lock. 'Can't be too careful.'

He walked towards the kitchen. 'Want a beer, Charlie? Young lady? Willy, is it? I've got some white wine, that okay?'

Brock nodded and noted that Willy had flashed one her best dazzling smiles at the footballer. Did she want to join the ranks of the WAGs? Willy turned to her companion. 'Did you hear that? "Young lady?" The lad's got manners.'

'He's also got bad eyesight.' Brock didn't see the dig in the ribs coming. Laird padded back through. He handed Willy a full glass of Prosecco. 'You would never get a job in a pub, Derek. Too generous with your measures,' she said rather naughtily.

'Aye, I've had that complaint before.' At least the AWOL footballer hadn't lost his sense of humour. A good sign, noted Brock, as he accepted a bottle of Stella Artois. Laird went back to retrieve a bottle of lager and sat on a comfy, well-worn chair by the unlit fireplace. Brock and Willy settled down on a tartan-bedecked sofa in front of him with a well-scuffed coffee table in between them. There was a five-second silence. The footballer looked at the sports reporter. Brock took the hint. 'Nothing to worry about, Derek. Willy is perfectly trustworthy, I can assure you.'

Willy smiled radiantly again. 'That's what you think, Charlie Boy.' The light-hearted comment helped ease what little tension there was in the room.

'I've created a wee bit of a kerfuffle, Charlie, eh?' said Laird.

'Kerfuffle? Aye, I suppose you could say that,' nodded Brock. 'It's not a word I've come across in the newspapers to describe your current situation, I must admit. It wouldn't be one I would use, either, to be honest. I saw a headline in the *Trib* proclaiming it was a **"MULTI-MILLION POUND MYSTERY"**. They also had a comment piece by Rodger James telling us all that Crazy Horse really WAS Crazy. Do you know him? Rodger James? Smiler?'

'Heard of him, don't know him,' said Laird. 'One to be avoided, I'm told.'

'At all costs, Derek. Shake hands with him and make sure you still possess a spleen. Nasty piece of work. Gives guys like me a bad name.'

'And you're doing a good enough job yourself.'

'I'm one of the guys wearing a white hat, you know me. I'm a human being first and a journalist second. Some others out there tend to get a bit confused. Presumably, Señor Horse, that was why you got in touch with me in the first place. *Si?*'

'Of course,' nodded Laird, taking a swig of beer. 'Look, I'm sorry for being mysterious, so please bear with me for the moment.

I can't tell you everything. Not right now. But I will and that's a promise. I bet you're dying to fire off a couple of questions.'

'Another great understatement.'

'But please hold off. You might wonder why I'm here in Millport?'

'Never crossed my mind for a moment,' grinned Brock. 'And, by the way, you are invited to the national newspapers' annual awards ceremony in London next week when I pick up my Investigative Reporter of the Year honour.'

'Yeah, knew you would walk away with that one,' laughed Laird.

Willy was fascinated. This was not how they conducted these interviews in the movies or on television. On screen, it was all hard-nosed stuff, probing questions, heavy debate and some pretty clever deductions along the way. Even she realised this was a monumental tale. Here, right in front of her a few feet away, was the highly-valued sportsman who had come off the radar and had the world searching for him. And, right beside her, the reporter with a breaking story at his fingertips. But they were talking a lot of nonsense, like two sozzled punters propping up a bar. Not what she had expected at all.

'Okay,' said Brock, 'I'll ask a few questions and you can answer the ones you want to and ignore the others. That seem like a plan?'

'Seems fair to me. On you go, give it your best shot.'

'Money problems?'

'Nope.'

'Drugs?'

'Heaven forbid. Nope.'

'Women?'

'Nothing there, either, I'm afraid. Perfectly happy with the women in my life although I might have some explaining to do when I get home.'

'Murdered anyone?'

'Been tempted,' laughed Laird, 'but held off so far.'

'Gun smuggling?'

Another smile. 'Ditto.'

'Mixed up with some bad guys? Gambling?'

'No chance. I give those guys a body swerve. Bad news, that lot.'

'Trouble at the club? Some friction between you and the players? The manager?'

'Nope, all clear on that front, too. Players are all good guys, well, most of them. And the manager is a lovely bloke.'

'Okay, why Millport? You could have gone anywhere, literally *anywhere*, and yet you chose to come here. Why?'

'I can answer that one straight off the bat. Solitude. My parents took me here on holiday about twenty years or so ago. I've always remembered it as a quiet wee place without any fuss. It's funny what sticks in your mind, isn't it? My mum ran out of milk one day. I recall she was making porridge. It was about one o'clock in the afternoon. She gave me some money and told me to get down as fast as I could to the shops to get another pint before they closed for the day. Shops closing in the afternoon. For the rest of the day! I was amazed. A place that peaceful and quiet. Daft

233

wee story, I know, but one that's been locked away in my memory banks. I realise now it must have been a Wednesday because I know from walking along the front that's the day the entire island completely shuts down and rolls up the pavements. Incredible, really. Shops closed everywhere. Couldn't they come to some sort of arrangement? Agree to alternate days? Anyway, that's the quirkiness of Millport and that's why I'm here.'

'You didn't have to phone me, Derek. Did you think I might recognise you and blow the whistle?'

'Genuinely, that did not cross my mind. Yes, you would have recognised me, that's for sure. But I didn't think for a second you would have gone running to the papers. More likely, I think you would have confronted me. But that was never an issue, believe me.'

'What was, then?'

'Do you want to know the truth?'

'That would help.' Brock encouraged Laird.

'When I saw you with Willy walking past the boatyard out there my first reaction was that of shock. I thought I had been rumbled. Then I recalled you were a decent bloke.' He hesitated and looked at Willy. 'You've got yourself a good one there.'

'Oh, I haven't got him.' Willy almost blushed. 'Not yet.'

Brock looked mildly surprised as Laird continued. 'You were one of the rare sports journalists I had met who had never tried to stitch me up. I know you could have, but I appreciated that you never did. That meant a lot to me. I just wanted someone I could trust. Even my parents don't know I'm here. Imagine that? I phoned them a couple of days before I "disappeared", if that's the word, to let them know I would be in the headlines. I stressed they were not to worry. I knew the reporters would be door-stepping them – that's what you call it, isn't it? – and I didn't want to burden them with too much knowledge. My old mum's such an honest person she would have probably told them, anyway. All they needed to know was that I was safe and not to worry. When I saw you and this lovely damsel' – he smiled at Willy – 'then I thought we should make contact. Someone I could talk to. I had your number from the call you made a few months ago and I prayed that you hadn't changed it. I copied it down and phoned you from this other mobile which I'll now drop into the Clyde. I suppose I surprised you, eh?'

'One day I'll sit down with you and spell out the difference between a surprise and a shock, Derek. A surprise is seeing a naked lady walking down the High Street. A shock is seeing that the naked lady is your wife. I think that's the best way I can put it.'

'Interesting analogy, Brock. I'll use it some day. But that's the truth of the matter. I suddenly felt very lonely. Yes, I know all this is my choice and I did the running away. I wasn't going to sit down with the club's shrink. I wasn't quite ready for the couch. And, anyway, I wanted to sort out my own head before I talked to anyone else. Sorry, Brock, I still haven't reached that stage. I will soon enough, I know that. Then I'll tell you first. I might even ask for some advice. After all, you are that bit older than me, aren't you?' He looked at Willy. 'In fact, a fair bit older than everyone else in this chalet.'

'Why, thank you, kind sir,' said Willy, violet eyes dancing, eyelashes fluttering.

'You kids want me to leave and come back in five minutes or so?' Brock smiled. 'Just pass me my zimmer.'

Willy and the footballer winked at each other. She could see why Derek Laird did so well with the femmes in Barcelona. The world appeared to be collapsing around his shoulders, but he still had time to be a charmer.

'So, Charlie, that's where I am at the moment. I'm not going to hide out forever. In all probability, I'll be back playing football in a couple of weeks. I'll take my punishment, pay my fine, accept the flak and get on with it. And, before you ask, my health is fine, mentally and physically. And, no, I do not have the dreaded lurgy or whatever the latest must-have designer disease is these days. I'm perfectly fine.'

'Well, you look okay to me,' said Willy.

'Why, thank you, kind lady,' returned Laird.

'Oh, for God's sake. Any chance of another beer?' smiled Brock. 'I've already seen *Runaway Bride*. Didn't fancy it and I fancy even less being an extra in the sequel.'

'*Runaway Superstar*,' said Willy. 'I like it. Wonder who gets to play the girl?'

'Just a passing thought, Derek,' Brock broke in. 'You're not on the run because you screwed the chairman's wife, by any chance? These things happen.'

'Have you seen the chairman's wife? A Greek pal of mine runs a fabulous restaurant in Barcelona and he has a saying for ageing folk. "They're so old they forget to die." I'm afraid she comes into that category.'

'And has the chairman got a daughter?'

'The chairman has a GRANDdaughter,' said Laird. 'But that's another story.'

CHAPTER THIRTY-TWO

4.52pm.Wednesday 24 November.

Largs, North Ayrshire Coast.

Miguel Araquistian, a portly middle-aged Spanish cop with La Guardia Urbana, and his nephew, Javier Sanchez, ambitious young sports reporter with *La Vanguarde*, stood at the Largs slip. The wind shrieked as it rattled its ferocious route along the promenade.

The frantic two-and-a-half hour flight from Barcelona to Glasgow had been a bumpy ride but, as Araquistian observed, 'it was relatively crash free'. The taxi journey from the airport to the North Ayrshire coastal resort had taken just under an hour. And had been just as jarring. Now all they needed to do was hop aboard the Cal-Mac ferry, get across to the Isle of Cumbrae, make their way round to Millport and find Crazy Horse. The cop could then reassure his police boss at the Barcelona bureau to call off the nationwide search for the missing footballer. And his nephew reporter could file his exclusive story. Everybody happy. As easy as falling off a log. Whatever that meant.

It was the Spaniards' first visit to Scotland and they had been warned of the 'savage' winters. Both looked as though they had copied the dress sense of Nanook of the North, with heavy tan hide coats down to their ankles, topped off with enormous fur-lined hoods. They had tucked their trousers into calf-length boots. One of their fellow-travellers on the ten-minute journey across the Firth of Clyde strip was Effie MacKenzie. She eyed the pair. 'Ye'll be lookin' fur a wee igloo then, Ah suppose, when ye get ower there?' she noted, smiling. Araquistian and Sanchez both had a reasonable grasp of the English language. They looked blankly at each other. 'Sorry, we don't understand,' said the cop, adding by way of explanation, 'We are Spanish.'

Wee Effie squinted from under the hirsute caterpillar that streaked across her forehead. 'Ye'll be frae Barcelona, then? Like Manuel? *Fawlty Towers*?'

Araquistian made out the word 'Barcelona', not pronounced properly but close enough. '*Si*,' he said, wondering how on earth this strange-looking little lady knew he and his nephew were from that particular location in Spain. 'Were all Scotswomen possessed of the devil?' He looked at his travelbag. Yes, the tag clearly showed his address in Barcelona; that must have been it. He nodded. Effie, determined to provide a little impromptu entertainment for the other twelve bored-rigid passengers waiting for the ferry to arrive, said, 'Aye, it's okay, they're from Barcelona.' She tried to sound like John Cleese as Basil Fawlty. Araquistian and Sanchez looked again at each other. The cop whispered, 'Are all women in this country like her? An *idiota*? An *imbecila*?' They frowned and looked out to the restless waves of the Firth of Clyde, doing their best to avoid the gaze of Wee Effie.

She strained to hear what the older of the pair had just said. Effie turned to Fran, her domino partner in Robbie's every Tuesday and Thursday afternoon, and said, 'Wid ye listen to that? Ah ken they're talkin' aboot me, aye they ur so they ur. Next thing ye ken they'll be wanting me tae go back wi' them to yon Barcelona. Ye ken whit these foreigners ur like. Ah'll need to put them right.'

Effie practically spun Araquistian off his feet as she grabbed him by the elbow. Before he had the chance to utter a word, she pointed to where he supposed her breasts may be located under the thick labyrinth of tweed clothing. 'See these, senior amigo,' she said emphatically. 'Nae promiscuity. Understaun? Nae promiscuity. Just cos Ah'm friendly ye shouldnae get the wrang idea. These ur fur ma Alfie and naebody else.' She pointed again to her well-hidden bosom. 'Nae promiscuity,' she repeated. Effie turned to Fran. 'There, Ah think that's got the message across, eh?'

'*Tonto*,' thought the cop. '*Completo tonto.*'

'Uncle, how difficult can it be to hide on such a small island?' asked Sanchez.

Araquistian shrugged, 'A magician can hide anywhere. There is the saying, is there not, that sometimes it is best to hide in plain sight? Maybe we will find him as soon as we land on this island. What is it called ... Isle of Cumbrae? He might be right under our noses.'

'Then, uncle, why are the Scottish police not doing anything about it? They must want to find him, too. Yes?'

'Oh, nephew, I have no idea how the police work in this country.' He grinned. 'Maybe they are too busy rounding up small crazy women and locking them away.'

Both laughed out loud. The closest Wee Effie had come to Spain was watching the sitcom *Benidorm* on telly and brushing against the paella shelf in Morrisons. She wondered why the foreigners looked so happy. And why the hell were they going to Millport in November? She had to solicit more information out of these visitors to her island. Once again, Araquistian came close to being yanked off his feet as she grabbed his elbow.

'Hey, senior amigo, ma pal wants to know whit yer daein' here. Who ur ye, anywey?' Wee Effie was a shade more inquisitive than normal; possibly the three dark rums, consumed in haste with Fran

239

in Smithies, were kicking in.

The cop looked to his nephew for some assistance. The reporter shrugged his shoulders. '*No comprendo*,' he mouthed.

'Fran, they've got somethin' to hide,' said Effie. 'They're no' answerin'. She hauled Araquistian closer. 'Yer no' a spy or onythin' like that, ur ye? We dinnae get too many o' yon spies in Millport.' She looked the cop up and down and decided. 'Naw, ye're too glaikit tae be a spy. Nae offence. Nuthin' wrang wi' glaikit people, Christ knows we've got oor ferr sherr o' them in Millport, but Ah dinnae think they wid make good spies, ye ken?'

Araquistian was known to have a fly trap mind that snapped up morsels of information in an instant. Every piece of material would be assimilated in moments, pieced together with impeccable precision. More often than not, it would lead to an instant arrest. He was not the commisara de La Guardia Urbana in Barcelona for nothing. He observed his wild-eyed antagonist with the bizarre eyebrows. She had him stumped. Maybe his English wasn't quite as good as he thought. His nephew wasn't much help, either. He shrugged his shoulders.

'Senior amigo,' menaced Effie, 'we'll be keepin' an eye oan ye ower there, ye ken? Step oot o' line and we'll a' come doon on ye like a ton o' bricks. Nane o' oor men ur chicken-hertit. Ma Alfie's a ferr fechter when he gets his dander up. Ye dinnae want to see him in yon mood wi' his dander up. He had wee brawl with a neighbour wance. Rigor mortis had set in for aboot four hoors before he wis brought roon. We're no' too keen oan dodgy interlopers wi' big, daft claes, ye ken?'

Araquistian smiled and nodded. His nephew smiled and nodded.

'Jus' so's ye ken,' said Wee Effie.

CHAPTER THIRTY-THREE

5.02pm. Wednesday 24 November.

Millport, Isle of Cumbrae.

'Bet you he's dead.' Vodka Joe, sitting in his personal neuk in Hugh's Bar, seemed fairly confident in his prediction.

'Who?' Bar owner Hughie Edwards emitted a tired, deep, groaning sound. 'Elvis Presley? The old King? Archduke Franz Ferdinand? The Archbishop of Canterbury? Mickey Mouse? Any chance you could be a tad more specific?'

'Crazy Horse, of course,' snapped back Vodka Joe, somewhat irritated. 'Keep up, Hughie. Who have we been talking about for the last few days? That rich bastarding footballer who's gone missing. Bet you he's dead. Stands to reason, doesn't it? Forget this kidnapping nonsense, for a start. Nobody's looking for a ransom. Why would anyone bother snatching him if they didn't want a couple of million? His chopped-off fingertips would be falling out of envelopes in every cop shop in Barcelona, wouldn't they?'

Hughie stopped scouring the pint glass for a moment. How many police stations were there in Barcelona?

'How many fingers do you think Derek Laird possesses?' he asked the regular incumbent of the sofa in the corner of his pub.

'And there have been no sightings of him, either.' Vodka Joe ignored the question and charged ahead. 'So where is he? Dead. At the bottom of a river somewhere.'

'Sleeping with the fishes, perhaps?' sighed Hughie, who had

heard it all before.

'Got it in one. He's upset the Mafia and they've sent round Luca Brasi to do him in.'

'How many times have you watched *The Godfather*, Vodka?'

'About fifty-odd by now. Why?'

'It WAS Luca Brasi who was done in. It WAS Luca Brasi who went to sleep with the fishes.'

'Never! You sure? Can't be! Not Luca Brasi. He's my hero. No way.'

'Go and watch the movie at least one more time and put yourself out of your misery. They nail Luca Brasi's hands to the table and then they strangle him ...'

'That was another guy.'

'No, it wasn't, take my word for it. It WAS Luca Brasi. Have you read the book, by any chance?'

'You know I don't have the time to read a book,' Vodka Joe sniffed indignantly, lifting another glass to his lips: he was now well into double figures for the day.

'Well, I have. A bloke called Mario Puzo wrote it. Did you know he did the screenplay for the first *Superman* film? Anyway, the way he writes it, Luca Brasi loses control of his bowels and slips on his own shit and pish. Or, if I remember correctly, as Puzo wrote it, "his faeces and urine". Either way, it WAS Luca Brasi who was strangled. And James Caan received a fish wrapped in a towel, which was the Sicilian Mob's way of saying Luca Brasi was sleeping with the fishes.' Hughie wore the smile of the triumphant before enquiring, 'By the way, are you ever sober when you watch movies?'

'Some of the time.' Again the outraged tone. 'I'm no' Barry Norman. I don't have to write about the damn things.'

'Give *The Godfather* another try. Maybe a good idea to do it before you come round here knocking on the door before I get a chance to open up in the morning.'

'Doesn't matter. Bet you this Crazy Horse guy is no longer in the land of the living. He's got everything on a plate and then he disappears. Birds, good-looking ones at that, with massive gazongas, flash cars ... and did you see the picture in the paper of his house? Christ, it was like a hotel. Swimming pool, saunas, a hundred bedrooms. And a fuckin' cinema. Christ, how lucky can you get?'

'He might not be feeling too lucky at the moment, my little friend.'

'Aye, and that's because he sleeps with the fishes.' Vodka Joe scratched the three-day growth on his chin. 'You sure Luca Brasi's dead?'

'Definitely, Vodka. He's gone to meet his Cod.'

A giraffe's arse; it was over Vodka Joe's head.

The door scraped open accompanied with its usual inconvenient sweep of uninvited cold air. Dr. Algernon Pendlebury peered into the pub. 'Is this a private party or can anyone join in?' he asked. Neither Hughie nor Vodka Joe responded.

The island's GP made his way to the bar. 'Hughie, I have heard such good things about a cheeky little white wine by the name of *Chateaunuef du Cumbrae* and I would like to get acquainted with such a beverage. I am of the belief there is the possibility of acquiring such a fragrant and captivating *cru* within this very establishment.'

243

'If you want a bottle of wine, why don't you just say so, Hick? Fuck's sake.' Vodka Joe was still trying to come to terms with the death of Luca Brasi. 'What's with all the fancy jargon? What did you say the other night when you farted? What nonsense did you come up with?'

'I didn't fart,' said the doc with a slight trace of exasperation. 'I expect farting from the likes of you. From me, it was an involuntarily and, admittedly, violent expulsion of wind from my anal passage.'

'Smelled like a fart to me and the rest of the pub,' said Vodka Joe.

'Hughie, can you please do something about the persistent pestilence problem or I may have to seek another drinking emporium where I will continue to indulge my fond relationship with the pleasing tartness of a fine grape?'

'That's as maybe, Hick,' replied the bar owner, 'but do they stock *Chateauneuf du Cumbrae?*'

'Yes, not worth it, I suppose,' said the GP. 'Vodka Joe, I want to go on record as saying I hate you. There, it's official.'

'You can take all your words and place them beside your next fart,' replied the resident of the coveted sofa.

Hughie placed the bottle of wine on the bar. 'Tall glass, please, barkeep,' said the doc rather haughtily. 'I would have thought you might be on my side on this one, Hughie. I'm disappointed.'

'Oh, go and sit on your anal passage and give us peace.' The bar owner felt like an extra in a bad movie when Hickory Dickory and Vodka Joe locked horns. 'All we need now is for Boring Brian to make an appearance,' he thought.

He squinted through the front window. 'Fuck!' he uttered. 'Looks like it's not going to be my day.'

CHAPTER THIRTY-FOUR

5.14pm. Wednesday 24 November.

Millport, Isle of Cumbrae.

Charlie Brock would often insist there was only one thing perfect about Rodger James and that was his personality bypass. Apparently, he had once applied for charisma, but had been knocked back. Brock's considered opinions had been relayed to Smiler. He had grinned, once again displaying his alarming array of disintegrating fangs. He approved of Brock's observations and had made a mental note to thank his fellow-hack one day. It meant all his vigorous backstabbing over the many years had not been in vain.

Within an instant of arriving at the Glen Mill Guest House on Miller Street in Millport, the *Tribune's* chief sports reporter had hardly endeared himself to Noreen Taylor, proprietor of the five-bedroomed establishment. 'Nice blouse, dear,' said Smiler, as he signed in as James Stewart. 'Pity you couldn't get one your size.'

Ms Taylor, stoutish spinster of the parish, sixty-seven years old and never been kissed, blanched momentarily, suddenly feeling very cold. Had she just heard correctly? Had this odd-looking man just said what she thought he had said? This was Millport and people normally waited until they had been properly introduced before they were allowed to be rude. Those were the rules.

Smiler smirked. She almost fainted dead away at the sight of the crumbling assortment of incisors. 'Maybe you'll get a blouse that fits you for your Christmas,' he added, accepting the key to room three. 'I'll see myself up. You stay here and remain fat. Can't have you burning off any of those precious calories you have so enthusiastically piled on over the years.'

Ms Taylor wondered if her late grandfather's old blunderbuss in the cupboard under the stairs was still loaded and in good working order.

Smiler looked around his room. Clean, at least, he thought. He put the holdall he always kept in the office for an emergency on the single bed. A crumpled shirt, an unironed pair of trousers, baggy underpants, some rolled-up socks and an oversized beanie hat that had more than a passing resemblance to an exploding tea cosy. No toothbrush. He never saw the need for such an instrument of torture. He put his gear in the wardrobe and grinned. 'I'm here, Crazy Horse. Where are you?' He would go for a bite to eat and then on to that source of all information, the pub. He pulled on his ill-fitting headgear that, in the blustery conditions, ensured that what was left of his hair wouldn't arrive anywhere five minutes before him. He reappeared at the reception desk just opposite the main door of the small boarding house. It was the best accommodation Marge Dawson, the long-suffering sports desk secretary, could find at such short notice; Smiler made a mental note that he would be having a word with her when he got home.

'Ah, Ms Taylor, you're still here,' he said. 'Thought you might be in the kitchen in pursuit of a snack to tide you over. I can ascertain by your ample girth that you are the very person I need to talk to. I've worked up quite an appetite today and I would like to know which of your fine eating establishments on the island you would recommend. Surely, with your generous proportions, you will have a fair idea.'

'It's November.' Ms Taylor spoke through gritted teeth.

'Yes, thank you, I am well aware of the calendar month. That doesn't help put food in my belly now, does it? You must leave some morsels for the other people on the island, you know.'

'Try the chip shop at Quayhead Street.' Ms Taylor could always phone ahead and tell the hippy owner to urinate in the chips.

'Yes, I may try some good old-fashioned fish and chips ...'

Maybe Ms Taylor could persuade the hippy to shit on the haddock, too.

'... and sample the delights of your little island. Toodaloo.' Smiler waved a hand in the air as he made to open the door.

'Mr Stewart,' called out the guest house owner. 'I'm afraid I'll have to ask you to vacate your room tomorrow, by midday at the latest. I've got a coach party booked in. Sorry about that.' She didn't like lying, but it was either that or the blunderbus.

'Not to worry, podgy one. I hope to be off your island as swiftly as possible. My business should be concluded this evening. I take it you don't wish me to bring you back a haggis supper or something like that? A small repast before you repair to your bed? Can't have your stomach thinking your throat's been cut now, can we?'

Noreen Taylor smiled back. She knew a place where she could acquire ammunition if the blunderbus was out of bullets.

CHAPTER THIRTY-FIVE

5.52pm. Wednesday 24 November.

Millport, Isle of Cumbrae.

In an instant, Noreen Taylor realised the blunderbus would not be required for this pair: they were an absolute delight. Miguel Araquistian and his nephew Javier Sanchez, happy to get in from the snell wind ruthlessly whipping along the promenade, were signing the visitors' register at the Glen Mill Guest House.

Ms Taylor smiled at them while admiring their sensible clothing. 'Welcome to Millport,' she positively trilled, her chins wobbling like a pile of pancakes as she spoke. 'All the way from Barcelona? I've never had anyone from Barcelona stay here before. It's so exciting. What a pleasure. Sorry it's a wee bit bleak out there. We might even get snow next week.' She paused. 'How on earth did you find me? My goodness, wait until I tell the sewing bee. Recommended, perhaps?'

Araquistian, struggling to disembark from the bulk of his heavy hide coat, was as delighted as Ms Taylor; he could actually understand her, unlike that apparently deranged little lady who maintained a steady stream of babble all the way over on the ferry. Thank God the trip had only taken ten minutes. He might have been forced to use his gun. He nodded, 'I saw your advertisement in the office where we purchased our tickets over in ...'

'Largs,' she said helpfully.

'Yes, Largs. *Gracias*, thank you. Your leaflet looked very inviting and your accommodation looked very comfortable. Very good prices, too. And now we are so lucky to have two rooms. We aim to stay one night, possibly two. Is that okay?'

'Oh, yes, of course. We're very quiet at this time of year.' She frowned. 'ANY time of year at the moment. This recession, you know, it's hurting everyone.'

'I come from Spain, *querida dama* ... sorry ... dear lady. I know what you are talking about, believe me.' He smiled. 'Let's cheer up and hope it all goes away. The sooner the better. *Si*?'

'Yes, I'll drink to that,' agreed Ms Taylor, who was known to partake of the odd sherry. And not just on the Queen's Birthday.

'Do you need our passports, dear lady?' asked the cop as he prepared to open his luggage.

Noreen Taylor looked quite surprised. 'Passports? Oh, we don't get a lot of those things around here. I'll check in the morning. No need for them tonight.' Another pause. 'Please don't think I'm being nosy, but may I ask what brings two such handsome gentlemen all the way from Barcelona to this small island? And in November, too. Not much to do.'

Araquistian looked the well-meaning owner of the guest house straight in the eye. And lied. 'My nephew and I are very keen golfers. We are looking around parts of this wonderful country and we intend to come back in the summer and play your excellent courses.'

'Oh, do you play golf in Spain?' Noreen Taylor looked genuinely surprised.

The cop laughed. 'Yes, of course. Maybe you have heard of Seve Ballesteros?'

The guest house owner thought hard before shaking her head.

'Jose Maria Olazabal?'

Another knitted brow.

'Sergio Garcia? Antonio Garrido? Manuel Pinero? Jose Maria Canizares? Jose Rivero?'

Noreen Taylor shook her head vigorously. It sounded as though her guest was reading through a pizza takeaway menu. 'I'm more of a lawn bowls person myself,' she said, almost apologetically. 'Maybe you've heard of Jamie McCarthy? He's the best on the island.'

It was the cop's turn to look quizzical. 'Jamie McCarthy? No, I don't think so. We have bowls in Barcelona, *si*. Very popular with the retired people. Many English play it. Very well, too, until they have too much to drink and then it becomes very dangerous. Then it is *carniceria*.'

Ms Taylor looked blank.

'Carnage,' offered the nephew. '*Si, carniceria* ... carnage. *Destruccion* ... wreckage.'

'Aye, it's a bit like that here, too,' nodded Ms Taylor. 'Big Tam Hughes has a little too much to drink and forgets what sport he's playing and starts throwing the bowls around like he's shotputting. Now that is very dangerous.'

'And my nephew tells me you have a golf course on the island, *si*?' The cop looked hopeful.

'I'm told it's one of the best in the world. Honestly, they come all the way from Dundee to play on our course.'

'Dundee?' The cop had never heard of the place and wondered if it was a small country in Asia. 'Must be good. I must see it for myself tomorrow in the morning light. Is it far from here?'

'*Nothing* is far from here. This is Millport, remember? No, a taxi will get you there in about five minutes; two if Jimmy's driving and he's had a wee drink. Lost his licence, you know. And he's still drinking and driving. Tut, tut. Wife's not happy. Never is, mind.' She wrinkled her nose and added, 'Or you could cycle there. You have cycles in Spain?'

It was Sanchez's turn to laugh. '*Si*, we have cycles in Barcelona; as many as Amsterdam. Yes, those two-wheeled nuisances are everywhere. Every day. The authorities keep adding new yellow lanes, but do the cyclists bother to keep to them? No. Is it like this in Millport?'

Noreen Taylor laughed. 'Oh, we've got cycle paths, sure enough, but no-one bothers with them. They cycle on the pavements here.'

'*Ay, caramba!*' exclaimed the sports reporter. 'The roads are so busy? On the pavements? Very dangerous, no?'

'Not really. Well, not if everyone's sober. And that includes the pedestrians.' She sniggered again as she passed over the keys to rooms four and five. She wondered if she should warn them about the occupant of room three. She decided against it; they looked too happy.

'Have you had anything to eat?' she asked. 'A lot of places are closed this time of year. I could rustle up a couple of bowls of Scotch broth if you want. My own special recipe.' The guest house owner could be as economical with the truth as the cop.

'Oh, yes, please,' said Sanchez. 'We'll take our stuff up to the room and we'll be back down in five minutes. Scotch broth? Is there whisky in it?'

'I could put a wee tot in if you want,' said Ms Taylor, who was

252

known to add the odd sherry to just about everything she cooked (which was mainly mince).

'That would be nice,' said the cop. 'So, everything I hear about the Scottish people is true? Whisky with everything?'

'Well, not quite. Not too good in omelettes,' answered Noreen Taylor. 'I take it you'll be going for a dram tonight?'

'Dram?' queried the cop. 'I don't know this word. Dram? What does it mean, please?'

'Oh, of course. Dram is a little glass of whisky. Or it could be a large glass of whisky, of course. The measure's your pleasure, as they say, if you know what I mean.' The guest house owner came close to giggling.

'Oh, *si, grande.*' The cop motioned with his two hands vertically apart by about ten inches. 'I very much like large.'

'Well, as soon as you've had your broth, you should get yourselves over to Hugh's Bar. It's on Stuart Street. Not far from here. Good wee howf ... pub ... bar ... and ask for Hughie. Good lad. Watch out for Vodka Joe in the corner. Don't say you haven't been warned.'

'Why is he known as this "Vodka Joe"?' asked the policeman.

'Oh, you'll know as soon as you see him. Believe me.'

The cop and the sports reporter mounted the steep tartan-carpeted stairs to their respective rooms.

'Maybe we should have asked her about Crazy Horse, uncle?'

'*Pah!* If she hasn't heard of Seve Ballesteros, what are the chances she knows of a Crazy Horse?'

CHAPTER THIRTY-SIX

8.15pm. Wednesday 24 November.

Millport, Isle of Cumbrae.

'Feel a bit guilty, leaving him on his own.' Charlie Brock and Willy were heading into another gale force wind along West Bay Road on their way back from Chalet Number Twenty and its mystery occupant. 'Is it just me or was the wind in our faces when we came along here to go to Derek's? Is there someone up there with a huge invisible fan following us around making sure we're always walking into the wind?'

'Yes, dear,' answered Willy, 'that's what it'll be.'

'You're beginning to sound like a wife,' said Brock.

'I AM a wife,' replied Willy. 'Just not yours.' She added teasingly, 'But you never know your luck.'

Brock felt her arm tighten around his as they huddled together for warmth on their way to Hugh's Bar. He didn't really know what to think. Willy was becoming as much a puzzle as Crazy Horse. A lot better looking, mind you, but still a bit of a conundrum, nevertheless.

'What's your take on Derek?' asked Willy, almost shouting to be heard above the din of the blustery conditions.

'Well, he doesn't look too confused, does he? Seems to know what he's all about. If we had turned up tonight and witnessed a shaking, slurring wreck we would have known what was the problem right away. But if he's doolally, his disguise is impeccable.

Looked perfectly normal to me. And just guessing here, but I think he looked perfectly normal to you, too.' He turned to look at his companion.

Willy smiled and said, 'Please continue.'

'So, what have we got? A very wealthy footballer who enjoys playing for one of the biggest clubs in the world, loves the lifestyle, adores the city of Barcelona, talks enthusiastically about his friends there, has his own private concubine, flash cars, fabulous home, adoring fans, good health, doesn't do drugs, not much of a drinker, would never last the pace at any Christmas sports desk outing I've ever been at, and has all his own teeth and hair. Plus he's twenty-five years old and could retire tomorrow and never have to worry about his next gas bill. I wish had problems like that.'

'So, what's his problem?' queried Willy. 'What – or *who* – is he running away from? Why is he in hiding? What's the big secret?' Brock's well-preserved companion enjoyed a good mystery with the best of them.

'What's his market value, Willy? Eighty million pounds? Well there you go – it's the eighty million pound question. Anyway, I need a drink,' asserted Brock as he pushed open the door to Hugh's Bar, the pair immediately confronted with Griff Stewart and Harry Booth; suspicious glances all round. The newsman was first to speak. 'Please grace us with your presence,' he said, motioning towards a wooden stool at the corner of the bar. 'And you can bring that tired old hack with you, if you must.'

'Very funny, R.I.P. And you say I should get some new material?' Brock pulled out the stool for Willy who perched on it, giving an appreciative Vodka Joe a ringside seat from which he could view her shapely backside.

'Still a Dry Martini and lemonade, dear girl?' asked R.I.P. as eloquently as possible. Willy nodded, 'Thank you.'

'Brock? Beer?' grunted the newsman.

'Let's all bunch round for a wee confab,' said El Cid. 'We've got something to talk about, have we not? We don't keep secrets from each other, do we, Charlie?' There was a glint in the cop's eye. He pushed his beer further up the bar to be closer to the other three. The four were crunched together which was rather strange considering there were only five other people in the watering hole, one of them a slyly-glancing Vodka Joe, dreaming of Gina Lollobrigida, but accepting Willy as a reasonable substitute.

'So, no secrets, Charlie? Nothing you want to tell us, eh? All quiet on the western front? No big stories about to break? No sign of a very famous footballer who may be on the run? Nothing like that happening out there?'

Brock said nothing.

R.I.P. picked up his brandy glass, sipped contentedly and then asked, 'Do you need a hand with a story, Charlie? Anything the News Desk can do to help you out in your hour of need? Struggling under the weight of a breaking story? Head in a fug? You only need to ask, you know that.'

Willy grabbed Brock's backside and squeezed. Hard. It was just as well Big Eric wasn't sitting at Vodka Joe's vantage point. The Gents loo in Hugh's Bar might have required urgent overnight redecorating.

The sportswriter wasn't sure how they knew or how much they knew, but he knew they knew. 'Fuck's sake, shut up, you two,' he hissed through grinding teeth. 'Christ, don't blow this.' He shook his head and gulped down some welcoming ale. He looked again at his best two pals in the whole wide world and wondered again about them. 'Okay,' he said under his breath, 'You're good, I'll give you that. How the fuck do you know? Who's been talking?' Brock had to admit he was baffled.

'We followed you,' admitted the cop in a matter-of-fact manner.

'What? When?' Brock's eyes narrowed.

'Earlier tonight,' answered the newspaperman. 'We thought we would have a bit of fun. Gets a bit quiet down here sometimes, just so much booze you can shovel away. Saw you and Willy taking off up Cardiff Street and we went after you.'

'Didn't have a clue, did you? Not a bloody clue,' chipped in the cop.

'We tracked you all the way along to the boatyard, making sure we kept our distance.' It was R.I.P.'s turn. 'You didn't look back once; not once. You were obviously far too distracted by this gorgeous girl' – he practically leered at Willy – 'and who wouldn't be? Feast your orbs on something that beautiful? Or two old farts being buffeted about in the wind?'

'It's a no-brainer, as they say in the football world, I believe.' The cop came in right on cue.

'And?' Brock looked from cop to reporter and back again.

'Well, we saw you turn off the road and up towards the chalets,' continued the policeman. 'We couldn't stop there, could we? We thought, well, we surmised ... we had a wee idea ... a notion ... that there might be some ...'

'Hanky panky?' Willy interrupted the tongue-tied cop. 'A bit of nookie? A little in-out, in-out?'

'That thought never crossed our minds, did it, R.I.P.?'

'Not at all,' lied the newsman. 'No we wondered ... in fact ... thought possibly you were ... ah ... house-hunting. Yes, that's right. House-hunting.'

'Is that the best you can do?' Brock was disappointed. 'House-fuckin'-hunting?'

'Best I could do off the top of my head. Sorry.'

'So, I now find my oldest buddies are a couple of Sneaky Petes? Dirty old men?'

'We couldn't help ourselves, mate. I'm a cop and he's a news reporter. Our antenna buzzed big-style. You would have done the same. Cut us a wee bit of slack, mate. Imagine the shock when we saw Derek Laird popping his head round that door. Christ, my heart nearly stopped. And give us a bit of credit for the snooping stopping right there when we realised it was important and we came straight back here. We haven't spoken to anyone. Not a soul.'

'Well, thanks a lot for that, guys,' said Brock, sounding not the least bit appreciative.

'Oh, let's not fall out, Charlie,' said the newspaperman.

'Let's not end years of friendship over something so trivial,' said the cop.

'Trivial?' Brock couldn't restrain himself. 'Fuckin' trivial? Sports story of the century. And you're following me about, around over at the chalets trying your best to queer the pitch? God protect me from my friends.'

Unfortunately, for the sportswriter his exclamation was just a little too audible.

And Brock hadn't taken any notice of the character balancing the baggy beanie hat hunched over the bar two yards away with his back to him.

It was also Brock's great misfortune that Rodger James possessed the hearing of a bat.

CHAPTER THIRTY-SEVEN

11.17pm. Wednesday 24 November.

Millport, Isle of Cumbrae.

Smiler, looking even more like a blood-sucking creature from a Grade B horror movie, was quite at home creeping along in the dark of Stuart Street, the stained collar of his shabby gaberdine overcoat pulled up, his sagging beanie hat tugged down almost to his nose.

He stopped briefly at the newsagents. 'Yes,' he beamed. 'Thought so.' A postcard had been sellotaped onto the inside of the shop window. 'Log Cabin For Rent. All Year Round. Reasonable Prices.' The *Tribune's* chief sports reporter guessed there would be only one location for such accommodation on the island. 'West Bay Road,' he mouthed as he read the card. Very helpfully, it also provided the information on how to get to the chalets. He nodded and grinned mirthlessly before setting off up Cardiff Street.

He took no notice of the interested occupant of the black Range Rover Evoque parked across the road at the pier.

Miguel Araquistian and Javier Sanchez were also well wrapped up to protect them against the raw conditions. They did not take any notice of the tall peculiar figure with the bizarre headgear who skulked past them. Noreen Taylor, the rather chubby and pleasant guest house owner of Glen Mill, had pointed them in the direction of Hugh's Bar if they were looking for a drink and some local colour. However, the cop found it impossible to go against his instinct and training.

'No, nephew,' he said, 'we will start at the other end of town. I saw a drinking house over there and that will be our starting point. Then we can work our way back here. That makes more sense, does it not?'

'I suppose so, uncle. I wouldn't argue. You are the expert. How many pubs did you count on our way in?'

'Three,' said the cop. 'Shouldn't take us too long to cover the ground. The pubs here close at 1am, so a couple of drinks in the first two places and maybe spend a little more time in this Hugh's Bar. Sounds like an interesting place, *si*?'

They both huddled into their hide coats and walked into the wind. Within ten minutes they were standing at the bar in Robbie's Tavern.

'My guid God, jus' look whit the wind blew in,' remarked the bar owner as the customers entered his establishment, wrestling to close the heavy, protesting door behind them.

The Spaniards' thoughts were in tandem. 'Was he related to that odd little woman from earlier in the day?'

Thankfully, veteran barman Hamish McNulty was awake enough to note the two swarthy gentlemen confronting him were not from his island. If they were, they had been spending an inordinate amount of time under the glow of sunlamps. He spoke a little more slowly and coherently for their benefit. 'Welcome,' he said. 'What's your pleasure?'

The two newcomers stared at him.

'Oh, sorry, what would you like to drink? What is your preference?'

'Two large whiskies, *por favor*,' requested Araquistian, he

261

pointed to the array of single malts on the gallery behind McNulty. 'I will let you choose. I think you may know the best brands, *si?*'

'Oh, *si*,' said McNulty, a serial visitor to Lanzarote. He went to the gantry and lifted two glasses to the optics. He poured generously and placed the drinks on the bar. 'I think you'll like this wee malt, distilled in far-off Islay.'

Araquistian, before paying, lifted the glass to his nose, sniffed expertly and then launched the entire contents down his throat. He coughed a little. 'Very good,' he wheezed. 'Another, *por favor*.' He winked at his nephew. 'You do not have to drink like a Scotsman, Javier. Leave that to me.'

McNulty took the glass from the bar and moved again towards the optics on the gantry. 'Large again, *señor?*' he said.

'Oh, *si*,' said the cop. 'One for yourself, too. Whatever you desire.'

The proprietor didn't need to be placed in a stranglehold when such offers were made. 'A gin and tonic would go down fine,' he said. The three chinked their glasses like long lost friends. '*Slainte*,' said the barman. '*Buena salud*,' said the Spaniards.

'The name's Hamish McNulty,' offered the bar owner.

'I am Miguel Araquistian and this is my nephew Javier Sanchez,' returned the policeman. 'Very pleased to meet you.' They shook hands.

'Well, lads, I take it you are Spanish, eh?'

'*Si*, from Barcelona,' said the newsman. 'You will want to know why we are here on your island, *si?*'

'Can't lie, laddie, it had crossed my mind. I would have to be – how would you say? – *muerto*, aye, *muerto* if I wasn't a little bit interested.'

'*Muerto?* Dead. You speak Spanish?' asked the cop.

'No, not really, only what I pick up in Playa Blanca for two weeks every January after I close this place down in the new year. Need a breather, recharge the old batteries and I love that wee part of the world. Been going there for about fifteen years or so. I know how to order up a San Miguel, right enough.'

The three smiled. 'So, why are you here, if I am not being intrusive? If I am, just let me know and I'll shut up. I've been serving behind this bar for forty years and I know when to be quiet.'

The cop and the sports reporter had decided honesty, on this occasion, was the best policy. They knew they were not going to walk into a pub and find their quarry sitting in a corner sipping an ale, playing draughts while balancing a large sign with an arrow pointing to him declaring, 'DEREK LAIRD THIS WAY'.

'You have heard of this Scottish player who has gone missing in Spain?' asked Araquistian. 'Derek Laird? Crazy Horse? You know him?'

'Aye, I read the newspapers, but, to be honest, I am a wee bit of a rarity for a Scotsman – I'm not that interested in football. I'm more of a gee-gees man.'

The Spaniards looked at him quizzically. 'Gee-gees?' both asked at the same time.

'Oh, aye, sorry. Horses. Horse racing. That sort of thing. Football, I'm afraid, doesn't do much for me. But, yes, I know the story about this bloke. Done a runner, has he?'

The cop nodded. '*Si*, I know this expression. I must tell you,

Hamish, I am a policeman. My nephew is a sports reporter. And we would both very much like to talk to Derek Laird.'

'And you think the lad is here? In Millport? Seriously?' It took quite a bit to startle Hamish, but Araquistian had managed it. 'Fuck's sake,' added the barman.

'*Si*, we have information that tells us he is here on this island. Javier, show Hamish a photograph of Derek Laird, please.'

The nephew handed his mobile phone to the barman. 'Isn't it just wonderful, eh? Technology today.' Hamish was impressed by the wonders of the twenty-first century. He took the phone and squinted at the image, an up-to-date photograph taken at the start of the football season. He shook his head. 'Sorry, lads, but, as I said, I'm not very good with footballers.'

He handed the mobile phone back to Sanchez. 'Technology today,' he repeated. 'You know, there was a young lad in here with a wee bit of plastic earlier this morning and he said he had about two hundred books on it. Called it a Kinsomething or other.'

'Kindle,' said Araquistian, alerted. 'You said "young lad", Hamish. Do you know him?'

'No, never seen him before in my life, my friend. Just came in off the street, had a couple of lagers and showed me this Kindle thing. He had it in his holdall. Left it with me while he went along to the bank to get money for the chalet ...' Hamish's voice drifted off. 'Let me see that mobile phone again, please, young fella.'

Once again he looked at the image. 'You know something, gents, this could be the very chap. Can't be one hundred per cent, but, yes, there is a definite likeness.'

'And you know where he is staying? You said something about a chalet?' pressed Araquistian.

'Aye, a chalet,' said the bar owner. 'Look, gentlemen, I don't want to get this youngster into any trouble. Maybe I've said too much already. I don't like sticking my nose in ...'

'Let me reassure you, Hamish, I am not here to arrest him. It's way out of my jurisdiction, anyway, but that is not why I am here. I can notify the authorities back in Spain and we can call off our search once I am sure it is Derek Laird who is here and he is safe.'

'And I want to write the story,' added Sanchez, finding it impossible to contain his eagerness.

'Plus I am a Barcelona fan,' said the cop. 'My nephew, alas, follows Espanyol. There is no hope for him. Can you help us, Hamish? I promise you we are not here to harm Derek Laird. They wouldn't let us back into Barcelona if we did anything to upset Crazy Horse.'

'Chalet Number Twenty' said Hamish. 'West Bay Road. Go out here, walk all the way back to the pier. You know it?'

'*Si*,' said the cop. 'We are at Glen Mill guest house. Noreen Taylor.'

'Okay, turn right up Cardiff Street and take the first left along West Bay Road, walk about fifteen minutes or so and the chalets are opposite the old boatyard. You cannot miss them. Chalet Number Twenty, right at the back.'

'Another two large whiskies please, Hamish, and a very large gin and tonic for yourself,' said Araquistian, beaming brightly.

'*Si!* Don't mind if I do, *señor*,' said McNulty.

CHAPTER THIRTY-EIGHT

11.48pm. Wednesday 24 November.

Millport, Isle of Cumbrae.

'A man walks into a bar. "Oof!" he says. It's an iron bar.'

Tommy Cooper?

Smiler froze abruptly. Something cold and metallic was forced into the back of his neck. 'Don't bother looking round. If there was anything to see, I would charge you.' Still the unmistakable Tommy Cooper tones.

Rodger James, the *Tribune's* chief sports reporter, had been prowling around in the dark shadows of the boatyard opposite the wooden chalets at West Bay Road. It was almost midnight and he was about to spring his surprise on the occupant of Number Twenty, the only chalet with its lights on and showing signs of life. He enjoyed catching people off guard. It was what made his work so rewarding. He had made a living out of it.

Now he was confused.

'Alright my, lovelies? Two sausages in a frying pan. One says to the other, "Blimey, it's hot in here." The other says, "Fuck me, a talking sausage!"'

Bruce Forsyth?

Smiler was tempted to look round. 'Don't think about it,' said Adam Crawley, still sounding like Brucie, while holding a cigar tube to the back of the newspaperman's neck.

'Let's see how we get on with my Irish accent. A drunk goes into a pub. "Bartender," he says, "buy everyone in the house a drink, pour one for yourself and give me the bill." So, the bartender does just that and hands the man a bill for £70. The drunk says, "I haven't got any money." The bartender slaps the guy around a couple of times and throws him out into the street.' Pause. 'Enjoying this, Smiler? There's more. Anyway, the drunk goes into the same pub the following night. This time it's even busier. He goes up to the same bartender and slurs, "Buy a drink for everyone in the house, pour one for yourself and give me the bill." The bartender looks at the guy and figures he wouldn't be stupid enough to pull the same stunt twice in two nights. He does as he's told. He gives the drunk the bill for £95. The guy says, "I haven't got any money." The bartender slaps him around a couple of times and throws him out into the street.' Another pause. 'Following the story so far, you skeletal monstrosity? Nod if want me to continue. Good lad. Okay, the next night, it's the same scenario. The drunk goes up to the same barman and says, "Buy everyone in the house a drink and give me the bill." The barman asks, "No drink for me this time?" The drunk replies, "You? No way! You get too violent when you drink."'

Dave Allen?

'Aye, it's the way I tell 'em.' Frank Carson? 'Oooh, shut that door.' Larry Grayson? 'Titter ye not.' Frankie Howerd?

'Now you don't have a fuckin' clue who's standing behind you, do you?' asked Crawley, back to Tommy Cooper. 'Does this give you a starter for ten? Here's another.' He cleared his throat. 'I saw six men kicking and punching the mother-in-law. My neighbour said, "Are you going to help?" I said, "No, six should be enough."'

'Did you get Les Dawson, Smiler? Not bad, eh? One of my

best.' Crawley continued as Les Dawson. 'I'm a star turn at office parties, you know. I play the piano by ear. Suppose it would be better if I used my fingers. Did you hear the one about the penguin that goes into the pub and asks the barman if he had seen his brother? The barman answers, "Don't know, what does he look like?"'

All was eerily quiet.

'Are you frightened yet, you fuckin' miserable shit? You should be. This could be the very night you meet your Maker. Don't think there'll be too much for you to chat about when you meet Saint Peter up at the Pearly Gates, do you? Trapdoor will be at the ready for you, turd features. Oh, here's a good one, you'll like this. Don't go away.' There was silence from the motionless, petrified figure in front of Crawley.

'Did you know heaven and hell sit right beside each other? God discovers Satan has been building on His land. He tells Satan. "Get off My land." Satan says, "What will you do if I don't?" God says, "I'll sue you." And Satan says, "Where will you find a lawyer?" Boom! Boom!'

Basil Brush?

'I do a mean Morecambe and Wise, too. Maybe we'll keep that treat for later. If there is a "later" in your case, of course. Let's stick to Les Dawson for the time being. You've made a lot of people suffer, haven't you?' Smiler hesitated. Crawley pressed the cigar container into the back of his head. 'YYYYYYYYES!' Smiler responded. 'So, guilty as charged, hog's breath?' Again the delay. 'Why ... why ... are you doing this to me?' came a pitiful squeak from the newsman.

'Can't you fuckin' guess, rodent features? What goes around

comes around. Right? Tonight it's your turn to squirm. Couldn't believe my luck when I saw you heading into the pub. Recognised you immediately despite that fuckin' stupid hat. You wearing that for a bet? That wonderful big window at the pub. I could see you when you came in and, unfortunately for you, all you could see was your own reflection. Hardly a fair exchange, eh? You came in the front door and I went out the side exit. I sat in my car across the road and waited for you. God's on my side tonight. What does that tell you? And out you came and, even better, you headed in this direction. Not a soul in sight. Thank you, Lord, I will make a contribution when the plate goes round on Sunday, I promise.'

'Now ... now ... don't do anything silly,' mumbled Smiler. 'I can explain.'

'For fuck's sake, Smiler,' said Crawley in his best Michael Caine, straight out of *The Italian Job*. 'I only came here to think about extinguishing your miserable life. I don't want a discussion or a debate. We're way beyond that, you odious reptile. Do you really think it is acceptable that you can get away with piling misery on so many individuals? Doesn't work that way, my friend. There are so many times you can kick a dog before it will bite back.'

'Maybe there has been a misunderstanding?' moaned Smiler. 'Can we not ... can't we talk about this?'

'So, you want to be a chat show host, do you? Think it's easy?' Michael Parkinson was now in the chair. 'Well, I find that quite remarkable. Yes, absolutely fascinating. Extraordinary. You are supposed to be an intelligent man, are you not? Your readers hang on your every word, every day. Yet here we are, standing in a deserted boatyard in the midnight gloom in Millport and I've got a gun at your head and I am seriously thinking about blowing your lonely grey cell out of your diseased cranium. That's not very clever, is it, Smiler? How on earth did it come to this? Maybe you've been too smart for your own good, eh? Possibly, this is exactly what you deserve. You've lived your life in the shadows, so how appropriate would it be if you ended your worthless existence here and now, without an audience? A lonely, misguided soul left for the foxes to enjoy a midnight feast? Plenty of them around here, my friend. They might never be able to identify you with what's left of your carcass. Normally, they can go by dental records. I think, though, they would make a special exception in your case, don't you? Can't believe you've ever visited a dentist. Have you?'

A pitiable whimper. 'I ... I ... don't like dentists.'

'And I'm sure they just adore you, my lovely.' Bruce Forsyth again.

'Right, now, do you feel lucky, punk?' Clint Eastwood as *Dirty Harry* was now in charge of the cigar holder. 'I haven't got all night, so let's just cut to the chase. I represent several individuals who are not at all happy with you; no, not happy at all. You've been threatening a lot of dangerous people. And they've hired me and I have to say I like my job, cleaning up scum like you. Are you listening, punk? Nod your head.'

A woeful, low whine came from Smiler. 'Can we talk about this? I've got money.'

'I only asked you to nod your fuckin' head,' Michael Caine again.

The newsman slowly motioned his head back and forth a couple of times.

'That's better, punk.' Clint Eastwood once more. 'The way I

see it, we've got two choices. I can drop you right here ...'

'Please, please don't,' sobbed Smiler.

'... or I can set you free. What's it to be? Dropped here or set free? I'm giving you the choice you don't give others.'

'Set free,' came the sorry reply. 'Please.'

'A wise choice, punk. Now all you have to do is give the right answers and by this time tomorrow you can be sitting in your relic in Pollokshields – yes, punk, I know where you live – and have your feet up enjoying your favourite music. Do you like music? Can't see you quite boogying on down to Lady Marmalade of an evening. "*Voulez-vous choucher avec moi ce soir*?" Don't think so. Who did you prefer? Labelle or All Saints? I was a Labelle man myself. You haven't got a scooby, have you? I bet your idea of fun is pulling the wings off flies and having a pull of your pud to Hitler's Greatest Hits. That more your sort of stuff, Smiler?'

'You're ... you're not funny,' came a sad whimper.

'Not funny? Not funny? You started it.' John Cleese had arrived. 'Let's get back to the choices before one of us dies and from where I'm standing there is a good chance that will be you and not me. I won't do Mel Gibson here, you'll be happy to know, but I see you have chosen your freedom. Well, freedom comes at a price, my tragic, undernourished, elongated string of depravity. Let's get serious. I am told by my clients, of which there are far too many, that you have obtained certain items that may embarrass them. Now this is the easy part. You agree here and now to lose that material, ALL of it, and you can walk away. Or sail away, more accurately. Told you it was easy. Disagree and, well, I'm afraid there can be only one outcome and that will mean the foxes of this little island dining well into the early hours of the morning.

271

It could be midday before what's left of you is found. What a wretched thought. And no-one to mourn for you. No Mrs Smiler at home wondering where you have gone. No-one to miss your very presence. No, gone, just like that. One minute here, the next minute your face being chewed off by a grateful pack of hungry little mammals in the middle of nowhere. I meant to ask. What are you doing here, anyway? There must be a good reason.'

A small, hesitant voice whispered back. 'I'm looking for Crazy Horse.'

'Yes, and I'm Buffalo Bill. I thought you'd do better than that.'

Crawley made an unexpected move and grabbed the sports reporter's wrists and pulled them behind his back. 'This won't take a minute.'

'What's going on?' Smiler yelled frantically, but no-one was listening.

'Fun's over for the night, my friend. This is where it all gets serious. You've chosen freedom and that's what you'll get. Am I to believe you agree to the terms and conditions of your release? Just nod your head, I can't be bothered with any more chat. Good lad. Now you know if you don't keep your word there won't be any second chances. I'll come back for you. And if I can find you here, you know I can find you anywhere. Agreed? Yes, I thought so. Now open your mouth wide.'

There was feeble resistance from Smiler. 'Do it, punk!' Eastwood took over from Cleese. 'Or no freedom. Think starving foxes.' Crawley pushed a sock into Smiler's mouth, shuddering while he did so, hoping not to catch anything contagious. 'That's a good boy. Won't take a minute. Don't bother to turn round, I've still got the gun and my trigger finger is mighty itchy. Now let's try a blindfold. Possibly not your colour, but it'll have to do.'

Crawley pulled a green and yellow polka-dotted scarf tight across the newspaperman's eyes. 'There, that's not too bad. See no evil, speak no evil. That'll be a first for you, punk. Now let's get you past these rocks and down to the shore. Don't bother struggling. Easy for me to knock you cold here and now and throw your limp body into the rowing boat, do you fancy that? Of course not.'

The footballer took the sports reporter by the elbow and propelled him roughly towards the water's edge, the Firth of Clyde's earlier rage becalmed at this time of night. 'Looks like a full moon, Smiler. Christ knows what you'll meet out there. Just let me know if you want to change your mind. No? Good lad. Willing to take your chances, then, with Mother Nature? Well, they do say the devil looks after his own, don't they? That being the case, you'll be home and snuggled up in your bed with that rotting corpse you keep in the spare bedroom. "Mother, oh, mother. What have you done?"' Anthony Perkins in *Psycho* made an appearance.

Crawley pulled and pushed Smiler towards the rowing boat. 'Take it easy, my old friend, there are a lot of rocks here. Don't want you breaking an ankle, do we?' He lifted the sports writer's right leg and placed it inside the boat. 'Okay, there you are. Next one, please. Good lad.' He manoeuvred him towards a seat in the middle of the small boat. 'Sit down,' he ordered. The newspaperman did as he was told. He was terrified and soiled himself, a putrid smell enveloping the immediate area. 'Fuck's sake, Smiler, couldn't you have waited and shared that with the seals? Is that stench coming from your mouth or your arse?'

Smiler perched on the seat. He tried to speak. A one-size-fits-all sock put an end to that. Blindfolded, gagged and his hands tied behind his back, he cut a pathetic figure. Adam Crawley didn't care a jot. 'With your hands out of commission, as you might say, there will be no need for oars, my horrible, boney old friend. I'll just get rid of them. So let's see where fate takes you.' With a fair degree of effort, he managed to push the boat out into the inky blue waters, in the general direction of Largs, he guessed. Smiler remained bolt upright as the rowing boat took a bit of a buffeting. 'Get used to the rhythm,' said the footballer. 'Move around and you'll be overboard before you can say "Jaws". Can't have the good old Firth getting polluted, can we? You're going to have to break the habit of a lifetime and not rock the boat.'

Adam Crawley stood on the stone wall and watched the rowing boat bob around for about five minutes or so. At least, he had chosen one that didn't have a hole in it, although he had been tempted. He had arranged with a friend, an old team-mate who owned a motor launch on Rothesay, to keep an eye on the developing situation. He really didn't want a death on his hands; Smiler wasn't worth that stain on his soul. A bit of fornication with a nubile teenager behind the wife's back was perfectly okay; compulsory, even, for a footballer. But murder wasn't in the script.

'Hey, Smiler, can you still hear me? Here's a little farewell song for you. "I'm Popeye the sailor man; I'm Popeye the sailor man; I'm strong to the flinch; 'Cause I eats me spinach; I'm Popeye the sailor man. I yam what I yam. Toot! Toot!" *Bon Voyage.*'

Crawley walked back through the boatyard, a good night's work done. As he strolled along West Bay Road, pulling his leather jacket tight and heading towards his parked Range Rover Evoque at the pier, he smiled. He was certain Smiler would not even attempt to tell the story to the authorities.

Who would believe someone had been held at gunpoint by

Tommy Cooper? Or was it Bruce Forsyth? Maybe Clint Eastwood? John Cleese? Michael Caine? And a whole host of others?

'Damn,' said Crawley, 'I forgot to do my Morecombe and Wise duet.'

He shrugged his shoulders. 'Maybe some other day.' He, and many more unaware benefactors, had a reason to smile that cold, winter's evening in the North Ayrshire coastal town of Millport. He knew his gift for mimmicry would come in handy one day. He also realised he had almost been recognised in the pub until he began speaking in a broad Irish brogue that bewildered the barman.

'They'll never take my freedom!' he cried at the top of his voice, echoes bouncing off the neat row of silent Victorian stone villas. He was happy. He got to do his Mel Gibson, after all.

CHAPTER THIRTY-NINE

12.45am. Thursday 25 November.

Millport, Isle of Cumbrae.

The Spaniards eased into the shadows, blending with the dull greyness of one of the villas. Both were more than a little disconcerted at what they were witnessing. As a policeman, Miguel Araquistian's immediate instinct was to act, to somehow attempt to intervene. He stood silently in the ghostly gloom alongside his nephew and watched the improbable scenario unfold. The tall skinny figure wearing a silly hat was being roughly manhandled by the other person. What was he holding to his head? Was that a gun? Was that a blindfold over the eyes of the big one? Why was he being shoved into that rowing boat?

Araquistian had made a career out of thinking swiftly on his feet, the ability to size up a situation and seize a solution. He said nothing. His nephew Javier Sanchez broke the silence. 'Should we go to the aid of that man, uncle?' he whispered. The cop deliberated for a brief moment. He shook his head. 'Hush. Be patient, please, nephew,' he returned in a low tone, his forefinger to his lips. 'Let me think.'

The unlikely scene was played out while they watched from about fifty yards away, at an angle opposite the boatyard which was bathed in moonlight. Now the boat was being thrust into the waters of the noiseless sea. The passenger was sitting bolt upright in the bobbing vessel. He was saying nothing; maybe he was gagged, too. Araquistian could not be certain in the murkiness. He stared ahead with a fair degree of incredulity. This does not add up, he thought. The cop did not subscribe to the proverb that 'he who hesitates is lost'. He was also only too aware of the saying 'fools rushing in'. He remained motionless, a mere observer in the dark, cheerless cold.

He and his nephew witnessed the rowing boat being tossed around, the occupant silent. Then the aggressor appeared to be singing. Araquistian strained to hear the words. 'Popeye?' he repeated. 'Popeye the sailor man?' This was all very odd.

'Uncle,' whispered Sanchez in almost muted tones. 'What are we going to do?'

The cop held up his right hand. 'Sshhhh,' he advised. 'Let's continue to watch for a moment.'

The antagonist in this bizarre exhibition was now walking along the road. His face became quite visible under the yellow glare of the lighting. Araquistian looked intently. The man was smiling hugely as he rubbed his hands giving the impression of someone satisfied with a job well done. 'They'll never take my freedom!' he boomed. And laughed.

'*Braveheart*? Mel Gibson?' The cop had seen the movie a couple of times. This entire enactment had now gone well beyond the curious. He watched as the shadowy figure walked along West Bay Road before vanishing in the general direction of the town. Then, and only then, did he gesture for his nephew to make a move. 'What is happening, uncle?' he asked urgently. 'What are we going to do?'

Araquistian and his nephew had travelled to the Isle of Cumbrae to confront a runaway footballer. Now they had just observed a person, bound and probably gagged, being thrown into a rowing boat and set off to sea by someone who, quite clearly, did not care about the outcome of his actions. Stealthily, the wraith-like figures came out of the dimness and hurried across the road to the boatyard. Sanchez, young, fit and athletic, began to unbutton his coat. 'Stop, nephew,' ordered the cop. 'Do not be too hasty. I would not advise a midnight swim in these waters. Let's just watch from the edge for a moment.'

The Spaniards stood and looked out to sea. The little rowing boat and its occupant were barely visible, a silhouette seesawing around aimlessly. The silence edged towards overpowering; the eeriness was absolute. Sanchez, frustrated at the lack of action, leapt down from their vantage point on the rockwall. He hauled over a rowing boat, resting on hard-caked sand, and began searching for oars. He found the ones discarded by Adam Crawley some ten minutes beforehand. '*Ay caray!*' he exclaimed when he noticed a hole the size of a fist in the hull of the vessel.

'Hush, nephew,' signalled the cop. 'I think I hear something out there.'

A low spluttering noise was barely audible. Araquistian wished he possessed a pair of night goggles. He stared ahead, his eyes watering in the wafting breeze. He squinted into the gloom and could just about discern a motor launch which was approaching the rowing boat. What on earth was this all about? he wondered. Surely, not some unusual nocturnal pastime for Scottish islanders? More silence. A minute or so passed. Then a putt-putt-putt sound and the motor launch now appeared to be towing the rowing boat. To safety? Araquistian dragged his fingers across his black curly hair and fished out a packet of cheroots from his inside coat pocket. 'How am I ever supposed to stop smoking, nephew?' he asked.

'And now we visit Señor Laird in Chalet Number Twenty,

uncle?' urged the sports writer. 'I do not care to be involved in any more strange goings-on in this part of earth.'

'*Si*, I think we better get our work done and get off this island pronto, nephew,' responded the cop. 'Maybe I will not come back here for golf, after all.'

CHAPTER FORTY

12. 50am. Thursday 25 November.

Millport, Isle of Cumbrae.

'Charlie, it's me. I need to see you urgently. Now!' A beseeching tone had replaced the composure of a couple of hours earlier. 'It's fuckin' important.' Derek Laird required immediate assistance.

'Where are you?' Charlie Brock snapped out the question, moving away from his companions at the bar and already heading towards the door. The sportswriter realised the situation was developing a lot more swiftly than anticipated. The footballer had agreed to sleep on the next move and had arranged to have breakfast with Brock and Willy, away from prying eyes in Chalet Number Twenty, early in the morning. What had changed?

'I'm over at the pier,' said Laird. 'I'm at the old ticket office. It's okay, there's no-one in sight.'

It was fortunate the owner of the black Range Rover with the tinted windows had pushed the driver's seat all the way back and nudged into a dead sleep. Adam Crawley wasn't about to attract attention to himself, signing into a hotel or a guest house. He would be on the first ferry at seven in the morning and would be back in Edinburgh a couple of hours later. He smiled as he dozed.

'Don't move,' said Brock. 'I'll be there in a second.'

He went back to Willy, the cop and the newsman. 'Give me a couple of minutes, people. Got to go.' Unexpectedly, he took a step forward and kissed Willy on the cheek. 'Love you,' he whispered.

And with that he was through the door and heading at pace across a deserted Stuart Street, dodging the parked Range Rover with its slumbering occupant.

'Christ, Derek, what's happening?' he exclaimed as the footballer emerged from the shadows. 'I thought we were seeing each other in the morning.'

'So did I, Charlie, but I had to get on my toes fastish,' said Laird, still slightly out of breath. 'Something was happening down at the boatyard and I wasn't hanging around to see what all the commotion was about. I saw two figures in long coats prowling around. I guessed they weren't autograph hunters. I got out sharpish, running across the back gardens of the villas.' He rubbed his right shin. 'Think I collided with about ten fuckin' stone gnomes. The amount of crap people leave around in their backyards.'

'Were you seen by anyone? The guys in the long coats?'

'No, definitely not. I had a quick look back, but they appeared too pre-occupied with something happening out in the water. I didn't stop to ask. And here I am. Any idea of what happens next, Charlie?'

'You're not going back to the chalet, that's for sure. You can sleep up at Schloss Adler ...'

'What is this Schloss ..?'

'It would take too long to explain, Derek. Maybe some day. Anyway, you're staying with me. It's a bit crowded because I've got Willy there, of course, and two good friends, a cop and a news reporter ...'

'Christ, you pick your company, Charlie. A cop AND a news reporter. And how do you intend explaining me to your mates?

"This is a guy who looks uncannily like that footballer who's gone missing?" Do you think they'll buy into that? Do you ...'

'They already know you're here,' interrupted Brock, holding up a hand.

'Oh, great! Why don't we just buy some advertising space in Times Square and tell the world?'

'You can trust them, Derek. They are genuine friends; no duckers and divers allowed in our little troupe of three.'

'How did they know I was here? I can't believe you told them.'

'I said I trusted them, Derek, I didn't say I wanted them to have my babies. No, they saw you earlier. They followed me and Willy when ...'

'I thought you said they were friends?'

'Aye, friends who sometimes make a great argument for birth control, but friends still the same; friends with disturbing senses of mischief.'

'A cop AND a news reporter?'

Charlie Brock thought quickly. He looked at his wristwatch, it was closing in on one in the morning. 'Let's go and meet them.'

'You're fuckin' joking!'

'My well of humour has dried up for the time being, I'm afraid. There's only Willy, R.I.P. and El Cid in the pub ...'

'R.I.P.? El Fuckin' Cid? What the hell's going on, Charlie? Who are these guys?'

'And Hughie will be there, too,' said Brock, ignoring the question. 'He's the owner. Oh, and Vodka Joe. I'm sure Hughie will grant us about an hour's drinking-up time, so let's put it to a good use. Time to come clean, Crazy Horse.'

'Aye, let's stop dancing around. How do you say it in journalism, Charlie? Time to spill the beans?'

'Don't want to upset you, Derek, but I've never heard anyone use that expression in newspapers.'

'Oh, who cares? I'm going to spill my guts.'

'Never heard that one, either.'

The footballer and the sportswriter trotted swiftly towards the front door of Hugh's Bar. Adam Crawley snored loudly in the black Range Rover. He was still smiling.

CHAPTER FORTY-ONE

1.05am. Thursday 25 November.

Millport, Isle of Cumbrae.

Miguel Araquistian and his nephew Javier Sanchez, cloaked in the dark, crept forward, careful not to make a sound in the stillness of the night. The lights were still on in Chalet Number Twenty. 'Okay, Javier?' whispered the cop. The sports reporter nodded, his lips seemingly unable to move. He was on the verge of the story that would assuredly launch his journalistic career. He realised he would be able to dine out at the top table on this tale forever. And he was nervous. Very nervous.

Araquistian took charge; he would make his nephew proud. 'Get them off guard,' he whispered. 'Move in when their hands are low and their chin is exposed.'

Sanchez wondered if he was about to enter a boxing ring. He merely sought an interview.

The cop banged on the door of the chalet. This was obviously essential training for police forces throughout the universe. No need to use a doorbell when you could splinter wood with brute force. THUMP! THUMP! No reply. 'Go round the back, nephew. Have a look in the window, tell me what you see.'

'Nothing,' came the reply twenty seconds later. 'The place looks empty.'

'Can't be,' said Araquistian, raising his voice above the earlier murmurs. He stepped forward again and landed two more sledgehammer blows on the door, a tactic he had perfected chasing Romanians in Barcelona. THUMP! THUMP!

All was quiet.

'I know you are in there, Derek Laird. My name is Miguel Araquistian and I am the commisaro du La Guardia Urbana of Barcelona. I am accompanied by my nephew, Javier Sanchez, a sports reporter of *La Vanguardia*. We are not here to harm you, do you understand? I wish only to ascertain that you are alive and well, that is all. There are a lot of people worried about you. All the Barcelona fans. Including me. I am Barca through and through.' The cop wondered if a little bit of flattery might do the trick. 'You are my favourite player, alongside Cruyff. And Maradona. And Messi. And ... oh, please, allow me to see for myself that you are fine and I can tell everyone back home the good news.' Another pause. 'And maybe you could take a moment or two to talk to my neph ... the sports reporter who has travelled with me. Is that possible?'

Not a sound.

'Is he hiding in there, uncle? It doesn't look like there is any movement.' The nephew tip-toed again to peer in the side window. 'I see nothing.'

Araquistian was running short of patience. His police training came to the fore; he walloped on the door twice again. THUMP! THUMP! 'Listen, señor Laird, we really do need to talk. Even for only a moment, *si*? We can talk and then we will go away. Maybe after a quick word with this sports reporter. Then we go. *Si*?'

Nothing.

'Uncle, have you tried the lock?' asked Sanchez.

'I do not have my special knife, nephew,' answered the cop. 'I left it at home, didn't think it would be required.'

'No, I mean the handle. Have you tried the handle? Maybe it's not locked.'

'Don't be silly, nephew. Laird has come this far undetected, covered his tracks with devilish cunning, do you really believe he would leave a door unlocked?'

He tried the handle and the door swung open. 'That's a first,' he muttered as he stepped into the chalet. He immediately noted its tidiness, apart from two empty beer bottles and a drained wine glass on a table. There was also a three-quarters-full bottle of beer. He looked at the arrangement of bottles. 'He's had company, nephew,' said the cop, trying to recover composure.

'How do you know, uncle?' asked the sportswriter. 'Are you sure?'

'Yes, nephew, I'm sure. Two people have been sitting on the sofa opposite that chair. Someone has had two bottles of beer and his companion has had a glass of wine. Presumably, that would mean two men and a woman; odds are that would be the case. I'll bet you'll find lipstick on the wine glass. Take a look.'

'Is this not evidence, uncle? Maybe the Scottish police ...'

'The Scottish police can go fuck themselves, nephew. They haven't shown any interest in Laird so far, so why should we care now?'

Sanchez picked up the glass and examined it. 'Yes, uncle, you are correct. Very slight trace of lipstick here.' He smiled. 'Could be a man wearing lipstick, of course.'

'I know they wear skirts around here, nephew, but I doubt if they parade around in the latest *Coco Chanel* fragrances.'

The cop stood back. 'Not much to see,' he said. 'Bedroom, shower and kitchen empty. Look in the wardrobe, nephew, see what's in there, please.'

Sanchez was now getting rather excited. There were on the trail of Crazy Horse. 'Just a couple of sweaters, jeans and shoes, uncle. Nothing suspicious.'

The cop picked up the bottle of beer that was almost full. 'You left in a rush, my friend. Poor Scotsman, leaving your drink behind. And you didn't lock the door, either. What startled you?' He thought for a moment, pushing a hand through his hair.

'And where are you now?'

CHAPTER FORTY-TWO

1.20am. Thursday 25 November.

Millport, Isle of Cumbrae.

'Okay, are we all strapped in and sitting comfortably? Then I'll begin.'

'Just a minute, Derek,' interrupted Hughie Edwards. 'I'll lock the doors. Anyone could wander in, you just never know on this island.'

The pub owner swept round from behind the bar, took the keys that jangled noisily from his belt and bolted the front door. He raced to the top of the bar and repeated the act with the side door. 'We're safe now,' he said contentedly. 'Right, Derek, fire away. Spill the beans.'

The footballer looked at Charlie Brock and smiled. So, too, did Willy, as intrigued as anyone inside the bar as to what was about to unfold. Griff Stewart, the newspaperman, and Harry Booth, the cop, pulled up their stools and settled comfortably at the bar. The contents of their glasses had been replenished and they were in the mood for a right good yarn. They had already explained their *noms de plume* to Derek Laird. The footballer thought the monikers fitted well. 'R.I.P. and El Cid,' he nodded. 'And I thought I had a daft nickname.' There was one other customer in the pub, but it seemed obvious Vodka Joe wouldn't have much of an input to the conversation. He was emitting the sound of a gentle buzz saw as he settled cosily into his private neuk by the window.

'Here goes, folks. Well, it's been fairly well documented that I like the company of women ...'

'Lucky bastard,' said Hughie before he could stop himself. 'Oops, sorry.'

'Aye, I suppose I can't complain, Hughie. I've done okay so far. Lots of nubiles in Barcelona who use me as much as I use them. Oh, I know it will end some day, maybe sooner rather than later, who knows? "Enjoy it while you can" everyone tells me, and that's exactly what I've been doing. Until ...'

The footballer hesitated. The five fascinated occupants of the bar seemed to lean forward as one towards Laird's couch seat at the window opposite the comatose Vodka Joe.

'And?' asked Hughie, rubbing furiously at a pint pot with a flannel.

'Well, that's when I met Martine. Yes, she's the so-called "mystery brunette". I had been seeing Erica Martinelli, Melinda Z and Anna Glow, but Martine seemed different somehow. I liked her in a different way from the other girls I had dated since arriving in the city. My God, she was stunning, a natural beauty. I had actually been with Anna when I met her.' Laird halted and added, 'I suppose you've heard all about these girls in the newspapers over the last few days?'

'Anna's the one who gets the fun bags out all the time on children's telly?' enquired Hughie, who already knew the answer.

'Aye, Anna's quite happy to display the mammaries any time the cameras are rolling ...'

A pint pot splintered under the robust force of Hughie's scrubbing.

'Can we let Derek get on with the story, Hughie?' pleaded

Brock. 'My deadline's been and gone, but I wouldn't mind an early start in the morning. A bit of hush, mate, eh?'

Hughie looked suitably chastened. He nodded and made a zipping motion across his lips.

'Okay, folks,' continued the footballer. 'Happy to get it off my chest, at last. Anyway, I was at some awards ceremony with Anna when I first saw Martine. I thought she was breathtaking, drop dead gorgeous. I hadn't felt like that for quite awhile. I managed to get a telephone number and I promised to call her. And I did that the very next morning before going to training. We arranged a quiet date. I trained all day with a stiffy – oh, sorry, Willy, forgive me – and I couldn't wait to see her that night. We went up to a place in the hills, a nice peaceful little restaurant. And we just chatted about this and that. She told me she had heard of this "Crazy Horse" footballer with Barca, but didn't know it was me. To be honest, she didn't look too impressed.'

'She told me she was a model. I asked her if she did nude shots, the tasteful sort, you know. She glowered at me. I thought I was about to be turned to stone. That was not her style, I was told. She was a proper model. And she also warned me not to call her a clothes horse. She was really unusual; no-one had spoken to me like that. I realised Martine was going to be a challenge.'

The footballer stopped to lift his glass to his lips. 'You pour a mean pint of draught, Hughie.'

'Best on the island,' said the bar owner. 'Tell us more about this Martine,' he urged impatiently, thinking it was fortunate Big Eric wasn't in the vicinity.

'Well, I saw Martine a couple of times over the next fortnight or so. It was quite a hectic schedule, you know. I was juggling with the other three and I didn't really need a fourth spoke ...'

'That's a new name for it,' interjected Hughie, not realising he was continually interrupting the flow.

'Shut up, Hughie, and let the lad have his say,' said El Cid.

'So I had a problem. What was I to do? I had great fun with Erica, Melinda and Anna, but somehow Martine was getting under my skin. And I knew I had to sort it out. As I said, Martine was different. Every other bird jumped into bed at the drop of a hat. Martine was not like that. A challenge, right enough.'

'I know how you feel, I can sympathise,' said R.I.P. working off memory.

'She kept telling me we would know when the time was right. Oh, I could footer about with her norks and so on; it was a bit like being back at school with Mabel. And what a pair of diddies she possessed, too. Sorry about this, Willy, but I've got to tell it like it is, hope you don't mind.'

'Don't let me stop you, Derek.', she smiled. 'It's all very educational.'

'I mean you're well stacked, too, if you don't mind me saying. You'll never fall flat on your face, will you? Well, Martine was the same. A photographer pal used to email me piles of pictures to let me know who were the hottest bods on the local scene. Quite by chance, he fired over a few of Martine, modelling bikinis. That girl could fill out a swimsuit, believe me. Very, very suggestive. However, on the romance front, we decided to keep everything quiet. I didn't even tell my team-mates. The manager didn't know, either. None of the guys who work for me had a clue. It was our little secret, Martine and me, and we would keep it that way until we both agreed it was appropriate to do otherwise. I knew the other three girls might be disappointed, but I realised it would take them about a nano-second each to get a new rich guy in tow.'

'And you didn't want to hurt their feelings?' asked Willy. 'That's quite noble in this day and age, I must say.'

'Thank you, Willy. Much appreciated. Aye, there was an element of that, but I couldn't help myself. Genuinely, I felt I was falling in love with Martine. Oh, I knew that it would mean having to give up so much if I settled down at twenty-five. But I knew my dear old mum would be happy. So I decided to ask Martine if she would move in with me. She turned me down.'

'And that's why you vanished?' Hughie asked. 'You couldn't take rejection? Your pride was hurt?'

'No, not at all. Martine still wanted to date me, but she asked for time to think things over. She had just turned twenty and wasn't too sure about a long-term commitment. To be honest, I could see her point of view. She was a fabulous-looking girl and she could have had her pick of the billionaires who populate this planet. She wouldn't have had to tolerate the aches and pains of an ageing footballer who, I had told her, has every intention of returning to Scotland once his playing career is over. Martine was actually born in Sao Paolo in Brazil and was taken to Barcelona by her parents when she was about six. Fairly certain neither Glasgow nor Edinburgh or anywhere else in Scotland might have figured too much in her thoughts as she was growing up. Millport neither, no offence, Hughie.'

'So, you had to part?' Hughie was enthralled.

'Yes, Hughie, but possibly not in the way you might imagine. Martine and I were due for a night in another restaurant tucked up in the hills. We were having a marvellous evening, as usual, when Martine told me she thought it was time we celebrated our love. That was the world she used; "celebrated". I thought that was lovely. I had waited about a month to hear those words and I can tell you I was ready for it. I was getting plenty off the other three, more than my fair share, but I was desperate to do the business with Martine.'

'And you couldn't perform and fled Barcelona in embarrassment?' Hughie had to know.

'No, Hughie, not quite as straightforward as that. Had that been the case, I would have been back in Scotland years ago, truth be told. I've pulled a few birds in my time and when we've got down to the nitty gritty I've been so knackered that the best I could manage between the sheets was a fumble and a smile before conking out.'

'Aye, we've all be there, Derek lad,' confided El Cid, extracting confused glances from his journalist pals.

'So what was the problem? You can't stop there.' Hughie was back to vigorously cleaning a pint glass.

'Well, we went to my place. I had the champagne on ice, played some cool Isaac Hayes, dimmed all the lights. We went up to the bedroom on the third floor. That's the one I keep for my special girlfriends: four-poster bed, black satin sheets and all that. And Martine was certainly special.'

'And?' Even Willy was eager for more information.

'Martine said she would slip into something more comfortable. I told her I would be quite content if she just remained in her skin. "Later," she whispered. Then she appeared wearing this really sexy number and practically glided into bed. "Ready when you are, *Caballo Loco*," she said. She had never called me *Caballo*

Loco before. Anyway, I practically shredded my gear as I slid in beside her. I have to admit I was more excited than ever before. I looked at her flawless skin, her brunette hair spread over the pillow, her smouldering blue eyes, her voluptuous red lips. She pulled me closer and took my left hand. She said, "Is this what you want?" and pressed my hand towards her crotch. I almost leapt through the ceiling.'

'An electric shock?' asked Hughie.

'I would have welcomed an electric shock, Hughie. Martine had the full set. Cock, balls, the lot. I couldn't believe it. I swept back the cover and there it was, a giant, blue-veined, ramrod-stiff, bald-headed, yoghurt-dispenser. Sorry, didn't mean to offend, Willy.'

'That's okay,' laughed Willy. 'Yoghurt-dispenser is my Sunday name.'

Laird grinned. 'And, even worse, she had a bigger dick than me!'

'So Martine was really a Martin?' asked Brock, already wondering about the angle he would be pursuing in this story.

'Actually, she was a Martinho.'

'And you never had an inkling?' asked Brock. 'No Adam's Apple? No stubble on the chin? Hair on the back of her hands? Bulge in her pants?'

'I'm telling you, Charlie, she was beautiful. I would have defied anyone to look at Martine and believe she was packing down there. She tucked it away, she told me once I had drained a fifteenth glass of champagne to settle my nerves. She – I just can't call her *he* – told me she thought that's what I wanted, that I was maybe bored with straight girls. She told me she had several friends – I was told not to call them "shemales" or, even worse, "chicks with dicks" – who dated bored, wealthy gentlemen.'

'I told her I wasn't *that* bored or *that* wealthy. I hoped I would NEVER be *that* bored or *that* wealthy.'

'Wow! What a story,' said Willy.

'And that, my friends, is why I am with you tonight. That's why I decided to get away for a while. You are the only people in the world who know that story. Except, Martine, of course. It's good to be able to tell someone, I thought I was going to explode trying to keep it all inside. Now I realise I will have to go back and face the music. I suppose I will be a figure of ridicule for a while, but I'll just have to accept it and ride out the storm.' Laird paused and looked at Brock. 'Well, Charlie, is that a good enough story for you? Will it earn you a few bob?'

'Pretty sensational stuff, my friend. Worldwide interest; front and back pages. I might have to get myself an agent. But let's not be hasty, okay? There's a lot to think about.' He swallowed the contents of his pint pot. 'Hughie, have we still time for a quick scatter?'

'Plenty of time,' said Hughie, who was grateful Big Eric wasn't around to hear Laird's story. A crowbar would have been required to prise him from the ceiling of the Gents.

Outside the pub, two Spaniards attempted to peer through the front window of Hugh's Bar. All they could see were their own puzzled reflections. 'Looks like we won't be having a late one in this pub, nephew,' said Miguel Araquistian. 'We'll try again tomorrow. Crazy Horse can't be far away.'

At that moment, Derek Laird was sitting on a couch barely two feet away on the other side of the glass.

Vodka Joe stirred to life. He yawned and stretched his arms above his head. Unsteadily, he got to his feet.

'Fancy a nightcap, Vodka?' asked Hughie, already heading for the upturned bottle of Rasputnik on the gantry.

'Aye, thanks, Hughie, and then I'm off up the road. Get ready for another day on Millport. Maybe something interesting'll happen tomorrow.'

CHAPTER FORTY-THREE

7.48am. Thursday 25 November.

Millport, Isle of Cumbrae.

'Thank Christ I'm not playing today,' exclaimed Derek Laird as he eased himself gingerly out of the rickety armchair beside the TV. 'I'd be running around like a deformed chimp with cramp.'

'You were the lucky one,' said Harry Booth, rubbing sleep from his eyes. 'I had to put up with R.I.P. snoring in my left ear all night.'

Charlie Brock entered the crowded living room doubling as an impromptu bedroom on his way to the kitchen of his top floor flat. 'Tea or coffee anyone? A brew is urgently required.'

'A new vertebrae is urgently required,' said Griff Stewart as he began to stir and unwind, crushed onto the two-seater lounge alongside El Cid.

'Where's the lovely Willy?' asked Laird. 'Don't tell me she's dumped you already, Charlie. Looks like I don't have the copyright on doing runners, then?'

'The lovely Willy, as you call her, Derek, is at this moment over at Mrs Pastry's picking up twenty crispy hot rolls to go with the mountain of rashers she bought earlier. Girl's got her wits about her. The way to a man's heart etc., etc. First, though, tea, the best drink of the day.' Brock checked the kettle, filled it with water from the tap and clicked it into action. He sat at the small table beside the window; a curious seagull perched on the windowsill outside, looking into the apartment. Laird stretched and made a growling noise. 'That's better,' he said, as he parked his backside on a seat beside the sportswriter, waiting for the water to boil.

'Well, now you know the truth, Charlie,' he said. 'Warts, willies and all. Some tale, eh?'

'Aye, you can say that again, Derek.' He laughed, 'A real cock and balls story if I've ever heard one. Sorry, couldn't resist. Seriously, now we have to see which is the best way forward with this information. I take it you will be contacting the club at some stage this morning? Wouldn't do you too many favours if the first they know of all this is when it hits the newsstands tomorrow. It'll be everywhere. PA, UPI and Reuters will be on it like a swarm as soon as it hits the presses. They check the first editions of every newspaper, you know, pick out the best stories and refile them. You can be sure they'll be whizzing **'CRAZY HORSE FOUND'** all over the place. So, it really would be for the best if your club are not caught on the back foot.'

'I was going to phone the boss, anyway. He's a genuinely decent chap, Charlie. I'll put him straight and, as I've already said, I'll take my dumps and I'll face the music. Won't be pleasant, but there's nothing else for it. I can't run and hide forever.'

'Let's see what we can concoct. I didn't sleep much last night...'

'How fortunate,' said the cop.

'... and I did a fair bit of thinking.'

'What a shame,' said the news reporter.

'There's absolutely no need for the entire world to know about you and Martine. Who's going to talk about this? There were seven of us in the pub last night and one was Vodka Joe who doesn't count. I think I can speak for myself, Willy, R.I.P., El Cid and

Hughie and say that our silence is guaranteed. No clipes in there. You're hardly likely to shout it from the rooftops, so that leaves Martine. I wouldn't think it would do her modelling career much good if advertisers realised she was built like a Sumo wrestler down there. Just a thought, Derek, but where does she put her manhood?'

'Believe me, there are ways of disguising that bloody thing. Take my word for it.' He shuddered.

'Okay, so where does that leave us? I've got a wee idea, so let's run it up the flagpole and see if anyone salutes. Have you got a granny tucked away?'

'Is this code for something?' The footballer was surprised. 'I never joined the Masons.'

'No, really, I'm serious, it's a straightforward question. Do you have a wee granny tucked away somewhere?'

'Yes, my mum's old dear is still alive. She's in her eighties, I think. Lives in Stornoway.'

'Absolutely perfect,' said Brock. 'She's been unwell ...'

'Hardly likely, Charlie, she still chops her own firewood.'

'No, for the purposes of this story, she's got to have been sick, at death's door, even.'

'My old granny Olive? She's as fit as a flea.'

'I'm delighted for her,' said Brock, 'but let's just say she was ill. You know journalists can bend the truth a little, don't you?'

'You mean you're lying bastards?'

'Exactly. Thanks for that. Okay, that's going to be my storyline, complete with quotes from you to confirm it. You were distraught when you heard about the plight of your dear old granny. She's always been your favourite ...'

'I've hardly ever seen her.'

'... you felt guilty about being so far away just when she needed you most. You panicked. You had to get back to Scotland.'

'What about slipping through customs? The cards I gave my pal Ricardo to dispense among his associates? The dollars, yen and bhat from the bank? How do I explain all that deception?'

'No problem. You didn't, in fact, slip through customs, did you? You weren't travelling on a fake passport. If the cops at border control can't do their job properly, then that is hardly your concern. The cards? You're a big-hearted guy. Who's to say anything else? And the money from the bank? So what? You were planning on a wee world tour when the season finishes. You got the cash now because you were told by your financial people you would get the best deal and not to wait. In any case, there is no way the police will ever admit to being duped. As Vodka Joe would say, the law of *omerta* would kick in.'

'*Omerta*?' It was Derek Laird's day to be perplexed.

'Yes, silence. The Mafia code. The rule that prohibits divulging information about certain activities. Have you never seen *The Godfather*?'

'No, never. Is it any good?'

'Almost up there with *Where Eagles Dare*, but that's another story. So, all you need to do is get in touch with your mum and get her to follow the bouncing ball. Tell her to take her lead from you. Keep her away from the press all day today and we'll sort out tomorrow when it arrives. Better still, tell her to get booked into a hotel or a guest house somewhere out of the way. Stay with a friend or a relative for a few days until this news becomes chip wrappers. Get your gran onside, too. I'll write the story of you simply being alarmed about the news of your granny. You were shocked, not thinking straight. Totally dismayed. Think of the headlines, **'HERO STAR RUSHES TO HELP SICK GRAN'**. It'll work, trust me. You'll end up getting the sympathy vote from the public. Old grannies everywhere will love you. Who wouldn't yearn for a grandson like you? You'll be mayor of Barcelona before the turn of the year.'

'And what about the club? What do I tell them?'

'The truth. You'll need them on your side for the next few days or so. If you both sing from the same hymn sheet, the problem will go away, I assure you. I've written more than a few tales like this one.'

'What? Players going out with birds with dangly bits?'

'Not quite. No, guys who have gone AWOL, led astray by good old *femmes fatales*, booze, drugs, gambling, you name it. A couple of days later they come to their senses and try to disguise their past forty-eight hours or so of debauchery. Trust me, Derek, I've helped out more than a few over the years. Okay? Happy to leave it with me?'

'It might just work, Charlie.'

'It WILL work, Derek. I'll file the story and I'll just say an island in Scotland. I won't identify Stornoway. News guys at every paper would see this story and begin sending their own reporters there. Turn it into a circus. So, we'll leave them in the dark. I'll follow that up with a quotes-driven piece by yourself complete with a heartfelt apology to the club and the fans. How you hoped that they would understand. That'll round it all off. I'll phone a few

301

sports editors, let them know the story is coming. And I'll leave my mobile switched on for an hour or so. Answer a few queries, but keep them at arm's length. After that, they can do what they like. They've got the information and the rest is up to them.'

'You're not going to sell it as an exclusive? You would get more money, eh?'

'Aye, could probably name my fee, but all that means is a scrum kicking off tomorrow as every other paper goes into overdrive to get their handle on the follow-up. They can be even more vicious when they have been left at the starting gate and they are forced to play catch-up. Your mum's house would be besieged with reporters wanting to know how your granny was keeping, where she lives, how close you are, any photographs? Try to persuade your mum to make herself scarce. She wouldn't stand a chance with some of those people. Ninety-nine per cent of them get the others a bad name. Don't think your mum needs the hassle, do you?'

'When you put it like that, I don't suppose so.'

'And don't worry about me. I'll still make a packet from this story, believe me. It looks like Christmas is back on. Could be good news for Willy.'

'Happy to have done my bit,' smiled Crazy Horse.

'Anyone for tea or coffee?' It was El Cid. 'I'll be mother.'

Brock groaned. 'What is it about men who want to be women?'

CHAPTER FORTY-FOUR

9.25am. Thursday 25 November.

Glasgow.

Larry Wilson could hardly believe his ears; Smiler was whistling happily with a fair old gusto. The taxi driver had picked up the *Tribune's* chief sports reporter at his home in Pollokshields and was now heading through the rush-hour traffic to drop him off at the newspaper's offices in the heart of the city.

The previous day Smiler had been his usual nauseating self as he prepared to get the train from Central Station for Largs on his way to Millport. What magical powers did this small island possess, that could transform this wretched character into something akin to a human being?

'Excuse me, cabbie,' said Smiler. 'I've never asked you your name, have I? Very remiss of me, my apologies.'

Wilson came close to veering his vehicle into a packed queue at a bus stop. 'Larry Wilson,' he said.

'Larry? Right, must try to remember, again please forgive me. Too much going on in my head sometimes. Feel an awful lot better today. Isn't today a wonderful day, Larry? Look at the crisp winter sunshine. You can almost touch it, can't you? So lovely. All those wonderful and vibrant colours. Makes you glad just to be alive, doesn't it?'

Rodger James didn't mention the previous evening's events which had brought about his remarkable reincarnation. Had that really been a gun against his head? Were the threats genuine? He would never know for sure. But he wouldn't take the risk. His aquatic adventure had been more than just slightly traumatic, too. Who was the kind gentleman who had picked him up and tugged his boat back to the beach at Kames Bay, then set him free? That knowledge would never be attained, either. The mystery rescuer insisted on Smiler remaining blindfolded until he had finished a very slow count to one hundred. Then, and only then, had he been allowed to remove the covering.

Wilson checked the rearview mirror; it looked like Smiler, but he sure as hell wasn't acting like Smiler. He ventured to talk to the newspaperman, something he had been warned against in the past. Attempting to engage the *Trib* reporter in any sort of small talk was simply asking for the immediate termination of your employment and at least forty lashes. 'Everything go okay in Millport, I take it?'

Smiler grinned. Unfortunately there wasn't much he could do about the rotting molars. 'Yes, an interesting time, I must admit. You could say I got close to God, Larry. I've been given a second chance, you know. I've seen the error of my ways. Oh, I've made mistakes, *many* mistakes. I know I can be a better person.'

Noreen Taylor, portly owner of the Glen Mill Guest House, had come close to a full-blown seizure earlier that morning, before the *Trib's* reformed character left to catch the first ferry back to the mainland. Thoughtfully, he had purchased a box of chocolates for his hostess, possibly the first time in his life he had bought confectionery. There was a note to thank her for kind assistance while also complimenting her on the comfy bed and spotless room. Noreen praised the Good Lord she had had second thoughts about bringing the blunderbuss out of mothballs.

As Smiler walked up the passenger ramp to the 7am ferry at Cumbrae Slip, he had been passed by a black Range Rover with tinted windows. Adam Crawley didn't even give a sideways glance to the character in the threadbare gaberdine overcoat.

Larry Wilson pulled over his cab outside the *Tribune's* old grey building, standing six storeys high. Smiler practically bounded out, full of verve and vigour. He said, 'Thank you very much for the safe journey, Larry. I am much obliged once again.' He leaned forward and deposited something in the taxi driver's jacket pocket. 'Have a drink on me, please.'

Wilson was dumbfounded. Later that day he investigated what had been placed in his pocket. It was a tea bag.

'Well, at least, it's a start,' thought the cabbie.

CHAPTER FORTY-FIVE

11.05am. Thursday 25 November.

Millport, Isle of Cumbrae.

Charlie Brock had to admit he was not a huge admirer of the works of Shakespeare, but he couldn't prevent himself. 'All's well that ends well,' he said, chinking his pint glass against Derek Laird's bottle of beer.

It was five minutes past eleven and the sports writer and the footballer were standing in Hugh's Bar, waiting to be joined by the usual suspects. Brock had filed both tales, the hard news story and Derek's 'first person' piece, to the UK's national press. They had taken him just over an hour to write. Two articles, two clicks of the send button on his laptop and the words streamed hither and yon.

He could see Willy making her way across from the Schloss Adler. El Cid and R.I.P. were no doubt scoffing the remains of the bacon butty extravaganza presented by their shapely benefactor. Hughie had already claimed his prized autograph. 'Can you make it out to me and sign it Crazy Horse?' was the request. Laird was happy to comply.

Vodka Joe was quite surprised to see he wasn't first in the drinking den as he made his way through the door, expecting a vodka to be waiting on the bar and today's copy of the *News* to go with it. He wasn't disappointed; a good start to the day. 'Morning, people,' he said, picking up his glass and newspaper without breaking stride on his way to his favourite neuk.

'You still think Crazy Horse is dead?' Hughie couldn't resist.

'Cert,' replied Vodka Joe. 'Sleeping with the fishes. No argument.'

Derek Laird hadn't a clue what they were talking about. He was leaning against the bar realising he was a mightily relieved guy. The footballer had phoned the manager, Rafael Castillo, on his private mobile number. He explained about Martine and went into every detail. Momentarily, after he had had his say, he held the phone away from his ear expecting a withering rebuke and all sorts of threats. He was taken totally by surprise to be greeted with gales of raucous laughter. Had the manager been tipped over the edge of reason? Had it all been too much for him?

'Derek,' said Castillo, 'you are so innocent, my young friend. You should have informed me immediately and I could have told you about the Italian player who came to Spain just over a decade ago. He arrived with a rather attractive transvestite who went everywhere with him. We all knew in football, of course, but it was never made public. No-one cared about his sexual preferences. It was no big deal just so long as he continued to perform on the football field. How he performed in the boudoir with his drag queen boyfriend was no-one else's business. Three of our top clubs bought him and they were all aware of his sexual desires. He was even photographed regularly with his lover. You have to say the transvestite did scrub up well. No-one guessed, not even the snoops in the newspapers. So, Derek, you are not so unique. Sorry to disappoint you.' The chortling faded and was swiftly replaced by a stern tone. 'Now get your backside back here and expect to be fined a month's wages and be put through some gruelling sessions, morning and afternoon. I want you fit for Valencia next week.'

Laird had arranged for Brock to email his two stories to the club's media office. Both tales would travel in tandem. A sick grandmother in a remote Scottish island and no mention of

Martine. Barcelona would endorse the story at a press conference at noon tomorrow, hopefully bringing a halt to the entire episode.

Willy, looking radiant as ever, swept into the pub, the morning chill trailing behind her. A Dry Martini and lemonade was waiting for her on the bar. She picked up the glass and clinked with Brock and Laird. 'Derek,' she said, 'when you chat up another girl you might think about adding a new line.'

'And what would that be, young lady?'

'How's it hanging? And if you get an answer, run like hell!'

'And try to be a bit more cocksure in the future, will you?' chipped in Brock.

'Yeah, I suppose I asked for that. But I don't feel too bad now I've had my chat with the manager. I know I'm not a freak show after what he's told me. I'm way down that pecking order. Didn't mean to say "pecking", sorry. Shit, I'm not even on the waiting list.'

Laird suddenly went quiet as he looked over Brock's shoulder and out of the huge front window of Hugh's Bar. 'Charlie, see those two guys I was telling you about last night; the blokes with the long coats? Unless I'm very much mistaken, that's them heading towards the front door. Fuckin' hell, they look like the KGB. All they need are Cossack hats.'

Brock glanced towards the pair, who were obviously foreign. 'Could be wrong here, mate, but I might venture they are Spanish. Do they have secret police in Spain?'

Laird's face was draining of colour at a rapid rate. 'Well, there's some organisation called Centro Nacional de Inteligencia. You don't think they would sent out secret cops for me, do you?'

'Maybe the big boss is a Barcelona fan. Wants you back in the team as quickly as possible.'

'Hughie, tell these blokes the toilets are out of order for the rest of the day, will you?' Laird made a hasty retreat to the Gents.

'Well, Willy, it's just you and me to hold the fort. Are you up for it?'

'You don't have to ask, Charlie boy, you know I'm up for anything with you.' Her persuasive, inviting eyes were dancing again as she sipped her drink.

The door eased open and in stepped Miguel Araquistian followed by Javier Sanchez. Both were dressed for a Moscow winter. Araquistian looked around him slowly before advancing to the bar. He smiled at Hughie. 'Two large whiskies, *por favor.*'

He gave Willy an approving glance before dismissing Brock. He noticed Vodka Joe in the corner, sitting quietly catching up with the news and, as ever, gearing himself for the first bell and the appearance of his daily sparring partner, Dr Algernon Pendlebury.

'Any particular brand?' asked Hughie.

'Oh, we had drinks from the pub along the way last night,' motioned the cop with his right arm. 'Something from a place called Islay, I believe. Very good, too. Do you have such a drink?'

'That's a choice between eight distilleries, my friend, but it could be the Bunnahabhain malt,' said Hughie. 'Yes, we've got that. Very nice it is, too.' Slight pause. 'And what brings you to our little island?'

'Where are my manners? Allow me to introduce myself, *por favor.* My name is Miguel Araquistian and this is my nephew Javier Sanchez. I am a policeman in Barcelona and Javier is a

309

sports reporter with a newspaper.'

'I'm Hughie,' said the bar owner, stretching across to the shake the hand of the policeman, still in the act of dragging off a massive buckskin glove. Hughie repeated the act with the sports reporter.

'You on holiday?' asked Hughie shrewdly as he passed over the malts.

Araquistian had decided honesty was the best policy the previous evening in the other pub. And it had also paid dividends. Wooden Chalet Number Twenty opposite the boatyard. He and his nephew had scouted the area first thing in the morning; still no sign of the missing footballer. Where was he? He went for the truthful approach again. 'I am looking for Derek Laird, the Scottish footballer known as *Caballo Loco,* Crazy Horse, who plays for Barcelona. Have you heard of him?'

'Aye, we are aware who you are talking about,' said Brock, introducing himself to the Spaniards. He realised his stories had yet to circulate before publication tomorrow. 'What makes you believe he is on this island?'

'We KNOW he is on this island,' said Araquistian putting a heavy emphasis on the word. 'I would like very much to talk to him, if it is at all possible. There is nothing to fear.' He grinned. 'We are not hunting him. My bosses in Barcelona are still searching for him and I would like to put their minds at ease. There are also thousands of Barcelona fans who are worried about his disappearance. Including me.'

'And your nephew?'

'Oh, *si*, my nephew. He would like the big exclusive story for his newspaper. Make himself a star, get promoted, talk to the main players, cover the huge games. You know what I mean?' Again the wide grin.

'Yes, I think so,' replied Brock, not inclined to show his full hand just yet. Hughie and Willy remained muted. Vodka Joe was now reading the women's problems page, engrossed in a debate over breast enlargement. He looked up briefly at the two strangers. 'Seen any polar bears out there?' he asked, passing comment on their dress code. 'Bloody global warming. We've got a penguin colony down at Kames Bay, you know.' The Spaniards shrugged. Vodka Joe went back to scouring Hughie's newspaper. He wasn't impressed by an email from Jane B, Oban, who actually wanted a breast reduction. 'Keep them meaty, beaty, big and bouncy, girl,' he advised. No-one took any notice.

'And what happens when you find Derek Laird?' Brock pushed ahead.'Would you even *recognise* Crazy Horse out of his working clothes?'

'Maybe,' said Araquistian, appreciatively sipping his malt. 'Maybe not. Oh, this is lovely. Yes, I see what you mean ... er ...'

'Charlie Brock.'

'Ah, yes, Charlie. I have watched him many times at the Nou Camp, but my usual seat is closer to the clouds than it is to the ground. And, of course, I have seen him on television, but that puts on ten pounds, so they say. I shouldn't tell you this, Charlie, but, as commisaro du la Guardia Urbana in the city, you would expect me to recognise most people, wouldn't you? One of my favourite opera singers is a female by the name of Maria de Hidalgo. She is absolutely beautiful. I would have crawled over broken glass just to touch her. And do you know she lived not far from me? I saw her practically every day and I never recognised her. Without all her wigs, make-up and finery, she was just another woman in the supermarket. Maybe Derek Laird is the same.' Another shrug of

311

the shoulders. 'Who knows?'

'And what about you, Javier? Would you know Crazy Horse? Have you ever interviewed him?' Brock was doing some ground work.

'I wish!' said the sports reporter with undisguised enthusiasm. 'But I am not so important. Maybe some day ...'

'All your dreams will come true,' completed Brock. He had a good feeling about the Spaniards. He slid off the bar stool. 'Hughie, keep my pint warm, I'm off to the loo. Back in a moment.' He winked at the bar owner. Two minutes later he returned with Derek Laird.

'*Ay, caramba!*' cried the sports writer. '*Caballo Loco!*'

EPILOGUE

11.02am. Friday 26 November.

Millport, Isle of Cumbrae.

'Charlie, give us plenty of warning the next time you're coming over, will you? Give me a chance to alert Steven Spielberg and then we can get everything on film.'

Hughie Edwards smiled as he energetically scoured a pint pot. Vodka Joe was sitting in his 'Sofa So Good' corner, engrossed in the morning's newspapers. Hughie had bought six dailies at Crawford's when he saw the banner front page headlines. **'CRAZY HORSE DISCOVERED'**, roared *The News*. **'CRAZY HORSE REVEALED'**, screamed one. **'CRAZY HORSE CAUGHT'**, bellowed another. **'CRAZY HORSE TRACKED DOWN'**, shrieked yet another.

Dr. Algernon Pendlebury, aka Hickory Dickory, sitting at his usual place beside the fruit machine, was secretly captivated by the *Gazette's* front page report on the story, **'MISSING FAMOUS SCOTTISH FOOTBALLER ESPIED ON UNNAMED ISLAND'**. They didn't quite subscribe to the punchy, smack-between-the-eyes headlines of the down-market red tops.

'EAT YOUR OWN BODY WEIGHT IN DIGESTIVE BISCUITS', offered the rarely-read *Sphere*.

'Looks as though you've cleaned up, Scoop,' observed Willy. 'I take it a couple of quid will be coming your way?'

'Sincerely hope so,' said the sportswriter. 'I'm not a big fan

313

of becoming the guy who put the word 'free' into freelance. I can't afford to work for nought. Aye, should be a nice little earner. Mind you, I'll still have to chase down a few of the rags who are always quite eager to run your stories, but not quite as enthusiastic when it comes to actually paying for them. I'll get it in the end. Just mention "Sue, Grabbit and Run", those well-known bad-ass lawyers, and it's amazing how quickly the coffers are opened.'

Brock prepared to heave his half-drained pint of lager in the general direction of his gullet before pausing. He wrinkled his brow. 'One thing that has surprised me in the papers this morning, and I wouldn't blame you one bit if you thought I was well past being surprised by the press. But the comment piece in *The Tribune* by my old chum Smiler is a real gaster of the flabber. I could hardly believe it; he's actually siding with Derek. Changed tack completely. He's saying the lad deserves our sympathy because he obviously had something weighing heavily on his mind. This isn't April the first, is it? Smiler writing something in support of someone? Just doesn't sound like our mate at all. What could possibly have persuaded him to pen such a piece? Aye, that's a puzzler. Must be God's work.'

'And, right on cue, here come Frank and Jesse,' pointed out Hughie. 'Stick them up a couple of drinks, Charlie? Can you afford a "Brandy, gentleman's measure, if you please" and a pint of heavy?'

'Don't you dare go splashing your money around, Scoop,' intercepted Willy. 'We may need it to pay for a couple of weeks somewhere nice in the sunshine to escape this winter. Tenerife is nice this time of year, I'm told. What do you think, Charlie boy?'

'Willy, I think this is the beginning of a beautiful friendship ...'

'Just "friendship", Charlie?'

'Have you never seen *Casablanca?* No? That's what Humphrey Bogart says to Claude Rains at the end of the movie. A classic line.'

Griff Stewart, chief news reporter of the *Daily News,* pushed open the door and was quick and to the point. 'You're a bastard, Charlie. Do you know that? A genuine one hundred per cent 24 carat bastard.'

'To be honest, R.I.P., I've never thought too hard about it. By the way, there's a glass of brandy on the bar if you're still talking to me.'

'I've had Martin Gilhooley on the mobile. He wants me to do a full follow-up to your Crazy Horse story. He knows Crazy Horse was in Millport and he wants a reaction from everyone, only EVERYONE, on this bloody island. And every other conceivable angle, as well. Am I not allowed a holiday?'

'Well, if you rush over to Miller Street you'll catch Araquistian and his nephew getting ready to catch the bus for the noon ferry to Largs. He could give you a good angle from a Spanish cop's perspective, don't you think? And, if he's come back to earth after his exclusive in his newspaper, young Javier will surely help out with the response from Derek's team-mates. And I'm positive Vodka Joe could give you a typical islander's feedback on the tale.'

'I was sure he was sleeping with the fishes,' came the mumble from the corner by the window. Vodka Joe sounded vaguely disappointed.

'Glad you got that one wrong,' said Derek Laird as he entered through the sidedoor. He was packed and ready to go. 'Hughie, have I got time for a quick round, please? What everyone's having? And a bottle of *Chateauneuf du Cumbrae* for the good doctor, of course.'

315

'Why, I'm much obliged, kind sir. You play for Barcelona? Yes? I'll make sure I look for your results every week. May the very best of fortune follow you wherever you go on your travels. May your balls fly straight and true.'

The footballer grimaced involuntarily for a moment, but regained his composure. 'Cheers, Hick,' he said. The island's GP didn't bother to correct him. 'Better stick up a couple of large malts from that place in Islay, too, Hughie, if you don't mind. Miguel and Javier will be joining us in a moment. We're all travelling back together, same flights, the lot. Strange game, isn't it?' Laird grabbed Brock by the hand. 'Shake, comrade,' he said. 'I'm in your debt.'

'You owe me nothing. I've made a couple of bob and Willy has instructed me to put it to a good use: a holiday in the winter sunshine for us both in Tenerife.'

Laird turned to Willy, threw his arms around her and kissed her smack on the lips. 'It's been a pleasure, lovely lady. Tenerife? You're both invited to Barcelona. I'll show you the sights; you'll love the place. Charlie, I'll give you a call when I get home, once everything has settled down. However, I absolutely insist you and Willy are my guests in Barca, stay as long as you want. Okay?'

Suddenly, the footballer adopted a serious, solemn expression. 'I've still got one worry, Charlie.'

'Fire away, Derek,' said Brock. 'Is there anything I have overlooked? I thought I had covered all angles.'

'As well as your arse,' added the evesdropper from the corner. No-one took notice.

'What if it is discovered the sick grannie was all a scam? What if the locals in Stornoway know old Olive is my only living grandparent and blow the whistle? Do you know the local press up there? Wouldn't they think that was a massive story? They could have photographs of Olive chopping up firewood, out on her daily five-mile jog …'

'Just make sure they don't have any snaps of her doing push-ups in the carrot patch,' Vodka Joe offered in a less-than-helpful manner.

Brock laughed. 'It's covered. Yes, they do have a local newspaper up there, but I've taken care of it. I know the local freelance. I've let it slip that Olive isn't your only living grannie. No, you've got another in some more obscure Scottish island. Her name is Muriel. And she was very sick recently. Trust me, they'll never bother checking.'

'Oh, Old Muriel, eh? Sick, you say? Must pay her a visit some time soon. Maybe wait until the end of the season.' Derek Laird was more relieved than he let on.

Miguel Araquistian and his nephew Javier Sanchez came in to say their fond farewells. Twenty minutes later, the Barcelona-bound trio, after extensive goodbyes, exited the pub. Jimmy Brogan was waiting in his taxi. He looked sober, but no-one could be sure. Araquistian hugged everyone, including Vodka Joe, and promised to take good care of *Caballo Loco*. He also enquired about the possibility of golf courses on this place called Islay. Sanchez followed his uncle's example and pledged his word to Brock he would stay in touch. Email addresses were passed around. 'I hate goodbyes,' said Willy. 'Me, too,' agreed Brock. 'Let's keep that in mind, eh?'

The taxi took off, just missing Noreen Taylor on her bicycle. 'Hope they make it all the way to the slip,' observed the doctor dryly. His words were drowned out. 'Fuckin' idiot!' shrieked the

317

stout guest house owner as she sought to bring her wobbling bike under control.

Hughie walked back behind the bar. He poured a Dry Martini and lemonade for Willy, pulled a pint of lager for Brock, sent over a vodka for his pal in the corner and asked himself, 'Hughie, do you deserve a drink? Do you deserve a LARGE drink?' He nodded profusely, placing the glasses on the bar for his guests before travelling the well-trodden path to the Martell optic. He helped himself to a gentleman's measure, then turned and said with an air of satisfaction, 'Cheers everyone.'

He moved to the bar beside Brock and Willy. 'So, it's been quite an eventful few days all round, eh?' He had also been informed Cob Webb had surfaced following his sexual jousting with Dirty Carrie. Apparently, there had been some involuntary projectile vomiting from both drunken parties in cubicle two in the Ladies' loo at the Legion. 'All things considered, though, it was a fairly successful first date,' observed Hughie.

The bar owner looked at Brock. 'First, Wild Bill Hickok. Now Crazy Horse. Who's next? Sitting Bull?'

Brock thought for a moment.

'Um heap no bad idea, *Kemo Sabe* ...'

Some other books from Ringwood Publishing

All titles are available from the Ringwood website and
from usual outlets.
Also available in Kindle, Kobo and Nook.
www.ringwoodpublishing.com

Ringwood Publishing, 24 Duncan Avenue, Glasgow
G14 9HN

mail@ringwoodpublishing.com

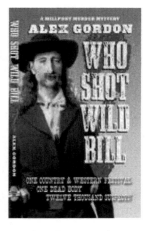

Who Shot Wild Bill?

Alex Gordon

One Country & Western festival. One dead body. Twelve thousand suspects!

The Millport Country & Western Festival is in full swing, with 12,000 would-be Wild West heroes dressed up as cowboys and Indians, complete with toy guns, headdresses, mock bar fights and gun slinging. Millport is starting to feel more like Tombstone, Arizona.

But there has never been a murder on the island. Until now.

A festival visitor, calling himself Wild Bill Hickok, has been found shot dead. Thousands of toy guns, but one of them must be real. Reporter Charlie Brock, on the island on holiday, is roped into solving this Millport murder mystery. With snappy dialogue and eccentric characters, *Who Shot Wild Bill?* is a quirky crime mystery and a homage to Millport. It is also the prequel to *What Spooked Crazy Horse?*

ISBN: 978-1-901514-31-5   £7.99

THE GREATEST STORIES NEVER TOLD

ALEX GORDON'S HILARIOUS ANECDOTES TAKE ME BACK TO A BYGONE ERA. WHEN THE EDITORIAL FLOOR COULD BE A BIT OF A BEAR PIT. BUT WAS BURSTING WITH TALENTED. MERCURIAL INDIVIDUALS. EVERY DAY WAS A GREAT ADVENTURE - AND SOME OF US EVEN LIVED TO TELL THE TALE! '
- ANNA SMITH

Jinx Dogs Burns Now Flu

Alex Gordon

Alex Gordon, after almost fifty years in the Scottish newspaper industry, spills the beans in a frank and candid manner!

Jinx Dogs Burns Now Flu is a rollicking, hilarious trip through the crazy world of Scottish newspapers. It's a journey that takes the reader behind the headlines of the biggest, most sensational stories of our national press. It also introduces the fascinating if madcap characters whose job it was to bring you your daily news. Prepare to be bewildered by their antics as they chase front and back page exclusives. Other stories here throw an entirely new light on what actually happened around many of Scotland's most famous sports stars; stories that will cause quite a few reputations to be reassessed.

ISBN: 978-1-901514-28-5   £9.99

A Man's Game

Alan Ness

On a Saturday afternoon in central Scotland, both Davie Thomson and Stuart Robertson have scored goals for their respective football clubs: Cowden United FC and Glasgow Athletic. Once team-mates in the Athletic title-winning side of 1997, their subsequent fortunes could not have been more different. Whilst Robertson had gone from strength to strength, winning titles and the love of the Scottish public, Thomson had slipped out of the team and down the leagues, with alcohol and a weight problem contributing to his fall. Whilst scanning the results, James Donnelly, reporter for the Daily Standard connected the two and remembered the tragic events which would forever link them and their team-mates from that ill-fated side.

ISBN: 978-1-901514-27-8   £9.99

A Subtle Sadness

Sandy Jamieson

A Subtle Sadness follows the life of Frank Hunter and is an exploration of Scottish identity and the impact of politics, football, religion, sex and alcohol.

It covers a century of Scottish social, cultural and political highlights culminating in Glasgow's emergence in 1990 as European City of Culture.

It is not a political polemic but it puts the current social, cultural and political debates in a recent historical context.

ISBN: 978-1-901514-04-9   £9.99

Between Two Bridges

Brian McHugh

New York, 1933. Prohibition is coming to an end, but not everyone is celebrating. A few astute businessmen realise that by legally importing liquor before the Volstead Act is repealed, they can net themselves a small fortune. Charlie McKenna, an Irishman who spent time in Glasgow during the Great War, is sent to complete the deal with Denholm Distillers in their St Enoch Square office.

Glasgow, Present Day. Still reeling from the murder of their pal, three friends are knocked off-course by the resurfacing of a battered diary. It soon leads them back into their investigation of Julie's grandfather, Charlie McKenna. More troubling tales of war, gold and gangsters begin to surface. The sequel to Brian McHugh's *Torn Edges*, *Between Two Bridges* is a fast-paced adventure with a well-researched historical setting.

ISBN: 978-1-901514-35-3   £9.99

The Activist

Alec Connon

When Thomas Durand embarks on a cycling trip around Britain with two fellow students, his life changes forever. A chance encounter inspires Thomas to leave home and drop out of university. As he roams, his eyes are opened to the harm inflicted by humans on the natural world. Driven by an increasingly passionate interest in marine conservation, what begins as a typical gap-year turns into a decade's worth of activism on the open ocean. Here the stakes are highest of all: Thomas enlists with Sea Shepherd, a controversial organisation dedicated to the protection of marine life. It is a commitment that will soon place his life in danger.

The story follows Thomas, from his first tentative steps into the life of an activist in Vancouver, to his battles with a Japanese whaling fleet in the Southern Ocean. An ecological thriller, *The Activist* will shock and inspire anyone with an interest in marine life, conservation and the splendour of the natural world. Without preaching, it is also a clear-eyed demonstration of why this cause is worth fighting for.

"Alec Connon's extraordinary adventures into the world of the whale epitomise the vast disconnect between the human and natural world. In this heartfelt novel, he explores the outer edges of the world which we have dominated, and the price it has had to pay for that domination. In picaresque episodes which are by turns funny, tragic and deeply moving, Connon addresses, in a highly personal and evocative manner, the ways by which we might make amends for what we have done."

Phillip Hoare, Samuel Johnson Prize winner and author of *The Sea Inside*

ISBN: 978-1-901514-25-4   £9.99